THE LAMP OF DARKNESS

DAVE MASON
with MIKE FEUER

LIONSTAIL PRESS

For Chana,
whose patience
was tried
many a time
by my six years of writing,
but who stuck by me
anyway
with undying support.
It wouldn't have happened without you.

Acknowledgements

As a reader, I always marveled at how many people were mentioned in the acknowledgements of books. After all, writing a book seems like such a lone undertaking. As a writer, I'm struck by the huge number of people who played a role in making this book come about. First of all, both Mike and I want to thank our wives Chana and Karen for supporting us throughout. My son Aryeh Lev, with his love of stories and desire to deepen his understanding, was a constant source of motivation. And of course our parents, without whom, none of this would have happened.

The origins of this book go back to when I was learning the books of the early prophets with Rabbi Aaron Liebowitz and studying the inner workings of prophecy with Rabbi Yaakov Moshe Pupko, both at Sulam Yaakov in Jerusalem. Most of this book was written within the walls of Sulam Yaakov, and I'd like to acknowledge the entire crew there, specifically Rabbi Daniel Kohn's, whose teachings have been crucial to the development of our understanding of many key points in the book, and David Swidler, whose encyclopedic mind filled in many a random fact.

I'd like to thank Barnea Levi Selavan of Foundation Stone for helping us understanding the historical context, Yigal Levin of Bar Ilan University for helping us identify the ancient city of Levonah, and Shoshana Harrari of Harrari Harps for teaching us about Biblical instruments.

Thank you to our editors, Shifrah Devorah Witt, who edited an early draft of the book, and Rebbetzin Yehudis Golshevsky who edited the final two drafts.

I'm incredibly indebted to the dozens of readers who offered comments, corrections, and direction over the years. I can't come close to mentioning them all. But I have to give special mention to: Rabbi Joshua Weisberg, Chaya Lester, Eliezer Israel, Michelle Cahn, Leia Weil, Beth Shapiro, Hadas and Gidon Melmed, Moshe Newman, David Shaffer, Jen Bell Hillel, Rachel Winner, Rabbi David Sperling, Rabbi David Fink, Eitan Press, Josh Fleet, Diana Maryon, and my uncle Sam Firestone.

Thank you all.

Two quick notes before you start reading:

1) We've created an introductory video for anyone who would like more background regarding the world you're about to enter, available at <u>TheAgeofProphecy.com/video</u>.

This video can be viewed at any time. It's not necessary to watch it before beginning. You'll also find both written and video notes on the website providing sources for ideas discussed in the book and deeper insights into key concepts.

2) We are constantly striving to improve the quality of our work as well as the readers' experience. The current publishing revolution not only provides authors previously unknown flexibility, but also allows readers to play a prominent role in the writing process. Accordingly, we've put a feedback form on our site at <u>TheAgeofProphecy.com/feedback</u>.

If there is a specific element for which you'd like us to provide an explanatory video, or if there's a passage that you find confusing, or if you find (Heaven forbid) a typo, please let us know.

579 Years after the Exodus
In the Cave of Dotan

What did I receive on my thirteenth birthday, when I came of age? The gift of light. A lamp, fueled by the residue of oil scraped from old vessels and pressed out of discarded wicks, threw dancing shadows over the earthen walls of my underground home. I knew those walls so well by touch, but I hadn't seen them for over a month. The sudden flare of light blinded me at first, and then illuminated a ring of haggard men circled around me. Their eyes squinted against the brightness, but radiant smiles spread across their wizened faces. Just as the last man placed his hands on my head to bless me on coming of age, the flame died out, plunging us all back into darkness.

Hillel said: If I am not for myself, who will be for me? And when I am for my-self, what am I? And if not now, when?

Pirkei Avot 1:14

1

A Shepherd's Inheritance

Twelve-year-old boys daydream—one day they're soldiers in King Ahav's army, the next they're nobles visiting his palace in Shomron, or even pilgrims risking the Forbidden Journey to the Temple in Yerushalayim—but those dreams pass like summer clouds. The daydreams that haunted my childhood were for things that other boys took for granted: a mother's love, a father's guidance, a share in the land. Those sweet dreams only fed hopes for a life that could never be mine. Playing my *kinnor*—the small harp that was my only valuable possession—provided my only escape from these hopes. When a *nigun* consumed me, it drove all thoughts, hopeful or otherwise, from my mind.

I don't know if sheep hope—if they do, it's only for fresh grass and cool water—but the *kinnor* calmed them, too. Whenever I played to my uncle's flock, even the rams didn't stray far. While other shepherds in Levonah corralled their sheep with a staff, spending long days on their calloused feet, I sat in the shade with my *kinnor*. My favorite place to sit was under a gnarled fig tree overlooking the road leading up to the town. No tree gives shade as cool as the fig tree, and its fruits ripen one at a time; in summer I could always find a few perfectly ripe figs to snack on. This spot also provided me with a first glimpse of travelers on their way into Levonah.

It was a hot market day in early summer when Seguv stepped off the shimmering road, leading his donkey up to my perch on the hillside. Seguv was only a few years older than me, and spent half his time traveling the Kingdom with his brothers, selling their father's dates from their great estate along the Yarden River. They came to Levonah three or four times a year, but that day was the first time I ever saw Seguv traveling alone. He approached me with a bounce in his step that told of news.

The sheep bleated—strangers spooked them. Seguv untied one of his saddlebags, and rummaged through a thick cushion of flax until he produced a tiny clay bottle. Its dust-colored exterior disguised the treasure within. His eyes sparkled.

Could it be? What else could be in such a small flask? "Is that it?" I asked, my eyes reaching toward the vial.

Seguv nodded.

I leapt to my feet. "Put just a drop in my hand. I want to feel it."

He gave a sly grin as he pulled the flask away. "A drop of this is worth more than one of your reeking sheep, and it would be worth my head if the King found out. I'll let you smell it though."

I reached out to take the bottle, but Seguv tightened his grip. Only when I dropped my hands, did he uncork it and hold it under my nose. The essence flooded my senses, overwhelming the smell of dry grass and stone with the sweetness of wildflowers. I closed my eyes and inhaled. Deeper notes of the scent—mineral, earth, spice—unfolded just as Seguv pulled the flask away. A hot breeze carried the sheep odor back under the fig tree. I opened my eyes, confused. "If it's so precious, why are you bearing it?"

Seguv's eyes widened, "My father wants the first batch to go directly to the King."

"But why are *you* taking it?" The roads were safe, and had been ever since the civil war, years ago. Even so, who would send a kingly tribute with a boy selling dates, even if he was of age?

I could tell from the way he smiled, with his tongue flitting between his teeth, that he was just waiting for me to ask. "It's early," he said, raising his dark eyebrows. "This is the first batch of afarsimon oil ever produced in the Kingdom. The King isn't even expecting a crop this year. My father says there's no better time for my first appearance at court."

Seguv was so accommodating, always stopping to speak whenever he passed through Levonah, that I sometimes forgot how prominent his family was. "So that's why you're making the trip alone?"

"Mmm?" Seguv was hardly listening, his attention focused on returning his precious cargo to his saddlebag, packing it deep into its flax nest.

"Is that why you're making the trip without your brothers? To win the favor of the court?"

"Oh." Seguv closed the saddlebag, his hands fumbling with the straps. "I forgot you didn't know." His breath seeped out of him, sinking his ribs into his chest. "We lost Aviram a few months ago, and now Onan is too sick to travel."

"What happened?" I couldn't help the question. Aviram's laughing face rose in my mind. Gone?

Seguv's teary eyes rose to meet mine. "It's the waters in Yericho." His chest swelled and collapsed in short bursts. "Many have died from them, but father says it won't stop the rebuilding."

Seguv tied off the last strap of the saddlebag as a fiery gust blew off the hillside, rustling the broad, handlike leaves of the fig tree. I wanted to comfort him, but feared saying the wrong thing. Who knew better than me how easily a misplaced word could hurt? I reached instead for my *kinnor*—it had soothed my own heart so many times. The *nigun* I had been playing when Seguv climbed up to me wouldn't work, it was too light, too playful. I lowered my eyelids and quieted my mind. A slow breath filled my chest, and my fingertips found a new melody. I plucked the notes gently, passing through the simple *nigun* a few times, and then opened my eyes—it was all I could offer.

The music filled the emptiness between us, its notes softening the silence under the tree. Seguv's head dropped forward as one, two droplets darkened the dry soil at his feet. With a hitch in his breath, Seguv mumbled, "Thank you," and then picked his way down the slope, drawing his donkey toward the town's gate.

"Go in peace," I called after him, then added, too quietly for him to hear, "and may the Holy One protect you from the waters of Yericho."

I closed my eyes back into the melody, playing it louder now. Although it was impossible, I hoped that Seguv could feel the song even in Levonah, and that it would bring him comfort there. Like a river, the notes flowed from my *kinnor* as my fingers swirled across the strings. The repetitive melody and the heat of the day settled down on me, on the road, on the sheep—like a dream. Still playing, a feeling came upon me, a tingling across my back. The dreaminess suddenly evaporated; I knew this feeling. I had felt this pricking of warning two moons earlier when a lion stalked the flock in the early morning. Had I responded right away with sling and stones, I might have fought her off. But I had dismissed the feeling—the sheep were quiet. And when the lion pounced, I was too late to keep her from making off with one of the lambs.

My back tensed up with the certain knowledge that something was behind me, but still I didn't open my eyes or stop playing. The first moment of facing danger was the most important. If only I could identify the threat, I'd gain some advantage. It couldn't be a lion this time—lions almost never hunt at midday. And one wouldn't come this close to the road, certainly not on market day.

I opened my eyes and spun quickly around, hoping to at least catch whatever it was by surprise. I was right, there was something there...some*one* there. I almost laughed when I saw that it was just an old man standing on the other side of the fig tree, swaying gently with his eyes closed. The heavy gray eyebrows, broad forehead and deep wrinkles mapping his weathered face signaled nothing but calm. He held his staff as if it were an extension of his hand, a sure sign that he had walked many a path. Even at some distance he appeared so very tall.

Yet, I couldn't shake the feeling that something was wrong. I hadn't seen the old man step off the road, nor heard any bleating from the flock. Where had he come from and why was he just standing there? Travelers walked quickly, their eyes on the road, rarely returning greetings with more than a glance and a nod. Even the ones I could persuade to share stories of their travels departed before the final words of their tales left their lips. But this white-haired stranger just stood there, swaying. Had he stopped to listen to the music?

Even as I studied the old man, my fingers kept their rhythm, never breaking from the *nigun*. The pricking in my back intensified. If the music drew him, would he leave when it stopped? I silenced the strings with the palm of my hand.

The old man stopped swaying and locked his gray-blue eyes onto mine. A stone grew in my throat as his leathery lips broke into a smile. My chest tightened, shortening my breath. I saw no danger, but the ominous feeling built, like an old memory trying to force itself to the surface. My gaze escaped his hold, finding a nearby ewe gnawing a clump of thistle from its wool. I knelt beside the creature, working at the thistle until the old man stepped away from the shadow of the fig tree, back toward the road.

He had left easily enough, but the tight fist in my stomach remained. I just knew that he would return—and return he did. By the time the old man emerged from the town gates the sun was edging down in the west, and he was followed close at heels by a young couple from town. His gaze found the flock first, then narrowed in on me. Our eyes met and even from a distance I knew: he was coming for me.

Though he walked with a steady pace, the couple remained behind as he began to scale the rise up to me. I knew neither of them well, but I would never forget their wedding a month before. The bride's father hired me to perform, the first payment I ever received for playing my *kinnor*. They stood beneath their wedding canopy, a nervous, joyous energy on their faces. Now they stood like stone markers at the edge of the road, huddled and still, waiting.

The sleeve of the old man's linen cloak whispered as he gestured at the trunk of the fig tree, silently indicating his intention to join me. My stomach clenched in a sudden dread, but this was common land—I could hardly pro-test. My fingers kept on with their melody as if moving of their own volition. A cold unease filled me. I could not help but watch him closely.

He sat down slowly but smoothly—not like the old men of Levonah, whose knees creaked and faces groaned as they lowered themselves to the ground. Positioning himself with just his fingertips, he leaned his back against the fig tree's trunk, pulled in his feet, and raised his knees before him. Once settled, he took a long and penetrating look at me—as if judging my merit. He then nodded in my direction, silently commanding me to go on with the mu-sic. Were it not for the couple watching from below and my strange disquiet, I might have thought he sought out the shade for a late afternoon nap. His head sank between his bent knees. He was perfectly still.

I played on in the still air, as if waiting for a sign from him, not knowing how long I played or even why. A butterfly came to rest on his motionless el-bow, extending and retracting its black and orange wings. The butterfly took flight in a flash of fiery orange as the old man shuddered. The hairs on the back of my neck bristled as a charge filled the air. His bent back trembled for what seemed an age. Was he in some small fit? Should I stop playing? Yet, my fingers kept plucking the strings of their own accord while thoughts spi-raled through my mind, like dust blown in an eddy. My fingernail caught on a string of my *kinnor*, slicing the string in two.

And just as abruptly as the shuddering began, the bent form stilled again. The back that seemed bent over in an impossible curve slowly straightened; the old man nodded again to me, charging me to stop. Without a word, the stranger unfolded from his position to an impressive height. His face was seamed by age, but his body was upright, his brow imposing. He raised his aged hand and crooked a finger toward the road, turning his gaze in the cou-ple's direction. "Come," he beckoned to them.

The young man and woman rushed up the slope to meet him. As they approached, the old man called out, "It rolled behind the wine barrel at the back of the house, and there it lies—dirty, but perfectly safe."

The woman put a hand to her chest, a giddy smile brushing her lips. Her husband said, "Now I know you are truly an *ish Elokim.*" The old man responded with a silent nod. "Shall we escort you back to the city?"

"I remain here with the boy. Go in peace with the blessings of the Holy One."

"Peace and blessings upon you, Master Uriel," the young man said, taking his wife's hand and starting back toward the town gates.

The old man turned his blue-gray eyes on mine, then shifted his gaze to my stilled hands on my *kinnor.* "It's time to water the sheep and pen them in for the evening. I will come home with you, Lev. I need to speak with your uncle."

I gathered my things, wondering, *"How does he know my name?"*

👑 👑 👑

The King's tower, empty of soldiers during these times of peace, was already casting its shadow across our small farm by the time we returned home in silence. I trudged through my evening chores, my eyes straying like a lost lamb's to watch my uncle in quiet parley with the imposing stranger. It wasn't until I saw the branches of the carob tree black against the flaming horizon that I pushed myself to work faster. I filled the watering trough and secured the pen as a curtain of darkness was drawn from east to west.

The rocky spring behind our farm was normally dry by early summer, but this year a trickle of the heavy winter storms remained. Farmers had cursed the late *malkosh* rains that soaked the barley crop, spoiling most of it before it could be stored, but I felt only gratitude now as the stream of cool water ran over my curly brown hair and down my sweat-salted, lean frame.

It was nearly full dark when I came inside, the evening meal mostly over. Only Uncle Menachem and my younger cousins Dahlia and Eliav remained at the table; Aunt Leah had already taken the three littlest ones up the ladder for bed. My bread steamed; Dahlia must have reheated it on the hearth when she heard me coming in. I dipped it in salted *labneh*, chewing quickly because it was so late. The old man was gone, but his presence was felt in the heavy silence of the table. None of us children would ask about him unless Uncle

Menachem mentioned him first, and he said nothing. When I finished, Dahlia rose to clean up while Eliav and I remained at the table for our nightly studies.

"And you shall sanctify the fiftieth year," Uncle Menachem began, chanting the verse that he too had memorized as a child, "and proclaim freedom in the land for all who dwell in it." Eliav and I echoed him, repeating not only the words but also the melody that strung them together like beads on a strand. "It will be a *Yovel* for you," my uncle continued, "you shall return each man to his ancestral land, and return each man to his family."

"It will be a *Yovel* for you," we repeated, "…you shall return each man to his ancestral land…" Dahlia, setting the crockery in the alcove, pushed a stubborn, russet curl away from her eyes and coughed, "…and return each man to his family." The cough was our signal—she had a question.

"Uncle?"

"Yes, Lev?"

The problem was, I never knew exactly what was bothering Dahlia. "When is the next *Yovel*?" Silence from the alcove—I guessed right.

Uncle Menachem ran his fingers through his wiry beard, newly streaked with gray. "I asked my father the same question when he taught me this verse."

"And what did he tell you?"

"That he had never seen a *Yovel*."

"Have you seen one?"

"No, Lev."

I gripped the edge of the table to contain my excitement. "Then the next one must be coming soon!"

Uncle Menachem shifted on his stool, but the coals in the hearth didn't shed enough light to read his face. "No, Lev. My father had seen more than fifty years when he died. Do not put your hope in the *Yovel*, it is not coming. The land will not return." He rose to his feet though we had recited just one verse. "That's enough for tonight, it's already late." I sunk my head, avoiding Dahlia's eyes. "Lev, see that the flock is secure and then get to sleep."

I bit my lip hard enough to taste blood. I ought to know better than to get excited over the *Yovel*—another stupid daydream. I grabbed my *kinnor* from its peg by the door on my way out, its broken string dangling dead at my side. The new moon's tiny sliver had already set, but the summer sky was always clear, and I could pick out shadowy forms by the light of the stars. I tugged first at the gate of the pen, testing that it was well fastened, then skirted the edge of the wall, feeling for fallen stones. There was one faint bleat at the noise, but the flock was settled in for the night.

I lifted a flat rock at the edge of the pen, withdrawing a skin pouch from the hole beneath. After a month nestled in cool earth, my new strings were fully cured. I sat on the ground with my back against the pen's low wall, and ran my hand across the top of the *kinnor* until I found the empty spot, a missing tooth in its eight-stringed grin. I threaded one end of the sheep gut through the hole in the olive wood frame, wound the bottom end around its groove at the base of the *kinnor*, then tied off the other end around its bone key. I began to stretch and tune, stretch and tune, searching for the right sound to match the other strings. When the eight notes were in harmony, I ran my fingers lightly across all eight strings, letting the voice of the *kinnor* ripple out into the night.

This was my favorite time of day, when I could be alone with my music. In these moments, there were no responsibilities and no thoughts. I could just follow the flow of the rhythm…and forget about my fate. But the music had barely taken hold when a voice broke my focus.

"You must have questions about today," Uncle Menachem said, hovering above me in the starlight.

I silenced the strings of the *kinnor* and stood up. "Yes, Uncle."

"Did you know that old man?"

I thought back to the dread I felt when he first appeared—it seemed rooted in a memory deep within my heart. I reached down for it, but nothing came. "No, Uncle, but he knew my name."

"His name is Master Uriel."

I said nothing, certain he came to tell me more than the old man's name. But why the hesitation?

"He is a *navi*." Again Uncle Menachem paused, breaking up a clump of dried dirt with the toe of his sandal.

I recalled Uriel's trembling beneath the fig tree, and the couple with their missing item. Was that the spirit of prophecy? Is that how he knew my name?

"Do you know why he has come?" my uncle asked.

Since I first laid eyes on the old man earlier that day, he had filled my thoughts. An idea struck me suddenly. The thought made no sense, but I couldn't drive it away: Uriel came to take me from my family. Yet, my face remained a blank—no word escaped me. My uncle taught me that silence is a fence for wisdom, so I kept my mouth shut and shook my head.

"The *nevi'im* have called a gathering in *Emek HaAsefa* and they need musicians. Master Uriel asks to hire you."

"Hire me?" So he did want to take me away. I pictured a hundred men like him, tall and foreboding, trembling in a circle. *Why do they need musicians? Do they dance?* "How long is the gathering?"

"Two months."

"Two months?" I hadn't slept even a single night away from home since coming to live with my uncle. "I can't leave for that long—what about the flock?"

"Eliav can look after them. You were also ten when you first took them out alone."

My breath came short. "What did you tell him?"

"I won't refuse a *navi*, Lev. Not without reason."

I said nothing. If having me at home wasn't reason enough, what could I say?

"This will be good for you," Uncle Menachem said, speaking fast. "It won't be long until you're of age, and..." he reached beneath his cloak and pulled out a small pouch, tipping the contents into his hand, "...look here."

It was too dark to make out more than shadows, but I heard the unmistakable sound as my uncle emptied the pouch: the clink of copper. I reached out, my fingers finding the heap of cold metal—there must have been thirty pieces at least. "Whose are these?"

"These are mine, but I weighed them out according to Master Uriel's word. You will receive the same amount at the end of the gathering." He dropped the pieces back into the pouch one by one, each piece ringing in the dark as it fell.

"So many..."

"Enough for a ram and three ewes, with some left over." He tightened the leather strap at the top of the pouch, tying it shut. "It's a shepherd's inheritance."

I flinched as the word fell like a stone between us: inheritance. "Uncle, tell me again what happened to my father's land."

Uncle Menachem crossed his arms and sighed. "It's as I've told you, Lev. Your inheritance was lost to the King in the civil war. Do not dwell on what was lost. The *Yovel* is not coming." He put his hand on my shoulder. "The Land is wide enough for all of us, if we each find our place."

I nodded, but knew I had no place. My uncle cared for me like his own, but his land would pass to his sons, not his nephew. I didn't even know where my father's fields lay. It had been foolish to get excited about the *Yovel*—just another futile dream.

"When you return from the gathering, we can start building you a flock of your own." He held the sealed pouch of copper in the palm of his hand, as if weighing it. "If that's still what you'll want."

I strained my eyes to read his expression, but it was too dark. Shepherding was the best path for one without land—my uncle taught me this from earliest memory. "Why wouldn't I want that?"

"I'm...I'm sure you will," he said, avoiding my eyes. "You should take that jar of spare strings with you and get to bed. It's late and you have a long journey tomorrow." He squeezed my shoulder—as much affection as my uncle ever showed—and turned back toward the house.

I lifted the flat rock and retrieved the jar again. When I stood straight, I found Dahlia sitting on the wall of the pen, a dark shadow in the moonless night. "So what does the old man want?"

I sat down next to her. "Weren't you listening?"

"Just tell me."

"He needs a musician for a gathering."

"For how long?"

"Two months."

Dahlia let out a low whistle. "Are you going?"

"Yes."

"Now you won't have to stop travelers to tell me stories of the Kingdom. You can see it for yourself."

I slid along the wall away from Dahlia. "Those are other people's stories."

"They don't have to be." She touched me gently on the cheek, bringing my eyes to hers. Dahlia was the opposite of her father—almost too affectionate. It was fine when we were kids—we were raised like brother and sister—but we were both nearly of age now. Soon we'd be separated, and all her affection would only make it harder. "What's bothering you?"

Dahlia would keep pushing me; she always did. "Your father didn't give me a choice."

"What did he say?"

I examined my hands so I wouldn't have to meet her eyes. "He said it would be good for me, but I know what he meant."

"What?"

I tapped my thumb against the frame of my *kinnor*, distracting myself enough to keep my voice calm. "That I have to find my place elsewhere because I have no land and can't inherit from him."

Dahlia pulled her hair away from her eyes, tucking a particularly obstinate curl behind her ear. "Neither can I."

"It's different for you. Your father will marry you to Shelah or someone else with land."

Dahlia said nothing, just stared out into the darkness toward the property of our unmarried neighbor and shuddered. She was younger than me, but would come of age first, reaching her twelfth birthday in less than six months. There was no telling how long her father would wait before seeking a match for her.

"I'll be thirteen in less than a year," I continued, still not looking at her. "Without land, I'll have no choice but to become a shepherd, following the grasses from pasture to pasture."

"You won't have to leave here when you come of age."

"Not right away, but your father's already sending me away so I can earn enough copper to start a flock. It won't be more than three years until it's too big to keep here."

"Where will you go then?"

I stared at the hills to the east, black against the stars. "To the edge of the wilderness, away from the villages."

"That's so far. When would we see you?"

I shrugged. "A shepherd doesn't just leave his flock." That was true, but there were other truths that Dahlia, who clung to her dreams as if they were the morning sun, refused to accept. Even when I did visit, I might not see her, and we'd certainly never be allowed to speak alone like this.

Dahlia tugged her knees to her chest. "You don't know what will be in three years' time."

Fire blazed in my chest. "You think I'll inherit my father's land? Your father already told me it won't be returned—I don't even know where it is. What will be different in three years?"

"I..." Dahlia's eyes glistened in the starlight. "I don't know, but when you come home—"

"What's going to change when I come home?"

"Well, if the *Yovel* is not coming—"

"If the *Yovel* is not coming, my land will never be returned."

Dahlia shook her head. "If the *Yovel* is not coming, then any land you buy will be yours forever."

I gave a bitter laugh. "Do you know how many years I'd have to herd a flock just to buy a small piece of rocky hillside? It's better not to dream at all."

"Is it?" Dahlia also had a fire in her—we were of the same stock, after all. "This morning you thought you were stuck in Levonah, and tomorrow you're leaving with the old man. You never know what can happen."

"His name is Master Uriel," I said, straightening up and picturing his piercing eyes. Blood rushed to my face at the mention of the prophet, and I was glad for the cover of darkness. "There's something strange about him."

"He's a *navi*. My mother told me."

The memory of him saying my name on the hillside brought a fresh dread down my spine. My voice faded. "There's something more."

"I knew it!" Dahlia lowered her voice and leaned in. "Your eyes were so dark when you came home." That was the annoying part about Dahlia: she could always tell my moods so easily. She always said that my amber eyes would darken to match my thoughts. Yet, how could I tell her about my unease when I first saw the *navi*? She would only tell me to trust my heart.

I kept my voice low. "Your father knows more than he says."

Dahlia sighed and lay down on the broad, stone wall of the pen. "The stars are bright tonight."

"What do you think he's hiding?" I pressed.

"Look at the stars, Lev. Aren't they beautiful?"

"Why don't you answer me?"

"I'm trying to." Dahlia pushed me lightly with her bare foot. "Look at the stars. Whatever's going to happen is already written there. It doesn't matter what my father's hiding, he didn't give you a choice."

I pushed her foot away, but turned my eyes upwards. "No, he didn't."

"Try to remember everything you see at the gathering. I want to hear all about it when you get back—it will give me something to look forward to."

◊ ◊ ◊

I woke to the drumming of my heart and shot upright. My forehead was clammy with sweat, my breath came fast. Waking from the dream was like a sudden burst to the surface after being submerged deep in dark waters. I knew this feeling, like a terrified little boy choking back a scream. It was the old dream, I could feel it, even as it evaporated from my mind before I could grab hold of it. How long had it been sincethe last time? A month? But there was a time when it had been with me night after night. A little boy, alone in the dark, learning not to cry out and wake the others.

I pulled my tunic over my head in the faint dawn light—today wasn't a day to dwell on dreams. I arranged my few belongings on my sheepskin sleeping mat: the extra strings, my pouch. Together with my *kinnor*, sandals, and tunic, this was all I owned. I started rolling them in a bundle when something heavy dropped on the mat.

"This was your father's knife," Uncle Menachem whispered, trying not to wake the younger children. "I intended to give it to you when you came of age, but it may serve you well on your journey."

My fingers trembled as I picked up the knife. The stone of the handle felt smooth in my hand. I brought the knife up to the high, square window that offered the only light in the loft. A worn ox-hide sheath pulled off with a tug, revealing a blade that was flint rather than iron, a full two handbreadths long. I had never seen one like it. A copper inlay decorated the hilt, the worn design resembling two claws with three toes each, the inner toe of each claw gently touching.

A lump blocked my throat. My father had held this knife.

"Lev…" My uncle sounded far away, but there was a quiver to his voice that got my attention. "The *nevi'im* are the chief servants of the Holy One. They mean only good; I believe that." I studied his face, confused by the mixture of emotions I saw there: love, loss, reluctance, even a touch of fear. Twice he looked as if he was about to say more, then turned to go so quickly that I had no chance to respond.

I watched him climb down the ladder. I sheathed the knife, added it to the pile on the mat, rolled it up and tied it together. All the while, Uncle Menachem's words turned over in my mind.

I descended the ladder to find Aunt Leah standing before the hearth. "Sit down and eat before you go," she said. There was a plate on the table with cheese and my special bread. Ever since I could remember, she had set aside the first piece of bread baked each day for me.

"Thank you, Aunt Leah," I said, then quickly washed my hands and sat down without meeting her gaze.

She sat opposite me, watching me eat, her eyes tinged with red, the same color as her woolen headscarf. Her scarves were the only dyed garments our family owned—my uncle bought her a new one each year after the rains. If asked, I'm sure he'd say he buys them to treat her to something special. But I also knew that anyone who saw her in them presumed my uncle to be a man of substance.

I ate quickly, mostly as an excuse to keep my attention on my food. The bread disappeared, but other than rubbing her eyes with the back of her hands, my aunt didn't budge, just sat watching me, expectant. There was no use putting it off, she wasn't going to let me leave without talking. Without looking up, I said, "You don't want me going, do you, Aunt Leah?"

Tears ran down her cheeks and she forced a half smile. "Yes, I do."

My eyes rose up to meet hers. "You do?"

"I do." She wiped the tears with her palm. "Menachem said you were too young, but I told him you were ready."

So my uncle hadn't wanted me going—that explained the reluctance. "If you want me to go, then why are you crying?"

She smiled, as two more tears spilled over her cheeks. "Hasn't your uncle taught you that more than the lamb wants to suck, the ewe wants to give milk?"

I just stared back. Why was she suddenly talking about the flock?

Aunt Leah laughed, releasing more tears. "You don't understand now, but when you're blessed with children you will. You're my sister's son, but you know you're the same to me as one of my own, don't you Lev?"

A wet stinging filled my eyes—I hoped my aunt didn't notice. "Yes, Aunt Leah."

"And no matter what happens, you'll always have a home here."

I nodded—no words would come.

There was a soft knock.

My aunt rose and opened the door. Uriel stood a little way off, his back to us, leaving us the space to say goodbye. Aunt Leah held me in a tight embrace, her quiet crying so loud in my ear, her tears wetting my face. I took a final glance at my home over her shoulder as I hugged her back, my eyes open and dry. Though I was destined to return, I would always remember this as the moment that I left home for good.

Shimon ben Azai said: Do not despise any person, and do not dismiss any thing, for there is no one who does not have his hour, and no thing that does not have its place.

Pirkei Avot 4:3

The Three Keys

Looking off into the brightening east, Uriel stood at the edge of Uncle Menachem's land, hands folded over the top of his staff. "Why have you come, Lev?"

I stared up into the prophet's ancient face, but couldn't read his eyes; his shaggy brows cast their own shadow. "My uncle told me I was hired…" I held up my *kinnor*, "…for my music."

The *navi* pushed himself to his full height, towering a full head and a half above me. I craned my neck to hold his eyes. "So you are here because you were sent?" His face was unreadable as a stone.

I hitched my sack higher on my shoulder, wishing I could put it on the donkey that waited at his side. I hadn't asked for this old man to come tear me from my family—what did he want from me?

"Know, if it is only by your Uncle's will that you come to join us, then it is my will that you remain here."

I glanced over my shoulder at the olivewood door of the house. My family's reactions to my early return flashed through my mind: my aunt's disappointment, Eliav's sly grin. Would Dahlia be happy I was back, or think I'd failed?

"You fear being shamed for turning back," Uriel said, giving voice to my thoughts. "Do not. Your uncle will be relieved. There is much you can do here to help your family."

"Are you offering me the choice?" The last word caught in my throat. My family's rhythms were ruled by routine, and my own life had been shaped by the decisions of others. I had never chosen to come live with my uncle, nor had I sought the life of a shepherd. I may have complained to Dahlia about not having a choice, but I never really expected to be given one.

Uriel's eyes kindled. "The *nevi'im* inhabit a world of devotion. Our Way is a path of choice; its servants are not for hire. So tell me now—do you choose to come with me, or are you being sent?"

A breath of eastern wind pushed the dry scent of the olive grove between us, carrying with it a vision of an unknown future. Was it true? Could I choose to let the prophet leave without me? But the breeze died and the illusion faded. This was just another daydream; this was not a real choice. My uncle had spoken, and I would not upset my aunt.

I glanced toward the King's Road in the distance; I knew that we would not move until I told the prophet what he wanted to hear. I drew in a deep breath, drinking in the smell of dew on the leaves of my uncle's grapevines. This narrow valley held the only life I knew. Straightening my posture to mirror Uriel's, I peered into the prophet's eyes and lied. "I choose to come with you."

Uriel held my gaze, as if he had heard all my thoughts, weighed my words, and knew them to be empty. "So be it," he said at last. "Put your belongings on Balaam." The sharp lines of his face relaxed as he stroked the lone, ragged ear of his ancient donkey, whose head sank with a murmur of enjoyment.

When I finished tying down my things, Uriel clicked his tongue and started down the path, his donkey following without being drawn. The footpath from my uncle's farm skirted the city walls. When it joined the cart track that zig-zagged down from the town gate, Uriel increased his pace and extended his strides, moving nothing like an old man. The donkey trotted and I pushed myself to keep up.

I knew every rock and tree along this stretch, the spots where the first shoots showed after the early *yoreh* rains, and where small pockets of grass could be found even in late summer. We passed my favorite fig tree, the heavy bottoms of its tear-shaped fruits already ripening to a reddish brown. In two months' time the fruits would be all gone, the low-hanging ones eaten by other mouths, the higher ones falling to the ground to rot. My eyes lingered on the shade beneath the leaves, the place where I had seen Uriel shaken by prophecy the day before.

I felt the prophet's eyes upon me. "You have a question?"

How did he know? "Yes..." I caught myself before using his name. The couple yesterday called him Master Uriel, so did my uncle—was it disrespectful for me to do so? I could just call him Master, but I was hired to play music, not serve. Grandfather? It worked for the village elders, but didn't seem right for a prophet. Better not to address him at all. "Yesterday, when the couple came to you," I glanced back at the fig tree, "You used prophecy to find something of theirs?"

"They lost a valuable ring."

"You find *rings*?"

Uriel chuckled, slowing his pace and turning toward me. "You thought *navua* was only for more important things?"

"Well...yes."

"I assure you," Uriel said, his eyes no longer laughing, "That ring was immensely important to them." He turned back toward the road, resuming his driving pace.

The silence felt heavy as I followed behind. I hadn't meant to say that what he did was unimportant—I was just surprised. I ought to keep silent.

But there was another question I wanted to ask, one that had been on my mind since I woke that morning, and hadn't my uncle always said that the bashful never learn? I increased my pace until I was back at the old man's side. "And then you received *navua* about me?"

The old prophet slowed his pace again, fixing me with a hard gaze. "About you?"

"Yes, about hiring me?"

Uriel's arrow-straight posture relaxed just slightly, and he again turned his eyes up the road. "No, Lev, I did not receive a *navua* about hiring you."

"Then why?"

Uriel watched me out of the corner of his eyes. "Why what?"

The tips of my ears grew hot as a faint smile pulled at the edge of his mouth. Was he playing with me? "Why me?"

"What do you mean?"

I took a few more steps in silence, sharpening my question. "I mean, why *me*? There must be better musicians. I'm just..." My voice trailed off. What was I?

The donkey's grunts were the only sound as Uriel contemplated the question. "So you want to know what, other than *navua*, would have driven me to hire a shepherd boy to play for the prophets?"

I nodded.

"That is a wise question, and thus deserves a response." Uriel stopped and faced me. "My heart told me."

His heart? Those blue-gray eyes scanned mine as I thought about his answer. I started walking again so I could drop my eyes. "You didn't want to..." I scratched the back of my sweaty neck, "...check?"

Uriel continued next to me, the clunking of Balaam's hooves following close behind. "I have learned never to use prophecy to question my heart."

"But prophecy—"

"An open heart knows more than you realize. At times its intuition is more valuable than prophecy. There is no faster way to dull its voice than to doubt it."

Even if he was right, what did it matter? How many times had I watched the distant hills, dreaming of a mother who would never return? How many times had I questioned my uncle about land that would never be mine? I learned long ago that an open heart could also betray. Why rely on his heart when he had a better tool? "Isn't prophecy more powerful than intuition? Your heart couldn't have found that lost ring, could it?"

Uriel combed his long fingers through his thick gray hair. "True, it could not. Yet, my heart is mine to know, while prophecy is not at my command. Yesterday I was unable to receive *navua* until I heard your *kinnor*."

"My *kinnor*?"

"Your music is pure and beautiful. It cleared away many barriers."

The road from Levonah dropped into a broad valley where it met the King's Road. An expanse of vineyards flowed into the distance all around the crossroads, on land owned by one of the noble families of Shomron, worked by farmers from the village. As we turned south, I recalled the stories my uncle told me about the prophets. Beauty was rarely involved.

"You are confused," Uriel said, again responding to my thoughts. "Your uncle told me you learn the stories of our Fathers. Tell me, after Yosef's brothers sold him into slavery, how did they deceive their father Yaakov?"

I had always loved my lesson in the warmth of the evening kitchen. "They dipped Yosef's coat in the blood of a goat. Yaakov thought Yosef was killed by a wild beast."

"Good, I see you know the story."

Every boy in Yisrael probably knew that story, but I still stepped lighter with the praise. I plucked a fennel blossom from its tall stalk off the side of the road, squeezing the seeds into my hand.

"Now, do you understand it?"

My hand paused on the way to my mouth.

"Yaakov was a *navi* and a wealthy man. Shouldn't he have known his sons were lying to him? Couldn't the Holy One tell him where Yosef was held in Egypt? Why didn't he go down and redeem him from slavery?"

I stopped walking. I had known this story most of my life—at least I thought I had. "I don't know."

Uriel continued on in silence. I followed, but didn't push myself to keep up, drifting further behind as I chewed on the prophet's question. I popped the fennel seeds into my mouth, savoring their pungent flavor. How could I know why Yaakov didn't ask the Holy One—and what did that have to do with my music? I focused on Uriel's back as if the answer lay somewhere between his shoulder blades.

My uncle told me that Yaakov mourned his son every day he was gone as if he had died that very morning. That was why the story stuck in my mind. I knew the darkness of grieving, like a black hole in my chest. What was left to me of my parents? A memory of lavender wafting from Mother's hair, the weight of Father's broad and heavy hands on my forehead—every shard of memory was shrouded with longing. Had Yaakov felt that way for twenty-two years? I tore ahead, slowing only when I drew even with the elderly prophet. "Was it his grief?"

Uriel slowed his pace without turning his head. "Are you asking me a question or giving me an answer?" *The prophet has no interest in making things easy for me.*

A hot breeze drove a parched thornbush across the road. *Where had the vineyards gone?* We had already crossed into wilder country, without my noticing. I inhaled deeply and replied in a clear voice. "Yaakov couldn't receive prophecy because he was mourning the loss of Yosef."

Uriel smiled, the first show of warmth I felt from him that day. "Indeed. Sadness seals the heart. Only in joy can it receive."

The road sank between low, terraced hills that blocked any breeze, and sweat ran down my neck as a white sun burned directly overhead. Ahead, a man sliced the last of his wheat, grabbing handfuls of stalks with his left hand and hacking at their bases with a curved iron blade. A young woman collected the cut wheat, laying it flat to dry. As soon as she caught sight of us, the woman dropped her stalks to the ground and smoothed her skirt. Her swollen belly nearly overwhelmed her narrow frame as she carefully picked her way down the uneven ground to the road. She bowed her head low. "Master Uriel, won't you turn aside and eat a meal from your maidservant?"

I felt a rush of affection for her. The handful of almonds we ate at mid-morning were long gone, the hour for the midday meal had passed, and even my aching legs were protesting their hunger. Yet the prophet had shown no signs of slowing. He nodded to her request, and I sighed as we stepped into the slim shade of a carob tree by the side of the road. The woman weaved her way back to her husband, whispering and gesturing off into the distance. He dropped his sheaves to the ground and ran through the fields.

She returned and led us across the furrowed field to a poor dwelling tucked into the shadow of the hills. Its mud brick walls marked them as among the humblest of Yisrael, but the roof was freshly thatched and a jasmine bush near the door gave off a welcoming scent. We entered a tight, dark room, the entirety of their home. She seated us at a low table, poured a small bowl of wine into a pitcher, filled the rest with water, and placed it before us with two clay cups.

"Thank you, Milcah," Uriel said, pouring for the two of us. She brought out a pot of freshly salted cheese, then quickly patted dough into two cakes and placed them directly on the coals in the hearth.

Soon after the bread was done, the husband returned leading a donkey carrying a second woman, like Milcah, but with a slight body and pinched face. Milcah's husband helped her off the donkey, and she stepped into the house, walking directly to the prophet.

"Peace unto you, Master Uriel," she said, her eyes resolute. "I have come for another blessing."

Uriel laid down his bread and swallowed the bit in his mouth. "Another, Rumah? Has the first brought what you sought?"

"Of course not!" The blood drained from her face and her eyes burned.

"Why then do you ask for another?"

Her shrill cry pierced the small room. "Any fool can look at the two of us and see why." She turned to Milcah, the fire in her eyes departing as they fell on her, and soon they brimmed with tears. "My sister and I received the same blessing from you nine months ago. Now here she is with her belly between her teeth, and I am just as I was, but for being older."

Uriel's only response was a slight nod, and her anger flared again.

"Why? Why her and not me? She'd been married for two years when we came to you, I for almost ten. People say you can work miracles. Why didn't your blessing work for me?"

"It is not truly my blessing, but that of the Holy One."

"What does that mean?" Rumah's voice cracked as the tears began to flow. "I told my pain to *you*. It was *you* who promised me a child. Of course the Holy One is the source of life, but *you* are a *navi*."

"I never promised you a child." Uriel rose from his stool, his thick, gray hair brushing the smoke-blackened rafters of the low roof. He peered down at Rumah, small and frail but unshrinking in his shadow. "There are three keys that the Holy One does not surrender to any servant, even the *nevi'im*: the key to the womb, the key to the grave, and the key to the heavens. Without them, there can be no birth, no resurrection, no rain. Even our father Yaakov turned away our mother Rachel when she wept before him, demanding a child. And despite what you may have heard, my power is as nothing compared to Yaakov's." His fist clenched around the handle of his staff. "I say his words to you now, 'Am I in the place of the Holy One who has withheld the fruit of your womb?'"

Even in the dim light, I recoiled at the hard glint in Uriel's eyes. His words shattered Rumah's anger into tears, and she wept into her empty hands.

"So then you can do nothing? I am lost?" she cried out.

"No blessing is in vain," he replied, his voice softer now, "but the blessing alone may not be enough."

"But the Holy One heard my sister's cry." Rumah glanced in Milcah's direction and wheeled back, stung by what she saw. "Why does she merit and not me?"

"It is not always a question of merit. There are many things that can block the channels of blessing. Perhaps your desires lead you astray, and you have not come into this world for the children you wish to bear. And perhaps you yourself are closed to the blessing which is ready to be born into your life. When I left here last, what did you do?"

"You know exactly what I did. I went to my husband—what else would I do to conceive?"

Uriel turned to Milcah, "And what did you do?"

"I also went to my husband." Milcah took the pitcher and added more wine to Uriel's almost full cup, her neck flushing as she spoke. "I'm not sure what else you mean?"

"I mean, when did you start preparing for the baby?"

"Well, it's silly," she said, pink blotches rising from her neck to her cheeks as she reached for a loosely woven fabric of heavy wool. "The next day I started weaving this blanket. At first my husband laughed at me, but then he started building that cradle."

"Yes, that is right." Uriel smiled as he contemplated the woven basket next to their reed sleeping mats.

The older sister pursed her lips and glared at the blanket. "You're not suggesting that if I wove a blanket I would have conceived too, are you?"

"Of course not. The blanket itself was insignificant, as was the cradle. Your sister's conviction made her a fitting vessel." Rumah's mouth was a thin line, and her eyes darted back and forth between the blanket and Uriel. "Milcah acted as if the blessing was already fulfilled. She created a space in her heart for the blessing to rest, allowing it to bear fruit." Rumah's hands unclenched as her eyes settled on his face. "Do you remember what you thought when you left me last?"

"I do." She bent her head with a short laugh. "I even remember talking to my husband when I got home. He asked me, 'Do you think it will work?' I told him, 'Who can tell? Milcah thinks it will. What harm could there be in going along?'" Her eyes rose back to Uriel's, filled with a new light. "So if I believe, it will work?"

"I cannot promise you that. As I said, the key of birth is beyond my grasp." Uriel's words extinguished the light in her eyes, but his face remained radiant.

"And if it fails? If there is no child?"

I knew the look in her eyes well; I imagine such a look also brightened my eyes whenever my hopes rose. Yet, despite the misery I'd suffered from dashed hopes, despite all the dangers, I wanted Uriel to keep her hope alive. Milcah turned away from her sister, as I held my breath.

"Then you have a choice. You can embrace your present state, receiving it as the will of the Holy One, an opportunity for growth, for *tikun* in this world. Or you can struggle against it. But know now that your struggle will not succeed. I cannot say that joy in this decree will provide what you desire, but bitterness certainly dries up the wellsprings of blessing."

"Master, is it true that our futures can be read in the stars?"

Hesitation lingered in the black air. Was it wrong of me to mention the stars, which my master surely knew he would never see again? I twisted a loose string on my worn tunic.

"It is true," he eventually responded, "…most of the time."

"Do the nevi'im read the future there?"

"No, Lev. We keep far from that path."

"Why, Master?"

"The stars are a bridge between this world and the one beyond. One skilled at reading their movements can see what is coming into this world before it arrives."

"Then why avoid them, Master?"

"Our father Avraham was a master stargazer, and read in the heavens that he and his wife were never to have children together. But the Holy One raised Avraham above the stars, promising him that they would no longer bind him and his descendants."

"So the fortunes of Yisrael do not lie in the stars?"

"Most of the time our destiny can be seen there as well. But when we choose a higher path, our destiny is taken in hand directly by the Holy One, bypassing the stars. That is why the prophets avoid their guidance: they do not wish to limit the future to the confines of the present."

Rabbi Eliezer said: Warm yourself by the fire of the Sages, but beware of their glowing coals lest you get burnt—for their bite is the bite of a fox, their sting is the sting of a scorpion, their hiss is the hiss of a serpent, and all their words are like fiery coals.

Pirkei Avot 2:15

Honoring the Calf

"When you find Yosef ben Avner," Uriel's voice was soft in the dawn light, but I heard the command, "tell him we shall meet tomorrow at the junction."

I peered across the mist rising from the valley, westward toward the ancient walls of Beit El, my morning meal untouched before me. "How will I find him?"

"Quite easily, I imagine. There is no other like him in the city."

"But where does he live?"

"He once lived in the weavers' quarter, but I do not know if he has remained there. I have not entered Beit El in upward of sixty years."

My head swung back to stare at the prophet. Sixty years? The men in Levonah who reached sixty years ground their food to mash before eating it, yet Uriel still had a full set of teeth. Just how old is he?

The prophet waved at my untouched bread. "Eat. There is no knowing how long you'll be gone."

I took a bite of the dry loaf, forcing myself to chew—I shouldn't fail in my task because of hunger. Uriel walked out to a precipice that cast the beginnings of a shadow over the junction below, and sat down on his heels on its rocky edge.

I eyed his perch as the first rays of the rising sun began to warm my back. "Are you going to sit here alone all day?"

"Probably, though sometimes visitors come to me even in this place."

I swallowed another bite. "Why haven't you entered Beit El in sixty years?"

The prophet shifted his eyes to a cloud of dust rising above the road in the distance, my question evaporating in the morning light, ignored. "That looks like a royal messenger riding toward Beit El. If you hurry you can catch him. There might be news."

I shoved the last chunk of bread into my mouth, slung my water skin over my shoulder, and raced toward the path. My legs ached from the long march the day before, their stiffness resisting every step. Hoofbeats echoed in the distance, and I pushed myself into a run down the steep, rock-strewn path. This was a mistake. I didn't notice a cluster of loose pebbles until my foot was upon it. My arms shot out for balance, a weak compensation for fumbled footing. My backside hit the ground first, and I slid down the hard packed trail until my left knee banged into a boulder.

I glared up at the old man. I was a musician, not a messenger. Why should I have to run after some horse and search out a stranger in a city I didn't know while he just sat and waited? But the prophet's eyes were closed, impervious to my anger or the pain in my knee. I got up, rubbing my leg, and limped carefully down the path.

By the time I reached the crossroads, my legs were loose, despite the throbbing in my knee. The road up to Beit El was steep, but far smoother than the trail that lay behind. I was only halfway to the city when the horseman reached the junction below. I pushed myself back into a run, but it was no use. The rider's tunic, emblazoned with the royal ox, whipped in the air as he thundered past, leaving me coughing in a cloud of dust.

The messenger rounded one of the massive stone towers flanking the entrance to the city and disappeared through its gates. Three ram's horn blasts echoed over the surrounding hills—a public announcement.

My lungs raging, I pushed onward. This was no longer just about Uriel's command. A public announcement directly from a royal messenger was something we heard in Levonah only three or four times a year. I rounded the tower and raced through the narrow gateway, past a guard who barely glanced my way. A crowd already surrounded the horseman in the city square, but some of the dignitaries were still making their way from the chambers in the city gate—the announcement wouldn't start without them. My lungs heaved as I hobbled to a stop, doubling over to get my breath. I had made it in time.

A thin beard shaded the messenger's cheeks; he couldn't have seen more than twenty summers. He and his mount were covered in dust, sweat tracing thin lines down his face. He sat stiffly, chin held high, gazing over the heads of the crowd. When the last of the officials reached the square, he brought a silver tipped ram's horn to his lips and blew a single blast. "By authority of the great King Ahav!" A hush fell across the square. "It gives His Majesty great pleasure to announce the royal betrothal!"

The rider didn't flinch, but his horse sidestepped nervously at the crowd's roar. Still gasping for breath, I added a feeble cheer. Aunt Leah always said, "It is not good for a man to be alone." To her, even a king was lacking without a wife. The last time she had said this, her words came with a sad glance at me.

The messenger cleared his throat, still gazing over the heads of the crowd, and waited for silence. "King Ahav will marry Princess Izevel of Tzidon on the ninth day of the fifth month in the royal capital of Shomron. Let all of Yisrael come and rejoice!"

I was ready this time and let loose a loud "Hedad!" but my voice was nearly alone. I cut my cry short, feeling the stares of the crowd.

The messenger lowered his gaze, meeting the eyes of the people for the first time, sneering at their stunned looks. He kicked his mount, swinging it around, and was not yet clear of the crowd when he pushed it into a gallop. I still stood bent over, catching my breath, when someone grabbed the back of my tunic and yanked me out of the horse's way. I tried to thank him, but he was already talking to the man beside him. The thud of hooves was soon drowned out by the babble of voices discussing the news.

I searched the faces of the crowd, seeking a friendly one I could ask for help. I wasn't sure why news of the King's engagement would incense the people, but the confused fury written on their faces extinguished my desire to approach any of them. Yet, with the messenger gone, now was the time to find out about Yosef ben Avner before the crowd dispersed. I bit my lower lip. I never liked asking for help, especially from strangers. But there was no other choice—I'd just have to pick someone.

"Are you Lev?"

I spun around to meet the smiling eyes of a squat young man, appearing some five summers older than me, with a bushy black beard and bent nose. "Yes, I am."

"Excellent. I am Raphael ben Eshek. Master Yosef sent me to find you. Come, he is waiting."

A warm glow spread through my chest; finding Yosef had gone far easier than I feared. Is this how it would be among the prophets? Would they simply anticipate all my questions? Without another word, Raphael turned to go and I hastened to follow, still hobbled by my bruised knee. I felt comfort with Raphael from the first, but as we entered the streets of Beit El my ease faded. If Yosef knew who I was and where I would be, what else might he know about me? Feeling suddenly exposed, I wrapped my arms across my chest.

Raphael interrupted my thoughts. "How long have you been with Master Uriel?"

At least Raphael didn't know everything about me. My first instinct was to tell him that I wasn't really with the prophet, I was just a musician he had hired for the gathering, but I swallowed the objection. "Two days."

"Ahhhhh," he chuckled. "My first week with my master, half the time I had no idea what was happening."

I laughed louder than I intended. "That's how I feel right now."

Raphael glanced down at my swelling knee, with the trail of dried blood that marred my shin. "Is this fresh?"

I nodded.

"We'll put something on that when we arrive. For now, let me help you." Raphael thrust his stout arm under mine, and supported my limp toward a narrow, stone paved street that radiated out from the city square.

As my body sank onto his shoulder, I caught a side glance at my new friend. He smelled clean, like a fresh rosemary bush. Could he tell that I had not properly bathed since the last new moon? I inspected his tunic; it was not the rough wool of a servant's. Who was he exactly? "Are you Yosef's assistant?" I asked.

"No," Raphael grunted at the burden of my weight, "his disciple."

"You're training to become a prophet?" My uncle's tales of the prophets were among my favorite stories, but I couldn't recall a single story that involved training.

"Yes." Raphael beamed, revealing a set of large, crooked teeth that filled his wide grin. I couldn't help but smile back; his eyes gleamed like those of my young cousins whenever Aunt Leah treated them to roasted nuts.

"How long have you been with Yosef?"

"Five years."

"Five years?" I spent only six months going out with my uncle before I was ready to take the flock by myself.

"Oh yes. Prophecy comes only after many years of training—if at all."

"And have you received prophecy yet?"

"No, I'm still counted among the bnei nevi'im, not the nevi'im."

We stopped in front of a flat-roofed house made from chiseled stone, its street side broken only by a plain wooden door. The door swung outward, and an old man stepped into the street, his coal black eyes fixed unblinking on my face. I turned away from the intensity of his gaze, inspecting him out of the corner of my eye. His gray hair and beard were darker and better groomed than Uriel's. The bright white of his linen robes contrasted with the raven black leather totafot boxes bound to his arm and forehead. Uriel also put totafot on briefly that morning, but had removed them before eating.

"Welcome Lev ben Yochanan, I am Yosef ben Avner. I am aware of Uriel's instructions to you; nonetheless, speak your message and fulfill your master's command."

It was one thing for Raphael to assume that I was Uriel's servant, but it was another for Yosef, a prophet, to call him my master. I wanted to protest, but thought better of it—I could already see that Yosef was not someone to argue with. "The time has come for the gathering," I said, my voice sounding hollow even to my ears. "Master Uriel has informed the others. He will await you at the junction in the morning."

"Very good. We will be there." Yosef continued to bore into my eyes, even as I turned away. I tried to catch a glimpse of what was happening inside the prophet's house, in vain.

"Raphael, I see that Lev's knee needs care. In my quarters you will find clean fabric and ointment in the remedy box next to my mat."

Raphael entered the house and Yosef turned back to me. "You would like to observe my disciples." He had the same unnerving practice as Uriel of telling me what I was thinking. "They are engaged in training now and it is not desirable to disturb them." His eyes flickered over me from head to toe. "Yet, there is a way you can help my disciples. Then you may enter and enhance, rather than disturb."

Curious though I was to see what was going on inside, Yosef's piercing eyes made me glad that I had a ready excuse. "My kinnor is with Master Uriel."

"No matter, you will not need it."

Raphael returned with a cloth and a bowl of water, and bent to the ground to carefully clean the wound. He then brought out from within his robe a small clay jar filled with some evil-smelling substance. I clenched my teeth when the herbs touched my knee, but the sting lasted only a moment. A layer of yellowish ointment coated the wound, which I could suddenly barely feel. I eyed the wooden doorway narrowly, asking Yosef, "What else would I do?"

"You will see a stool in the middle of the room." Yosef nodded to Raphael, who entered the house, closing the door behind him. "All you must do is walk in and sit down."

"That's it?"

"That is all."

I had no more excuses to give Yosef, and it did seem a small price to satisfy my curiosity, yet my tongue turned pasty as I stepped toward the door. How could sitting on a stool help the disciples in their training unless they were to do something to me while I sat defenseless?

My moist palm took hold of the iron door handle. A floor of beaten earth met my footfalls inside, where the room was heavy with quiet. Eight disciples were ranged along the walls, each seated on a reed mat, legs folded, eyes closed. An alcove high in the wall contained over a hundred scrolls, far more than I had ever seen, many brown and cracking with age. In the middle of the room sat the sole piece of furniture, an empty stool.

I limped quietly to my place, and sat down, my knee protesting. No one reacted to my entrance. Other than one disciple who scratched his nose, no sound or movement disturbed their rhythmic breathing. Yosef leaned against the doorframe and watched.

I rubbed the back of my neck, suddenly hot and itchy. I could not see that they were acting upon me in any way, but these were not ordinary men; they were bnei nevi'im, disciples of the prophets. Uriel and Yosef both knew things about me without being told, sensing my thoughts as if they were spoken aloud. Is that what the disciples were doing now, reading my thoughts? Would I even know it if they were? I fought the desire to press my hands over my ears as if to block the way to my mind, knowing how useless such a move would be.

I had agreed to help, but my thoughts were my own. My forehead creased as I tried to empty my mind. It didn't work. Memories came pouring in on me, the very ones I least wanted to share: Dahlia surprising me while I bathed at the spring; almost losing the flock in a thunderstorm; the feel of Mother's hair on my cheek. Sweat beaded on my forehead, but my failed efforts only proved I couldn't clear my mind by force. My kinnor provided my only refuge from thought, but at this moment it was far away. The silence pressed down on me. My kinnor. The kinnor channeled my music, but it wasn't the source of it. Closing my eyes, I reached for a nigun to play in my mind. A melody whispered in my ears, and my shoulders relaxed. Thought and memory faded as my fingers worked strings they could not feel, plucking the notes sharper in my mind than I ever had with my hands.

Yosef finally broke the silence. "What can you tell me about our guest?"

The disciples turned toward their teacher, eyes still closed. I blushed, hoping no one would mention the incident with Dahlia at the spring. One replied, "He is a boy, Master."

"Why do you say so?"

"His footsteps. It took him eight steps to get from the door to the chair. It takes me five or six. Also, his steps were soft, lighter than a man's, but not hesitant like a woman's would be on entering."

"But slightly uneven," the disciple next to him added, "as if he's walking with a limp." I touched my left knee, still aching from the fall that morning.

Yosef was not yet satisfied. "What else?"

"He's a musician, Master."

"Interesting. Why do you say so Nadav?"

"He's tapping his feet." I peered down at my feet; I hadn't realized they were tapping out the melody in my head.

"Do only musicians tap their feet?"

"No, I even do it myself sometimes." The disciple cocked his head to the side. "But there's something different about the way he taps, the rhythm is more...complex...than when I do it."

"I see." Yosef's voice gave nothing away, but he was smiling. "What else?"

The navi's eyes swept back and forth across the disciples, but no one responded. Finally, the one who scratched his nose earlier said, "He's uncomfortable with us speaking about him."

"What tells you this, Elad?"

"When Nadav described him tapping his feet, he stopped, and he's breathing faster than he was before." Instantly my cheeks grew hot.

"Very perceptive."

This was my first experience with using the ears to see, and I was amazed at how much the disciples were able to learn just by listening. Yet, within half a year, the skills of these disciples would seem basic to me. When one enters a place that light cannot penetrate, his ears become his eyes. I would learn to hear the difference between a wall and a doorway, and to distinguish the footstep of friend from enemy.

"The time has come to take mercy on our guest who has provided an opportunity for so much insight. Open your eyes and greet Lev, a musician that Master Uriel has hired to play for us during the gathering." Yosef smiled at Nadav, the one who had guessed I was a musician, and from the look of gratitude on his face, I gathered that a smile from Yosef was a rare reward.

"I must ask you to excuse us now, Lev. We will meet again tomorrow at the junction."

👁 👁 👁

The sun had not yet reached its midpoint in the sky when I left Yosef's house. I walked back, barely thinking about where I was going, mulling over everything I had seen and heard. In all the stories my uncle had taught me, the Holy One simply chose the prophet—there was never any mention of disciples or training. Yet, Raphael said that all the prophets, every single one of them, had trained. Some could have learned from other prophets, as Raphael was learning from Yosef, but what about the others? Avraham and Moshe had been alone, cut off from any other prophets—where could they have trained?

Unbidden, an image of sitting on the ground in our sukkah rose in my mind, listening to Uncle Menachem tell the stories of the prophets. This was my favorite time of year, after the grape harvest, when we moved outside for the seven-day festival, sheltered only by a roof of fallen branches. During Sukkot, we worked as little as possible, spending our time inside the sukkah, singing, feasting on a roasted ram, and telling stories. I could not remember having my nightmare even once while sleeping inside the fragile walls of the sukkah.

These days, most men considered shepherds little better than illiterate thieves, respecting no man's boundaries, and ignorant of the ways of Yisrael. But on each night of Sukkot, Uncle Menachem told the story of one of the seven shepherds of Yisrael: Avraham, Yitzchak, Yaakov, Moshe, Aharon, Yosef and David. It always seemed strange that our greatest leaders came from a trade so widely despised. But I never thought to question how they became prophets. In the stories the Holy One just addressed them—that was all.

I turned the stories over in my mind as I wound through the streets of Beit El. It couldn't just be coincidence that they were all shepherds—could they have trained for prophecy while in the wilderness with their flocks?

As my mind wandered, my feet led me back to the gate of Beit El. I stopped just inside the heavy wooden doors, realizing that Uriel would not look for me much before sundown. I had time for myself, a rarity in Levonah. I turned my head up and sniffed—the scent of roasting meat hung in the air. I immediately knew where I wanted to go; I just needed to get there.

Hurrying back to the main square, I stood watching until I spotted what I was looking for—a farmer drawing a lamb up a wide thoroughfare. I crossed the square to follow, and the enticing aroma of sizzling fat and meat thickened as I left the open plaza. I was on the right trail.

I followed my unwitting guide through the winding alleys of Beit El. The road climbed gently, the stone pavers underfoot polished by the steps of countless feet. Flights of two or three stairs occasionally broke its smooth incline. Before long, we had walked enough to cross all of Levonah twice, yet we weren't even at the center of the city. Of course, Levonah was little more than a farming village compared to the Holy City of Beit El, where Yaakov—one of the seven shepherds himself—built an altar a thousand years before. The street broadened into a marketplace. Open storefronts lined the sides and free-standing stalls ran down the middle. The man leading the lamb disappeared into the crowd, but it no longer mattered—I had arrived.

A familiar animal odor filled the air, and sheep bleated from a storefront on my right. I stepped in, seeing that the store opened out to a pen in the back, where lambs lapped water from a trough. "How much for one of those?" I asked, though I knew I didn't have enough copper to buy one.

The burly shopkeeper eyed my dirty tunic. "The lambs start at three shekel silver, the rams go up to eight."

"Eight shekel silver? We get only half of that for a ram that size."

"A shepherd on your first trip to Beit El, eh? The sheep you sell are for eating; it doesn't matter if they have a bad eye or walk with a limp. Mine have no flaws. If you get any big ones in your flock like that bring them to me. I'll give you a lot more than you'll get from the slaughterers."

A rhythmic cooing rose from dozens of holes between the white stone blocks of the wall. "How much for a dove?"

"I can give you a good one for half a shekel." He pulled a small iron weight from a pocket of his smock and put it on one end of a scale. On the second pan, I dropped a few copper pieces, my earnings from the wedding earlier in the summer. Just as my fourth copper piece landed on the pan, it sank, bobbing up and down until it came level with the iron. It was most of what I owned, but I couldn't miss this chance—plus a hefty sum awaited me at the end of the gathering. An image of Dahlia floated into my mind, her nose crinkling with envy when she heard I'd gone to Beit El a year early.

The shopkeeper stepped onto a short ladder, untied the reed cover over one of the holes, slipped both hands in, and deftly pulled out a dove. It struggled, then relaxed in his grip. "Hold it like this, with both hands over its wings," he said, passing me the brown bird streaked with its purple feather-tips. "You don't want it to fly away." I gripped it the way I was shown. The small body squirmed in my hands, its heart beat wildly. Its feathers barely contained the bird's fine bones; I felt as though they'd crack if I squeezed too tightly.

"Hold it firm," he chided me. "If you let it struggle, it might get hurt. A pity to waste your copper on an unfit offering."

I tightened my grip and the bird relaxed. "What do I do now?"

"Take it to the altar. Follow the crowd uphill toward the smoke." Unable to contain my excitement, I snorted out a laugh. The shopkeeper's eyes narrowed, and his beefy hand clapped onto my shoulder. "Wait, I forgot to ask. You're of age, are you not?"

I shook my head. "Not for another year."

He wrapped his big hands around mine, taking control of the passive dove and shaking his head with a half-smile. "I should've asked first. You can't make an offering until you're of age. I'll not have you sin on my account." He stepped up the ladder and returned the bird carefully to its hole, then placed my coppers back in my empty hand.

A stone rose in my throat. "Is there nothing I can do?"

"Go and bow before the Holy One. Anyone can do that."

I stepped out of the shop and continued up the center of the marketplace, picturing Eliav laughing at me if he ever heard about the dove—I'd have to tell Dahlia when we were alone. As the street rose, the scent of incense overpowered the musky reek of sheep. Once I cleared the last of the stalls, the clamor of the caged animals faded and a new sound caught my ear. Floating above the hum of the crowd was a song unlike any I had ever heard. The precision and delicacy of notes weaving into one another bespoke exceptional skill and countless hours of practice. I closed my eyes and filtered out the noise of the marketplace to better focus on the music. An elbow in my back broke my concentration as a thickset farmer stumbled against me and cursed. I'd chosen a poor spot to stop and gawk.

Slipping through the crowd, I sought the source of the music. The street leveled, opening out into a large square. Across the plaza, I found what I was looking for: seven musicians standing on a wooden platform, brilliant red robes falling to their feet. In the open air of the plaza, the incense was no longer just fragrant; it was intoxicating. Music floated on a cloud of cinnamon, clove, and myrrh, filling the open square, unchallenged by the hushed crowd.

The cry of a frightened sheep tore my attention from the melody. With the instincts of a shepherd, I sought out the distressed animal, but the thick cloud of smoke billowing up from the incense altar obscured my sight.

There was another sharp bleat, cut short by a grunt, and I spotted the lamb. Its blood flowed out in jets into a stone bowl held ready to receive it. The creature's body sagged, lifeless, as a barefoot priest robed in white hoisted it on his shoulders and carried it up a ramp to the altar. A second priest lifted the bowl of blood and splashed it in a stiff-armed arc across the base of the altar.

Just beyond the bloodstain, a tall, painted banner fell from the horns of the altar to its base, displaying the royal ox of the House of King Omri. As I stared, the cloth billowed out in the breeze, revealing a crack in the stone hidden beneath. The fissure ran almost the entire height of the altar, with a thin trail of ash surfacing from its depths.

As I stood there, observing the crack, Uriel's words from the morning before came back to me: The prophets live in a world of devotion; the places they go are reached only by choice. I hadn't really chosen to follow the old prophet; I only told him what he wanted to hear. But it was my choice to come to the altar and bow down before the Holy One.

I crossed the square and ascended to a platform of massive stone blocks towering over the plaza. A second platform stood above the first. Four limestone pillars supported a roof of woven reeds shading the sacred object: the Golden Calf.

The Calf wasn't as immense as I had imagined. Its eyes would barely have reached my knees, but the burnished gold reflected the sun as brightly as a mirror. Its expression was exactly that of a real calf wishing to nurse, and even from where I stood I could see the texture of its hide.

I always expected my first trip to Beit El would be with my uncle, during the annual pilgrimage, and now my pride at coming on my own was tempered by not knowing what to do. My face grew hot as I avoided the gaze of the priests guarding the Golden Calf. A gray haired man ascended next to me. From the corner of my eye, I watched him stand for a moment, as though gazing up into the Calf's eyes. Then he lowered his knees onto the chiseled stone. I copied him, wincing as my bruised knee hit the ground.

I felt the Calf's eyes watching over me, over all the faithful of Yisrael, as it had for generations. How many prayers had it heard?

This was my chance to speak directly to the Holy One. I recalled my earliest memories of tefillah, of how I would cry out for my mother to come back. I wasn't sure how long that went on, probably for years, until one day Uncle Menachem took me aside and explained that wasn't the way prayer worked. "We don't pray for the impossible," he explained, "and we don't pray to change what already is. But we can pray for things that haven't happened yet, like strong rains, a good harvest, or that the flock should be safe."

So for years I did just that; I prayed that the flock would be safe from lions and wolves, and in the two years I led the flock, I had lost only three lambs. But now, standing before the Holy One, with the flock so far away, the same old prayers sounded hollow to my heart. This was my chance to pray for what I really wanted. Not the return of my parents or the inheritance of my land—it was still forbidden to pray for the impossible.

Yet, how quickly our visions of what is possible can change. At the last new moon, I would have said that I was destined to become nothing more than a lowly shepherd. Yet, perhaps Dahlia was right, perhaps circumstances could change, even for me. After all, here I was, just a few days later, bowing down in Beit El. If the altar of the Holy One, the holiest place in the Kingdom, could have a crack, then could I, with all of my flaws, also attain holiness?

Raphael said that his master had put him on the path five years ago—the path to prophecy. When I asked Uriel yesterday why he had taken me for the gathering, he said it was for my music. But there was something he was holding back—I was sure of it. Could this be it? Had he brought me to the gathering so that I could catch a glimpse of a different future? Had he put me on the path to prophecy without my even knowing it?

This was finally something meaningful to pray for, a path of devotion to something greater than just my sheep or my stomach. If it was my fate to become a shepherd in the wilderness, then I wanted to be like the seven shepherds of Yisrael, a shepherd-prophet.

My fellow worshiper was already stretched out on the flagstones, arms extended before his head, legs trailing out behind him. I copied his position, placing my palms flat before me. Lowering my forehead to the cold stone, my hands trembled at my first act of devotion.

The Knife

"Darkness is rising upon the land."

These were the only words the prophet uttered when I told him of the King's engagement. For the rest of the night he just sat on the precipice, deep in thought. I didn't even get to tell him about bowing before the Holy One.

We met Yosef and his disciples soon after dawn. The two masters embraced, then led us off eastward on the broad road toward Yericho. The disciples and I waited until the masters were far enough ahead to speak without being overheard, then we started off behind. Our route led down the dry wilderness slope that bridged the fertile mountain plateau, where I had spent my entire life, and the Yarden valley below. A herd of gazelles leapt along the ridge, leaving gray tracks on the barren terrain. One stopped to nibble at the dark green leaves of a lone hyssop bush that had fought its way through the rocky soil. Halfway down the slope we turned north onto a smaller track, hardly more than a footpath, that followed the ridge-line along the edge of the wilderness. A hot wind lifted the dust, and I tasted grit between my teeth. Only the toughest creatures could call the steep, arid country home. Two rough, migrant shepherds clicked their tongues to guide a flock of coarse-haired goats toward a patch of brown grasses growing in a catch-basin between the hills.

This is me in a few years' time.

At what point had my family made clear to me that this was my future? Was it all at once, or only little by little? But this was my first time in the true wild. The grass was sparse and the springs distant from one another, making shepherding here strenuous work. Yet, a quiet serenity rested between the hillsides. Though life here would be hard, my decision the day before to train for prophecy bolstered me. It was the perfect place for learning to hear the words of the Holy One.

My enthusiasm for wilderness life lasted only until mid-day, when we finally passed a shepherd's tent close enough to see more than its brown hide exterior. Outside its goatskin walls, the shepherd's wife sat baking their bread directly on the coals of her fire. She responded to Uriel's greeting with a ghastly smile, baring her toothless gums, and drawing tight the weathered skin of her face. There were no children around the tent—she hardly looked healthy enough to have any. Was her blighted condition a result of the harshness of their lives, or were the prospects of a wilderness shepherd so poor that her husband could marry no better? Either alternative was enough to make me cringe.

Long after we passed the shepherd's tent, even as the springs came closer together, returning a haze of green to the landscape, I still couldn't clear that image of the shepherd's wife from my thoughts. Perhaps I should bring Dahlia here to see the worn woman herself? Then she would abandon her silly dream of following me on my path, and leave me to walk it alone.

I was torn from my thoughts of Dahlia only when Raphael announced, "Welcome to Emek HaAsefa, Lev." He swept his hands toward a valley nestled between the hills below us, its gently sloping clearing already in shadow.

My eyes were drawn to black openings along the steep rock face opposite. "Are those caves?"

"Yes. They will be our homes during the gathering." Raphael stepped off the road onto a trail down to the valley, "…and those are just the ones you can see."

Raphael descended directly to the clearing where white-robed servants were laying out food. I stopped first at the animal pens to find Balaam already in the enclosure, snuffing loudly while eating alongside twenty or more donkeys and three horses. As I retrieved my belongings from the saddlebags, my eyes appraised the horses—had nobles come to the gathering?

The Knife

In the eating area, I found a table laid out with hot bread, chickpea mash, and beet tops lightly cooked to a bright green. A Yisraelite indentured servant spooned out food for the disciples, while another baked bread over a clay dome. It was my first time seeing a man baking bread, and my first time having food prepared by an eved ivri. In Levonah, there were only avadim canaanim, non-Yisraelite slaves whose servitude was for life.

The eved ivri took one glance at me, and his eyes narrowed. "Are you Lev?" I nodded. "Master Uriel had us set this aside for you." He retrieved a piece of bread from behind the cooking area, dotted with small amounts of the chickpea and beet tops. After a full day's march, I had hoped for more food than this. The eved must have caught my expression for he added, "You can take more. I don't care." He put down his spoon, with the handle facing toward me, then went to help with the cooking, leaving me to serve myself. I added only a modest amount, remembering my uncle's resentment at how much the hired workers had eaten during last year's olive harvest.

Food in hand, I gazed around until I found Raphael, who sat with two other disciples on the gently sloping hillside. The disciples ate in silence, chewing each morsel dozens of times before taking another. When he saw me approach, Raphael swallowed the bite in his mouth, interrupting his chewing, to greet me. "Hi Lev," he said with a warm smile, "Looking for the musicians? They're sitting over there." I caught myself before sitting down—did the musicians not eat with the disciples?

I followed Raphael's gesture and saw three people sitting together in a corner of the field. Their garments immediately caught my eye; they were all dressed in heavy woolen tunics like my own. The whole time we walked together, I hadn't thought how much my clothes, so hot and itchy in the summer heat, must have made me stand out from my companions, who undoubtedly wore wool only in the wintertime. As I weaved through the disciples, I became intensely aware of my tunic, its dank odor, and how it had been crudely stitched together by Aunt Leah and Dahlia. The linen garments of the bnei nevi'im were doubtless made by master weavers. I kept my gaze ahead on the musicians so I wouldn't have to meet the eyes of the disciples.

Two of the musicians were youths, one a thickset boy about my age who sat hunched over his food. The other, a few years older, leaned back on one of his elbows and ran a hand through his wavy hair as he watched me approach. The third musician was a man, younger than my uncle, who sat erect, his narrow beard almost reaching his waist. "Are you Lev?" the man asked. I nodded and sat down next to him. "Excellent, then we're all gathered. I'm Daniel ben

Eliezer, the master musician here. This is Yonaton ben Baruch," he pointed to the younger boy, "and Zimri ben—"

"Just Zim," the wavy haired one interjected, his mouth half full. Juice and vegetables dripped from the bottom of his rolled up bread, and he ate at a pace that made me wonder how long it had been since his last meal.

Yonaton offered a hesitant smile. Like me, he'd just taken small amounts of each dish, and sat with his flatbread spread out on his lap, the different foods on it not touching. I sat down next to him and bit into my bread, glad for the distraction of food that excused us from conversation.

As the first stars appeared in the sky, the chatter among the disciples died down, and all turned their attention toward the serving table where Uriel, Yosef, and a third white-haired sage stood between three torches in a circle of flickering light. "May all who have come be blessed," Uriel began.

"Many are the paths we have walked to reach this point and many are the places from which we have come. Together, we seek dveikut—a true bond with the Holy One. In dveikut, the Divine Light will flow to Am Yisrael, and through them to all of creation. The hour is late, and for many of you the journey has been long; nevertheless, our time is short, our task is great, and our Master is pressing." He gazed over the crowd of disciples, torchlight glittering in his eyes. "Know too that the reward is great if you pursue the Way with discipline and commitment. We expect nothing less from each of you."

Uriel stepped back into shadow as Yosef replaced him in the torchlight. "When you are dismissed, you will go directly to sleep. You will be woken in the second watch of the night to begin your training. Remember your dreams; even ordinary dreams are one sixtieth prophecy. Each night you will discuss your dreams with a master to decipher their—"

"This isn't for us," Daniel whispered. "Come, we can speak in the musicians' cave."

I stood and reluctantly followed Daniel. I knew that prophecy could come through dreams—Yaakov's vision of the ladder came in a dream—but I had never known that my own dreams might contain prophecy. I longed to hear about unlocking their secrets, but as I followed Daniel away from the eating area, I realized that it didn't matter much. Yosef said that to decipher your dreams, you needed to remember them. There was only one dream I really wanted to understand, but I could never remember the slightest detail of my old nightmare. Besides, if I ever could remember what the dream contained, I was pretty sure I wouldn't need a master to help me interpret it—it felt more like an evil memory than a prophecy.

Pale blue light still filled the western horizon, but with the moon only a sliver, the trail was little more than a gray smudge on dark ground. Daniel led us, walking with the comfort of one who knew his way.

"Will they also wake us in the middle of the night?" Zim asked.

"No, they don't need us until an hour or two after sunrise."

"Good, because the second watch is when I normally go to sleep."

Thistles snagged the hem of my tunic as the path narrowed at the foot of the cliff. It wound upwards, in some spots little more than a ledge bound by a sheer drop, widening out as we passed cave openings. We stayed close to Daniel, the darkness forcing us to rely on his position to avoid a deadly misstep.

"Why do you go to sleep so late?" Yonaton asked Zim.

"It's when I play my best music—there's a special energy to the night."

"I wouldn't know," Yonaton replied. "In my house, we go to sleep as soon as we can after sunset and wake before dawn. My father says sleep is the body's reward. I couldn't get up if I stayed awake playing."

"That's why I never rise before the third hour of the day if I can help it."

My jaw dropped. "Are you royalty?"

Zim laughed, "Why would you say that?"

"Whenever I'm slow out of bed, my uncle tells me that only princes sleep until the third hour of the day."

"No, I have no noble blood. My father's a farmer, and so was his. But farming's not for me. I left home for good a year ago."

The path flattened out as we stepped onto a rock ledge at the mouth of the highest cave, the cliff face rising above it into the darkness. Even in the dim light I could see a circle of boulders out front, surrounding a fire pit dark with charcoal.

"Then how do you eat?" Yonaton asked.

"My music." Zim retrieved a drum from inside the cave and sat down on one of the boulders, gently tapping the taut hide with his fingertips. Though hardly focused on his drumming, it was already clear that his sense of rhythm was excellent. "I've found enough work between weddings and festivals."

"What kind of festivals?" Yonaton asked.

"All kinds. The best is coming up at the full moon in Shiloh—I never miss it."

I swung my kinnor off my shoulder and straddled one of the boulders. "But you'll still be here then, won't you?"

"When Master Yosef hired me I told him I'd come only if I could still play Shiloh."

"How about you, Daniel, is that what you do too?" Yonaton asked.

"Me?" Daniel chuckled as he sat down next to Zim, clutching his nevel, a standup harp twice the size of my kinnor. "No, I have a wife and three daughters; I can't be running around to festivals all the time. It's only while my wheat is drying that I can devote myself to music."

"Isn't it hard being away from your family?" Yonaton asked.

"Sure it's hard, but my nevel is easier to work than my land, and copper doesn't spoil." Daniel began to pick out notes and tighten strings.

Zim cocked his head toward Yonaton, "First time away from home?"

Yonaton nodded, "I've never even slept away before."

"How far did you come?" I asked.

"Not far. We live just on the other side of that hill."

"So why not go home at night?"

"My father told me I can't expect the prophets to send someone round to the farm every time they need me. Still, it's nice to know I can run home if I need to, and my sisters said they'd visit." Yonaton pulled a halil, a wooden fife two handbreadths long, from his belt. "How about you, Lev? Do you play festivals or do you also work your father's land?"

I plucked the strings of my kinnor, feeling their eyes but not looking up. "My father's dead. My mother too. I shepherd my uncle's flock."

My words killed the conversation. I knew this moment, having experienced it so many times in the past—the awkward quiet, the eyes turning away. Zim filled the silence with his drumming, increasing his pace and power. Daniel joined in, picking up Zim's beat, with crisp plucks against the long strings of his nevel, the notes reverberating into the cool evening air. Only Yonaton remained silent. My eyes were dry—I learned long ago that tears would neither bring back my parents nor water the flock—but I was surprised to see that Yonaton's warm brown eyes reflected more of the night sky than my dry eyes ever could. I smiled and raised my kinnor, indicating that there was no more to say. Yonaton wiped his eyes across his sleeve and smiled back, raising his halil to his lips.

♆ ♆ ♆

The stars were already bright in the sky when I saw twinkling lights ascend the trail toward the caves. "What are those lights?"

"Lamps," Daniel said. "The disciples are going to sleep."

"And they carry their own lamps?" At my uncle's house, lamps were reserved for holy times—olive oil was too precious to burn during the week.

"I'm glad I'm not one of them," Zim said, watching the lights go out as the disciples reached their caves.

My hand dropped from the strings of my kinnor and I stared across at Zim. "Is it really so hard to go to sleep early?"

Zim laughed and leaned into his drum, tapping out higher pitched notes with the fingertips of his right hand on the drum's edge as his left palm pounded the center with a booming bass.

And then it suddenly occurred to me: there could be only one explanation for his lack of interest. "You've never seen them taken by prophecy, have you?"

Zim reacted to the challenge in my voice, meeting my eyes without breaking his rhythm. "No. Have you?"

"Yes." That one word was enough to silence Zim and draw the stares of Daniel and Yonaton, but I wasn't done. "When you see it you'll understand—"

"Don't envy the prophets, Lev." Daniel let his hands rest on his nevel and our song unraveled—only Zim kept up the beat.

I turned on Daniel, "What's not to envy?"

Daniel sighed, "Theirs is a path that will lead you nowhere."

"Why nowhere?" Yonaton asked. "Look at the masters—"

"Yes, Yonaton, look at the masters. Take Master Uriel. Where do you think he'll be come harvest time when our backs are bent with labor? Out in the fields with us?" Zim gave a snort, and Daniel turned to me. "Can you imagine him chasing your sheep over the hillsides?"

Daniel leaned over his nevel to press his point. "I've been playing here for twelve years. The first day, there's always a musician or two who dreams of becoming a prophet; but they learn soon enough that's all they are—dreams. And you'll learn too."

I recalled my last conversation with Dahlia, how she said that there was no telling where my future would lead. "But even dreams can come true—can't they?"

"Not this one. It's as King Solomon said: Wisdom is good with an inheritance."

I winced at the word inheritance. "What does that mean?"

"It means that it doesn't matter how wise or holy you are, Lev, you'll never become a navi. Look at the bnei nevi'im, servants preparing their food, lighting lamps just to walk back to their caves—some of them even rode in on their own horses. They don't dress like you. They don't smell like you." Zim chortled. Yonaton quietly sniffed his tunic. "Most of the disciples study for years before receiving navua, if they receive it at all. Who do you think watches their farms or their flocks while they're searching for the Holy One?"

I just shrugged.

"You have to be rich to become a prophet, there's never been one that wasn't. As far as I can tell, it's part of their Way."

I opened my mouth to respond, but shut it again. What could I say? Uncle Menachem always told me that the smart man learns from his mistakes, but I never seemed to. When would I stop falling into the trap of clinging to dreams that could never come true? I was like the fool in Eliav's favorite story, the one who sat by a pool of still water, the moon reflected in its surface. Such a beautiful stone, he thought, if he could only get it for himself, he'd be a rich man. But when he grabbed for it, his hands plunged into the cold water and the moon disappeared. He cursed himself for his stupidity, but when the water calmed, the moon reappeared, and he thought that perhaps this time he'd be lucky.

Daniel watched me closely. "Don't look like that. You have a surer path open to you."

"What's that?" I asked, daring him to tout the joys of shepherding.

"The nevi'im use your music to lift themselves beyond this world. You may not reach prophecy, but it can uplift you as well. You just need to learn to play properly—start with this." Daniel leaned his nevel against the boulder, came around behind me, and laid his hands over mine. He pulled my left hand further down the front of my kinnor, placing it in an unfamiliar hold. He then twisted the angle of my plucking hand, my right. I didn't like the feel of his hands on mine—after what he just told me I would have preferred to be left alone—but I didn't fight him. "Grip it like this, firm up your hold in your left hand, but loosen up on your right. Now listen." Daniel plucked the highest string and the kinnor let out a crisp, clear note.

"It feels awkward." Worse than awkward...painful, almost.

"You're used to doing it wrong. Give it time—you'll bring out the full voice of your kinnor. It's a fine, fine instrument."

Yonaton pulled his halil away from his lips. "They don't smell like us?"

Daniel laughed, "Sniff one tomorrow. They're obsessed with purity. Most bathe at least once a day." He returned to his nevel and picked up the melody again. "The way I see it, how much do they really have to tie them to this world? That must be why they can rise above it so easily."

"It's not so easy," Zim said, drumming now with his fingertips so as not to drown out his voice. "They need us."

"Just the disciples—the masters don't need musicians."

"But Master Uriel did," I said, sitting straighter now that I knew something that Daniel didn't. "The day we met, he came to me when I was with my sheep for my music. That's how I was hired."

Daniel inclined his head to the side and stared at me again, then turned his eyes away and shrugged. "I've never seen a master use a musician before."

Zim waved off our words with the back of his hand. "Enough of this, we may not be prophets, but we know what we need." He stepped up his playing, and the rest of us followed his lead, bringing the conversation to an end.

The music indeed was unlike any I had ever played. Few in Levonah had the time or the patience to play instruments outside of festivals and celebrations. For the first time in years, I found myself in the presence of clearly superior musicians in Daniel and Zim, and even Yonaton harmonized beautifully, if quietly, on his halil. I closed my eyes into the rhythm, feeling a tingling in my fingertips as they plucked out the melody, leaving my concerns about the navi'im behind.

🪕 🪕 🪕

A servant shook each of us roughly by the shoulder the next morning. "Master Uriel requires you," he said, then stepped out of the cave before I'd even sat up.

I squinted in the sunlight. I'd never slept so far into the morning—nor had I ever stayed up so late. By the time Daniel finally made us go to sleep, the eastern sky had already brightened to a dark gray. All through the night, I was telling myself I'd regret not getting to bed, but the music fixed me there. Guided by Daniel's nimble nevel and driven by Zim's rhythms, I discovered sounds in my kinnor that I never knew existed.

Several buckets of water awaited us outside the cave, and we quickly washed our hands and faces. The cold water chased the sleep from my eyes. I examined our cave, the daylight offering me a chance to see my new home properly. The niche in the wall where I slept seemed carved out for that very purpose. In fact, none of the cave walls were smooth like the ones near Levonah; they were all grooved, as if hewn out with iron tools. They couldn't have been made for the annual gatherings—caves were hardly necessary in the summer, and the grooves had rounded edges, not the sharp lines of freshly cut stone—they looked old. Hundreds of years old, maybe? But who would have gone to so much trouble to carve out caves in the wilderness?

As the others started down the trail, my eyes fell on the outline of my father's knife beneath my sleeping mat. I wasn't afraid of anyone taking it—but it didn't seem right leaving it behind. I took out one of my spare strings and used it to secure the sheath around my waist, under my tunic. Then I ran down toward the valley floor to catch up with the others.

Twelve disciples sat in the shade of a large carob tree, its branches heavy with green pods browning in the early summer heat. Daniel directed us toward a smaller pomegranate tree nearby, where we immediately warmed up. Uriel acknowledged us with a nod, then addressed the disciples.

"Envision your nefesh like a pool of water. When the soul is perfectly still, it reflects what is above. The slightest ripple on the surface, however, distorts the image, and destroys any hope for vision. Music helps us quiet the mind and calm the pool." I grinned at this description, thinking again of the fool who tried to grab the moon, but erased the smile as the prophet faced us. "Daniel, just a simple melody, this is the first trial for many."

Daniel plucked a slow tune, and the rest of us joined in once we caught the rhythm. I took advantage of the easy pace to practice the holds that Daniel had taught me the night before—my wrists ached from the strange position. The melody barely held my attention. Was it the simplicity of the music, our lack of sleep, or was Zim correct that there was just something special about the night?

If Uriel noticed anything absent, he didn't show it. He walked among the disciples, correcting their posture and whispering advice. One disciple appeared older than the rest, with milky scars mapping his face. He sat upright with legs crossed, eyes closed, swaying gently with the nigun. He listened to Uriel's whispering, nodded once, then returned to his swaying.

My heavy eyelids kept fighting to close. All the things I normally did to keep myself awake—pacing, talking, even playing faster or harder—would have disturbed the disciples. Only one of the bnei nevi'im appeared to be struggling with sleep himself, despite the fact that the disciples had woken at the second watch of the night and were now doing nothing more than listening to our dull music. I recognized him as Elad, the disciple of Yosef's who had scratched his nose two days earlier during their training, the one who surmised that I was uncomfortable with the disciples discussing me. Elad's head kept drooping forward and jerking back up as he fought off sleep. The rest of the bnei nevi'im indicated through their straight posture and gentle rocking that they somehow remained engaged.

It was a relief when the session finally ended and we were given a break before the midday meal.

"Do you mind holding my pipe?" Yonaton asked me. "I want to run home, I'm sure that my mother is worried."

"I don't mind," I said, suspecting that Yonaton was running home less for his mother's need than his own.

He handed me his halil, a delicately whittled piece of olive wood out of place in his thick farmer hands. "I'll be back in time for the meal."

I watched him go until he passed over the hill, out of sight. I wondered how my family was doing in Levonah. Eliav would be out with the sheep, Dahlia would already be baking the midday bread—did they miss me?

I lay down on my back, enjoying the sun on my face, thinking about what I would tell Dahlia at the end of the gathering. The look of awe in her eyes was the last thing I saw as I drifted off to sleep.

I awoke to Yonaton's figure standing over me, a melon in his hands. "We're going to miss the meal."

"What? Oh, right." I sat up, stretched my arms above my head, and followed Yonaton down to the eating area, hazy from sleep.

Bread, cheese and bright green leeks were still laid out on the serving table. Again, one of the servants handed me a prepared dish, but only me, offering no explanation why he had not done the same for Yonaton. My portion was a bit bigger than the night before, but lacked cheese. Did Uriel really feel that I deserved so little, especially when Yonaton was allowed to take as much as he wanted? Well if he objected to my taking more, he'd have to tell me himself. As Yonaton helped himself to everything from the serving table, I took more leeks and laid a big spoonful of cheese over the top. Food in hand, we sat down next to Zim, who was already finishing his meal.

"So that was prophecy?" Yonaton asked, dipping his bread in the runny cheese.

I shook my head, fighting back a smile. "No one there received navua. It looks more like this—" I put down my bread, leaned over, and trembled the way Uriel had done. Two passing disciples flashed me cold stares.

"Whoa," Yonaton's eyes went wide. "So what do we do when it happens?"

"We keep playing, right?" Zim said through a mouthful of bread. "If they need us for prophecy, we have to keep going."

"I don't think it matters. When Uriel had navua it didn't seem as if he'd notice anything, really."

"So he was completely vulnerable?" Zim asked. "Anyone could just come over and slit his throat?"

I recoiled at the brutish question. "I guess so."

"But he's a prophet," Yonaton said. "He can see things no one else can. He would know if he's in danger."

"You think?" Zim asked. "From what I've heard, prophets see only really important things."

"But if someone wanted to hurt him, that would be really important to him—don't you think, Lev?"

"It would be," I said, trying to sound confident, but feeling shaken. Zim might actually be right: Uriel had seemed completely removed from this world while receiving prophecy. But if Uriel was vulnerable, it seemed best not to share that information. "Besides, prophets see things all the time that aren't so important, they just don't tell stories about them. I saw Uriel find a lost ring."

Zim stood up to leave, his remaining bread still piled high with more leeks than Yonaton and I had taken together. "You're not finishing your meal?" Yonaton asked.

"These are almost raw," Zim said, pointing to the leeks. "They've got all these servants, why don't they cook their food?" He walked off toward our cave, shaking his head.

The two of us were the last to finish eating. When we were done, Yonaton hefted his melon. "You want to split this with me?"

"Sure."

Yonaton took the fruit over to a large rock and lifted it over his head.

"Wait, no need to smash it, I've got a knife." I reached under my tunic and pulled out my father's knife, then hesitated as Yonaton stretched out his hand. I hadn't shown it to anyone, nor even used it myself. But I'd already offered—it wouldn't do to refuse now. I turned the blade around and held out the hilt, hoping he hadn't noticed the hesitation. He cut off two pieces, then thrust the knife back into the melon.

Yonaton bit into his slice, but his eyes were on the handle sticking out from the fruit. "Where did you get that knife? I've never seen one like it."

I turned away, wishing I hadn't brought it out. "This is a great melon. Did you grow it?"

"It's from my own plot." Yonaton said, his grin as wide as the melon slice. "I just saw it was ripe when I went home."

"Where did you get that?" We both jumped at the rumble of the deep voice behind us. We turned to see the disciple from that morning's session, the one with the milky scars marring his face, pointing at the melon. The three of us were now alone in the clearing.

"From my family's farm on the other side of the hill. Cut yourself off a slice if you like."

"Not the melon, boy. The knife." He plucked it out of the fruit and held it up before his eyes, turning it this way and that. The flint blade absorbed the sun's light instead of reflecting it back.

My mouth went dry as I held out my hand to take it back. "It was my father's. Now it's mine. Give it here."

The man ignored my outstretched hand. "Your father's you say?" His eyes moved from the knife to me, the scars knotting and flushing as he spoke. "And what's your name?" The exposed blade in his hand made the simple question a threat.

"Lev."

"Lev ben?"

There was something about him I didn't trust. "Lev ben Menachem," I lied. "And yours?"

His scars stretched as he let out a harsh laugh. "Shimon ben Naftali. Very wise to use your uncle's name, Lev ben Yochanon." He took a step toward me, holding my blade in his left hand, and pulling a dagger from his belt with his right. I was defenseless.

Yonaton reacted immediately, jumping to his feet, snatching a rock from the ground, and cocking his arm back, ready to throw at the first sign of attack.

I stood paralyzed, hand still extended, gaping at this stranger who knew my father's name.

Shimon ignored both our reactions, his eyes returning to my knife as he turned his small dagger around and offered me the hilt. "Take this."

I reached out and took the weapon—though if we were going to fight I'd rather have my knife back. But Shimon simply wiped my knife clean on the hem of his tunic and laid it down next to the melon. He bent down, bringing his eyes even with mine. "Never let anyone see this knife. The danger it brings is very real." I was mystified by his words, but saw the truth in his eyes. "Besides, this is not a tool for cutting fruit. It has only one purpose, and should be used for nothing else. If you want to cut melon, use that one," he pointed to the blade in my hand. "You can keep it. I've got another."

Without another word, Shimon turned and headed down the hill, in the opposite direction from where the disciples were gathering. As he retreated, I examined the bronze weapon in my hand. Its value was equal to two sheep at least, probably three. Even if the disciples were rich, as Daniel said, surely they didn't just give away such valuable gifts for nothing? My eyes moved to my father's knife, sitting on a rock, still moist from the melon. It didn't look dangerous—what was he afraid of? But I had a more pressing question. "Wait!" I shouted at Shimon's back. "How did you know my name?"

Shimon didn't break his stride down the trail, only turned his head to reply over his shoulder. "I brought you to your uncle."

Rabbi Elazar HaKapar said: Envy, desire, and the pursuit of honor remove a person from the world.

Pirkei Avot 4:28

The Song of the World

"What just happened here?" Yonaton's arm dropped to his side, but his fist still gripped the rock he'd picked up to defend me.

My eyes remained fixed on Shimon's dagger in my hand, avoiding Yonaton's stare. "My parents were killed when I was two."

"Killed? By who?"

"I don't know. It was during the civil war." I didn't look up—I couldn't bear seeing the pity in his eyes. "All I know is that a stranger left me at my uncle's house...after. I guess now I know who that was." I pushed my thumb into the edge of the dagger, not hard enough to draw blood, just enough to distract myself from the dark hole in my chest. "Are we playing again today?"

Yonaton's shoulders relaxed at the change of subject. "No, the masters gave us the rest of the day to prepare for Shabbat. I know a spring not far from here where we can bathe."

It was the best answer I could have hoped for. I was in no mood for the slow music we played that morning for the *bnei nevi'im*—music like that left my mind too free to wander. I tucked Shimon's blade into my belt, picked up my father's knife, and followed Yonaton toward the hills at the edge of the valley.

"I've never seen a knife like that—what's it for?"

For Yonaton, who could run home to his mother between sittings, it must have seemed obvious that I knew the purpose of my father's knife. But there was so much I didn't know. "I've never seen one like it either. My uncle gave it to me the day I left, but he didn't tell me anything about it. Just that it belonged to my father."

"Can I hold it?"

It was a natural question, but I still recoiled, weighing the knife in my hand as we walked. It was my father's—my only inheritance. Yonaton threw the rock in his hand at a distant boulder, and was rewarded with the resounding clap of stone on stone. He had good aim and a strong arm; I couldn't have hit that boulder even if I could have thrown that far. Yet Yonaton hadn't picked up that rock to throw it at some boulder, he picked it up to defend me from Shimon. I turned the knife around and held it out, handle first.

Yonaton received it with open palms. He ran a finger over the dark, gray edge. "I never knew stone could be so sharp. It looks ancient." He turned his attention to the insignia on the hilt. "Are these claws?"

"I think so, but I don't know what they mean."

"It looks like a small sword." He swung the broad blade in short, chopping arcs.

I thought back to Shimon's warning, "But who would get so upset about using a sword to cut a melon?"

Yonaton shrugged and handed back the knife. My chest relaxed as I slipped the knife back under my tunic, nestling it safely against my thigh.

We reached the foot of the hills and eased down a well-worn path leading into a shaded ravine. The gorge was lined by stunted oak trees, a sure sign of water. A disciple stood by the side of the path, hands extended toward the sky, eyes squeezed shut, tears flowing down his cheeks, mumbling something I couldn't understand. I forced myself to look away as we passed, fighting the desire to stare at his indecency. Daniel was right, whatever these *bnei nevi'im* were involved in was not for the likes of me.

Our trail wound through high brush as the ravine walls narrowed around us, ending at a crumbling, white cliff. Clear water bubbled out of a crack at its base and flowed into a pool formed by a cut in the bedrock.

Yonaton stripped quickly, wincing as he slipped into the frigid spring. I hung the knife over a branch of an olive tree, laid my tunic over it, and sat down at the edge of the pool. Despite the bright sun and appeal of cold water,

I didn't enter. My mind was fixed on Shimon. *He brought me to my uncle. Does he know how my parents died?*

"Come in!" A splash of water hit me in the face. Yonaton smacked the surface again and I put my hands up in a useless attempt to block the spray. I peered down at my attacker, submerged up to his chest, with his head still dry. My legs kicked a waterfall down on Yonaton. I soaked myself in the process, but no longer cared. Yonaton fought back with the full force of both arms, drenching me. I pushed off the edge of the pool, dove under the water, and pulled my new friend's legs out from under him.

🎵 🎵 🎵

We were still laughing when we returned to our cave late in the afternoon. Zim stood at the entrance, back to the waning daylight, a polished bronze mirror in one hand, shaping his long hair into a wave with the other. He had changed his tunic of plain wool for one of reddish brown that left watery red marks on his neck—he must have stained it himself with berries. Anything dyed with madder or henna would have been expensive beyond even his wildest dreams. Zim nodded as we walked in, without glancing up from his mirror.

"Have you ever seen a boy with his own mirror before?" Yonaton whispered in my ear.

I shook my head. "My aunt has one, but she doesn't look in it this long."

"If I was your aunt, I wouldn't either," Zim said, entering the cave. "You should be more careful if you're going to talk about me. I may drum loudly, but my hearing is excellent." My ears grew hot and Yonaton turned away, but Zim wore the same carefree expression as always. "Laugh if you like, but if you ever want to feed yourself with your music, you should think about getting one yourself."

"A mirror won't help our playing," Yonaton said.

"True, but it will get you more work. All eyes are on the musicians—you get hired for more festivals if you look right." Though answering Yonaton, Zim held out his mirror to me.

I took the sheet of flat, shiny metal. It had been a long time since I'd seen my reflection, and the mirror was clearer than any pool I had peeked in. My brown hair was curled from the water, the hairs on my lip were thicker, like a long shadow under my nose, but I was mostly struck by my eyes. They were light today, the color of bee honey, and seemed older than I felt.

From the valley rose the blast of a ram's horn, the signal of the coming Shabbat. The three of us headed down to the clearing where we joined Daniel. Like Zim, he had a second tunic for Shabbat, made from finer wool than the one he wore during the week. The food was a measure better than the night before; the vegetables were still barely cooked, but the smell of roasted lamb also filled the clearing. My mouth watered. Aunt Leah prepared meat only for festivals.

Again a servant handed me a piece of bread and portion of beet greens that had been set aside for me behind the cooking area, where they had already turned cold. I received no meat, and the amount, though larger for Shabbat, didn't come close to meeting my appetite. Daniel, Zim, and Yonaton all eyed my food curiously; none of them had rations set aside. I took the bread and piled meat onto it, making sure the servant saw I wouldn't quietly accept such meager portions. But my greed still seemed small next to Zim's, who crowded as much lamb on his bread as it would hold, not wasting any space on the vegetables. Daniel pointed out a spot for us closer to the *bnei nevi'im* than we had sat the night before. As soon as his bottom hit the ground, Zim raised a chunk of lamb to his mouth, but Daniel grabbed his wrist. "On Shabbat we wait."

Uriel stood in the middle of the clearing holding a goblet of wine. His voice rose in a chant that spoke of the six days of creation and the day of rest. I was familiar with the words from my uncle's house, but not with the drawn out pace of the prophet's melody. It was hard to concentrate on the words with such savory smells wafting up from the food.

When the blessing was complete, Uriel drained the goblet in a single motion, and handed it to a waiting servant. "Now can I eat?" Zim asked Daniel.

"Patience."

The prophet now held up two loaves of bread, one on top of the other. "The Holy One tested our fathers with manna in the wilderness, giving them each morning enough food for that day, but no more. On the sixth day, they received a second portion for Shabbat. The blessing of Shabbat is that we do not receive; it is the blessing of knowing that we already possess what we require. I bless us all on our quest for holiness to know that the Divine light we seek is already within us."

Uriel had barely broken the bottom loaf when Zim's hand starting moving toward his mouth. "Now?"

"Yes."

My hand hadn't been poised like Zim's, but my stomach was just as ready to pounce. The meat was pink and tender, and the vegetables were so well flavored that I almost didn't mind that they were undercooked. Though I had taken a large portion, I soon went back for more of everything.

I was just finishing my second helping when conversation among the disciples died. Tzadok, the ancient, third master, stood by the fire in the center of the eating area. Zim still ate, but Yonaton and I stood, knowing that when the masters spoke it was time for us to go. Daniel put a hand on each of our shoulders. "On Shabbat we stay."

Tzadok closed his eyes, filled his chest, and opened his mouth in song. I would never have guessed that such a resonant voice could emerge from so frail a body. The melody was simple and repetitive. Daniel and a number of the disciples joined him immediately, and more of us merged with them as we picked up the *nigun*, until we all sang together. Swept up in the current of the song, my body swayed and I closed my eyes.

Our voices echoed in the open air of the valley. The melody folded over on itself, and amplified the collective energy with each turn. For the first time since coming to the gathering, I felt united with the *bnei nevi'im*. When Tzadok reached the end, he lifted his voice higher, holding the final note until his breath ran out. His silence brought the song to a close, and quiet settled over the clearing.

I opened my eyes to see Uriel standing alone, his face illuminated unevenly by the red light of the dwindling fire.

"There was once a man who lived in a kingdom in the middle of the desert." The prophet spoke softly, but in the stillness of the night, his voice carried across the open ground. "Every day, this man walked past the King's palace in the morning as he went out to his field, and again in the evening when he walked home. Each time he wondered, 'Why is it that the King has so much while I have so little?' His envy of the King grew and grew, until he was unable to pass the palace without anger.

"The man formed a plan: he would dig a tunnel under the palace, come up inside the treasury, and take just a tiny amount for himself. He worked for years and years on his tunnel, and as his labors grew, so did his desire, until he no longer felt the need to leave the King anything at all. Finally, the tunnel was complete, and he broke through the floor of the palace in the middle of the night. He expected to see piles of gold and gems, but found himself in an empty hallway, just outside the treasury. If he kept on digging, there was a chance that he could still access the treasury and escape before dawn. But now that he had broken through the floor, fear struck his heart—he could be discovered at any time, and discovery would cost him his head. So he stepped back into his tunnel and fled the palace with nothing.

"It happened that a second thief, who knew nothing of the first, had formed an identical plan to rob the King, and tunneled into the palace on the very same night. Unlike the first, he emerged inside the treasury itself. He saw mountains of gold and streams of jewels, and filled his bags and pockets with treasure. As he was about to leave, he spotted a large ruby in the corner of the treasury, so beautiful that he could not imagine leaving it behind. Lacking any room for it in his bags or pockets, he placed the gem in his mouth.

"The thief lowered his bags into the tunnel and was about to jump in, when he stopped. He spit the gem back into his hand and restored it gently to its place. Then, he emptied his bags and pockets, returned the treasure, then climbed into his tunnel—leaving the palace with nothing.

"The next morning, the two tunnels were discovered. The head of the guards came running to the King. *My King, two thieves tunneled into the palace last night.*

"The King was shocked, no one had ever broken into his palace before. *How much did they take?* he asked.

"The guard said, *It is unfathomable my King—they didn't take anything. One thief missed the treasury and left with nothing. The second thief entered the treasury, but we've counted the reserves and nothing is missing.*

"The King said, *I want to meet these two men. Let it be known that they will not be punished if they come forward.*

"Such was the power of the King that both thieves presented themselves at the palace by day's end. The guards brought the first thief before the King. *Explain how it was that you broke into my palace and left with nothing?*

"The thief stood shaking before the King and said, *I planned to tunnel into the royal treasury, but when I came out I found that I had not dug far enough. I feared that if I ventured further, I would be caught, so I went back into my tunnel and fled.*

"The King said, *Very well. Had you remained, you might have caused me great loss, but as it transpired you turned away from the evil. As promised, you will not be punished. I reward your honesty today with your life. You may go.* The first thief was removed from the King's audience.

"Guards then escorted in the second thief. The King turned to him and asked, *Explain how it was that you broke into my treasury and left empty handed.*

"The second thief dropped his head. *I did intend to rob you, sire. When I emerged inside your treasury, I filled all my bags, my pockets, and even my mouth with your treasure. Then, when I was about to climb into the tunnel and escape, an image of your face came to my mind. You have been a just and generous king to your people. I should be proud to serve such a king. How could I rob you? So I returned all the treasure to its rightful place and left the way I came.*

"A tear came to the King's eye. *Guard*, he called, *I want you to take this man into the treasury and let him take anything he wants.*"

Uriel paused, staring into the glowing coals. "There are two ways to turn from evil in this world. If we right our way from fear of punishment then, like the first thief, we are forgiven. But there is a higher way—to rectify our deeds out of great love for our King. Then our very sins bring us merit, for the Holy One knows how far along the path of evil we have gone and how great an effort it took to reverse our course. If we return in love, our *tikun* will be great indeed."

The prophet rose taller in the dark, his voice loud in the silence. "Some of you are here because you desire the prophets' power. You want to cry out, to correct the errors of the people, and when your cries are not heard, you will be tempted to coerce. You must remember that the Holy One seeks true service of the heart. To threaten the people, to give them a glimpse of the awesome power of the Holy One, may sway them, but only through fear.

"Yisrael is a holy nation. The task of the *nevi'im* is to guide them to the highest level of service, to inspire their holiness to elevate all of creation. To do this, we must awaken in them the desire to rectify their deeds out of love. I wish you all a peaceful Shabbat."

𝄢 𝄢 𝄢

"Blessed is the One who divides between the sacred and the mundane," Uriel chanted the following evening at the close of Shabbat, "between light and darkness, between Yisrael and the nations, between the seventh day and the six days of creating—"

"And between the *nevi'im* and the musicians," Zim chortled, just loud enough for the three of us to hear.

I ignored him, gazing up at the stars first breaking through the dark sky. The sun had set some time ago, leaving an inky stain on the western horizon. Uriel lifted the goblet of wine in his hand, sanctifying the end of Shabbat as he had its beginning. When he marked the division between light and darkness, a disciple touched together the wicks of two lamps, merging their flames into one.

"Can we play now?" Zim asked.

"Yes," Daniel answered, his voice strained. "Let's go back to the cave."

When he and Zim played music together, they worked off each other beautifully. But instruments were forbidden in Emek HaAsefa on Shabbat, and had sat idle the past night and all that day. Throughout the Shabbat day, while I enjoyed the quiet, walking through the valley with Yonaton and playing Stones, Zim lay in the cave, his eyes straying again and again to his untouched drum in the corner.

At midday on Shabbat, Daniel had sat with eyes closed, listening. "I love coming to this valley," he said. "It's so peaceful. When our music is stilled, you can really hear the song of the world."

"The world has a song?" I asked.

"Each thing in the world has its own melody. Together their notes rise to form the song of the world."

Zim, who had said little since the morning meal, rolled over at this. "Call it the noise of the world if you must—what you're hearing is too much silence. You're right that there's beautiful music in the world, and you'll hear it as soon as I can get my drum."

Now that Shabbat was finally over, Zim sped up the dark trail and was already seated outside tapping at his drum when the rest of us reached the cave. I retrieved my *kinnor*, took my place on one of the boulders, and fell into rhythm with Zim. Yonaton piped in with his *halil*, but Daniel still did not come out to join us. Would the tension left over between Daniel and Zim from Shabbat keep them from playing together? The thought had hardly been formed in my mind when Daniel stepped out, *nevel* in hand, and sat down between Yonaton and Zim.

Zim gave a last roll, and removed his hands from his drum, bringing our brief song to an end. He waved toward Daniel in a gesture that said, "You lead." Daniel tightened his strings, then struck up the *nigun* that Tzadok had led us in the night before. He began the song slowly, increasing his pace with each pass through the melody. We played on into the night, not speaking, letting the music reunite us in a way that words could not. On our first night together we had jumped from melody to melody, but tonight Daniel never strayed from Tzadok's *nigun*, just kept incrementally increasing the speed and intensity with each round.

It was rare in Levonah that I found the time to play my *kinnor* without having to keep one eye on my sheep. All I had were those few precious moments after the evening meal each night when I could let myself dive fully into my music. But even those moments were short-lived, as it was never long before my uncle, or exhaustion, called me in for bed. That night in Emek HaAsefa, Daniel drew me deeper into music than I had ever ventured before. We must have passed through the melody a hundred times or more, but it never grew old. Before long, the notes came of their own off the strings, without thought. I felt the notes flow through me, vibrating up through my chest, and saw them behind closed eyes in tones of blue and orange. For the first time I sensed what the prophets were seeking in our music, and why Daniel had said the night before that it could transport me as well.

It was not until well after the moon set, after the ram's horn sounded to wake the disciples, that Daniel finally broke off the *nigun*. My eyes scanned Zim's expression, expecting a protest; his energy had only increased as the night went on. No disappointment registered on his face, though. It was only after I lay down, when I heard neither snoring nor tossing from the bedroll next to me, that I realized Zim had not rejoined us in the cave.

Sometime later, a hand shook me awake. "Don't make a sound. Get dressed and follow me," Zim whispered in my ear.

I knew how much time had passed only when I stepped out of the cave and saw how far the stars had wheeled across the sky—I guessed we were late into the second watch of the night. The hair on my arms stood on end without the comfort of my warm bed. "Why did you wake me?"

"I want to show you what I found. Come." He turned without further explanation, and I was too clouded by sleep to protest. Zim all but ran down the path, and I hurried to keep up, careful not to stumble into the darkness below. It was only when I paused to catch my breath and the sound of my footfalls ceased that I heard it: a low, bass hum. "Zim, what's that sound?"

"You've finally heard it? I was beginning to wonder whether you three were deaf or I was crazy. I've heard it every night since we've arrived, but tonight I finally found the source. Come."

We reached the valley floor, continued along the base of the cliff and onto a faint trail that rose to the black mouth of a cave. The sound grew deeper, its rhythm vibrating along the stone walls of the cave. When we stepped inside, I could feel the sound reverberating in my bones. The cavern floor sloped steadily down into darkness. Sightless, I kept one hand on the wall and followed Zim's breathing.

There would come a time when I would grow used to the underground world, but at this moment I was still a child of the sun. As we descended deeper toward the source of the sound, I felt the weight of the rock pressing above me. Had I been alone, I certainly would have fled back to the comfort of the starlight. But I continued on after Zim, preferring to tremble in darkness rather than face his scorn.

Salvation came in the form of a dim, yellow light in the distance, growing brighter as we approached, and finally taking the shape of a lamp burning in a niche carved into the blackened rock of the tunnel wall. Below it was a short drop of less than a body's length; the lamp was surely there to prevent any-one from falling. Zim climbed down first, then silently showed me where to place my hands and feet. As we moved on, the security of the light tugged at me from behind, but in a few steps the tunnel turned and once again we were dependent on our hands and feet to see.

I lost count of my footsteps as we descended into the earth, the deep notes expanding as they echoed up to us. As we approached the source, it assumed a layered quality. The complexity was beyond anything but a stringed instru-ment, no number of voices woven together could accomplish that. *Could they?* A second light gleamed in the distance, and the tunnel widened out to meet it.

Torches high on the wall lit the floor of the cavern, but its roof remained shrouded in deep darkness. Flickering light danced over three circles of men swaying in rhythm, mouths pouring out their song. The power of the *nigun* that Tzadok sang the night before and that Daniel led us in earlier that evening was in its repetition, in its slowly building pace. Yet this *nigun*, sung under-ground, had a fullness that the other one lacked. Somehow, I knew the chant was ancient, each voice a thread in a fabric that stretched back ages. Tones stitched endlessly on themselves, notes braided into sacred layers, building ever more elaborate structures of sound. The song vibrated in harmony with the echoes thrown back by walls of the cave, and the torchlight seemed to grow brighter as the intensity built.

I edged toward the swaying men, eager to join them in their song. Before I made two steps, Zim grabbed my arm and pulled me back into the shadows, shaking his head. In my desire for the music, I had forgotten that we were in-truders—the prophets would not welcome trespassers. I nodded that I under-stood and Zim released me. Holding our breath, we crept along the cool and damp wall of the cave, outside the circle of light, and tucked ourselves into a crevice where we could see, but not be seen.

Tzadok again led the *nigun*, his hands on his knees, his body loose as he rocked forward and back. Even Yosef swayed with the melody, his dark eyes hooded by closed lids, the sharp lines of his face softened by the warm light.

What had saved me from drowning in my grief? Music. What had freed me when my pain was too much to bear? Music. But here I felt a new power: I saw the prophets and their disciples attaining a true unity on the strength of the *nigun*. I saw that music that flows from the heart can convey a depth of emotion that words cannot.

The song had been steadily building since we entered the cave, and now the momentum came to a head. Their voices rose to a peak in a unity that almost brought me to my knees—then ceased all at once. The silence deep in the earth held me like a newborn child.

The disciples' clothing rustled as they stood. Once they left the circle of light, we would no longer be hidden. Zim's voice trembled in my ear, "We have to get out of here."

We crept back along the wall, moving as quickly as possible without making a sound. Zim and I reached the tunnel without mishap, though I could not be sure we had escaped unnoticed. We scurried faster now, still careful to muffle our footsteps, but taking comfort in being out of view.

The breeze from the cavern's mouth flowed toward us in a cool stream. I raised my hand to my face, surprised to find a touch of moisture on my cheek, and quickly wiped my eyes. I did not risk my first words until we were beneath the stars again. "Warming to the prophets now, are you?"

"I had no idea they had music like this," Zim replied, shaking his head. "Imagine having such power and keeping it hidden underground!"

We increased our pace now that we were out of the total blackness of the cave. "What else should they do with it?"

"What else? You heard Uriel on Shabbat, he said that the prophets must uplift the people. So what do they do? They travel the land teaching the Law. If they want to inspire, they should bring their music out into the daylight!"

"It looks as if they don't agree with you."

"Of course they don't, and the more fools they are. They don't know how to use what they have—but we can." Zim's face glowed in the starlight.

"We work for them."

"Just for the gathering. In two months we'll be free."

"Free? Once the gathering ends I have to go home."

Zim led the way up the narrow trail crossing the cliff face. "You mean to your uncle's? And how long will that last? I heard you talking to Yonaton yesterday."

I scratched the back of my neck. "I thought you were asleep."

"I told you, you have to be careful what you say around me." Zim grabbed my arm and yanked me away from the edge of a precipice. "You have three years left at most in your uncle's house. Then what will you do? Wander alone through the wilderness, dreaming only of green grasses and fresh water for your flock?"

The words stung, and I hung my head. "What choice do I have?"

"Fool, you have your *kinnor*! If we spent our nights in this cave, learning the ancient *nigunim* of the prophets, just think what it would do for us. We could go anywhere—even to Shomron to play for the King."

"The King?" Zim was clearly repeating some fantasy of his.

He stopped in his tracks and faced me. "Yes, the King! Why not? Come with me."

Suddenly, I understood why Zim handed *me* his mirror the other day, even while speaking to Yonaton. It was the same reason that he woke me alone to hear the prophets' chant. I was the one with no future. I could go anywhere and hardly be missed. And two wandering musicians would be better than one; we could keep each other company, perhaps even find more work. As we reached our quarters, I was glad for an excuse to break off the conversation. "I don't know, Zim."

Zim appeared ready to say more, but Daniel rolled over in his sleep, and he held back.

I dropped exhausted onto my sleeping skin, eager for sleep. But neither of us got what we wanted. Zim never did make it back to the chanting cave, nor did I get a good night's rest.

The stars were fading when I next opened my eyes, my mind still cloudy from lack of sleep. I didn't know what woke me a second time before the sun, but there was a simple solution to such a problem. I wrapped myself more tightly and turned away from the dim light at the cave's opening.

As I drifted back toward sleep, my mind floated on the tide of birdsong rising from the valley below. The first trills and whistles were rhythmic enough to be a *nigun*, the blending together of so many voices strangely reminiscent of the song in the chanting cave. The world began to fade back into a sweet swirl of sound and light when I felt a hand on my back. I rolled over and saw Daniel's lanky body silhouetted by the deep blue pre-dawn glowing at the entrance. I stared up with blinking eyes and cocked my head to the side in an unspoken question. He put a finger to his lips and beckoned me to follow. I slipped my tunic over my head, wondering for the second time that night why I was leaving my warm nest behind.

Out now in the open air, the birdsong grew expansive. I hugged my arms to my chest, stepped out into the lightening morning, and inhaled the fresh scent of dew. Daniel hurried along one of the trails, and turned to wave me on without a word. I kept my eyes on my feet, trying hard not to stumble as I sped down after Daniel. What could be so pressing at this hour?

At first I thought that Daniel was bringing me back to the chanting cave, but then he left the path and slowed his pace, stepping through the tall yellow grass, heavy with dew. "What are we doing here?"

He put a finger back to his lips. A few paces on he stopped, dropped to his knees, and crawled on the ground, his eyes fixed on a single point. I followed behind, my tired eyes registering only a blur of brown and yellow. Gradually I gained focus; there, on a stalk of wild barley, sat a grasshopper, its green body muted to dark gray in the morning light. I turned to Daniel and mouthed, "What are we doing here?"

Daniel put a hand to his ear and pointed to the grasshopper. I closed my eyes to listen. The birdsong of the morning was so strong that it overwhelmed the high-pitched chirps of the tiny grasshopper. I leaned in closer, focusing on its piping, steadily blocking out all other sounds. As the rest of the world receded, I sensed deeper rhythms and more tones in the grasshopper's calls. I felt a gentle touch on my back and brought my eyes up to Daniel's. "Why are we here so early?"

"The birdsong is loudest before sunrise."

"But doesn't that make it harder to hear the grasshopper?"

"You think I woke you to listen to a grasshopper? To hear the song of the world you need to hear everything—the grasshopper and the birds."

I closed my eyes and leaned back in, listening without filtering out the birdsong. But I couldn't hold the two sounds at once—the song of the birds was so powerful, the chirps of the grasshopper insignificant. I gave up and got back to my feet. "Why did you bring me here?"

"I told you, to hear the song of the world."

"Why didn't you wake the others?"

"Not everyone can hear it. Look at Zim, he has no interest in listening to birdsong or the sound of the wind blowing through the trees."

"And why not Yonaton?"

Daniel placed a hand on my shoulder. "Yonaton will be a farmer. His time is better spent learning to sow than learning to listen."

"You think I'm different because I can play music while watching my sheep?"

Daniel shook his head. "Yonaton's an only son, just like I was. He has no choice but to inherit his father's farm and care for his parents when they grow old. You have a choice."

I snorted, "The choice to be a landless orphan?"

"The choice to pursue your music."

I suddenly understood why Daniel woke me a second time: He over-heard the end of my conversation with Zim earlier. "So you also think I should leave my sheep to play festivals and weddings with Zim?"

Again, Daniel shook his head. "That's a desolate life. Besides, to play festivals and weddings you don't need to hear the song of the world."

"Then what?"

"I saw your face the other night when we were speaking about the prophets. It's not only in the summer that they need musicians. One who can hear the song of the world could play for them all year round."

"I couldn't hear the cricket and the birds together. I'm not even sure what I'm listening for." I once again thought how similar the birdsong was to the *nigun* from the chanting cave. Was that the secret? Were the *nigunim* of the prophets somehow connected to the song of the world?

"It takes practice, but you can learn. I already hear the song of the sheep in your music—it's subtle, but it's there."

"Sheep sing?" I understood why Daniel termed the bird-calls a song, but the bleating of my sheep—that was music?

Daniel started back across the meadow toward the path. "I heard a story many years ago from my master, who played before the prophets for forty years, and who first taught me to hear the song of the world. When King David finished writing the Psalms, he said to the Holy One, 'Is there any creature in this world that sings more songs and praises than I?' A frog came and said, 'Do not become proud David, I sing more songs and praises than you do.'"

"The frog could talk?"

"It's a story. But after hearing the frog, David set out to discover the songs and praises of other creatures. How he understood them I don't know, but he wrote their meanings down in a scroll." Daniel studied my face. "You find this hard to accept?"

"I've never heard any praises from my sheep."

"Neither have I. But we can hear the rhythms of the animals, and we can help the *bnei nevi'im* hear them too. Listening to the world is one of their tools, it helps them find their place in the Way."

"I thought we play to bring them joy?"

"True, but joy is only one thing that we can do for them." Daniel yawned, stretching his arms up over his head, clearly intending to go back to sleep.

"So are the songs we play part of the song of the world?"

Daniel paused at the cave mouth. "I don't know if we sing in the song of the world. You'd have to ask one of the masters that."

I lay down and spread my tunic over me. As I settled in, the bulge of my father's knife beneath my mat dug into my spine. It seemed that everyone had an opinion on my future. I hadn't always liked what my uncle taught me, but I always believed it: that without land I had one choice—to become a shepherd. Since arriving at the gathering, new paths had opened before me, but did they hold any greater promise?

Zim wanted me as a companion; we'd wander from place to place to place, looking for enough work to feed ourselves. A desolate life Daniel called it. Daniel thought I should learn to hear the song of the world and play before the prophets. Perhaps that was a little better: I wouldn't have to move so much and it would be easier to build a family. But even if I could hear the song, wouldn't I be just like the grasshopper, whose chirps were drowned out before the powerful birdsong? Was that my destiny—to become the servant of prophecy, playing a part no one would notice?

As a shepherd, at least I could be my own master, have my own flock, and my successes would be my own. One last thought floated through my mind as I drifted back to sleep: my uncle had chosen wisely.

Rabbi Akiva said: All that will be is already known, yet one still has the power to choose.

Pirkei Avot 3:19

The Rogue Vision

It began as a halting vibration in Raphael's hand, like the twitch of a heavy sleeper. I exhaled to relax my chest muscles, a technique Daniel had shown me the night before. I sucked my breath back in quickly as Raphael's back arched, his forehead extending upward as if drawn by an invisible cord. Zim increased his pace, reaching for the power of our nighttime sessions. I pushed myself to keep up, feeling Zim's energy in the raw blasts of rhythm pouring off his drum.

The invisible cord snapped, and Raphael slumped forward, motionless. As I stared, a tremor crept up his arms, meeting at the base of his neck. His head snapped up, and convulsions overran his slack body like a powerful tide. This was more than I had seen when Uriel received *navua* outside of Levonah.

Yonaton stopped playing and stood mouth agape. He caught my eye with an expression that said, "Now I see what you mean." He quickly returned his *halil* to his lips, blushing at having stopped playing. But the music was hardly necessary; Raphael could no longer hear it. The other disciples broke out of their meditations, some as dumbstruck as the musicians, watching the first storm of prophecy since the gathering began.

Raphael's arms gave a final jolt, then went limp, the convulsions ending more abruptly than they had begun. The tension slowly returned to his body, and he pushed himself into a sitting position, his eyes wide and unfocused. Only when his gaze fell on Uriel did he really seem to return to us. "I saw the King's servant," he said, his voice flat.

"Ovadia?" Uriel asked, eyebrows raised.

"Yes."

"What was he doing?" Uriel probed.

Raphael's forehead creased and his eyes narrowed, as if examining a picture only he could see. "He is coming." Raphael closed his eyes and rocked gently, as if trying to launch back into the vision. "And there was a voice."

"A voice? What did it say?"

"Heed his request."

Uriel's forehead tightened, the lines gathering above the bridge of his nose. "Who should heed his request?"

"You should, Master."

"*Me*?" Uriel pulled the collar of his tunic away from his throat. "Was there anything more?"

"That's all I heard."

In the heavy silence that followed Raphael's announcement, hoofbeats thudded faintly in the distance. The tremor grew to a rumble, indicating steeds driven hard. Four chestnut horses, with one rider apiece, turned off the road at the head of the valley and descended toward the clearing. Yosef and Tzadok emerged from their caves to join Uriel, and they stood like a wall, awaiting the arrival of the riders.

Three soldiers reined in their horses at a distance, their flanks heaving from the sprint into the valley. The fourth rider approached the masters, his eyes scanning the area rapidly as he dismounted, pausing briefly when his gaze fell on the musicians. He had thick red hair, ruddy skin, and was dressed like no servant I had ever seen. He wore an embroidered blue tunic adorned with silver, a leather belt studded with copper, and a short sword at his hip. A beam of sunlight glinted off a seal hanging from his neck. I knew from watching Yoel ben Beerah in Levonah that the King's men wore seals around their necks—but I had never seen one that reflected the sun.

He embraced each of the masters, holding Uriel longer than the other two. "Is there a place we can speak?"

"Let us go to my cave," Uriel said. "You are hungry after your journey, Ovadia?"

"I'll eat when you eat; I never have much appetite after a hard ride." There was a nasal tone to his speech—was the servant of the King not of Yisrael?

Uriel's eyes fell on me, and I felt the same sense of foreboding as when we first met. "Lev, please bring us wine."

I laid down my *kinnor* and ran to the cooking area where fires burned in three large, earthen hearths. I approached a harried servant, sweating over the midday meal. "I need a wine skin."

The cook's lip rose in a sneer. "If the musicians desire wine, they'll just have to wait." He turned back to his cook fire abruptly.

Observing his profile, I wondered what he had done to become a slave. The *avadim ivrim* were debt slaves, usually thieves sold by the court into servitude for up to six years to pay back double what they had stolen. Why would the prophets surround themselves with such people? "It's not for us, it's for the masters and an emissary from the King."

"Ah, you should have said so." The sneer disappeared and the *eved* retrieved a skin and four clay cups.

I ran to Uriel's cave and found the prophets and their guest seated around a low table. "So Ovadia," Uriel said, "To what do we owe your visit?"

"Let us wait until we're alone," Yosef said, nodding in my direction.

"No, no, it is fine that he hear," Ovadia said lightly, "It concerns him as well. You see, I've come for the musicians." I was filling the cups and nearly splashed a stream of wine on the table.

"Why would you want the musicians?" Yosef asked.

"For the wedding, of course. The King heard that the prophets assemble excellent musicians for their gathering, and he wants the very best in the land for his wedding."

"Interesting," Uriel said, leaning forward to take one of the cups. "Thank you for the wine, Lev." The wrinkled skin between his eyes creased in thought. "It's a little dark in here, would you mind lighting the lamps as well?"

Sunlight shone into the mouth of the cave, making it quite easy to see. Yet, in my eagerness to hear more, I neither argued nor hesitated to fetch fire from the cooking area.

"I won't consent to send them," Yosef said as I reentered the cave. I stepped quietly toward a lamp in the back of the cave and took my time lighting it, extending my opportunity to overhear as long as possible.

Ovadia's eyes widened as his hand clenched. "How can you refuse your king? He has the right to anything in the land that he desires."

"He may be the King, but the full allegiance of the *nevi'im* is not to any king of flesh and blood. I've heard about Ahav's bride, and I can only imagine what this wedding will be like. Are we, the *nevi'im*, meant to contribute to such a travesty? And we also have a duty to the musicians in our service. They come here to play before disciples striving for holiness." Yosef turned now to Uriel. "How can we expose them to such practices?"

Uriel broke eye contact with Yosef, and focused on Ovadia. "There are two things I don't understand. I'm surprised to hear that the King is even aware of our gathering, and all the more that we hire talented musicians to play for us. And even if he is aware and wants our musicians, why not send a simple messenger to retrieve them? Why send the steward of the palace on such a journey?"

"Two excellent questions," Ovadia said, grinning just as Eliav would when caught taking extra wine. "The King knows about the gathering and the caliber of your musicians because I told him. He sent me here because I advised him to handle the *nevi'im* tactfully before the wedding, something we could not depend on an ordinary messenger to do. I convinced him of this so that King Ahav would suggest that I go personally."

"Why would you do such a thing?"

"Because there are serious matters that I need to discuss with you, and I needed a reason to come."

The cave fell silent as the prophets pondered Ovadia's words. Yosef cocked his head toward his guest. "Ovadia, you have come to us many times in the past. Why should you suddenly need an excuse?"

The King's steward raised his cup to his mouth, but returned it to the table without tasting it. "Everything's changed since the King's engagement. He knows that many oppose the marriage and fears that his servants will turn against him as well."

"And this is why the wedding has been so rushed…?" Yosef posed, more of a statement than a question.

Ovadia nodded. "He wants it over before opposition can be raised. He is constantly on the watch now for who is loyal and who is not. For me to meet with you there needed to be a reason, otherwise it would arouse the King's suspicions. He assumes that you are opposed to the match."

"That still doesn't justify taking our musicians to play before such a ceremony," Yosef responded. "Uriel, you must agree with me?"

Uriel held Yosef's gaze for a long moment, then dropped his eyes to his cup. "I'm inclined to let them go. Whether the request is fitting or not, King Ahav has the right to anything in the land. And now is not the time to make an enemy of him."

Yosef scowled, but didn't respond. He turned to Tzadok. "We have given our opinions, it is up to you to decide."

There was a pause as Tzadok shut his eyes to consider the issue. Opening them, he glanced at each of the masters, and then, without a word, nodded in Uriel's direction.

"Very well," Yosef said, "I won't oppose both of you. The musicians may go. Now tell us Ovadia, what is so important that you had to invent such an excuse?"

Uriel cut across Ovadia before he could speak. "Thank you, Lev, that is enough light for now. Please make sure that the soldiers are fed and their horses are looked after."

Yosef surveyed me with his dark, unblinking eyes. Had he forgotten my presence, or was he simply annoyed that Uriel had allowed me to stay and listen? I turned away but felt Yosef's eyes following me. I kept my expression blank as I walked toward the mouth of the cave. Once outside, though, I broke into a run. I just had to find Yonaton; I had a lot to tell him—and we had to pack.

🪕 🪕 🪕

"What do you think they're talking about?" Yonaton asked me for the third time as we gathered our things.

"I wish I knew, but I don't think that we're going to find out. Master Uriel seemed to want me to hear the first part, but not the rest."

"My father always said my time would be better spent working the land than playing my *halil*. I wonder if this will change his mind?"

"What are you packing for?" Zim asked as he and Daniel walked into the cave. "Does this have anything to do with the King's servant and the mysterious request Raphael was talking about? Lev, did you overhear anything when you brought them their wine?"

"Yes," Yonaton said, his voice cracking with excitement. "Ovadia came to get us to play at the wedding."

"We're going to play for the King?" Zim snatched up his drum with one hand and pounded it with the other. "I knew it! I knew my moment would come!"

Daniel sat down, his forehead furrowed in thought. "If that's all he came for, we should be leaving already."

"Well—" Yonaton began, but I cut him off.

"Yosef didn't want us to go. They were still discussing it when I left." Yonaton shot me a glance that the other two missed, but I had overheard a private conversation; it wasn't my place to tell Zim and Daniel everything that I'd heard. Somehow telling Yonaton felt different.

Zim turned to Daniel. "You don't sound so excited."

"I've played for the King before. As soon as he came out of mourning for his father he celebrated his coronation and gathered musicians from around the land. But don't think we're going to play before the King as we play before the prophets. There will be many musicians there. We may not even see the King."

"I've never even been to Shomron," Zim said, tapping the edge of his drum with his fingertips. "The King keeps a small group of musicians to play in the palace," he added with a wink in my direction. "You never know what could happen…"

Ovadia spoke with the masters until the sun burned a fiery gold in the western sky. When they emerged from the cave, Uriel sent word that we would leave in the morning.

"I'm going to tell my parents," Yonaton told me. "Do you want to come? They want to meet you anyway."

I nodded and laid my *kinnor* on my sleeping mat, but when we stepped out we saw one of the servants climbing the path toward us. "Master Uriel wishes to speak with you, Lev." His tone was soft, with none of the brutishness of the cook I spoke to earlier in the day.

"Me?"

"Yes, he awaits you in his cave."

I waved goodbye to Yonaton and followed the white robed *eved* down the trail. As we turned on one of the switchbacks on the path, I noticed a puncture in his right ear; not a piercing of the lobe, but a hole in the ear itself large enough to see through. Only one thing could have mangled him in that way. I shuddered at the thought, a motion that was not lost upon the servant.

"You are staring at my ear?"

I turned red, but the man's smile did not waver. "Does that mean—?"

"That when my first service was complete, I chose not to go free. Yes, I am a slave until the *Yovel*…if it ever comes. Forever, probably."

"And your master…?"

"Master Yosef stood me up against a door and drove an awl through my ear, yes."

I couldn't tear my eyes away from the mark of bondage. "But you could have been free."

"Free to do what? Go back to being a thief?" His smile grew broader, showing no signs of shame. "We all serve, Lev. Before I served my appetites. Now I serve a worthy master."

When we reached Uriel's cave, the servant gestured to me to enter alone. Uriel sat in the same spot I had seen him earlier that day. He waved me toward the stool opposite him. I sat, my chest suddenly tight. "You heard quite a bit today."

I nodded, my eyes on the table. Was he upset that I lit the lamps so slowly?

"There is something on your mind, Lev. You may speak."

"I was surprised you let me hear as much as I did," I said quietly.

"As was I."

So Uriel had wanted me there. Then why did I still feel the pressure in my chest? "Why did you let me stay?"

"My heart told me I should." I raised my eyes as far as Uriel's beard. "I can see the question on your face; you want to know the real reason why."

I nodded in response.

"It began with Raphael—such an unusual way to receive a prophecy."

"It didn't seem very different from when I saw you, just more intense."

"True, it is not at all unusual for a *navi* to receive a message for others. But *nevi'im* are rarely given messages to deliver to other *nevi'im*. If the Holy One wished to send me a message, why not send it to me directly? This is the first time I've ever received a prophecy through another prophet." Uriel bent his head forward so that his eyes met mine. "Questions are the gateway to wisdom. You may ask."

What did he want from me? I dropped my eyes to the table again and asked the next logical question. "Why do you think you received the prophecy this way?"

"I wondered the same. It could be that the end of my life is drawing near. *Nevi'im* often lose their *navua* near the end of their lives. Or it could be that the Holy One has decreed that I no longer deserve *navua*." His right hand raked through his beard and held it. "But my heart tells me that neither was the cause of today's events."

"What then?"

"I believe that the prophecy was not directed to me alone."

"Then why didn't you tell Master Yosef about the prophecy? Wouldn't that have been easier than arguing?"

"Yes, it would. And since Raphael spoke publicly, I could have shared his words if I desired. But the fact that the message was not addressed to Yosef gave me pause. I was told to heed Ovadia's request, but he was not. He was right to rely on his own understanding."

"But you said the message wasn't intended only for you. If not for Master Yosef, then who else?"

Uriel paused until I glanced up. "I believe that it was for you."

A shiver passed through my body. "Me?"

Uriel hesitated, as if weighing his words. "I noticed Ovadia looking intently at the musicians when he arrived. He clearly had an interest in the four of you."

Even if that were the case, the prophecy could just as easily have been for one of the others. "There's more, isn't there?"

"Yes," Uriel replied, but said no more.

I felt blood rising to my cheeks and reached under my tunic for my father's knife, which I now kept with me at all times. The weapon hit the table with a dull thud. "It has something to do with this, doesn't it?"

Uriel picked up the sheathed knife with a faraway look in his eye. At that moment, I was certain that he had seen the knife before. "Yes," he replied, gazing directly at me, but offering no more information.

"What are you hiding from me?" I asked, my voice rising.

Uriel sighed. "I understand how difficult this must be, but it is not yet safe to tell you all that I know."

"If it's my safety, shouldn't I be able to decide—"

"No!"

My head jerked back at his sharp word.

Uriel's eyes glinted as he leaned across the table at me. "When I took you with me, I promised your uncle I would look after you. I question his judgment in giving you this knife. I can only conclude that he is unaware of its significance. You heard what Ovadia said—we are entering dangerous times!"

Uriel lowered his forehead into his hands, as though needing their help to carry its weight. When he lifted it, there was a softer expression in his eyes. "Much as I would like to protect you, Raphael's prophecy shows that there is a greater will than my own involved. I must...I will allow events to take their course."

The prophet met my eyes again. "Do the others know your father's name?"

I sat up at the question. "Only Yonaton and Shimon, the one with the scars."

"Good. From now on, call yourself Lev ben Menachem. Tell Yonaton so he won't be surprised, but instruct him not to tell the others. I'm not concerned about Shimon."

Uriel rose. "Be careful in Shomron. Darkness is rising in the Kingdom—I have felt it building for some time. Trust your heart. If something feels wrong to you, it probably is. And keep your eyes open. I won't be in Shomron to see for myself, so I'm counting on you to be my eyes and tell me everything when you return." Uriel walked me to the mouth of the cave, placing his hands on my shoulders. "Perhaps it is best if you leave the knife here with me?"

I shook my head—it was my only inheritance.

"Very well, take it with you, but show it to no one."

🎵 🎵 🎵

"Put your gear on the donkeys," Ovadia told the four of us the next morning. "We'll be riding the horses."

The prophets lent us two donkeys for the journey, and I hitched my sleeping roll and *kinnor* to the smaller one. "You can ride with me," Ovadia said. I stepped onto a large boulder and mounted behind him.

Uriel walked toward us from one of the caves, and Ovadia kicked his horse forward, out of earshot of the soldiers.

"I have given more thought to your question," Uriel said.

"You have not changed your mind?"

"No, but there is something more I want to tell you."

"Should we speak privately?"

"There is no need, it is just a story."

This didn't seem to me like the time for stories, but Ovadia didn't appear surprised.

"A fox once walked along the banks of a river. Looking down, he saw fish swimming frantically back and forth. *Why do you rush about from place to place?* he asked them.

"*We are fleeing the nets of the men,* they replied.

"*Come up onto the land with me,* said the fox. *Here you will be safe from the nets of the men, and we can live together as my ancestors lived with your ancestors.*

"*You are supposed to be the cleverest of animals,* replied the fish, *but you talk like a fool. If we are afraid in the water where we know how to live, how much more is there to fear on dry land where we will surely die?*"

Uriel paused. Ovadia said, "I'm not sure I understand."

"Both paths before you are perilous. When forced to choose, remember that the fish may die even in the water, but leaving it brings total destruction."

Taming the Bear

Exhausted, I slumped forward and gripped the horse's flanks with my knees in a vain effort to save my sore backside. More hills of Yisrael rose before me that day than I had seen in my entire life as the horses raced past Beit El, then north on the King's Road. We continued past Levonah, then finally headed west until we reached Shomron on the very edge of the mountain plateau. I always imagined Shomron as the largest city in the Kingdom, and was surprised to see that it was less than half the area of Beit El. Yet, despite its smaller size, Shomron was not lacking for fortifications. The walls were twice the height of the walls of Levonah, and there were three gateways, one inside the next, inside the next. We slowed our pace to pass through the triple gate, and four soldiers, each with the royal ox emblazoned on his tunic, stood at attention. Ovadia reined in our horse close to the one carrying Yonaton, and spoke in a low voice. "While you're in Shomron, the two of you will stay with me."

"What about Daniel and Zim?" I asked.

"They will be in the musicians' quarters."

"We don't mind being with the musicians too," Yonaton said.

Ovadia shook his head. "Master Uriel made me promise to look after the two of you while you are here. He would not agree to send you without my giving my word."

The day before, Uriel had insisted that he would let events take their course without interfering. Yet, as the horses carrying Daniel and Zim turned off the main road immediately inside the city gates while Yonaton and I were carried farther up the hillside, it seemed to me that the old *navi* was not done interfering after all. And I was sure of it when we reached Ovadia's house, the largest and most beautiful I had ever seen. There was an arched entranceway to the courtyard, and the walls were built of hewn stone, containing windows as broad as my arm. While two maidservants prepared a stew and kneaded dough in the wide kitchen, an *eved canaani* carried our meager belongings up the ladder to a room reserved just for us. Ovadia and his wife Batya saw to it that we wanted for nothing, yet they hardly spoke in our presence, even to each other. As I soaked up the last of my stew with my bread, Batya said, "You two look exhausted; you ought to get to sleep."

Though the sun had not yet set, Yonaton nudged my shoulder as if to say, "Don't argue." It was clear that the family wanted its privacy. We said good-night and climbed the ladder to our room where the amber light of late afternoon streamed in through an open window. It shed a soft and inviting glow over two fresh straw beds. I had never slept on straw before—in my house, only my aunt and uncle enjoyed such luxury. I leaned out of the window and took in the view of the palace, which stood upon a raised rock platform cut out of the hilltop. Its high walls glowed, reflecting the setting sun. Soldiers stood guard, stone-faced, at the corners of the parapet. I watched until darkness fell and the palace disappeared from view. Only a week ago, my sheep were my sole audience; now I was in Shomron, about to play my *kinnor* before the King. Perhaps Dahlia was right: our lives could change in an instant.

In the morning, the *eved canaani* directed us to the visiting musicians' quarters, a single room that could comfortably sleep six, but with more than twice that number crammed inside. Aside from a wine barrel standing upright in the corner, the floor was completely covered with bodies. We stepped gingerly over the other sleeping musicians to reach Daniel and Zim against the far wall. Daniel sat right up when Yonaton jostled his shoulder, but when I shook Zim he just opened his eyes, moaned, and rolled back over.

"Have a late night?" Yonaton asked.

"More like an early morning." Daniel stretched his arms over his head and yawned.

"Well, help us wake the others, we've got to get down to rehearsal." I shook Zim's shoulder again. "Come on, Zim, you've always managed to get up to play for the prophets. This time it's for the King."

"Yes," Daniel mumbled, pulling on his clothes, "But our prophets water down their wine."

After much wrangling, Daniel managed to get all sixteen visiting musicians up, dressed, and out through the city gates. The sodden bunch could barely keep their eyes open as we headed toward an open field where the six court musicians waited with some amusement.

"I'm sure you're all good musicians, otherwise you wouldn't have made it here," said Dov, the chief musician in the King's court. Despite his bearish build, Dov had soft eyes and a warm smile peeking out from behind his graying beard. "We have only two days to learn to play together, so we're going to have to be diligent. The court musicians have been working on the music for the wedding ever since the engagement, so we'll lead. When you feel that you've caught on, join in."

Dov picked up his tall *nevel* and counted into the first melody—a rousing dance tune that kicked off with strong percussion and two *nevelim*. The other court musicians set right into their parts without hesitation. The rest of us, one after the other, meandered into the tune as it became more clear. As soon as all of us were well into the melody, Dov laid down his instrument and circulated among us, offering comments and corrections. "You need to slow down," he said to Zim. "Focus on staying in time with the rest of us." Zim, who was still struggling to keep from nodding off, scowled at the criticism, but he did slacken his beat.

Yonaton, whose turn was next, watched the exchange out of the corner of his eye. "I think you've got it," Dov said to him. "Play louder, I want you to come out clearly." Yonaton's shoulders relaxed, and I saw a grin from behind his *halil*. Dov then stopped in front of me, closing his eyes to filter out the other musicians. He opened them, nodded, and walked onto the next player without saying a word.

Once he had finished his rounds, Dov returned to his place, picked up his *nevel*, played through one full measure with us, then brought the piece to a close. He immediately started a new *nigun*, and the process began again from the beginning.

Taming the Bear

The King's Road was packed with people pouring in for the wedding when Yonaton and I headed back in through the city gates. Apparently, not all of Yisrael was as opposed to the match as the people of Beit El. Merchants hawking their wares to the milling crowd lined the main road as it climbed the hill toward the palace, sitting proud and stolid upon its summit. Yonaton stopped before a man selling iron tools and picked up a two-pronged plowshare. "My father could plow twice as fast with one of these."

I grabbed his arm, pulling him away from the cart, "Come on, you can't afford that." Yonaton shrugged and released the plow point, which clanked against the others in the cart. I stopped in front of another cart loaded with milky rocks. Licking my finger, I touched it to the rock, and brought it back to my mouth. "Salt!"

"From the Salt Sea itself," the merchant said. "Don't go eating it, and mind your hands now that you've touched it—you could blind yourself if you rub your eyes with this on your fingers. But I promise you, friend, sheep love it. So do shepherds—keeps the flock healthy like nothing else."

I put my hand on the rock again, feeling the sharp points of the crystals pressing into my palm. No shepherd in Levonah had a rock like this. Yonaton tugged on my arm. "You were right, we can't afford this stuff."

"Now, you don't know that," the salt merchant held up both hands to stop us. "A little one costs just this much copper..." He held up a small iron weight and dropped it on one side of a scale.

Yonaton pulled on my arm again, but I couldn't take my eyes away from those rocks. Would it really keep the flock healthy? If we were paid well for the wedding it might be only two years now until my flock grew too large to keep at my uncle's house. Would I have to take final leave of my family at only age fourteen?

Then, unbidden, a new image rose in my mind. It was Dov's face from that morning, smiling at me, the lone musician among our group that he hadn't criticized even once during the rehearsal. True, I mainly stood out because I wasn't suffering the effects of wine like the others, but Dov didn't know that. Without even meaning to, I had impressed the most influential musician in the Kingdom. Perhaps Dov would offer me a place in the King's court if I proved myself? Then being a musician wouldn't mean moving around, hunting for work wherever I could find it. It wouldn't mean living in a cave, playing for prophets who would use my music to enter realms forever closed to me. I could stay in Shomron, play before the King and nobles, and find my place among the elite musicians of the land—even Zim dreamed of that.

Dov's face faded from my mind, replaced by one younger, sweeter, and so much closer to my heart, with stubborn red curls forever falling over a pair of hazel eyes. I was closer to Dahlia than anyone in the world, but she just wouldn't see the fact that I could never ignore. There was a stone wall between us. It was something we never talked about, even though I had gone over what I would have to say endless times in my mind.

The stone wall is like the wall of the pen. I'm on the inside, locked in with the sheep. You're on the outside, feet planted on the soil. The wall is only waist high now—we can gaze at each other, talk together, even touch as we did when we were children—but only because we're young. As soon as we're both of age, this wall is going to rise right over our heads.

We had been raised like brother and sister, but that was just another part of the illusion. As brother and sister, we could stay close—what husband would be jealous of his wife's brother? But no man would tolerate such closeness with a cousin. Yitzchak married his cousin, Yaakov married his cousin. Cousins could make the ideal marriage partners—they share family and their lands are often side by side.

But Dahlia and I were the exception. Uncle Menachem would never accept the life of the nomadic shepherd for his daughter. A traveling musician or even a player for the prophets would seem no better. But what about a member of the King's court? There was certainly no comparison between a life in the wilderness and a life in Shomron, the seat of nobility.

And then there was the copper. Daniel told me that the King paid visiting musicians well—surely he did no worse for members of his own court. It might take me twenty years as a shepherd to save enough to buy a piece of rocky hillside, but all the court musicians that morning were dressed in linen tunics, not the woolen ones that farmers and shepherds wore. Perhaps as a court musician I could buy land in ten, maybe even five, years. And Dahlia was right; if the *Yovel* was not coming, then any land I managed to purchase would be mine forever. *Would it be enough, though?*

The salt merchant hadn't taken his eyes off me this entire time. No doubt, he thought I was dreaming of returning to my flock with one of his rocks, but I was no longer interested. Here, finally, was a dream worth leaving my flock over, a path that even a landless orphan could take toward a normal life.

A shrill scream shook me from my thoughts. A woman shrieked in the distance, her voice immediately drowned out by the rough cheers of a crowd of men. As the cheers faded, her cries rose again, only to be drowned out a second time by a deep roar.

The salt merchant laughed.

"What's that noise?"

"Go see," he said with a wry grin.

Yonaton and I followed a throng heading off the main road in the direction of the commotion, on a path that looped around a pile of boulders jutting out of the hillside. There was another shrill scream, and we scampered up the boulders to peer down on the scene below. I fell behind because of my *kinnor* slung over my shoulder and called ahead to Yonaton when he reached the top. "Is she all right?"

"The *woman's* fine," Yonaton replied, flinching as the crowd roared again. "It's her husband that's got the problem."

"What's wrong with him?"

"He might be torn apart by a bear."

"A bear's chasing her husband?"

"No. Her husband's chasing the bear."

Sure enough, an enormous iron cage stood in the clearing below. Inside the cage, a powerfully built man edged closer to a shaggy, brown bear. Over a hundred people stood around the cage, cheering him on while his wife pulled at the bars, berating her husband. He ignored her, his eyes focused on the bear that was crouched on four legs, its head reaching as high as the man's chest. As the animal threw open its jaws and roared, glints of sunlight sparkled off its neck.

"Yonaton, is that bear wearing…?"

"Jewels," he whispered, stupefied.

The man in the cage stepped forward, and the bear reared up on its hind legs. One more step, and the beast swung yellowed claws as long as my fingers, like a set of curved knives, a handsbreadth from the man's face. A spectator reached his hand between the bars of the cage, trying to grab a golden bracelet off the bear's wrist. The beast turned with a snap of its jaws, and the challenger in the cage advanced, arm outstretched.

The bear spun back to him, swatting with its massive, brown paw. He jumped back, but not far enough. A sharp claw caught the end of his nose. He brought his hands to his face as the crowd gasped, his wife's cries reaching a frenzied pitch at the sight of blood pouring through his fingers. "Get out of that cage!"

Retreating to the corner, the man removed his hands from his nose and wiped the blood on his tunic. He advanced again, circling around to the right of the angry bear. The smell of blood only provoked the beast. It launched forward, slashing its paws. The man ducked under its arm and lunged for the back of the bear's neck. His greedy fingers closed around the golden chain of a ruby necklace. The beast whirled around, the back of a paw slamming into the side of its opponent's head. The blow lifted the man completely off his feet. He crashed into the iron bars of the cage, and slid down the bars, collapsing at the bear's feet.

Two soldiers with spears leapt into the cage. The bear growled, but retreated before the sharp iron points. A third soldier dragged the challenger out and left him in the dirt outside the cage. Awareness slowly returned to his face, now swollen purple. He opened his eyes and sat up, blinking furiously to clear his eyes of the blood flowing from a gash on his forehead. He unclenched his fist and surveyed his palm. It was empty. The bear was pressed against the far side of the cage, the red stone still suspended from its shaggy neck.

Someone from the crowd helped the man to his feet. As he staggered forward, his wife pounced, hitting him in the chest with both fists, less powerfully than the bear, but no less fierce. The crowd's laughter mingled with the wife's screams as she pulled him away. A scrawny man with large, bulging eyes climbed to the top of the cage and the laughter immediately ceased. "A handsbreadth away from a lifetime of riches! Who will be the next to try?"

Two men stepped forward from different parts of the crowd. "One at a time," the announcer said. "You. You climb in. You can go next. Unless…Ovadia, have you come to try? I'll let you go first!"

The crowd turned to watch Ovadia approach the cage. He stared long and hard at the bear, now back on four legs, circling its enclosure. The crowd was quiet, silenced by the prospect of seeing the King's steward in a death struggle for treasure. "Not today, Aviad," Ovadia replied, his calm gaze meeting the shaky eyes of the announcer.

But his refusal only excited Aviad. "Come, come…surely one who enters the throne room of the King isn't afraid to step into a bear's den?" The crowd laughed at the bold taunt but Ovadia just shook his head. Aviad raised his voice higher, "Can any man have too many riches?"

"A fool may be blinded by the jewels Aviad, but a wise man sees the claws."

Ovadia turned away and his eyes fell upon the two of us. "Ah, boys, I was hoping to find you here. Can you come with me?" We nodded and followed him away from the crowd. Once out of earshot, Ovadia pulled out a sealed scroll. "Please take this to Uzziah ben Hanan. He is the foreman in charge of readying the gates. Wait for his response, then come report to me at the palace. I'll instruct the guards to allow you entry."

I was anticipating a meal after a long morning of practice, but could not bring myself to refuse. We found the city gates thrown open and people streaming through, most on foot, some on donkeys, and quite a few nobles riding horses. Workmen washed the gates and smoothed out rough patches in the road under the supervision of a tall man who walked among them, inspecting their work. Yonaton approached him, "Are you Uzziah ben Hanan?"

He nodded, taking the scroll from Yonaton's outstretched hand and examining the clay seal in the image of a footstool. "So, what does Ovadia want now?" He broke the seal, read the scroll, then turned to one of the workmen washing the gates. "Shama, take your horn and position yourself on that hill. When Tzidon's caravan comes into view, sound three long blasts." Turning back to Yonaton, he said, "You may tell Ovadia that everything has been arranged."

The first part of our task done, we headed back up the hill toward the palace at the top—but something about our errand didn't feel right to me. "Does it seem strange to you…" I asked Yonaton, "…that Ovadia would use us as his messengers?"

"He's far too busy to go himself," my friend said simply.

"Of course he is, but he must have other servants."

"Look around, everyone's busy." Indeed they were. All around us the pavers were being washed, bushes trimmed, and even a canopy erected below the palace. "He probably needs all the help he can get."

"Maybe." But something still didn't feel right to me. Uriel may have convinced Ovadia to take us into his house, but why would he make us his messengers as well? *If he needs extra help, why not use his personal servants?*

Three guards blocked the palace entrance. One put out his hand to stop us. "We're looking for Ovadia," I said.

The guard caught sight of the *kinnor* hanging over my shoulder and nodded. "You're the musicians?" He smirked, probably expecting men, not boys. "Go through. You'll find Ovadia in the entryway."

From Ovadia's house, I had seen only the top of the palace, but as we stepped through the gates, I entered a city within the city. All of the houses inside the Levonah town walls combined together would hardly equal the size of the palace. It was at least five times as wide as Ovadia's house, and rose to a full three stories. In the courtyard, a double row of thick limestone columns led up to the palace gate. The whole enclosure was buzzing like a beehive: slaves sluiced down the broad flagstones of the courtyard, gardeners pruned the grapevines, and servants darted from place to place, each one burdened by his own load.

Under the arched and pillared entryway to the palace, Ovadia inspected a stately oak throne, oiled and buffed to a warm glow in the sunlight. Beside him, a man in linen robes specked with sawdust gestured to an elaborately carved cedar tree on the back of the throne. "Had there been more time—"

"Nonsense," Ovadia said, cutting him off. "No visiting king could expect more. King Ahav will be pleased." He turned at our approach. "Ah boys, everything's been arranged? Excellent. I'm sure you're hungry. You can return to the house and Batya will make sure you're fixed something to eat. I may join you there soon, once I find servants to carry this into the throne room."

I eyed the throne of dark-tinted wood. It looked heavy, but not too heavy for us to carry. The next time I saw Seguv, he would surely tell me about his appearance in the King's court. How I would love to tell him that I'd been there as well.

I might be dreaming of spending the rest of my life playing music at the court, but I know how much my dreams are worth. This might be the only chance I ever get.

Yonaton read my face and nodded—he wanted to do it too. I spoke up, in the deepest tone I could manage. "We can carry it."

Ovadia's lips curled into a bemused smile. "You probably can. But the King is sitting on his throne and will be watching. For all the world, I would not be the one to drop this throne in front of King Ahav."

"We won't drop it," I said, trying to sound more confident than I felt. The craftsman shifted from foot to foot, clearly displeased with the idea of mere boys carrying his creation. But he would not voice his opposition before Ovadia.

Ovadia ran his eyes slowly over my face, then down to my chest and hands. He gave the same inspection to Yonaton, who was shorter and more solidly built. I expected Ovadia to refuse, but he raised his eyebrows and nodded, appearing pleased with our proposal. "Very well, two stout hearts are worth many strong arms. The throne belongs next to the King, on his left side. It is unacceptable to set it down in the throne room or to show any strain. If you feel it slipping, say 'Where would you like it, sir?' and I will come to your aid."

We picked up the throne, immediately discovering that it was heavier than it looked. The effort I saw on Yonaton's face mirrored my own. Ovadia hesitated, but then took a step backward, directing us forward. At his nod, servants opened two tall wooden doors, and Ovadia backed into the throne room. It was long and narrow, with black basalt columns, carved like date palms and just as tall, marching in two lines down the center of the room. Dust danced in beams of light shining through windows high in the southern wall. The King, a crown of woven gold on his head, sat on a raised platform three steps above the stone floor. The room held noblemen in dyed linen garments, soldiers bearing the emblem of the royal ox, commoners waiting to petition the King, and scribes recording all that occurred—about twenty people in all. We entered, and with great effort wiped the strain from our faces.

Ovadia walked in reverse ahead of us, twisting slightly to avoid showing his back to the King. His approaching presence parted the crowd as he directed us up the long aisle. I could see the tension creeping back into Yonaton's face, and the muscles of my own jaw tightened. Both of us leaned forward, using the back of the throne to hide our faces from the King, but this only made its weight harder to carry. My arms burned, my back was screaming, and I could no longer keep the distress from my face. Hunched and struggling, we carried the throne between the columns to the foot of the dais, but in order to place it on the platform, we would have to lift it waist high and pass right before the King.

"Where shall we put it, sir?" Yonaton asked. The strain in his voice rang out like a bell.

Ovadia grabbed the back of the throne with two broad hands and lifted it with surprising power. "Right over here," he said, his voice light and easy. The three of us carried it over the steps with ease, and Yonaton and I were able to relax our expressions before passing the King. We set it down next to him and backed away, bowing as we went.

"Nicely done, Ovadia. It is truly as beautiful as you claimed." A loud cheer came from outside, and everyone but the King turned toward the sound of the commotion. "Has someone just taken a jewel from the bear?"

"I believe so, my King."

"A rather brutal form of entertainment."

"Apparently quite popular in Tzidon. Princess Izevel thought it would amuse our guests."

"They do sound as if they're enjoying themselves. Still, we don't need any more cripples in Shomron—I'm feeding quite enough already."

Three long blasts echoed from outside the city. The King sat up tall and stately, a match for any of the pillars lining his great hall. "Could Tzidon have arrived already?" He sank back into his throne. "Ovadia, go and meet him outside the walls and escort him to me."

"Very good, my King. What of his wife and daughter?"

"Show them to their accommodations first. Women are not fond of holding audience immediately after a long journey." Ovadia bowed and turned to take his leave, motioning to the two of us to follow. "Wait a moment," the King said, noticing the *kinnor* slung across my back. "These boys. Are they the musicians that you fetched from the prophets?"

I heard the probing question in the King's voice, and recalled the smirk from the guard at the palace gates. Now that the King saw that we were just boys, would he guess that Ovadia's journey had nothing to do with musicians?

If Ovadia was ill at ease, his face belied it. "Yes, my King. These are two of the four I brought."

"You said they are quite talented, correct?"

"Superb, my King."

That was a risky thing for Ovadia to say. What if the King asked us to play and found us wanting? But the King had other ideas. "Bring them with you. It will make a nice impression for them to play upon his arrival."

"An excellent idea, my King." Ovadia bowed again and exited the throne room, with the two of us trailing closely behind.

Once out of the palace, we broke into a run, covering the distance down to the city gates in a quarter of the time it had taken us to climb up to the palace. My stomach growled—I hadn't eaten since before the rehearsal. *No time for food, though.*

We passed through the gates, and Ovadia directed us to a small, grassy hill overlooking the western road. Hearing from Seguv and other travelers about Shomron, I had always imagined it perched atop the highest mountain in Yisrael, but that was not the case. Shomron was guarded by higher mountains on the north, east, and south, each surmounted by a watchtower. Only from the west, where there was no higher peak, could the chariots of Tzidon approach. I raised my hand to block the glare and strained my eyes, peering past the rich, brown coastal plains, and caught my breath as I saw for the first time in my life a smudge of distant blue along the horizon. *The great sea!* Until that moment, I knew it only through stories. Teeming with life and dangers, it was the gateway to the rest of the world.

"The two of you will play from here," Ovadia said. "When they come into view, I will descend to greet them at the bottom of the hill."

"Who are we waiting for?" Yonaton asked.

"King Ethbaal of Tzidon and his daughter Izevel, who is to marry King Ahav in two days' time."

"Where's Tzidon?"

"It's to the north of Yisrael, on the sea. The people of Tzidon are great sailors. King Ethbaal has made his capital city into the greatest port in the world."

"Is that why the King wants to marry his daughter?" I asked.

"Yes. An alliance with Tzidon will expand our ability to trade. The King expects this to bring great prosperity to the land."

"Do you think it will?"

"The King's reasoning is sound."

Ovadia had not really answered my question, but before I could ask another, a standard marked by a majestic cedar rose above the horizon, whipping in the wind coming in from the sea. A wedge of horsemen trotted up the hill, each bearing a pole flying identical banners. Behind the horsemen thundered chariots, each carrying a spearman and a bowman. They scanned the sides of the road, weapons gripped at the ready.

"I thought this was a wedding," Yonaton said. "They look as if they're going to war."

This vanguard was followed by a single, gilded chariot, much larger than the rest, carrying three passengers seated side by side. In the middle sat an older man, draped in purple robes, with a high forehead and neatly groomed beard. He held his chest high as he gazed off into the distance. At his right sat a woman with coronets of steel-gray hair, the sun flashing off her many jewels. On his left sat a woman in a dove-gray dress, her face and hair covered by a white veil. A second line of chariots stretched down the road behind them. At the end of the caravan rode at least a hundred soldiers on horseback, with more coming into view. Each bore the cedar emblem on his chest.

Ovadia signaled to us with a wave. Yonaton looked to me to start, and I began the first melody that came to mind, the one we had practiced that morning when I first earned Dov's approval, a fast, dancing melody. It was too cheerful for a march, but Yonaton joined in without objection, and I doubted King Ethbaal could even hear us over the din of the horses. Ovadia walked down the hill and positioned himself by the side of road, bowing respectfully and approaching the royal chariot. He spoke with the King, then climbed in beside the driver, beckoning us to follow. Without stopping our music, we stepped down to the road and returned to the city as part of the royal retinue.

The main road of Shomron was too steep for the chariots, so the party dismounted at the city gates where a large crowd was assembled to catch a glimpse of the bride. As she descended, four soldiers came forward with a covered litter. She stepped gracefully into a padded seat, and drew the curtains around her, displaying nothing more to the disappointed crowd than a thin wrist and long, elegant fingers. The King and Queen walked slowly at the side of her litter as they ascended to the palace, followed by a winding trail of soldiers.

The procession stopped in front of the palace. Another servant ran forward to place steps before the litter, and the bride stepped down, still veiled, holding the hand of a maidservant for support. As Ovadia escorted the royal family into the palace, the maidservant followed, carrying nothing but an intricately embroidered sack made from some rich indigo fabric.

I wasn't sure what we should do, but as no one had told us to stop the music, we continued playing, trailing the royal family toward the palace at a respectful distance. The plaza showed none of its earlier activity, standing empty except for guards. At the inner gates, Ovadia turned to King Ethbaal and asked, "Would the King like to be shown to his room to refresh himself before meeting with King Ahav?"

"No, I'll see Ahav immediately."

"Very well, my master awaits you. Please follow me. I will return immediately to accompany the Queen and the Princess to their chambers."

Once her father had gone, the Princess pointed around at the plaza and columns and said something to her mother in a foreign tongue. Her words were meaningless to me, yet there was a melody to her voice that aroused a desire to glimpse beneath her veil. My eyes rested on her hands, the only part of her not hidden from view. Her skin was an olive tone that shone, as if rubbed with oil.

"You will be Queen of Yisrael soon," her mother replied in halting Hebrew. "If you wish to enter hearts of people, you must speak their tongue."

"As you say, Mother," the Princess replied, in a Hebrew far more fluid than her mother's. Izevel swept her hand across the plaza again. "It's little more than a fortress."

The Queen examined the carvings around the entrance. "It has some beauty. Remember, palace is Queen's domain. You cannot expect unmarried King to keep it properly."

"I'm so glad you were able to make the journey, Mother. I will miss your wisdom once you are gone. You are right. The dignity of the palace is my responsibility now." The Princess turned to her attendant. "Put it there," she pointed to a painted vase atop a pedestal opposite the palace entrance.

The maidservant put the vase on the floor and replaced it with the indigo sack, untying its top so that it fell in a heap around the object it held. She then stepped away reverentially. On the pedestal stood a bronze statue of a man, a jagged lightning sword grasped in his upraised hand. A helmet as long as his torso extended above his head, reaching toward the sky. "Yes," the Princess almost sighed. "That's better already."

I inhaled sharply and bit my lip. *A statue—an idol—in the palace of the King of Yisrael?* The shocked silence of the crowd in Beit El returned to me like a cold, ill wind. Even as I stood beneath the summer sky, gooseflesh ranged up my arms.

My sleep was broken that night, but not by the old nightmare.

The caged bear, larger and fiercer than before, roared. It reached up its great paws and pounded the iron bars above its head. The sun sparkled off the jewels hanging around its neck, but the ruby pendant was gone—in its place hung the Princess's bronze statue, its upraised arm ready to strike.

The bear curled a paw around a bar above its head, pulling down with all its weight until the bar snapped in its grip. It reached for another bar on the side of the cage, pulling until it broke as well. It grabbed another bar, then another, breaking each one in turn. Once the cage lay in ruins at its feet, the beast stepped free.

No longer confined, the animal grew at a terrifying pace. It climbed uphill, distending with each step until it reached the height of the palace itself. And it kept on growing. Paws the size of chariots whipped along the palace courtyard, hooked yellow claws ripping paving stones from their moorings. The monster grabbed the sides of the palace, tearing it from its foundations. It raised the palace and placed it on its head, now fitting it as tightly as a crown. In one colossal step, the bear breached the walls of Shomron, and lumbered north.

I startled awake, my heart pounding. Unlike my old nightmare, there was no forgetting this time; every detail of this dream remained deeply etched in my waking mind. Slipping out of bed, I went to the window, relieved to see the palace still perched on the hill, bathed in moonlight. Still trembling, I reached for my *kinnor*. Nothing calmed me like music.

Growing up in a home where everyone slept in the same loft helped me learn how to quietly slip down the ladder and step out into the cool night air without waking anyone. I didn't want to play near the house lest I disturb others' sleep. It took only a moment to decide where to go.

No one was awake in the streets, though I passed numerous bodies snoring by the side of the road. Ovadia had mentioned that there were not enough places for everyone to sleep in anticipation of the royal wedding. The city was only ten years old and had never before held so many people.

The bear slept, its shaggy back rising and falling with each breath. I approached the bars of the cage, assessing the great beast. Its finery was gone, somehow removed for the night, and a deep musk radiated from its hunched form in waves on the night air. I crouched nearby and plucked a *nigun* my aunt used to sing to me when I woke from a nightmare, confused and afraid. Despite my delicate picking, the music roused the bear; it sat up and snuffed at the air. I stopped playing, but it was too late. The beast rose to its full height and growled, thrusting its paws between the bars at me. I retreated as it snarled, blinking in the dark.

Standing at a safer distance, I closed my eyes and listened to its voice. Daniel said he heard the song of the sheep in my music. The bear was no different than my sheep, really, only larger and more dangerous. It had a rhythm, slower and more powerful than that of the sheep. I plucked again at my *kinnor*, searching for the right sound.

After a few fumbling moments, a simple melody began to emerge from the lower register of my instrument. It just felt…right. I opened my eyes to see the bear standing silently, no longer lunging for me through the bars. I stepped forward, closer, but it still did not move. I began to hum, adding my voice to the notes of the *kinnor*. The beast tilted its head and released a groaning sigh. I took another step forward—the bear was now within my reach, which meant that I was within its reach too. Still humming, I removed my hand from the strings and extended it between the bars. The bear didn't move. I laid my hand on the back of its mammoth paw, probing the thick fur.

The animal turned its head—I pulled my hand back, fearing a strike that never came. I returned my hand to the strings, quietly strumming the bear's song. The animal closed its eyes with a low grunt. It crouched and lay down, resting its head on the back of its paws. I reached in again through the bars, scratching the bear behind its neck, the same place where the man grabbed for the ruby necklace earlier that day. I continued to stroke the spot until the bear sank again into a deep slumber.

The Alliance

The High Priest's presence filled the wedding canopy, under which he stood alone. His commanding eyes peered from beneath thick, black eyebrows set within a broad forehead. A heavy beard hung upon white linen robes hemmed with golden bells, which tinkled as he smoothed a golden sash at his waist. The plaza in front of the canopy was wreathed in living boughs and heaps of summer fruits, blending a threshing floor at harvest with a king's table at feast time. A mass of torch-bearers stepped into the plaza, slicing a path through the crowd of noblemen. Dov struck the first three notes alone and the rest of us joined in on the fourth, just as we had rehearsed a dozen times the day before. An expectant silence fell over the crowd as all turned their attention up the aisle.

King Ahav appeared first, dressed in snowy white linen for his wedding day. No father nor mother to stand by his side, he proceeded alone, eyes focused straight ahead, never turning toward the crowd until he took his place next to the High Priest. Only then could I get a good look at his face, which reminded me of Uncle Menachem's when selling a ram for slaughter.

Next appeared a towering man in violet robes that billowed out over husky arms and a muscular chest, his hand cradling the handle of a sword at his side. Unlike King Ahav, his eyes swept across the aisle, examining the crowd with each step. I knew there were many in Yisrael opposed to the marriage— is that what he was looking for? Did Princess Izevel need protection at her own wedding? As the man's eyes passed over the musicians, a chill swept through my body, but the cold eyes did not pause. With a swirl of vivid cloth, he stepped under the canopy and positioned himself next to the High Priest, who took a half step away from the body-guard and peered at him from the corner of his eye.

The royal family of Tzidon now appeared. Princess Izevel stood veiled in the middle, her smooth black hair flowing over her shoulders, dark against the white of her dress. King Ethbaal's proud face tipped upwards, honoring neither crowd nor king with his attention. He led his wife and daughter forward in step with the music. I recalled the harsh gaze that Yosef had fixed upon Ovadia, insisting that he in no way wished to add to this celebration. Yet here I was playing the music that was drawing Izevel, step by step, closer to becoming queen. I swallowed the stone that formed in my throat, trusting in Raphael's prophecy.

At the end of the aisle, King Ethbaal dropped his gaze to his daughter, lifted her veil and kissed her gently on the forehead. A soft pink flushed in Izevel's light olive cheeks. She appeared only a few years older than me—she couldn't have been more than sixteen. A familiar scent of wildflowers surrounded the Princess, and I suddenly knew what had become of the afarsimon oil Seguv brought to Shomron. The Queen drew her daughter under the canopy and led her in a circle around King Ahav.

The High Priest stepped forward. "May all who have assembled here be blessed. We are the children of Avraham, whose tent opened to all sides to welcome guests. We placed our canopy under the sky, recalling the Holy One's blessing to Avraham that his children would be as abundant as the stars of the heavens…"

I was barely listening, my attention drawn more to the scene around me, to the royal families and the crowd, than to the words of the High Priest. King Ahav tipped his head upwards, mirroring King Ethbaal. Neither king watched Izevel, still circling King Ahav. But her eyes never left the face of her future husband as she walked the traditional seven circles, each one tighter than the last.

"...Marriage is the joining of two halves, destined from creation to be one. The first woman was separated from Adam and then returned, so they could bond together as one flesh. From this union came all men..."

How different my own wedding would be if Uncle Menachem ever allowed me to marry Dahlia. Two of my younger cousins would precede us up the aisle carrying a rooster and a hen; the canopy would be supported by poles cut from the four trees planted when Dahlia was born; we would be surrounded by family and friends, not strangers and dignitaries. I glanced at Dov, leading us with his *nevel*, who in the final days of rehearsal continued to be impressed by my playing. I had not yet asked him about returning to play in the King's court—I would have to do that after the wedding.

A murmur ran through the crowd. Princess Izevel, who now stood beside King Ahav, motioned to the High Priest. He broke off his speech and leaned in, allowing the Princess to whisper in his ear. The priest turned to King Ahav, who nodded. The High Priest winced, but restored the calm to his face by the time he stood upright and faced the crowd again. "This marriage is more than a union of two people, it is the joining together of two nations. The High Priest of Tzidon will bless the union as well."

The man in the garish robes, who I had mistaken for the Princess's bodyguard, stepped forward, his hand still resting on the hilt of his sword. "I am Yambalya. I serve Baal, the mighty storm god, patron god of Tzidon." His voice resonated with the deep tones of a bass drum.

"Long ago, when the heavens were young, the children of El fought for mastery. In his struggle against Ya'am, lord of the seas, Baal turned to Koshar, the craftsman, for weapons that would make him invincible. With these tools in hand, Baal threw down the lord of the seas into the depths, and climbed supreme into the heavens." Yambalya raised his arms skyward, revealing scars running up his forearms.

"As Baal's faithful, we follow his ways. Baal was mighty on his own. But he did not achieve victory until he formed an alliance joining his power with the strengths of another. So too, Tzidon and Yisrael apart are mighty nations. But their union will be incomparable. With the blessing of Baal, the fertile soil of Yisrael and the merchants of Tzidon will bring the nations of the world to our feet." A cheer erupted from the crowd, and Yambalya stepped back to the side of the platform.

All eyes again turned to the High Priest of Yisrael, standing pale and silent. He did not resume his speech, but rather nodded to King Ahav, who took a ring from a waiting servant and slid it smoothly onto Princess Izevel's outstretched finger. The High Priest faced the crowd, announcing, "I give you

King Ahav and Queen Izevel." The crowd cheered as the King and his new Queen clasped hands, stepped out from under the canopy, and headed toward the palace.

Three court musicians escorted the King and Queen while the rest of us followed the guests out through the city gates and into the fields around the city. As long as the King and Queen were in seclusion, the musicians were allowed to eat and enjoy the festivities. The feast area was divided into three sections: one for the soldiers, one for the nobility, and one for the commoners, who were invited to the celebrations but had not been allowed into the city for the ceremony.

The aroma of sizzling fat reached my nose, making my stomach rumble, and bringing to mind the altar at Beit El. Zim grabbed my arm, "Did you see the size of those cows they're roasting?"

"That's for the nobility," Yonaton said. "Come on, the food on our side looks fine. I'm starving."

"We could get in there if we wanted to," Zim said, staring beyond the guards at the roasting pit.

"How?" I asked.

"With these." Zim indicated our instruments and the dark red sashes that we had been issued for the wedding.

"Look at us, we hardly dress like nobility." I had borrowed Zim's mirror before the wedding, and thought that the dyed sash served only to highlight the plain weave of my tunic.

"As long as we look as if we're supposed to be there, the guards will let us pass through."

"I don't know," Yonaton said. "That one on the left looks pretty mean."

"Stop worrying. Just start playing and follow me—and remember to stare straight ahead." He launched into a weaving rhythm and started off, stepping to his own beat as he approached the guard.

Could Zim be right? If we acted as if we belonged, would the guards let us pass? I glanced at Yonaton, who arched his eyebrows as he raised his *halil* to his lips. I lifted my *kinnor*, my heart drumming in my chest, feeling the thrill of the challenge. When we reached the guards, Zim stepped up his beat and closed his eyes. *Just hold the rhythm*, I told myself. *Ignore the guards. Keep moving forward.* Despite his rough tunic and wild hair, Zim passed through, drawing the two of us after him.

"Wait." The guard on the left stepped in front of Yonaton—he had looked. The guard turned to Zim, then back to me, his face knotted in confusion. I stopped playing and took a step back, not waiting for the outburst that was sure to come.

Zim called back to us, "Don't lose the tempo, they're waiting for us." My hands leapt back to the strings—Zim wasn't admitting defeat. His voice carried so much confidence that the guard looked sheepish and stepped out of the way. Once out of earshot, Zim struck a final drum roll, ending in a belly laugh. "Remember: if you believe it, it's true."

The nobility merited a far wider space than the commoners. In the center was a roasting pit, spanned by two whole oxen and numerous lambs, surrounded on three sides by trestles piled high with roasted meats, breads, and salads. My mouth watered at the smell of spices mixed with the smoke of the roasting meat. Zim walked straight to a serving table, wrapped a chunk of roast lamb in bread, and bit into it like a wolf, letting the juices flow down his chin.

My hands were sweating from the ruse we used to get past the guards. Though excited at our success, I couldn't bring myself to touch the fare. If I ate the nobles' meat I'd be just like the shepherds in Levonah who grazed their flocks across furrowed fields. "I want to go back and eat in our area," I said. Zim laughed, but Yonaton's shoulders relaxed in relief.

"If you two want to go back, I'll come with you. Let me take a little more meat first—it's delicious. Who knows when I'll get another chance at a roast this good?"

Yonaton pointed to the far corner of the nobles' area where a small crowd stood gathered around a table. "What's over there?"

"Don't know. Let's see."

From one end of the table to the other lay a carcass covered in scales with sharp teeth and bulging, lifeless eyes. The animal was split open down its middle, and five servants stood shoulder to shoulder dispensing its flesh, steaming and fragrant. "What is it?" Yonaton asked.

"I don't know." I ran my hand over the animal's skin, feeling the smoothness of the scales on the skin that crackled between my fingers. "I've never seen anything like it."

A fleck of meat hit me in the ear as someone behind me laughed. "Mountain boys. Go back to your goats." Zim extended his bread to one of the servants who balanced a piece of the creature on top of his already overflowing pile of meats. "Never seen a fish before?" He held his bread in front of us. "Sure you don't want to try?"

Yonaton glanced at me.

"No," I said.

"Just try a bit of mine. I've already taken it and I'm not taking any more, so no one will lose if you taste it."

I reached out and broke off a small piece of Zim's fish—just a taste.

"See, it's no fun being holy all the time. Isn't it nice to grab what you want just once?"

I put the fish back on Zim's pile of meat, and wiped my hand on my tunic. "I don't want it."

Zim laughed. "Please yourself. Just be careful. You don't want to wind up righteous and alone like Uriel." Zim led us back out past the guards, who paid us no heed.

In the commoners' section, Yonaton and I waited in line to get our food. There was no fish and the meats weren't spiced, but it still smelled wonderful. Food in hand, we rejoined Zim, who handed us each a clay goblet. "I got us wine," he said, his own goblet already half empty.

Again I hesitated, remembering our first morning in Shomron, when I could barely rouse Zim for all the wine he'd drunk the night before. The only reason I distinguished myself at the rehearsal was because I hadn't stayed up drinking with the musicians. Now Zim was handing me a goblet with far more wine than had ever passed my lips. This was my last opportunity to impress Dov—I couldn't take any chances now. "I'll pass."

"Don't worry. I got it from this side, you don't have to feel bad about drinking it."

"It's not that. I don't want it to hurt my playing."

"A little wine isn't going to hurt your playing—it might even improve it." Zim downed a quarter of his goblet in one gulp, then wiped his mouth with the back of a greasy hand. "You're not with the prophets now. You're at a feast—probably the biggest you'll ever enjoy. Everyone is drinking and having a good time. Stop thinking so much." He held out the goblet again.

Slowly, I reached out and grasped it, then sipped at its pungent sweetness. It was much stronger than I was used to—not watered down at all. All around me people were drinking and laughing. I closed my eyes, took a large swallow, and felt my nervousness melt away.

☙ ☙ ☙

I was swallowing the dregs of my second goblet when three sharp trumpet blasts sounded from the palace: the signal I was waiting for. The world tilted as I rose to my feet, the wine sloshing in my stomach. Not up to running, I did my best to slip quickly through the crowd.

I arrived at the gates before they opened, slung the *kinnor* off my back, and joined the other musicians in my rotation. We fell into the same upbeat dance tune I had played when the royal caravan arrived at Shomron. The trumpets sounded a long cry, the palace gates were thrown open, and King Ahav and Queen Izevel came forth to loud cheering. A crowd careened around them as they strode hand in hand down the hill of Shomron, out of the city gates, and over to the mass celebration.

They were led to chaises right near the settee on which the royal couple of Tzidon lounged, upon a dais at the edge of a large clearing. I joined the rest of the musicians in our position just below the stage. Adjacent to us was the section reserved for the sick and crippled, who, according to the King's custom, were given seats at the very front of the commoners' area. Ovadia stood next to the stage, commanding a constant stream of servants, who converged on him and ran off in every direction. He had been working non-stop since returning to Shomron. Yonaton and I had helped him as much as we could when we weren't in rehearsals, delivering messages and lending our hands to the endless details to which he attended personally. I hadn't even seen him at the ceremony—he must have been too busy preparing the celebration to attend.

A clamor arose at the rear of the commoners as a line of torch-bearers snaked through the crowd. They pushed the crowd back as they advanced, forming the perimeter of an open space before the royal families. A single man stepped into the opening, so thin that his white robes swayed as if empty, wearing a matching white turban in the same style as the High Priest of Tzidon. Approaching the platform, he bowed deeply to King Ahav. "Your Majesty, I am your humble servant Avidah. My performers and I were brought by the dyers' guild of Tzidon in honor of the royal union. With the King's permission..." King Ahav nodded in assent, "We will begin."

Dov struck the first note and the musicians jumped into the music that we had prepared for the performance. It was a wild piece in parts, with a foreign rhythm, and despite all our practice, I feared I wouldn't keep up with the driving pace. But the wine loosened my fingertips, my dizziness was gone, and I felt a wonderful sense of freedom in its place.

Avidah withdrew to the side of the circle, standing just in front of the section set aside for the infirm. One of his performers carried a cedar torch into the clearing; its flame illuminated his blue robes and matching turban, the scent of its burning resin almost overpowering. He raced around the circle, his torch swinging close to the crowd, forcing people to step back to avoid the flame, pushing them farther and farther until he had more than doubled the size of the clearing. With a loud "Hiyah!" he threw his torch high in the air where it broke apart into six, smaller flames. He caught each one in turn, but each barely grazed his hand before it was back in the air again. Once he controlled all six torches, he began to run, keeping to the edge of the clearing, catching and throwing the torches as he went. The crowd cheered, stomping and clapping their hands. Back in front of the stage, he caught the torches one by one, catching three in his right hand, two in his left, and the final one in his mouth. He then put all six torches back into his right hand and took his place next to Avidah.

A second performer, a sword suspended from the belt of his pink robes, stepped toward the stage, holding a woven reed basket. He bowed before Ahav and Izevel, then removed several gourds from his basket, placing them on the ground before him. He drew his sword from its scabbard and held it above his head for everyone to see. The jeweled handle and polished blade glittered in the torchlight. In a flash, he slashed the sword down upon the gourds, splitting each one cleanly in two, and leaving no question: this sword was sharp.

Falling to his knees, the pink-robed performer held the sword straight above him, tipped his head back so far that the tendons on his neck stood out like ropes, and opened his mouth wide. A gasp issued from the crowd as the point of the sword descended toward his wide-stretched mouth. Only hours of steady practice kept my fingers from freezing on the strings of my *kinnor*. How could a man kill himself just to entertain the King and Queen on their wedding day? Watching the torchlight dance off the polished blade, I swallowed hard—why would he draw out the pain by doing it so slowly?

As the point of the sword entered his mouth, I turned away, not wanting to watch. Women screamed. I plucked furiously at my *kinnor*, grateful that the complex rhythm demanded so much concentration. Silence fell over the crowd and I glanced up, expecting to see the man writhing on the ground. My fingers faltered on the strings. The performer was still on his knees, gazing up, with half the length of the sword sticking out of his mouth. How could it be anything but torture? Yet the blade kept descending.

His jaw worked as the sword sank until nothing except the jeweled handle remained visible. Head tipped back, he rose to his feet with outstretched arms, spinning in a circle so that all could see. Turning back to the stage, he fell to his knees, and grasped the hilt with both hands. In one smooth motion, he drew the sword from his mouth, and held it high in the torchlight, showing that it was clean, without a trace of blood.

The swordsman returned his weapon to his belt and called out something in his guttural tongue. The juggler approached and handed him a flaming torch. Again he threw back his head and lowered it into his mouth. He removed the extinguished torch and handed it back, receiving another one in return. When the final torch was extinguished, both men bowed toward the stage.

King Ahav nodded stiffly, his lips curled in the slightest of smiles. Queen Izevel clenched her hands in her lap, swaying to the music. She beamed at the performers, following them with her eager eyes as they moved to the edge of the clearing and stood next to Avidah. Then her eyes fell on those seated behind the performers, on the special section allotted to the sick and crippled. The Queen stopped rocking and her eyes narrowed upon the neediest of the land. Her serpentine look was hideous, but it lasted only half a moment. A contortionist entered the clearing walking on his hands, back and neck arched impossibly so that his feet dangled before his face. The crowd bellowed with laughter. The Queen's attention returned to the performance, her expression regaining its graceful composure.

The musicians didn't pause for a moment. Zim was right; despite my initial dizziness, the wine hadn't hurt my playing at all. I felt an unfamiliar looseness, playing faster and with more passion than usual. Dov perceived the change as well—he kept turning to watch me. Every time his eyes fell upon me, I felt a jolt of energy, picturing myself dressed in a dyed linen tunic, playing in the King's court during the day, and coming home to Dahlia at night.

But the transformation in me was nothing compared to what came over Zim, who drummed with an abandon I had never witnessed before. His closed eyes were turned toward the sky, and his hands were a blur. Sweat poured down his head and neck, and he seemed unaware of his surroundings. I wasn't the only one who noticed. Yambalya worked his way over to the musicians, drawn by Zim's ferocious rhythm, and danced to the beat of his drums.

More and more performers came forward to carry out their feats, one after the next. The contortionist was followed by a man who wrestled a bear. He received a terrible blow to the face, but walked away erect and bleeding to the roar of the crowd. The wrestler was followed by a lean man in orange robes who charmed two poisonous snakes and allowed a massive green serpent to wind itself around his body. When the performers finished, they all came forward and stood in a row opposite the stage. Avidah fell to his knees and pressed his forehead to the ground, followed immediately by his troupe.

The performers stood as one, then exited the clearing in a line. Dov signaled for the musicians to pause. I stretched my fingers and rubbed my palms, never having pushed my hands so hard before.

From beyond the edge the crowd, a chanting rose in the guttural tongue of Tzidon. It grew louder and the crowd parted to allow Yambalya to enter the clearing. Ten men dressed in identical violet robes, all wearing swords at their sides, followed behind. Four of them carried a large wooden chest suspended from poles on their shoulders. Yambalya directed them to lower the chest to the ground before the stage.

We hadn't rehearsed any music for this and we all watched Dov for a signal, but for the first time that evening he had no plan. With a quick strike of his *nevel*, he started us back into the piece we had performed for the juggler, but we didn't get far. Yambalya waved his arms at us and the song died on our strings. He put his arm around Zim's shoulder. "Just you. You come play." He drew Zim into the clearing, positioning him next to the wooden chest.

Yambalya faced the stage and raised his arms. "We must now give thanks to Baal for arranging this union, binding it with blood." His voice boomed across the clearing. "We must humble ourselves before Baal. Ask that he bless this union. And bring prosperity to this land." A murmur rippled through the crowd. Yambalya signaled Zim, who began a high paced rhythm.

The violet robed priests lifted the heavy cover of their box. From inside, they removed a carved pedestal. Then, with heads bowed, they placed a golden statue upon it. It was a larger version of the bronze statue that Izevel had stationed in the palace, with a jagged sword in its upraised arm and the same helmet rising straight behind its head. Two priests approached Yambalya with a jar and a torch. He raised the jar, chanting in his native tongue, his words rising in a gut-wrenching cry as he splashed blood red wine before the pedestal. Then he knelt, torch in hand, and lit a pile of incense before the statue.

Yambalya touched his forehead to the ground. No longer distracted by the music, my eyes fixed on Yambalya, riveted. When he arose, he tightened his belt and slipped his arms out of his sleeves. The top of his robes fell away, revealing deep scars that snaked across his back and chest. His fellow priests likewise shed the top of their robes, revealing more ropes of scarred flesh.

"We are the servants of Baal!" cried Yambalya, in a voice that shook the air. He drew the weapon from his scabbard and I gasped as he held it high above his head. It wasn't a sword at all, but a broad, flat knife. Had it been stone rather than iron, it would have been nearly identical to my father's.

"We have no master but Baal!" Yambalya waved the knife in a wide circle above his head. His thick muscles shone in the torchlight, displaying almost enough power to split the statue in two—but no stroke against the idol ever came. Instead, the High Priest of the Baal brought the weapon slowly down, drawing its blade across his own chest. Screams arose from the crowd as blood flowed down his torso. He slapped the flat of the blade against his chest, speckling the golden statue with red.

The other priests now drew their own knives, cutting themselves and each other, screaming out, "Baal answer us!" Their knives were identical to Yambalya's, almost indistinguishable from the one I felt bulging against my thigh. Shimon told me my knife had only one purpose and should never be used for anything else. Could this have been the purpose? Was this the reason that Uriel didn't want me to know what it was for?

The priests formed a circle around the idol, the ground growing muddy with their blood. As they slashed and howled, Zim's drumming surged in intensity. The priests circled their god in a gruesome dance, stopping at intervals to tear at their flesh and call out to the star-filled sky. The crowd stood silent now, too stunned to do anything but stare.

Yambalya faced the royal couples. "The offering of blood has been made. We must now bow down. We must humble ourselves before Baal. Then Baal, master of the storm, will hear our pleas. He will bring rain upon this land. And it will flow with his blessing."

Queen Izevel fell quickly to her knees, pressing her face to the ground as her dark hair spread like a stain around her head. She was followed by both her parents, who moved more slowly, but with similar resolution. King Ahav remained seated, his eyes on the crowd, his fingers rubbing the hem of his sleeve. He glanced back and forth between his prostrate bride and the crowd around him. Ovadia stood next to the stage, glaring at Yambalya.

Yambalya turned a slow circle, blood trickling down his chest, scrutinizing the crowd. Few met his gaze. "People of Tzidon," he called out in his booming voice, "Humble yourselves before Baal." There was a rustling of clothes as the foreign guests dropped to the earth.

Yambalya faced King Ahav, whose eyes still jumped between his queen, the priest, and the people. "Great King! You wish prosperity for your land. Humble yourself! Bow down before Baal, most powerful of gods! Only he can fulfill your desire."

Queen Izevel raised her face from the ground. Ahav's eyes stopped straying and sank into his wife's gaze. His hands, held tightly in his lap, loosened. Green eyes wide, Izevel reached toward Ahav with one slender arm rising from the sleeve of her bridal dress. Tapered fingers reached toward him, beckoning. He rose at the coaxing of his young bride, reeling like a man overcome by wine, or half asleep. His eyes still on hers, he knelt to the ground, bowing until his forehead touched the wood of the dais.

"People of Yisrael. Your King and Queen want rain and prosperity for you. Show Baal that you desire it for yourselves and you will be answered." The crowd remained silent. Zim's drumming filled the clearing, the ecstatic beat echoing off the mountainside. Heads turned to observe each other, seeking guidance. One by one, noblemen lowered themselves to the ground to bow before the Baal.

Dov hesitated, but once most of the nobles prostrated themselves, he too knelt and pressed his forehead to the ground. At this act of leadership, the rest of the court musicians bowed as well.

My mind focused on the knives wielded by Yambalya and his disciples. *They drew their own blood so easily—would they hesitate to shed the blood of those who defied them?* My hand dropped to my tunic, feeling the bulge of my knife beneath. It would be so easy to join them, to drop to the ground and be spared their wrath. Yonaton's hands trembled on his *halil*. My knees buckled, as if my body had already made up its mind to yield, but my stubborn heart was not ready to give in. Daniel stood resolute, clutching his *nevel*. Seeing his defiance fortified me. *If he could resist, so could I.* Yonaton moved in closer, and we remained standing together. I gazed toward the stage to see what Ovadia would do, but he was gone.

Most of the nobility were now on the ground, but the majority of the commoners still stood. I glanced at the section next to ours, that special section reserved for the destitute, many of whom depended upon the kindness of King Ahav for their very bread. Yet, among the dozens of broken and poor, not one bowed down. One man, bent with age, who had sat throughout the entire performance, pushed hard upon his walking stick with a trembling hand, and drew himself to his feet. He stared at Yambalya, a fiery challenge in his eye.

The High Priest of the Baal surveyed the crowd. He nodded approvingly at the Yisraelite nobility, but shook his head as he scanned the rest of the people, almost none of whom met his eyes. He gazed upon the lame, united in their defiance, his eyes meeting those of the bent old man. Their eyes locked. I focused on Yambalya's knife, waiting for him to strike. But Yambalya only shook with laughter, and turned his back on the old man. He sheathed his knife, lowered himself to his knees, and touched his head to the ground before the golden statue.

When Yambalya stood, everyone on the ground rose with him. He raised his arms again, shaking the dirt and blood from his chest, and danced to Zim's frantic beat. His brother priests joined in, drawing others into the clearing to dance.

On the stage, the two kings and their queens returned to their seats and smiled upon the revelers. Izevel twirled her long, thin wrists in time to the music. Order broke down as people on all sides entered the clearing to dance. Dov signaled that we musicians were on our own. Some picked up their instruments and tried to keep up with Zim, while others jumped into the circle to join the revelry.

I picked up my *kinnor* and started to play, but Yonaton tucked his *halil* into his belt and said, "Come on, let's dance." My eyes scanned the clearing— the box holding the Baal was gone. What could be the harm in dancing now? I slung my instrument onto my back and followed Yonaton right into the thick of the crowd.

Whoever leads the people on the right path will not come to sin. But one who leads the people astray will not even get a chance to repent.

Pirkei Avot 5:21

The Dispersal

The tight grip on my shoulder woke me, but it was cold rain on my face that forced my eyes open. I lay on my back, squinting dumbly at the clouds hanging just above the mountaintops. Heavy drops pocked the ground and a fresh wind stirred dust across the clearing.

My head throbbed—I wanted nothing more than to slide back into sleep, rain or no—but Yonaton grabbed my hand and pulled me up. The world tilted as my body came to a sitting position. Bitter bile rose in my throat, bringing with it memories of dancing around the huge bonfire late into the night, whirling until the wine got the better of me. I could not recall lying down.

The rain fell heavier, rousing sleepers all around us. Grunts gave way to groans and curses as farmers staggered to their feet. It wasn't just the wet awakening that tried them: it was the season. Still mid-summer, the early *yoreh* rains were not due for another two months. All across the Kingdom, the abundant wheat harvest—blessed by the same late *malkosh* rains that had destroyed so much of the barley crop—was cut and drying in the fields. If a downpour soaked the grain, it could rot in storage, destroying the year's harvest.

As this knowledge set in, the farmers stared wildly at the looming sky above them. Only one man could help them now, and they moved in a pack toward the sound of drumming which still echoed from the clearing. "Come on," Yonaton said, pulling me to my feet. I followed, stumbling behind him over the uneven ground. The motion made my stomach roll, but cleared some of the fog from my head.

The mob swelled on the path, and stifled cries of "The *yoreh*, the *yoreh*!" filled the air. The strands of gray cloud hanging down from the sky evoked no fear in me, though. I had never seen rains this early before, but had heard other shepherds call them *matnat ro'im*, the shepherd's gift. Even a brief downpour now would bring up grasses in pockets and hollows all around Levonah, perfect grazing to nourish a flock until the winter rains. Farmers might tremble, but to a wise shepherd it was a treasure.

In the clearing, Yambalya and his disciples danced on to Zim's thunderous rhythm, which somehow held strong through the entire night. Their chanting took on new strength as the crowd flowed back like a tide, and they called out in celebration of Baal's speedy answer to their prayers. Yambalya's belly shook with laughter at the panic on the farmers' faces. He stretched his head back so that raindrops fell into his mouth. "Baal is merciful," he called out. "He will not destroy your crops. Not yet. This is but a sign. A sign..." he lowered his gaze to the crowd, "...and a test." The last word came out with a hiss that sent a shudder right through me.

"You will bring in your harvest before Baal unleashes the power of the storm wind." He pointed his finger at the farmers like a father reprimanding his children. "He who fails to heed Baal's power and leaves his grain in the field will surely see his harvest rot."

A circle of cowed Yisraelites surrounded Yambalya. He raised his muscular arms and his eyes rolled back into his head. A single drop of blood rolled down one arm from his wrist. As it reached his elbow, he gave a final triumphant shout, and the rain came to an end.

The royal family would continue to celebrate for a full seven days of feasting up at the palace, but the wedding's end signaled the end of the festivities for all but the highest nobility. Most of the revelers had already planned to leave that day, but now, with Yambalya's threat ringing in their ears, they ran to gather their belongings and begin their journeys home straight away.

Yonaton and I walked silently toward Ovadia's house. We were also leaving that day; the court musicians would suffice to play for the week of celebrations, and we were still needed at the gathering. The streets of Shomron were flooded with people, many running past us up the hill and more already heading out.

"You look awful," Batya said as we crossed the threshold. "You boys get ready to go and I'll fix you something."

When we descended the ladder with our sacks, one of the maidservants poured out two steaming cups of steeped herbs. "Drink that," Batya said. I took a sip and gagged. "I know it tastes awful, but it will help. You boys should also have something to eat. You have a long journey ahead."

We had barely begun our meal when Daniel arrived. "Finish up," he said brusquely. "The donkeys are ready. If we start soon, we might make it back before nightfall."

"We haven't been paid," Yonaton said.

Daniel held up a leather pouch bound with a thong. "Dov came to pay us this morning. I collected for both of you."

Daniel's pouch held more copper than I'd ever owned, almost as much as promised for the entire gathering. I tried to look pleased—if Daniel read the disappointment on my face he'd ask questions. I remembered all too clearly the first night of the gathering when he had smashed my dream of studying for prophecy. Even if I was deluding myself with thoughts of playing in the King's court, I wasn't ready for Daniel to crush this dream as well—certainly not with my head already pounding and my stomach barely holding down my morning bread.

No, if this dream was going to collapse, I wanted to hear it from Dov himself. Only he could tell me if there would be a place for my *kinnor* or not. I hadn't seen him since the dancing began the night before, when he still had a smudge of dirt on his forehead from bowing before the Baal. And it wasn't just him—every one of the court musicians bowed as well. Was that what it would mean to play in the King's court—bowing before the Baal? Would that be the price of getting Dahlia?

The pounding in my head grew more insistent, in a way that had nothing to do with last night's wine. Daniel wouldn't need to smash this dream—it caved in on its own. I hadn't bowed last night, even when I feared that Yambalya's men would run their blades through any who refused. I made my choice, and once my stubborn heart decided on a path, it was set. I wouldn't bow now either, despite the possible rewards.

I took my last bite and rose to follow Daniel, hating myself for falling into another silly dream, but no longer regretting missing Dov. More disappointing was leaving without seeing Ovadia. He was close to both the prophets and the King, the one person I really wanted to ask about the wedding, the Baal, and the rain. But Ovadia was at the palace and there was no time to find him. We thanked Batya, who handed us a sack of rations for our trip, and hurried out after Daniel.

While we packed the donkeys, Zim strolled over to the house, clutching his drum under one arm. His eyes were glassy, but his smile was wild with joy.

"Hey Zim," Yonaton called. "Where are your things?"

"They're still in the musicians' quarters."

"You better run and get them. We're leaving."

"I'm not coming with you." Zim took his drum out from under his arm, tapping it gently with his fingertips. "I came to say goodbye."

"You're staying for the week of celebrations?" I asked, a pang of jealousy knifing through me.

"Longer. Yambalya invited me to join him."

"You're not coming back to play for the prophets at all?"

"Playing for Yambalya all through the night, I poured all of my body and soul into my drum." Zim's eyes had a faraway look. "That's what devotion should look like."

I winced at the word *devotion*. Uriel used the same word to describe the Way of the prophets. I pictured Yambalya drawing his knife across his own chest. *Is that what devotion looks like to you, Zim?*

"We'll miss you," Yonaton said.

"I'll miss you too. But I have a feeling it won't be for long. You've both got talent, and you're only going to get better. From what I've seen, good musicians rarely stay in one place for too long. Unless they decide to marry like Daniel here," he added, giving Daniel a slap on the shoulder.

"So you'll be moving up to Tzur?" I asked.

Zim shook his head with a grin.

"Isn't Tzur the capital of Tzidon?"

"It is, but Yambalya isn't going back. Queen Izevel asked him to stay. She promised to build him a temple right here in Shomron."

Zim put down his drum and threw one arm around me and the other around Yonaton, drawing us both roughly to his body. When he released us, he picked up his drum, and stood playing while we rode away.

🪕 🪕 🪕

Beyond the mountains ringing Shomron, the road curved south and flattened out. Daniel dismounted and tied our donkey to his with a lead rope. "Your eyes are barely open," he said in response to my protest. "This way you can sleep and let the donkey do the walking."

The animal's slow plodding drew me wistfully back to our swift ride to the wedding. On horseback, the journey took less than a day, even with the lightly burdened donkeys following along behind. Now I couldn't see how Daniel hoped to get us back to the gathering before nightfall. The donkey rocked and swayed as we ambled over the bumpy road, and before long Yonaton's head slumped forward against my back. I fought to keep my eyes open, but sleep overtook me as well.

I awoke to a shaking, like a tremor at my back. Opening my eyes, I saw steep-sloped mountains surrounding us. Daniel trotted confidently, singing quietly to himself as our donkey followed close behind. What woke me was Yonaton, weeping quietly against my back. I lifted my head, but he immediately choked off his soft cry.

"What's wrong?"

"Nothing," Yonaton replied, sitting up and wiping his eyes on his sleeve.

"You can tell me." I twisted on the donkey's back so that I could catch Yonaton's eyes over my shoulder. *Tears—as if they'll help anything.* The Holy One knows I cried plenty when I was younger. But the tears never did me any good—I was no better off when they stopped flowing than when they started. Aunt Leah cried often, and I always found it hard to look at her when she did. Dahlia mostly stopped a few years ago at the same time I did. She learned quickly that tears were the fastest way to lose my interest.

On that first night of the gathering Zim and Daniel both turned away at the mention of my parents' deaths. But Yonaton hadn't looked away; his eyes had actually teared, even though mine remained dry. I forced myself to hold Yonaton's eyes. He hadn't looked away then, and I would stay with him now. "What is it?"

Yonaton hesitated, but only for a moment. *He's no orphan; trust comes more easily to him.* "It's my father. I know what he's like. He won't gather in his grain early. He'd say it's betrayal to fear the Baal. What if our harvest is ruined? We don't have enough stored to get us through winter."

"You think Yambalya can make the rains come early?"

Yonaton gazed up at the dark patches of clouds moving across the summer sky. "What if he can?" he said softly.

I didn't know what to say—I was a shepherd, not a farmer. I was about as far from sharing the farmers' worries about the early rains as Yambalya; I looked forward to them. I was no more concerned about the *yoreh* spoiling wheat than I had been a few months earlier when the *malkosh* ruined so much barley. The late rains made grazing easier this summer than in summers past. The early rains would do the same: replenish grasses, keep the flock healthier, and make my life easier.

But Yonaton's pain struck me in an unfamiliar way. A few months ago, it was the farmers who suffered when the barley spoiled. This morning, it was the farmers who would suffer if the rain soaked the wheat. It was easy to bear the pain of farmers I didn't know—especially when they had land and I had none—but it was much harder to gaze into the teary eyes of a friend. *Did his father really fear the Holy One so much that he would let his family starve? Were there many more like him in Yisrael?* Still not finding any words, I reached back and squeezed Yonaton's hand.

By early afternoon, the clouds burned off, leaving the sky a bright blue. The sun baked the moisture from the ground and Yonaton's melancholy dissipated with the clouds. "You know, I think the wheat will be fine," he said. "The prophets look out for Yisrael. They wouldn't let Yambalya destroy the harvest of whoever doesn't fear the Baal."

Yonaton's new attitude sounded forced to my ears, perhaps covering up for the shame of having shown his fear. Either way, I breathed more easily, relieved I no longer had to console a weepy friend.

We left the mountains south of Shomron behind and rode through the massive brown hills that I knew so well. When we passed the turnoff to Levonah, I searched the road leading toward the gate, hoping to catch sight of my flock on the hills. The land was quiet and empty.

We ate the midday meal under a carob tree just past Levonah. "We're making good time," Daniel said. "With a little luck we'll arrive before dark."

"But when I came with Master Uriel it took us two days from here," I said. "We were walking, but we weren't moving much slower than we are now."

"You went through Beit El. Our path will be more direct."

Yonaton swallowed the bread in his mouth. "Then why did Ovadia take us on the Beit El road?"

"Our way is too rough for horses. But the donkeys can make it if we lead them."

After the meal, we continued south on the King's Road for a short stretch, then Daniel turned the donkeys onto a narrow path that climbed up a broken hillside before the road to Shiloh. Once over the ridge-line, the path dropped into a gully, and we dismounted to lead the donkeys down the descent. We picked our way down a series of ridges and valleys, dropping ever lower, the hillsides gradually shifting to lighter shades of brown as the vegetation thinned, finally taking on the yellow tone of the hills around Emek HaAsefa. Daniel was right; this way was far shorter than the road through Beit El. I recalled how my legs ached from walking those first days with Uriel. *He couldn't have led us that way just to alert Master Yosef; a simple messenger could have done that.*

When I asked Daniel, he laughed. "How many people have we passed on this path?"

"None."

"There's your answer."

"What do you mean?"

"What do you think Master Uriel does when he's not at the gathering?"

I had never given any thought to the prophet's life before. "Return home to his family?"

Daniel shook his head. "He travels the land. People go to him for prophecy, for advice, for blessings, for judgment of their disputes. It's not his way to seek the shortest path."

I thought back to Zim's comment at the wedding—if I wasn't careful, I'd wind up holy and alone like Uriel. *Did he not have a family?*

The sun dipped below the hills, casting a pink and orange glow across the sky as we descended into Emek HaAsefa. As the caves high on the hillsides came into view, my eye sought out our cave, the highest of them all, with its rock ledge out front where the four of us had first played. I was surprised at a sudden blossoming of warmth in my chest—like coming home.

Daniel approached the servant with the punctured ear who was cleaning up the cooking area after the evening meal. "Is there anything left? We just returned from Shomrón."

"Yes, Master Uriel had us put aside dishes for each of you." The servant gestured to a table with three large portions of bread and lentils. A grin curled up my cheeks as I wondered if the prophet had received a vision that Zim wouldn't be returning with us, or if this was another instinct of his heart.

The servant approached me and spoke quietly, so that I alone could hear. "The portion on the right is for you." This pattern of food being set aside for me had recurred at every meal since the gathering began. I always received a small portion of the most basic foods, never any meat or cheese. Why I was the only one restricted in what I could eat I didn't know, but each time I took my meager portion and rebelliously added anything I wanted. Yet this time, the portion set aside for me was no smaller than the other two, and even had a helping of cheese. Was Uriel warming to me?

After the evening meal, we walked to our cave in the twilight. "I'll be back later," Yonaton said, just as I rolled out my mat. He laid his belongings beside mine. "I promised my mother I'd tell her when we got back."

"You're going in the dark?"

Yonaton peered out at the indigo sky. "The moon's still up, that'll give me enough light."

I finished laying out my bedroll and retrieved my *kinnor*. "Then Daniel and I will just have to start playing without you."

Daniel chortled. "You can play on your own." He lay down on his sheepskin mat. "I'm going to sleep."

"You're going to bed already?" Yonaton asked.

"I need the sleep if I'm going to make it back to my farm tomorrow."

I turned to Daniel. "You're leaving too?"

"I've got to get home and bring in my harvest before it rots in the field. You heard Yambalya, this morning's rain was only a warning. If we fail to heed it, we may not be so blessed in the future. I'm leaving at dawn. Yonaton, if I were you, I'd tell your family to bring in theirs as well."

The thin veil of confidence that masked Yonaton's face all afternoon melted, exposing his raw fear of the morning. Without another word, he ran out of the cave toward home.

Zim's reaction to Yambalya was one thing—but Daniel? "After all these years playing for the prophets, you're going to heed the Baal?"

Daniel shook his head. "All these years with the prophets have shown me that all kinds of things are possible."

"But you refused to bow at the wedding."

"True, but I also felt the rain on my face this morning." Daniel folded his arms behind his head. "If Yambalya is wrong and I bring in my crops early, what have I lost? But if he's right, and I leave them in the fields..." Daniel sighed, put down his head, and closed his eyes.

I rested my *kinnor* next to my sleeping mat—I didn't feel like playing alone. I left the cave hoping to catch Yonaton, but he was out of sight—probably halfway home already at the pace he was moving. I made my way down to the valley floor, unsure what I was searching for. All was silent; the servants had finished cleaning up, the disciples were all asleep. I strolled with a heavy step toward the pomegranate tree under which we played, its unripe flower-tipped fruits just visible in the moonlight, and sat down with my back against its smooth and slender trunk. A dark hole opened in my chest, swallowing down the excitement of Shomron and the wedding that had bloomed there. They seemed like a distant memory now. Zim wasn't coming back and Daniel was leaving. Would Yonaton be next? *Will I have to play on my own for the rest of the gathering?*

I had barely sat down when I stood up again—there was no point in staying awake on my own. I returned slowly along the path, its worn track a pale gray in the light of the two-thirds moon. A lone, tall figure strode ahead of me, reaching the musicians' cave first and stepping inside. I hurried into the cave and almost ran into the man, already turning to leave.

"Ah Lev, I was looking for you," Uriel whispered, resting his hand on my shoulder. "I want to hear about the wedding. Let us go to my cave so that we don't wake Daniel."

Uriel led the way back down the path, and I followed behind in silence. Four lamps burned inside his cave, dazzling my eyes as I stepped in from the dark night. I sat opposite Uriel, whose slate-blue eyes fell upon mine, expectant. I wasn't sure what he wanted me to say, so I started at the beginning.

"When we got to Shomron, Ovadia told Yonaton and me that we'd be staying with him, not with Daniel and Zim in the musicians' quarters." I paused, hoping he would direct me, but he didn't speak, just nodded for me to continue.

As words spilled out, I found myself saying more than I intended, talking about things of no importance. Why would the prophet care about us delivering Ovadia's messages, or the commoners wrestling the bear? I kept scrutinizing the *navi* for some sign of what he was after, but he just met my eyes with a steady gaze that drew the stream of images out of me.

When I finally ran out of words, two of the lamps had burned out—the charcoal smell of their wicks filling the cave as I slumped forward on the stool, exhausted. Uriel stared at me in silence, his face unmoving. The prophet's gaze felt heavier now that I was no longer speaking, and I dropped my eyes to the table.

"So Queen Izevel and her family all bowed before the Baal?"

A knot clenched in my stomach. "Yes."

"Then King Ahav bowed?"

In my mind I saw the King's hesitation give way before his bride's coaxing. "Yes."

"Then the people bowed as well?"

"Many of them."

"And Ovadia?"

"I looked for him, but he had gone."

"Then in the morning, there was rain?"

"Yes."

"The people were afraid, and in their fear they turned to the priest of the Baal."

This wasn't a question, but I still answered, "Yes."

Uriel's gaze rose to the ceiling of the cave. "The lamp of darkness is burning brightly once again," he said, more to himself than to me. The creases on his face deepened in the unsteady light. "May the Holy One protect Yisrael."

I examined the prophet, who never before seemed so old and frail. "The lamp of darkness?"

Uriel didn't answer; indeed, he seemed unaware that I had spoken. He stood quickly, knocking over his stool as he rose. He lowered himself onto a reed mat on the floor with his feet before him, his knees bent to his chest. "I would like you to play for me. We may need to end the gathering early."

"Why?"

"As you said, the rains might be coming. Whoever leaves his crops in the fields risks ruin. Many of our disciples are farmers. We cannot cause them to suffer such losses."

I thought back to what Yonaton said on our journey back to the valley. "But can't the prophets stop the rains?"

"Even if I could, I wouldn't do so."

"Why not?" I couldn't keep the challenge out of my voice. The image of panicked farmers gathering around Yambalya rose in my mind, and the taste of bile returned to my tongue. It was strange—I had cared little for their panic that morning; I was even looking forward to the early rains. But I must have swallowed some of Yonaton's fear on the ride back to the gathering. *Was the prophet also afraid of the Baal?*

"If we stop the rains, it will only bring the people to fear us more than Yambalya." Uriel said with resignation. "It becomes a battle of one fear over another."

"Isn't that what you want, that the people should fear the Holy One more than the Baal?"

"No! A true turning to the Holy One is the end of fear, not a step down its path."

"So none of the prophets will do anything to stop this?"

The old *navi* hesitated. "I don't think so."

I would have said no more, but I heard uncertainty now in Uriel's voice. Did this mean that not all the prophets agreed with him? Was there was still a chance to stop the rains? Perhaps if Uriel knew, if he really understood how much fear the threat of rain was causing, he'd decide that closing the gathering early was not enough—that this was a time to stand up to Yambalya. I had held back only one detail of our journey, one that I left out so as not to embarrass a friend. But even that would be worth it if it could make Uriel comprehend the humiliation of the people...and hold off the rains.

"When we were riding home from the gathering, Yonaton cried. That's how scared he was that his father would refuse to listen to Yambalya and their harvest would be lost." I flushed as I spoke, horrified to think of Yonaton's embarrassment if he ever found out. "Without the wheat harvest," I explained, "They don't have enough grain to get through the winter. And they are not the only ones."

Uriel slipped out of the position he had assumed in readiness for prophecy, shifting his feet and crossing his legs so that he could sit up on the reed mat to face me. "And you feel that Yonaton's tears show what?"

"They show suffering. They show fear."

"And weakness?"

I didn't want to call Yonaton weak, but Uriel was right—in that moment riding together, that's exactly what I thought. "Yes."

"You have much to learn about strength, Lev. Would you consider the constipated man strong?" Uriel fixed me with a penetrating glance. *Could he see that I, who cried so much as a child, had blocked my heart, and not cried for over five years?* "Yonaton's tears are not a weakness—they're his greatest strength. Indeed, if all of Yisrael could cry out as Yonaton has, we would have nothing to fear from Yambalya." Uriel stretched his long legs before him again, rubbing the underside of his thigh. "Now, if you could please play for me."

I swallowed, my body tense. *How would tears hurt Yambalya? The more our tears flowed, the deeper he'd laugh. He'd brush them aside as easily as he had the glare of the old, bent man the night before.* But the time for discussion had passed. I needed to play, which posed a different problem. "I don't have my *kinnor*."

"I'm sure you will manage."

I surveyed the cave, hoping to find something to make music with. Lacking anything better, I drummed on the table. Tension flowed out through my hands with every beat against the heavy wood, and soon a rhythm took hold. I opened my mouth in song, weaving deep vocal tones into the beat. It wasn't the best music I ever made, but it seemed to work. By the time the third lamp burned out, Uriel trembled with the spirit of prophecy.

I stopped drumming. In the silence, an image of Yambalya rose in my mind, his taut skin covered in scars and sweat, drawing his knife across his chest, showing all of Yisrael that he didn't fear spilling his own blood. Next I saw farmers' faces as the rain fell upon the celebrations, and heard Yambalya's deep laughter at their terror. Then I observed Uriel, old and gray, trembling in a heap on the floor. It was easy to guess which of the two the people would follow.

Uriel pushed himself to a sitting position, his face ashen, the creases in his face like knife cuts in the light of the remaining lamp. "The rains are indeed coming," he said, stretching out a hand for me to help him to his feet. His palm felt rough, like the scales of the fish at the wedding. I overestimated his weight, pulling harder than necessary, causing him to stumble. The prophet regained his balance and smoothed his tunic. "I must speak to the other masters about ending the gathering early."

"You really won't do anything to stop the rains?"

"I will not." Uriel placed both hands on my shoulders this time, holding my eyes in his. "There is no greater blessing than *shalom*, Lev. It is a peace so great that for its sake the Holy One overlooks our failures, even the people bowing to strange gods. But once peace is broken, there is little left but judgment. In a time of judgment, our sins are recalled and accounted for. The devastation may be great indeed. You are too young to remember the wars that ravaged this kingdom not so long ago. Believe me; it is nothing we want to return to."

Uriel took several steps toward the entrance, then turned back to face me. "I know that your words come from your courage as much as from your youth. This courage will serve you well. Indeed, it already has. It was no small thing refusing to humble yourself before the Baal."

I stood straighter. "No, I did not bow." Uriel nodded and stepped toward the entrance. I added proudly, "I've bowed only before the Holy One."

The old *navi*'s brow furrowed, as he half-turned back to me. "You bowed to the Holy One?"

"Yes," I nodded. "In Beit El. When you sent me to Master Yosef, I also visited the altar. I wanted to make an offering," I added with a sigh, "But I'm still too young."

Uriel turned to face me fully, his eyes narrowed. "But you bowed?"

"Yes."

A tremor passed through me as the prophet's glare pinned me, helpless. My earlier thoughts of Uriel as a weak, old man disappeared. In his suddenly hard eyes, I sensed an untold strength within his aged body. That strength, boiling with anger, now concentrated itself on me. I felt as I had the night before, watching Yambalya, knife in hand, glaring at those who refused to bow — anticipating a strike.

Finally, he turned away, stepping toward the cave entrance, his body sinking back into weariness. "You may sleep now."

The rasp of hide against stone woke me from an uneasy sleep. I opened my eyes to see Daniel rolling up his sheepskin sleeping mat in the gleam of an early morning sun. I dressed quietly so as not to wake Yonaton, stepped out of the cave, and sat on one of the boulders where the four of us first played music together. Clouds colored the eastern sky with shades of watered wine as Daniel emerged, his *nevel* in one hand, a sack slung over his shoulder. "I'll see you next year?" he asked.

I pictured Uriel's expression of the night before. *Would the prophet even want me back?* "I don't know."

"Return if you can." Daniel hitched his sack higher. "But even if you don't make it back, even if you have only your sheep for an audience, never stop playing your *kinnor*."

I didn't need anyone to tell me to keep playing my music; it was the one thing that brought me joy that I could carry with me wherever I would go in the wild. But Daniel's eyes were suddenly hard, and his beard stiffened on his chest. I had seen him this serious only once before, two nights ago when he refused to bow to the Baal. It was this that made me ask, "Why not?'

Daniel rubbed a hand along the wooden frame of his *nevel*, and stared out over the valley. "Twelve years ago, my master told me the same thing I told you, that I could stay with the prophets, playing for them year-round, just as he did."

"But you didn't want to?"

"I did." His head dropped as he spoke. "I stayed with them for over a year."

"Why did you leave?"

"My father was getting old—he could no longer handle the farm by himself. One day he fell and injured his leg. I had to go back—I had responsibilities. My master was disappointed, but he understood. Before I left he told me what I've just told you, that I must never stop playing."

"Why not?"

Daniel lifted his head and caught my eye. "The power of music surged inside me. Every power a person has must be expressed, otherwise it decays, and decay is a small death. The Holy One forbids us to resign ourselves to death."

"So that's why you return?"

"That's why I return each summer, even though I now have a family of my own and my responsibilities have only grown."

Uriel's stern countenance again rose in my mind's eye. I felt even more certain that he would not want me back. "So even if I can't return—"

"Even if you can't return, you must continue to play. Never let this spark inside you die. But I believe that you will return. You didn't receive a *kinnor* like that to play it alone in the wilderness."

My hand slipped to my side where my *kinnor* normally hung, feeling only empty air. "What do you mean?"

"The workmanship is unmistakable. It's prophet-made."

"Prophet-made? But I got it from my uncle."

Daniel's beard quivered as he shook his head once. "That *kinnor* was made by no local craftsman. I don't know how it reached your hands, but I doubt whoever gave it to you aspired for you to play before sheep."

"What do you mean 'whoever?' I told you my uncle gave it to me."

Daniel allowed himself a half smile. "I see. And your uncle is quite the musician, is he?"

My head cocked to the side. "No, I've never seen him play."

"A collector then? Your uncle has many fine craftsman-made objects lying about the house that he has no need for?" Daniel didn't bother keeping the scoffing tone from his voice now, and I allowed myself to smirk along with him—we both knew I didn't come from nobility.

"Admit it, Lev," Daniel's tone grew serious again, "even if you did receive that *kinnor* from your uncle, there's more to the story than you know. When a prophet's treasure winds up in one's hands, it's rarely happenstance. If you ever learn more, let me know, I always appreciate a good story. But now, I must start for home before the sun gets any higher—I have much work ahead of me." Daniel raised a hand in farewell, and turned down the trail.

I stepped into the cave and retrieved my *kinnor*, then sat back down outside, examining it in the growing daylight. I ran my fingertips along the olive wood frame, as if seeing for the first time the smoothness of its surface, the precision of the carving, and the flawless joints. Truly, there was nothing in my uncle's house that approached the fineness of it. I had been so fixated on everything I lacked that I failed to notice all those years that I held a treasure.

Yonaton stepped out of the cave into the brightening day, his arms raised in a yawn. "Has Daniel gone?"

"Yes, he's just left for home."

"Too bad, I would have liked to say goodbye."

"How are things with your family?"

"Not good. My father refuses to take in the harvest—he got angry that I even suggested it."

"Well he might change his mind now. Master Uriel saw last night that the rains are going to come early."

"Oh?" Yonaton's shoulders relaxed and a smile brightened his face. "If a *navi* says so, that will be enough for my father."

"They're serving the morning meal in the clearing if you want to go."

"Sounds good." Yonaton stretched his arms above his head again. "We've never made it to the morning meal here before."

The sun was rising over the eastern hills and the disciples were already sitting in the field eating by the time we joined them. One of the cooks handed me a small piece of bread, a single dried fig, and twelve kernels of toasted grain from where it had been set aside in the cooking area. The portion was the smallest I had ever received. Was this a further sign of Uriel's displeasure? I stepped forward to help myself to more of everything, and again none of the servants protested. Both Yonaton and I took much larger portions than we had on the first night of the gathering. This made me think of Zim, though neither of us could compete with his appetite. I felt suddenly lonely despite Yonaton's presence.

Silence fell over the disciples and we all shifted our attention to the center of the eating area where the three masters now stood. "We have received word," Uriel began. "The rains will indeed come early this year. The gathering will come to a close so that disciples can return home and attend to their harvests." There was a barely audible sigh from the *bnei nevi'im*—had they already heard what had happened at the wedding?

Uriel and Tzadok both appeared calm, their faces serene as they met the searching gazes of the disciples. Yosef scowled at the ground.

Uriel continued, "I will remain here with any wishing to stay and continue training. To those who are leaving, may you be blessed with an early and abundant harvest. You are now free to go."

Most of the disciples hastened to prepare for the trip home. Yonaton and I turned our attention to our meal, and were soon among the only ones in the clearing.

A tall disciple named Tuvia approached me. "Master Uriel asked me to escort you back to your uncle's. I need to ride past Levonah on my way back home."

"But I'm not a farmer. I don't need to go back for the harvest."

"Then speak to Master Uriel—but do it fast, because I need to go. He also asked me to give each of you one of these." He handed each of us a pouch of copper.

Yonaton turned his pouch over in his hand and examined the contents. "This is how much we were supposed to receive for the entire gathering, but we haven't even played for a week."

I poured out my pouch and counted as well. Yonaton was right—the entire summer's wages were there.

Tuvia gazed up at a small cloud in the otherwise clear sky. "I'm just the messenger. Speak to Master Uriel if you want, but you'll need to do it quickly."

Uriel was on the far side of the clearing talking to Yosef, his back to us. He wouldn't have arranged a ride home and paid full wages for the entire summer if he wanted me to stay. "I'll get my things."

Tuvia nodded. "I'll wait for you at the top of the hill."

"Master Uriel might not realize that you're not needed for the harvest," Yonaton said. "Maybe you should speak to him."

"He knows," I replied, avoiding his eyes. "If he's sending me home, he doesn't want…" I swallowed, "He doesn't need me." I didn't understand why bowing to the Holy One would anger Uriel, but I had no desire to talk about it—not even to Yonaton. "We should go pack."

Neither of us spoke as we gathered our few possessions and descended the trail back to the clearing. Yonaton kicked rocks along the ground. I searched for the right words—saying goodbye to Yonaton felt different than parting from Zim or Daniel. But words were never my strength. I stepped forward and embraced my friend. When I let go, I offered Yonaton a weak smile, and turned up the hill.

Tuvia was waiting for me at the top, mounted on a horse. "Tie your things down and climb up."

"How do I get on?" I asked as I strapped my rolled-up sleeping mat on top of his belongings. My only other time on a horse, I used a boulder to climb on behind Ovadia.

"Place your foot in that strap there, and give me your hand. No, your other foot." Tuvia pulled and I brought my leg over the horse. "Now hold on." I wrapped my arms around Tuvia, and with a kick to the horse's flank we started off toward the road. By the time I thought to glance back, I saw nothing but the hills behind us.

"Until I arrived at the gathering, I thought prophecy was simply a gift from the Holy One."

"Indeed, it is a gift."

"I mean, I never realized that nevi'im trained for it."

"We must train, for even gifts can harm one who is ill-equipped to receive them. Under a trained rider, a fast horse is a powerful gift indeed. But it can also throw off and break the back of the untrained."

"So all nevi'im have trained before receiving prophecy, Master?"

"I know of only one exception."

"Who was that?"

"Balaam, who called himself the man with the open eye."

The name Balaam made me think of Uriel's old, one-eared donkey. It lived longer than any beast of burden I had ever known, but was probably gone by now, at a time when so many animals perished from lack of food. Had Uriel really named a donkey after a prophet? "Why did Balaam merit navua if he had not trained?"

"Merit? I'm not sure that Balaam did merit, but he received it nonetheless."

"I don't understand."

"What training do you recall from the gathering, Lev?"

"Mostly that the bnei nevi'im had to quiet their minds."

"Yes, only a quiet mind is a fit vessel to receive. Music is a particularly good tool for achieving that. What else?"

"Dreams. I remember Master Yosef saying that dreams were one sixtieth of prophecy, and that all disciples must discuss their dreams with a master."

"Correct, they must also learn to understand the visions of their heart. What else?"

"I cannot think of anything else, Master."

"What remains is the most important step, the path that Balaam could never pursue: the complete refinement of the self."

"I don't understand."

"Many of the new priests of the Baal first began their training with us."

"They were bnei nevi'im?"

"Indeed. Some were drawn to the nevi'im because they wanted power, to control others, to be feared. Others had a desire to serve, but foundered because they failed to master themselves."

Though my master could not see me, I nodded, fully aware of how tempting the Baal was to those desiring power or seeking to satisfy their lusts. "Then how did Balaam succeed?"

"Because Balaam needed to exist. When we left Egypt, the Holy One wanted the nations to see that what made us distinct was not our circumstances, but our choices. We were led by Moshe, who spoke to the Holy One face to face. The nations needed a prophet of equal power to dispel any belief that only Moshe's navua set us apart. So Balaam was given tremendous powers of navua, so great that the nations could never claim they misunderstood the Holy One's will."

"But why choose him? There must have been one among the nations with a pure heart."

"There were many. But what would happen to one of pure heart who received the prophetic powers of Moshe?"

I bit my lower lip as I tried to picture a prophet as great as Moshe among the nations. What would he have done when he saw the splitting of the sea? "He would have joined Bnei Yisrael."

"Indeed. Look at Ovadia, who left his nation to join us even without navua. The Holy One needed to choose a man whose lusts were so strong that even receiving the Divine Will would not make him change his ways."

"But surely prophecy must have refined him somewhat, Master?"

"I do not believe so. We are refined by our choices. For him, navua remained a mere gift."

Rabbi Shimon said: Do not be wicked in your own sight.

10

Eliav's Choice

Ascending on foot from the King's Road to Levonah, I drank in the smell of young shoots sprouting in the valley. Now that I was forced to return to my flock, the farmers' dread of the rain faded; the prospect of shepherding again was eased by the promise of early pastures. I scanned the hillside for my flock, but it was nowhere to be seen.

I hiked up to the fig tree where I had met Uriel less than two weeks before. Picking a fig that was still green on top, I split its reddish brown bottom with my fingers. Its flesh wavered before my eyes as thin, white worms fled from the light. I dropped the infested fruit with a shudder and didn't reach for another.

Every rock and tree on the footpath that hugged the city walls whispered of home, yet the familiar landmarks brought constriction to my throat. A different sun shone on everything I knew, casting it in an unfamiliar light, including my uncle's house. It appeared smaller than I remembered. Dahlia saw me first, peeking around the mud dome of the oven. "Lev!"

"Lev?" Aunt Leah stepped outside, two-year-old Ruth grasping the back of her skirts. Tears were already on her cheeks as I hurried forward into her embrace.

ꭷ ꭷ ꭷ

"Tell us about the man eating the sword again," six-year-old Shimi asked for the third time.

"As I said, he didn't exactly eat it." I dropped my spoonful of lentil stew — everyone else had finished eating, but my bowl was still half full. "He bent his head back like this and held the sword over his head," I held my spoon over my upturned mouth in demonstration, "Then he lowered it down his throat." I lowered the handle until I gagged, "But he kept it going all the way down."

"How long was the sword?" Eliav asked.

"About this long," I held my arms out.

"But it must have gone down to his stomach." Dahlia wrinkled her nose at this. "And it came out without any blood?"

"Not a drop."

"I think you should all let Lev eat," Aunt Leah said. "You can ask him about his adventures tomorrow. He's home now. Come Ruth, Shimi, Naamah. To sleep."

The youngest children followed their mother up the ladder as Dahlia cleared the table. Uncle Menachem did not recite verses, as was our nightly custom; instead, Eliav went outside to check on the flock and Uncle Menachem stayed at the table while I finished. He had passed the meal in silence, hardly taking his eyes off me as he ate.

Eliav returned and climbed the ladder without a word. I wiped the clay bowl with the last of my bread, handed it to Dahlia, then turned toward the door.

"Eliav's already seen to the sheep," Uncle Menachem said.

"I know, Uncle." But I walked outside anyway and leaned against the edge of the pen, patting the head of the nearest sheep, which stared up, then pulled away.

"You didn't mention the rest of the wedding," my uncle said, coming up behind me.

"I didn't want to scare them. I wasn't sure if you even knew."

"We felt the rain here too, Lev. It didn't take long to learn the reason why. Everyone's in a panic to gather in their crops." Uncle Menachem tugged at the gate of the locked pen, checking that it was secure. "What does Master Uriel say?"

"The rains will come, just as Yambalya promised. He ended the gathering early."

"That's why he sent you home?"

"No, Uncle. That's not why he sent me away."

"No? What did he say?"

"He didn't say anything. He closed the gathering and told everyone they could go home to bring in the harvest."

"But if the gathering was closed, it was closed."

"No, Uncle." I fought the tremor in my voice. I wanted to understand the truth, and to do that, I needed to tell my uncle everything. "He stayed behind with any disciples wishing to remain."

"Then it probably wasn't worth paying a musician for just a few disciples."

"No, Uncle. He paid me for the entire summer." One of the sheep crossed the pen to lick my hand. I felt bolstered by the sudden affection. "He sent me away because he's angry."

"Angry?"

"On the way to the gathering, Uriel sent me into Beit El to deliver a message. I finished earlier than I expected. I had time, so I went to the altar to bring an offering, but they wouldn't let me. So I went and bowed to the Holy One. I told him this last night when I returned from the wedding."

Whatever response I may have expected, it wasn't the burst of laughter I received. "You told a *navi* that you bowed to the Golden Calf?"

My face grew hot. "Why not? You taught me that bowing to the calf is bowing to the Holy One. You go every year."

"Yes, yes I do," he said, no longer laughing. His smile melted, and even in the fading light I saw a shadow grow in his eyes. "I'm not proud of it. But I go. And I bow."

"Why wouldn't you be proud? And if you're not proud," I could tell he wanted to look away, but I held his eyes, "Then why do you go?"

He sighed, turning aside and resting his arms on the pen. "I used not to. Of course, when I came of age, my father took me. But once I married your aunt, your father wouldn't hear of it."

I started at the mention of my father; my uncle almost never spoke of him. "What do you mean?"

"The tale of the calf is a troubled one. Have I ever told you why the Kingdom was split?"

I sensed a story coming and sat down on the wall of the pen, shaking my head.

"When King Solomon died, the tribes called his son Rechavaum to Shechem to crown him King of all Yisrael. Now King David was a mighty warrior, and the people followed him with all their hearts. His son Solomon was a great builder who set the people to build the Holy One's Temple and his own palace in Yerushalayim. Twenty years of sending people north, thousands at a time, to fell trees and cut stones in the mountains of Tzidon. Twenty years of fathers gone from their families, husbands from their wives, sons from their farms.

"So when Rechavaum came to Shechem, the tribes said to him, 'Your father placed a heavy yoke upon us. Lighten our burden and we will serve you as we served him.' Now it is no small thing to make demands on the honor of a King. Unwilling to answer right away, Rechavaum took three days to consider.

"The elders who sat at Solomon's feet advised Rechavaum to heed the people. They promised that if the King bent to their will, the people would bow to him all his days. But Rechavaum's friends, the children of the palace, did not agree. They told him that it was dangerous to meet demands with weakness. They advised him to say, 'My little finger is thicker than Solomon's loins. My father laid a heavy yoke on you, I will add to it. If Solomon beat you with sticks, I will whip you with scorpions.'" Uncle Menachem shook his head with a mirthless laugh.

"Why would they say that?"

"I think they were afraid."

"Afraid? Afraid of what?"

"Of what the tribes would do. Of having to hold together the Kingdom without King Solomon." He stroked his beard and sighed. "And when men are afraid, they feel safer if they can make others afraid as well—afraid of them."

"So he listened to his friends?"

My uncle nodded. "His friends convinced him that the strong hand is the one that holds the whip. But he didn't count on the strength of the tribe of Ephraim. They killed his tax collector and sent Rechavaum fleeing back to Yerushalayim. Only his own tribe of Yehudah and the small tribe of Binyamin stayed loyal to the House of David. The other tribes chose Yeravaum as their king, and he declared the new Kingdom of Yisrael, independent from the Kingdom of Yehudah."

"But how could they do that?"

"As I said, Ephraim is a powerful tribe, and the northern tribes resented twenty years of forced labor to build a capital in the south."

"But you told me the Holy One granted an eternal kingdom to the House of David."

Uncle Menachem's eyes narrowed. "Well, this is where your friends, the prophets, enter the story."

"They fought against Yeravaum?"

He shook his head. "King Solomon's weakness for foreign women raised the wrath of the Holy One. Achia of Shiloh, Uriel's master, was sent to anoint Yeravaum as king even during Solomon's lifetime."

"The prophets declared Yeravaum king even before the people rejected Rechavaum?"

My uncle nodded.

"But what does this have to do with my bowing to the calf?"

"Well, Yeravaum had the support of most of the people, especially after it became known that he was anointed by a prophet. But there was one thing he didn't have: the Holy Temple. All the men of Yisrael are obligated to go up to the Temple for the three yearly festivals: *Pesach, Shavuot,* and *Sukkot.*"

"So?"

"So, only a king from the House of David is allowed to sit in the Temple, all others must stand. Yeravaum was afraid that if he allowed the people to go to Yerushalayim, they would see Rechavaum sitting in the Temple courts while he stood. Who would look like the greater king then? He feared their loyalty would return to the House of David. So he closed the roads to Yerushalayim and forbade the people from making the pilgrimage."

I pictured the faces of the nobles bowing to the Baal at the wedding. "Yeravaum was afraid, so he frightened the people?"

Uncle Menachem nodded. "He put soldiers on the road. After he killed the first few who defied his orders, most stopped trying. But Yeravaum understood that he couldn't stop the people from serving the Holy One. Their connection was too strong—attack that and the nation would rise against him. And he was not opposed to the Holy One, just to the people going to Yerushalayim. So he crafted two golden calves, placing one in Beit El in the south of the Kingdom and one in Dan in the north, and declared: 'Here are your gods that brought you up from Egypt.' Then he created a new pilgrimage festival one month after *Sukkot.*"

"Why did he choose the calf?"

"I think it was because our ancestors already worshipped the calf in the desert—it was already in our hearts. Your father had some other explanation that I never understood."

"What was that?" I couldn't keep the eagerness out of my voice. I had never before heard a teaching from my father.

"He said that the calf represents the animal half of our souls. That worshiping it was turning toward our animal self, away from our higher destiny."

I rolled the statement over in my mind, wanting badly to understand my father's words. "I don't know what that means," I admitted at last.

"Neither do I."

I ran my hand across the back of one of the sheep, where the wool was just starting to grow in after the spring shearing. "Uncle, if you know all this, why did you start going again?"

Uncle Menachem dropped his eyes. "It's what everyone does, Lev. It's a time for the people to come together and strengthen our connections to each other and the Holy One. I loved going with my father when I was young. Is it better to go to the Temple? Of course. But the road to Yerushalayim is closed." He cleared his throat, yet held his gaze low to the ground. "Your father made me ashamed to go, but when he was no longer here, I started again."

I nodded, glad my uncle had answered, but not wanting to push him further.

"So you'll be taking out the flock in the morning?"

Now it was my turn to look away. The question had been on my mind the whole journey back. "No," I said, and my uncle's eyes shot up to mine. "I'll go, but only to help Eliav. He leads the flock now."

"Lev, you know you are no less to me than my own children, don't you?"

I swallowed, but didn't reply.

"It's true that you can't inherit the land. But your aunt and I have spoken. We want each of you to inherit part of the flock. You needn't give way to Eliav. You're the elder and the better shepherd. He should help you."

My lower jaw trembled, but I had decided my path—there would be no more silly dreams. "No, I'll help him. Between the prophets and the wedding, I have enough copper to buy seven ewes and two rams in the spring." Uncle Menachem raised his eyebrows. "I'll go out with Eliav through the winter, then start a flock of my own."

Uncle Menachem pulled on his beard. "This is what you want?"

"Yes," I said, though my tone didn't ring as clearly as I intended.

"Very well. I'll give you another ram and three ewes from the calves. With that many to start, you should have a strong flock by the time you're ready to marry."

I knew he would want to help, but hadn't expected such a generous gift. "Thank you, Uncle."

Uncle Menachem stepped back toward the house, then turned to face me. "You're sure this is what you want?"

"Yes," I said with confidence I didn't feel. "Eliav should take the flock."

He peered deeply into my eyes. "I meant, are you sure you want to be a shepherd?"

My gaze rose toward the sky, lit by the last rays of the setting sun. The dream of playing in the King's Court still called to me, but not if it meant bowing to the Baal. "What else would I do?"

Uncle Menachem shrugged. "That morning when you went off with Master Uriel, you didn't see me. I was working in the olive trees and watched you go. I saw your face and wondered if you'd ever return to this life. You have a lot of your father in you."

Three mentions of my father in one conversation. Was Uncle Menachem suddenly willing to talk? "Uncle, what really happened to my parents?"

Uncle Menachem sat down next to me on the stone wall of the pen and stared down at his hands. When he spoke, it was just above a whisper.

"The truth? I don't know most of it. A man came to us in the night with cuts all over his face. Didn't appear as if anyone had treated his wounds at all. He was carrying you. You just kept screaming. You weren't hurt, but it looked as if you'd not been fed all day. Leah was nursing when he came. She handed Dahlia to me, and nursed you instead. He told me that he saw your parents killed. He wouldn't say any more. I tried to convince him to stay, to eat something and let us care for his wounds. But he refused. He just refilled his water skin, took a little food, and left."

I nodded, not trusting my voice—I hadn't known that Aunt Leah had nursed me. Menachem rested his hand on my shoulder, then stepped back toward the house. I sat alone with my thoughts as darkness fell.

♬ ♬ ♬

"Where's your *kinnor*?" Eliav asked me the next morning.

"I'm not bringing it." I held a shepherd's staff, which I hadn't carried in over a year. "You're in charge of the flock now. We'll do it your way."

Eliav didn't respond, just stared at me with a blank expression, as if unsure whether to be happy about this change or not. With a shrug, he turned his back, unlocked the pen, and let out a sharp "Yah!" that brought the sheep pouring out. I hemmed in the flock with my outstretched staff, and Eliav turned them downhill toward the fields on the back side of the town.

"The rain brought up fresh grasses by the road," I called from behind the flock. "No one's grazed there yet."

Eliav didn't turn. "The rain brought up grasses everywhere. This way's closer."

"But you need to go through Zimmah ben Merari's field this way. They might eat from the cut grain."

Eliav stopped and the sheep bunched up behind him, bleating and snorting. "All the shepherds pass through his field and no one grazes there, you know that. But if you'd rather go to the road, we can go to the road."

"It's your flock—I'll follow you."

Eliav spit on the ground, then turned the flock back up toward the road. I took up the rear, keeping the sheep in a tight group with light taps on the hindquarters of the stragglers. Without my *kinnor*, my mind drifted quickly. How long had it taken Eliav to change my grazing spot? Had he done it the very day I left? And why? Was it because the road was farther or because all the other shepherds went behind the town?

We found good pasture on the slope immediately below the town's gates. Eliav was more confident now with the flock, but he still stood periodically and rushed at any sheep that threatened to stray.

"Don't do that!" I shouted when Eliav popped up for the third time. "You're just as likely to scare them away as bring them back. If you want to tighten up the flock, go past the sheep and just walk back toward the center."

"All right," Eliav said, but he avoided my eyes as he spoke. I didn't offer any more advice after that.

By the time the sun passed its midpoint, I missed my *kinnor*. A staff might keep the sheep in line, but was a poor tool for occupying heart and mind. I watched puffy clouds drift by in ones and twos, high over our heads. Clouds like these weren't so unusual this time of year, but they made me think of the coming rains.

I brought my eyes down to earth just in time to notice a rider turning up from the King's Road below, dressed in violet robes. Bile rose in my throat. A priest of the Baal in Levonah?

Astride a black mare, the rider made much shorter work of the steep road than I had the day before. Eliav gaped, and I elbowed him so that he wouldn't stare. I needn't have bothered—two shepherd boys were beneath the priest's notice. He approached the gate and addressed the guard loudly in poor Hebrew. "I want Yoel ben Beerah."

Yoel ben Beerah was the King's minister in Levonah—what could a priest of the Baal want with him? Without thinking, I motioned to Eliav to watch the sheep and slipped up to the town wall. I crept along the footpath that hugged the wall, stopping in the shadow of the gate where I could hear without being easily seen. Memories of the wedding celebration flooded my mind, and I fought the urge to spit the bitter taste from my mouth.

The guard slouched in the gate, but sat up at attention as the priest approached. "Who seeks the King's officer?"

"A messenger of the Queen." The priest dismounted in a fluid motion, holding out a scroll in one hand.

The guard shot a skeptical frown at the priest, but when he examined the seal on the scroll, the defiance in his eyes died, his face turned pale, and he bowed his head before answering. "He is here in the gatehouse. I will summon him."

The guard retreated into the gate, and I was gripped by an internal battle. A voice in my gut screamed to retreat—I had no business with the Baal or the King's minister—but my curiosity pushed me closer to the gate, yearning to hear what the message contained. Yet, the knife at the priest's side drew my eyes. My heart pumped only fear—if he was willing to cut his own flesh, what would the priest do if he caught a spying shepherd boy?

Yoel ben Beerah stepped into the gate, trailed by two soldiers. He walked with a deliberate step, examining the priest as he approached. "I am Yoel ben Beerah. You may deliver your message."

The priest handed over the scroll and Yoel ben Beerah hastily broke the seal and glanced at the contents of the parchment. He scanned the gate plaza around him, causing me to shrink back against the stone wall. "Come, we must discuss this."

"Lev!" Eliav hissed from below.

I cringed at the sound and scurried down from my perch.

"What were you doing?"

"That's a priest of the Baal bringing a message to Yoel ben Beerah."

Eliav's eyes widened. "How do you know he's a priest of the Baal?"

"I recognized him from the wedding."

A smirk played at the corner of Eliav's mouth, then it turned down into a frown. "You have no business with him, what were you doing? If he had seen you…"

Eliav was right—it was a stupid risk to take. Why did I feel such a strong need to know what they were saying?

"What did he want with Yoel ben Beerah?"

"I don't know." I glared at Eliav. "I had to stop listening."

Eliav gazed up at the clouds. "Do you really think they can bring the rains?"

"Master Uriel says that they will come early."

Eliav grinned. "That'll be a blessing."

I leaned away from him. "But what about all the farmers whose crops will be ruined?"

"What about them?" Eliav planted his staff before him and stood. "Let their blood be on their own heads. Yambalya granted them enough time for the harvest, you heard him yourself. It's only those who don't listen whose crops will be ruined. And any rain is good for us, right?"

Again Eliav was right—hadn't I thought like him when I first felt the rains? Yet, now a fury rose within me that I couldn't explain. Not knowing what to say, I stalked off to gather in a stray ram.

The next day was Shabbat. I passed the time feasting with my family and repeating the stories of my travels, mostly at the request of my younger cousins. On the first day of the week, Eliav again directed the flock toward the fields behind the city. This time I didn't bother protesting.

After the evening meal that night, I retrieved my *kinnor* for the first time since returning home. It was not to "keep the spark inside me alive," as Daniel had pressed me to do. No, I needed music to smother all those voices rising in my head since my return: my anger at Eliav, my disappointment in Uncle Menachem, my aching desire to be more than a shepherd in the wilderness. I'd made my choice, and my *kinnor* was my best tool to quiet the tempest within and remain on my path. I leaned against an olive tree opposite the house and gently plucked the strings, trying to replicate the sound of the leaves rustling overhead, imagining myself alone in the wilderness.

"There was no music while you were gone." Dahlia stood over me, a bowl in her hands. "I brought you some toasted wheat."

I grabbed a few wheatberries, still warm from roasting, and popped them into my mouth.

Dahlia sat next to me, pulling her dress down over her feet, and resting the bowl in her lap. "Do you want to sing to me?"

"I don't feel like singing."

"Want to tell me about the wedding again?"

"No," I said, louder than I intended.

She pulled away. "Do you want me to go back in?"

"No, you can stay." We sat silently, listening to the whisper of the leaves and the soft notes of the *kinnor*. In the distance there were three heavy thuds, the sound of wood striking wood.

Dahlia broke the silence. "Are you happy to be home?"

I kept on strumming quietly. Had anyone else in the family asked, I would have offered a quick "Yes," but it was different with Dahlia. "I was when I first got back."

"You don't seem happy now." Again the thudding sound disturbed the twilight peace, this time closer. "I don't think my mother expected you to return."

"Is that why she cried so much when I left?"

"Probably."

"One of the musicians I met was like that. He left home over a year ago, moving from place to place, playing for weddings and festivals."

"He didn't get lonely?"

"I don't think so."

"Would you?"

I closed my eyes, picturing myself moving from festival to festival, carrying a mirror like Zim, never spending more than a couple of weeks in any one place. Maybe if Yonaton was with me it wouldn't be so bad. "I'd get lonely."

"I don't think she saw you becoming some wandering musician."

"No, she thought I'd stay with Master Uriel," I said, clamping my hand on the strings of the *kinnor*. The music died. Whenever I thought of Uriel now, I saw his cold narrowed eyes after he learned that I'd bowed to the calf.

"Yes," Dahlia replied, and we sat in silence once again.

Two men crossed Uncle Menachem's property and approached the house, taking no notice of Dahlia or me in the growing darkness. The man in front raised his staff and banged it three times against the door.

"Who's there?" my uncle called, anger and worry in his voice. We did not get many visitors at night—certainly not ones who knocked so loudly.

"It is Yoel ben Beerah," the shorter man answered in a voice that carried into the night.

Eliav opened the door and soft light from the hearth shone from the house, revealing the violet hue of the other man's robes. Uncle Menachem appeared next to Eliav in the doorway. "Good evening, Yoel ben Beerah. Please come in."

"There is no need, we want just a word." His voice was quieter now, but still had the tone of command. "Queen Izevel invites all of Yisrael to humble ourselves before the Baal prior to the rains so that we will be blessed with a bountiful year."

The priest put a box on the ground, opening a flap in the side facing the house.

"I see the Baal. And I see his servant's weapon," my uncle said, staring at the long knife at the priest's side. "Are we being forced to bow?" Eliav turned to his father, mouth agape.

"Certainly not. Queen Izevel only invites us. Already tonight several men have declined. If they're not concerned for their crops, I cannot help them. We are here for your sake."

The priest fell to his knees in front of the box, stretching out his arms and pressing his face to the ground. Yoel bowed next to him, supporting himself with his staff until his knees touched the ground, then laying his arms flat.

Dahlia clutched my arm. Would Uncle Menachem bow to the Baal as he did to the Golden Calf?

Uncle Menachem hesitated. Not a sound rose from the priest or the King's servant. I held my breath as Dahlia's grip tightened. This was not like the Calf. Even if Uncle Menachem believed bowing to the Calf was bowing to the Holy One, he could claim no confusion here. It was from my uncle's mouth that I learned the verse, "Do not bow before their gods, do not serve them, do not follow their practices; rather, tear them apart and destroy their monuments." My uncle's wavering form filled the door—but Eliav moved first. Turning away from his father, Eliav fell to the ground beside Yoel, stretching himself out in the dirt of the doorway.

Uncle Menachem eyes fell on his son.

Dahlia's nails dug deep into the skin of my arm. I choked back a cry.

Uncle Menachem's knees buckled, as if he was trying to hold up a weight greater than himself. Drawn by Eliav, his shaky knees gave way. Once his knees struck earth, his back curved into the same position that I took before the Golden Calf, with his arms reaching out in servitude, his forehead humbled to the ground.

Yoel stood first, brushing dirt and twigs from his cloak. Uncle Menachem followed, grasping at the doorpost for support. Eliav did not lift himself from the dirt until the priest stood and closed the shrine.

"You are a prudent man, Menachem," Yoel said. "May you receive much blessing for it. Peace to you."

"And peace unto you, Yoel ben Beerah," Uncle Menachem replied, without lifting his face.

The priest handed an object to my uncle. "Gift from the Queen," he said, then followed Yoel away into the darkness.

Uncle Menachem stood in the doorway, watching the two men disappear down the path. As he turned back toward the house, his glance paused under the olive tree where Dahlia and I sat. His chin fell to his chest; he stepped inside, and closed the door.

Dahlia's shuddering form shook mine. "I didn't think my father would bow."

"He doesn't like to be different."

The moonlight reflected in two lines down her cheeks. "You're different, but you never seem to mind."

"If I'm different, it's not because I mean to be." I shied away from her tears. "Don't think it's easy."

"If it's not easy, why did you come back?"

"Where else was I supposed to go? I told you: I don't want to be some wandering musician." I still avoided Dahlia's gaze, wishing she would dry her eyes.

"You said Master Uriel stayed behind with a few disciples. Why don't you return and play for them?"

My eyes shot back up to Dahlia's. "Uriel doesn't want me!"

The bowl of wheatberries toppled to the ground as Dahlia fled toward the house. I yearned to go after her—I hadn't meant to shout. But I didn't move even as she flew in and shut the door fast behind her. Instead, I lifted my eyes to the fluttering leaves of the olive tree, and plucked aimlessly at the strings of my *kinnor*.

"When you received your kinnor, you were still too young to play it."

"Then why was it left with me, Master?"

"Lest your neshama need release that your life could not provide."

"So that I would dream of more than my sheep?"

"Precisely."

I thought of all the misery that my daydreams had caused me over the years. I always thought that my kinnor helped me silence my futile aspirations. I never realized that it was responsible for creating them.

My Master said softly, "Song is the language of the soul. When music speaks through you, it reveals that the ears that hear and the hands that play are merely garments for the neshama."

Rabbi Elazar HaKapar said: Against your will you were created, against your will you were born, against your will you live, against your will you die, and against your will you will come to give an accounting of your deeds.

Pirkei Avot 4:29

11

The Vinyard of Shiloh

A hand gently shook my shoulder, rousing me from sleep. I awoke to total darkness.

"Get dressed," my aunt whispered against my ear. "Pack your things. Wake no one." Her dress swished down the ladder.

Eliav moaned in his sleep as I pulled my tunic over my head. I rolled my sheepskin sleeping mat as quietly as I could so as not to rouse him further. Holding my things under one arm, I slipped down the ladder. The flickering light of the hearth illuminated a clay statue set in a niche in the wall: the gift from the Queen.

Even in the half-light I could see that Aunt Leah's eyes were red and dark blotches marred her face.

"Aunt, have you slept?"

"No," she said, her head sinking into her chest.

"What's happening?" I rubbed my eyes to force them awake.

Aunt Leah breathed in a whispered cry as she struggled to maintain eye contact. "It's time for you to leave this house."

"Leave?" The word leapt out of my mouth too loudly. My eyes rose to the loft, but no one stirred in the dark house.

"Eat. You'll need your strength." Aunt Leah laid a plate of bread and cheese on the table. I sat opposite her and took a small bite, though I had little appetite.

"Do you remember how, before you left with Master Uriel, I told you that you are the same to me as my own children?"

I struggled to swallow the unchewed morsel in my mouth. "Yes."

"Well, I heard everything that happened last night. I know that Menachem and Eliav bowed to the Baal. Dahlia told me that you saw it too. I couldn't sleep thinking of you. I wish Menachem and Eliav hadn't bowed, but Menachem is my husband and Eliav my son, and I love them. I'd rather not have a Baal in the house, but there it is. I don't want to bow down to it, but if my husband insists, I will.

"I love you too, Lev." Aunt Leah stuffed bread and hard cheese into a sack. "But you're not my son." Tears now rolled freely down her cheeks.

I stared at my food as she sobbed.

"Your parents never would have raised you in a house with that abomination of an idol. My poor sister would never forgive me. For their sake—for yours—you cannot stay." Aunt Leah's head sank into her hands, her body shuddering.

I ate despite my lack of hunger, finding it easier to focus on bread than on its tear-stricken baker. Sleep was still heavy on my eyes, and I wanted nothing so much as to return to my bed.

Aunt Leah sat up, dried her eyes with the back of her hand, and gave me a weak smile that squeezed out two last tears from her eyes.

"Where will I go?" I asked, remembering this time to keep my voice quiet.

"You could return to Master Uriel—"

"I'm not going back to him."

"Why not?"

"I'm not going back." My words were final. "There must be another choice."

Aunt Leah laid a fragment of parchment on the table before me, brown in color, tattered at its edges. I tilted it to read by the red light of the coals. *Elazar ben Amram, Beit Shemesh* was all it said. "What is this?"

"This is the name of your uncle, your father's brother. He lives in the Kingdom of Yehudah. You can go to him and still be with your family, just…" She bit her lip to hold back a new wave of tears. "Just…away from all of this."

"Go to Yehudah?" It was the first mention I ever heard of family across the border.

"The road is guarded, but there are many paths through the mountains. Take this," she put a small pile of copper on the table. "Go to Mitzpah. Search there for a guide to lead you through the passes out of the Kingdom."

Ignoring the copper, I lifted the parchment, my heart pounding. "Whose writing is this?"

"It's your father's. He wanted you raised with his family in Yehudah. Menachem deemed it too dangerous to move you during the war, and then…" Aunt Leah wiped her eyes again on the back of her hand. "But now I see that your father was right. It will be better for you there than here."

"Why?" I could feel years of unanswered questions welling up inside. "Am I from the tribe of Yehudah? Is that why I have no inheritance here?"

"No, you're not from Yehudah. You have no land there either."

"There's something you're not telling me."

Aunt Leah didn't turn away as she normally did when I asked about my parents. "Master Uriel made us swear never to tell. He said that knowledge would put you at risk. But once you get to Yehudah you will be safe. Your family there can explain everything."

My eyes narrowed. So, Uriel was responsible for the secrets—for no one telling me the truth about my family.

A cough disturbed the quiet of the dark house. "That's your uncle waking. Go now. I won't have the strength to send you away with him here."

Aunt Leah added more bread to the sack and laid it on the table with a full skin of water. "Take the copper. It will get you across."

"I don't need it. I was paid more than that just for the wedding."

"Take it anyway," she said, her eyes pleading. "For me."

I collected the dull pieces of metal and added them to my pouch. It held more wealth than I ever dreamed I'd have at this age. It felt heavy against my thigh, but brought me no joy.

Aunt Leah opened the door. The pale gray predawn light illuminated the dirt path before me. Uncle Menachem's heavy foot appeared on the top rung of the ladder, and I hurried through the open doorway.

"I love you, Lev," was the last thing I heard as Aunt Leah closed the door behind me.

An orange glow backlit the eastern mountains as I headed down to the King's Road in the valley below. I fought the desire to turn and look at my house one last time. I was on a path I had not chosen and it seemed best to keep my feet moving; if I hesitated now I might not start again. As the trail dipped downhill, birdsong echoed around me. Thinking of Daniel, I considered stopping to listen, but it felt invigorating to just walk. I took my first deep breath of the morning, my chest expanding with dew-filled air.

The slip of parchment still tingled in my hand. I hadn't looked at it since learning that it was my father's writing—but I hadn't let go of it either. There was a message in the note, but what was it? I studied it now and my step faltered. My legs grew heavy at the thought of crossing the mountains into Yehudah—I had never heard of anyone trekking that dangerous path. Who would I even ask to help me? Aunt Leah said they would explain everything in Yehudah. Explain what? Possibilities swirled in my mind and I stumbled on a rock in my path.

I had to stop.

I dropped down onto a flat boulder by the roadside. Staring at the scratchy handwriting on the parchment, written in a brown ink I had never seen before, I willed it to reveal its secret. No guidance came. My face crumpled into my hands. I'd left so many places in the past weeks, but always with a clear destination. But now…now I was all alone.

The impossibility of this journey suddenly descended on me; I squeezed my eyes tight and bent over my trembling knees. Images whirled through my head: jugglers, prophets, musicians. My throat ached, each breath coming in labored gasps. Uriel rejected me; Aunt Leah sent me away. Who was left?

The pressure in my chest swelled and a groan rose up from deep inside. A shudder passed through my body, and for the first time in five years, I began to cry. It started off slowly, the first drops barely squeezing out with each heave of my chest, as if my eyes had forgotten how. Their salty taste hit my tongue, evoking memories of a past when they had flowed freely. A wail rose in my throat, and the tears broke free.

My shoulders shook as the chalky soil at my feet grew pockmarked with droplets; my sobs silencing the last birds of the morning.

I don't know how long I cried, but when I gazed up, the wind blew cool against my cheeks. My chest felt loose as I inhaled. My uncle's words echoed in my mind, "Yisrael is wide enough for us all, if we each find our place."

My head lifted toward the sky, a plea welling up within as I blinked away the last tears. My heart, no longer blocked, called out to the heavens as it never had before, *"Where is my place?"* I squeezed my eyes shut and sent all my will after the call.

The warmth of the newly risen sun caressed my face. As its golden rays penetrated my eyelids, I stood up from my cold stone seat. I slipped the parchment, damp with tears, into my pouch, slung my sack over my shoulder, and continued down the hill.

The junction with the King's Road appeared ahead, and I paused to gaze back up at Levonah's walls, reflecting the dawn light. I shook myself like a dog emerging from a cold spring. An image of Uriel rose in my mind—not stony with the anger of our last encounter, but suffused with the compassion and wisdom I had come to know. I could almost hear his advice about trusting my heart.

I reached the junction just ahead of a group of men walking down the King's Road from the north. They were all older than me, wearing the worn summer clothes of farmers. *What were seven farmers doing on the King's Road at dawn?* "Peace upon you," I called to the one leading the pack.

"Upon you peace," the man replied.

"Where are you headed?"

"To the festival at Shiloh. And where goes the young man?" he answered with a smile.

I opened my mouth to say Mitzpah, but held myself back. The parchment with my father's writing burned in my pouch—it was the key to all my questions. Yet, once I crossed into Yehudah—if I managed to make it alive—I'd probably never return. That piece of parchment sat in my uncle's house for ten years, another day or two wouldn't make any difference. And hadn't Zim said that Shiloh was not to be missed? Besides, Shiloh was one step closer to Mitzpah. "I'm also going to Shiloh."

"But you're far too young," one of the farmers laughed.

Now the whole group was staring at me—Zim never mentioned anything about age. "I'm a musician," I said, hoping that made a difference.

"Oh, I see. Walk along with us if you like."

"A musician, eh?" a particularly dirty farmer chuckled. "Why don't you play us something?" I wasn't interested in being their entertainment, but it was good to have company. I drew my *kinnor* forward and played the sheep's watering *nigun* as we walked.

� ♪ ♪ ♪

Dozens of men milled around the hill below Shiloh, and all seemed to be between the ages of twenty and forty. A second group gathered at the east side of the hill, but the two groups didn't mix. Nervous laughter ran through the crowd. One of my companions laid a hand on my shoulder and pointed to a cluster of trees at the foot of the hill. "The musicians are over there."

I approached the trees, finding five musicians playing as an older man scrutinized them, dropping comments and critiques. "Excuse me," I said to the man, who took no notice. "Excuse me," I called a little louder.

The old man turned, first looking over my head, then down until he met my eyes. "Yes?"

I had never asked for work before. "I'm wondering if you…" I started, brandishing my *kinnor*.

"Ah, you'd like to play with us." He smirked. "I'm sorry, I've got all the musicians I need." The other musicians watched me now, a couple of them grinning. "Keep working on your music. Perhaps in a few years you can come join us."

I nodded, my cheeks burning, and walked away, their music mocking my retreat. The musicians were good, but no better than me. The leader hadn't even listened to me play. Their song faded as I approached the King's Road, all but the drumming, which grew louder with each step.

I pulled the piece of parchment out of my pouch. It was stupid to think I could just show up and play—at least I hadn't lost much time. If I moved quickly, I might still be able to reach Mitzpah by nightfall. All I could hear now was the drum, pounding louder and louder.

"Lev, you came!"

"Zim!" He stopped drumming and wrapped one stout arm around me, squeezing my face into his shoulder. "I thought you were staying in Shomron?"

"I told you, I never miss Shiloh. Yambalya said I could come." Zim released me and I rubbed my nose, which itched from scraping against his rough tunic. "You're going the wrong way. The musicians set up over there."

"They didn't want me. The leader didn't even listen to me. He thinks I'm too young."

Zim laughed. "I was barely older than you when I started coming. You're not too young—you just look terrified. Come on." Zim walked past, waving for me to follow, "Emanuel!" he called with his habitual confidence.

The old man saw Zim, a genuine smile stretching across his face this time. "Zimri. I was hoping you'd come back. We can use your drum." Emanuel caught sight of me. "I told your friend to come back in a couple of years. We don't need any boys playing."

Zim shook with laughter. "You must have some group this year if you think your musicians are better than the King's."

Emanuel started, his eyes lit with curiosity. "The King's?"

"This is Lev ben Menachem. I played with him at the King's wedding. I told him to come to Shiloh—I figured you could use the help."

"But he's just a boy."

"You judge too much by appearances." Zim said, running a hand through his wavy, dark hair. "Have you listened to him play?"

"No." Emanuel scratched his beard.

"Lev, let's do that song we played for the juggler. You start and I'll join in. If the rest of you think you can follow along, feel free to try."

All eyes were on me again, but now it felt completely different. I took my time preparing to play, first stretching out the fingers on my left hand, then on my right. No one spoke as they waited. I closed my eyes and let my fingers go.

Zim picked the right tune. It was fast and the melody jumped around a complicated rhythm. If I hadn't spent so much time practicing before the wedding, I would never have been able to lead it. As it was, I struggled to play it on my own. Zim let me start solo, then filled in the rhythm underneath. After one round, a *nevel* added its voice, not quite in rhythm. A *halil* joined in with a high, warbling note, but struggled to stay in tune and fell away.

Before long, all seven musicians were playing—the quality of the music nothing near the caliber of the wedding. I played the notes as crisply as I could in order to guide the others—suddenly aware of how much my abilities had grown since the gathering began. All of Daniel's lessons had taken hold. I had more power and speed than before, but that wasn't all. I was playing more loosely now, as I did at the wedding after two goblets of the King's wine. This time, though, the freedom couldn't have come from drink. *It must have been from that morning's flood of tears.*

We played through the melody twice, then Zim departed from the rhythm into short rapid beats. I brought the tune to an end, sealing it with a bold final note that continued to reverberate even as I removed my hand from the strings and opened my eyes.

Emanuel's attention was locked on me, eyes wide and mouth slack. Zim held back a laugh. "You can stay," Emanuel said. "Let's try that song again. We can add it tonight if the rest of you get it sharper."

The Vinyard of Shiloh

👁 👁 👁

A molten sun faded in the west as a full moon rose over the ridge on the eastern horizon. The crowds on both sides of the hill continued to grow as the day wore on, but still hadn't mingled. The musicians set up on a hillside overlooking an expanse of trellised grapevines, their avenues or arbors forming shadowed lanes over the land that lay between the two gatherings. An old man approached the near group, and chatter ceased as they surrounded him. I could tell that he spoke loudly, but we were too far away to hear what he was saying.

When the old man finished, he left the first group and walked along the edge of the vineyard toward the second, passing directly below the musicians.

I nudged Zim and pointed. "Hey, that's Master Yosef!"

"That's right. He comes here every year. That's how I got hired to play for the prophets this summer—he heard me last year and asked me to come to the gathering."

"I'm surprised to see him at a festival."

"He likes to come and make sure everything happens in '*the right way.*'"

"What has to happen in the right way?"

Zim cocked his head and examined me slyly out of the corner of his eye. "You really don't know what happens here?"

"No, what?"

Zim threw me a mischievous grin. "You'll see soon enough."

The second group now gathered around Yosef. When he finished speaking, only a smudge of color remained in the western sky, and the moon glowed white and immense above the eastern hills. Yosef waved a flaming torch back and forth above his head.

"That's our signal." Emanuel said as he raised his hand. "Lev, lead us in that song from the wedding." I struck the first notes and the others joined in, sounding smoother than before, but still struggling.

The signal was not just for us. When the torch waved, both groups moved toward the vineyard, spreading out as they approached. Some men of the near group hesitated before walking under the bowers, but there was no such hesitation from the far-off crowd. Even from a distance, I could see that they were dancing, moonlight reflected by their brilliant, white garments. Yosef sat beside a bonfire on the hillside below us, next to two of his disciples.

As they reached the edge of the trailing vines, I got a better view of the dancers. "Hey, those are girls!"

"That's right." Zim snickered, his head bobbing to the beat.

"How can Master Yosef agree to this?" I said, scandalized.

Zim's laughed louder. "He says it's one of the holiest days of the year."

The last of the girls danced into the vineyard, and I could no longer make out anyone clearly. Hundreds of shapes moved beneath the vines, limbs twirling, their garments silver against the darkened ground. We performed our fastest songs, one after the other, and my energy surged as I imagined hundreds of girls dancing to my music.

Toward the end of our third song, a couple emerged from the vineyard, walking side-by-side up the hill toward Yosef. They stopped before the prophet, faces lit by the fire, staring into each other's eyes. The man appeared neither young nor old, with a severely crooked nose that distorted an otherwise handsome face. She was much younger than he, wearing an elaborately embroidered dress, her long braids falling from a white scarf upon her head. She was very pretty, and there was something unnervingly familiar about her.

I continued to stare until it came to me—I knew her. Her name was Hadassah, the daughter of one of the poorest families in Levonah. She looked so different tonight that I was surprised that I had recognized her at all. She must have spent hours, if not days, cleaning herself and braiding her hair. I had seen her only in dirty, tattered clothes. *How could her family afford such an ornate dress?*

Yosef addressed them, but his words were lost in the music. The couple glanced at each other and nodded with the expression of children getting away with something forbidden. They bowed their heads, and Yosef placed one hand on the man's head, holding the other just above Hadassah's. When he removed his hands, they gazed at each other again, clasped hands, and withdrew from the fire.

More couples emerged from the vineyard, ascending the hill toward Yosef, and waiting in a line that began to stretch down to its very edge. "What is he saying to them?" I asked Zim.

"Go listen."

"I can't do that."

"Why not?"

Something about the expression in Zim's eyes made my fears seem childish. I peered around for Emanuel, but he was nowhere in sight. With six other musicians playing, I wouldn't be missed if I went quickly. I left my *kinnor* and crept down the hillside, stooping under a rocky shelf that projected out just behind Yosef. A new couple stood before him now, both rather short and broadly built.

"It's hard to see in the vineyard," Yosef said, "So I want you to take a good look at each other in the firelight." The couple peered at each other and smiled. "You are certain of your choice?"

The man said "Yes," and the woman nodded.

"Very well. Bow your heads. May the Holy One bless your home to be like the tent of Yitzchak and Rivka, to raise righteous children, and to eat from the bounty of the land." Yosef lowered his hands, indicating the two disciples at his side. "These men are your witnesses that you have been bound today in holiness. You may go." The man stepped away from the fire first, and his bride followed him into the darkness.

I returned to my place among the musicians, my thoughts a whirl. "They're getting married?"

"That's right," Zim said.

"But I've been to plenty of weddings, why—"

"Nobody wants to get married this way. But some families can't find good matches for their children. They might have no wealth, no connections. And look around, some of these people are just plain ugly. But they all come to Shiloh and find each other in the vineyard."

"I recognized that first girl; she's from my town. Her family is really poor, but she was wearing a fancy dress."

"All the girls borrow dresses—it's part of the rules of Shiloh. No one can tell who is rich or poor in the vineyard."

"So how do they find each other?"

"The girls just go under the vines, dancing and calling out to the men. The pretty ones say 'Come find yourself a beautiful wife.' The ones from good families say 'Find yourself a wife to build a family with.' Inside that vineyard is the only place where the people of Yisrael don't hold back."

"So what if they aren't beautiful or from good families?"

"They say 'Choose a wife for the sake of heaven,' though I'm not sure why heaven should prefer an ugly wife!"

A place in Yisrael where no one holds back—no wonder Zim was drawn to it. "Did you ever think of going into the vineyard and finding a bride for yourself?"

"Me? Get married?" Zim threw back his head with a loud laugh. "I'm living in Shomron now."

"So?"

"So Baal isn't the only god that Izevel brought down with her from Tzidon."

"Who else is there?"

"There's Ashera."

"Who's he?"

"She. She's the mother of Baal, the goddess of the Earth."

"Yeah? Do her priests also cut themselves up?"

"Priestesses. And no, they don't."

"So what's her worship like?"

"A bit like this. Except in the morning you don't wake up with a wife."

* * *

The sun already blazed above the mountains when Zim shook me awake the next morning. My first thought was how strange it was for Zim to be awake before me, and then I realized that I was bathed in sweat.

"You were screaming."

"It's nothing," I said, sitting up, "Just a nightmare." But it wasn't nothing. For the first time, I remembered a detail from my old dream. There was a horse, driven fast. I wanted to close my eyes, to hold onto the vision, to see more.

"You sure you're alright?" The concern on Zim's face appeared so out of place.

If I was going to talk about my nightmares with anyone, it wasn't Zim. I opened the sack of food my aunt had prepared and pulled out bread and cheese, giving up on any hope of slipping back into the dream to learn more. "Come eat," I said. Watching Zim help himself to a piece of bread and a hunk of cheese, I felt grateful that at least it was Zim and not Yonaton who had heard me screaming. Yonaton's concern wouldn't have been pushed aside so easily, certainly not with a bribe of food.

In the vineyard and the surrounding fields, couples were sitting and walking together. Two groups again formed on opposite sides of the vineyard, each much smaller than the night before. These must be the ones who failed to find a match. *Would they be back next year?*

"So you're heading back to the gathering today?" Zim asked between bites.

It hadn't occurred to me that Zim wouldn't know. "No, the gathering was closed after the wedding."

"Why?"

"So that everyone can bring in their harvests before the rains."

Zim's eyes gleamed. "So even the prophets have begun to fear Baal? Yambalya will be pleased."

My first instinct was to defend them, but I held myself back. It did feel as if the prophets were giving way to the Baal.

"So you're going home then?"

I stopped eating and stared down. "I can't go home."

"Can't go home? Why not?"

"My aunt sent me away."

"Why? What happened?"

My throat suddenly felt dry, and I swallowed hard. "My uncle brought a Baal into the house. My aunt said that my parents would never accept me living in a house with an idol, so she made me leave. She told me to go to my father's family in Yehudah."

"Yehudah? How are you supposed to get across the border?"

"My aunt gave me copper. She said that, in Mitzpah, I will be able to find someone who will take it to guide me over."

"So that's it? You're going? And you'll just hope that whoever takes your payment can get you there alive?"

"What choice do I have?"

Zim shook his head. "Just because your aunt sent you to Yehudah doesn't mean you have to go. You're almost of age, Lev—it's time to become a man."

I turned away, my heart feeling like a cold stone in my chest.

"She threw you out—it's no longer her choice. Come back to Shomron with me."

"Shomron?"

"Yes, Shomron. Queen Izevel is building two temples, one for Baal, the other for Ashera. The nobility are competing to offer the biggest feasts each day. There aren't enough musicians for all the ceremonies and banquets. Two nights ago I even played for Uriel's son."

"Uriel's son?'

"The Chief Priest of Yisrael." Zim laughed at the look on my face. "Didn't you notice their likeness at the wedding? It might have been Uriel forty years ago!"

I pictured the face of the priest. If the thick brows were white and the skin across his broad cheekbones wrinkled, it would have been Uriel. How had I not noticed? "But Uriel hates the Golden Calf. How can his son be its priest?"

Zim shrugged. "You can ask him when we get to Shomron."

"I couldn't do that!"

"Why not? I did."

"You did? What did he say?"

"He said he used to walk in his father's ways. But his father was always traveling, tending to the needs of the people. He wasn't there for his own family. Ten years ago, he decided he'd had enough."

"And you're playing for him?"

"I'm playing for everyone. There aren't enough musicians in Shomron. They need you there."

I dropped the bread in my hand, my hunger forgotten. "You heard what my aunt said—my parents wanted me far away from the Baal."

"Your parents are dead, Lev."

My crying the day before must have unblocked the channel of tears, for fresh drops clouded my vision.

"I know it hurts, but it's true."

My eyes strayed toward the lone men leaving Shiloh with heavy steps.

"You can't live your life for them. Do you even remember what they look like?"

"You don't understand," I said, my voice flat.

"Maybe I don't," Zim placed a hand on my shoulder. "But you need to hear this. Didn't you learn anything last night?"

I shook off Zim's hand. "What do you mean?"

"I mean, look at those couples down there. Every one of them would have preferred to get married in the usual way, but it didn't work out for them. They could have stayed at home and cried about being alone—but they didn't. They decided not to let a rotten past force them into an empty future."

I gazed at the men and women holding hands under the trees.

"They went into that vineyard with all they had, and they left everything they didn't need behind. Now look at them, most of them aren't alone anymore. How do you think they feel?"

"I don't know…Happy?"

Zim shook his head. "Scared. They're starting a new life with someone they hardly know. But they know one thing: It's better to jump into an unknown future than hold onto a dead past."

I cocked my head. "What are you saying?"

"You were one of the best musicians here last night."

I snorted at the flattery.

"No, really. But if I hadn't come along, you would have walked away and never played a note. Emanuel took one look at you and decided that you were too young. What did you say back to him?"

"Nothing. I left."

"Exactly! Emanuel tells you to leave and you go, even though you're better than his musicians. Your aunt tells you to leave and you go, even though you don't really know why. Did you ever stop to think about what you want?"

Zim stood up. "Learn from the girls of Shiloh. Go into that vineyard and leave the past where it belongs. Come out ready to decide your own future, and let nothing stand in your way."

I picked up a piece of cheese. "I hear what you're saying."

"Clearly you don't, because you're still sitting here." Zim grabbed my arm and drew me to my feet. "Go on, and don't come out until you're ready to claim your life."

Zim pushed me downhill. I continued on my own, then turned back to Zim. "Don't eat all my food while I'm gone."

"Don't worry," Zim said, breaking off another hunk of cheese. "There's plenty to eat in Shomron. Go!"

As I ducked under the trellised vines, the smell of warm earth rose up from the ground between the rows to greet me. Rays of sun peeked between broad, green leaves, painting the thick, twisted vines with swaths of light and shadow. Rows of grapevines stretched out in every direction, the outer world felt far behind.

What Zim said made sense—I was on my own now. I didn't choose to leave, but now every choice was mine. Hadn't I come to Shiloh rather than going right to Mitzpah as my aunt wanted? I could just as easily go to Shomron—or anywhere else for that matter. Leaves trembled around me as a breeze swept off the hills above. I followed one path into the vineyard, but there were countless ways out. I settled myself at the base of a solid, olivewood post, around which two vines were entwined. The young grapes, maroon and growing heavy with juice, hung above my head.

What do I really want? And what path will get me there?

A grasshopper landed at my feet. The wind died, and its rhythmic chirps rang loud on the still air. I closed my eyes and other sounds emerged, the rustling of leaves, a distant dove's cry. I laid my head back against the knotty wood, the notes of the vineyard clear in my mind, and descended into their song.

Though I had walked far into the vineyard, it was easy to find my way back out, I just followed the bass notes of the drum. The sun was high and my sack of provisions lay empty on the ground by Zim's side. Zim beat out one last flourish on his drum, and got to his feet. "If we want to get back tonight, we'll need to go now," he said.

I nodded, picking up my belongings and following Zim toward the road.

"Put out your hand." Zim dropped three pieces of copper into my palm. "Emanuel paid us while you were gone. It's nothing compared to the wedding, but not bad for a night of music. Are you still going to Yehudah?"

I inhaled more deeply than I could ever remember. "No. You were right. That's what my aunt wanted—not what I want."

"Excellent. Yambalya lent me a donkey for the trip. If we both ride, we should be able to make it back before they close the gates."

I stopped Zim with a hand on his shoulder. "I'm not going to Shomron either."

Zim cocked his head. "No?"

"No. You go on your own."

"Where will you go?"

"On my own path."

Zim's face glowed. "Good. Then for the second time in a week, we part as friends." Zim embraced me with both arms this time. "Until our paths cross again."

Rabban Shimon ben Gamliel said: All my days I was raised among the Sages, and I never found anything better for a person than silence.

Pirkei Avot 1:17

The Rains

I filled my lungs, soaking in the dry desert air as the green speckled valley opened out below me. It was late afternoon, and my legs still felt strong. I shook my head at the memory of the exhaustion I had felt when I first took sight of Emek HaAsefa. I hitched my sack higher and stepped lightly down the trail.

Uriel paced beneath the carob tree, five disciples sitting before him, heads bowed between their knees. The old man's focus turned uphill, and his sharp eyes fell on me. Neither of us spoke. I went directly to my old spot under the pomegranate tree, swung my *kinnor* forward, and held my fingers over the strings, awaiting his signal.

The rhythmic whisper of the disciples breathing was the only sound as the old prophet stood motionless, his face a mask. I waited, undeterred by the quivering of my chin. I was so afraid that Uriel would drive me off again. Walking from Shiloh to Emek HaAsefa, I realized that fear had been my constant companion since losing my parents. But knowing this didn't relieve my fear; it only made it stronger. My teeth began to chatter like a *navi* receiving vision as I imagined Uriel rejecting me again. But for the first time I could bear, and even take a strange pleasure in the trembling, having resolved—like the girls of Shiloh—not to let fear stand in my way.

A flock of thrushes circled an oak topping the ridge on the far side of the valley. Their day's end jabbering filled the hollow valley with song just as Uriel relented, dropping his chin in the slightest of nods.

I closed my eyes and softly rippled my fingers across the strings of the *kinnor*, not wanting to startle the meditating disciples. At each pass through the melody, I increased the pace, the clear tones of the *kinnor* deepening and the music unfolding. The *nigun* flowed off the strings, through my bones, and settled in my heart as I lost myself in its rhythm.

A firm hand clasped onto my shoulder, and I opened my eyes to find myself alone with the prophet in the clearing. His creased face was expressionless, showing neither the kindness nor the anger that I recalled. "You have returned for the rest of the gathering?"

I nodded.

"And after that?"

"If you desire my service, I will go where you go. Master."

One eyebrow lifted at the title. All called him Master Uriel, but only a true servant or disciple called him Master. My stomach churned—would the prophet reject me?

"You have chosen to return. I accept you into my service," Uriel said at last. "Is there anything else you wish to say?"

"Yes, Master. If there are times that you do not need me, I would like to help Yonaton's family bring in their harvest before the rains."

"A generous thought. Come and play for us in the mornings. You may spend the rest of the day helping your friend."

"Thank you, Master."

"Put your things away and come eat. You've had quite a journey."

"Lev!" Yonaton dropped the sheaves in his hands and ran out to meet me. I held onto Yonaton's embrace for a long time, my arms wrapped tightly around his back. After being thrown out by my aunt and Uriel's cool reception, being held by an enthusiastic friend felt like coming home.

"Are you back to play for the disciples?" Yonaton asked.

"Yes, and Master Uriel says that I can help you with the harvest too."

"We could use it. Come meet my father and sisters." All eyes were on me as we approached their donkey cart. "This is my friend Lev. He came to help us with the harvest."

"You are welcome, Lev. I'm Baruch ben Naftali. Yonaton told us much about you." Baruch had a strong, stocky build and deliberate speech, giving me the impression that he didn't talk much. But he met my eyes with a smile that felt sincere.

"These are my little sisters, Yael and Naomi."

I waved to the girls. Naomi blushed and turned away, but Yael, the younger, continued to stare.

"So what can I do?"

"Right now we need to load the grain onto the cart and bring it to the threshing floor." Yonaton swiped the back of his arm across his sweaty forehead. "What made you come back?"

I glanced toward his father and sisters, working near me in a tight group. "I'll tell you later," I said, collecting a bunch of crackling sheaves and tossing them onto the cart. Yonaton's eyes burned with curiosity, but he held his tongue.

I had never harvested grains before. The sheaves of summer wheat were light, and the bending and stretching felt good. As I warmed up, I quietly sang an old shepherding song. Yonaton picked up the tune and joined in, and even Baruch started to hum along. Seeing that the song wasn't a disturbance, I let my voice soar.

🪕 🪕 🪕

I arrived at the farm the next day to find that Yonaton wasn't in the fields. "Morning, Lev," Baruch called, pointing to the hilltop overlooking the farm. "Yonaton's at the threshing floor. You can join him there."

"I thought we weren't starting threshing until tomorrow?"

Baruch scanned the western sky. "The morning clouds keep getting darker and burning off later in the day. The sooner we start threshing, the more we'll be able to save when…if the rains come." He sighed and returned to gathering the cut wheat.

I climbed up the terraced hillside, past dusty, green grapevines, and through a grove of olive trees until I reached the broad threshing floor at the very top.

"Good, you're here," Yonaton called out, raising his voice over the wind. "This is a lot easier with two people. You want to lead the team or ride the sled?"

Now that's an easy choice. "I'll ride the sled."

Yonaton hopped off the threshing sled and circled around to the front of the oxen, taking the reins. Until I arrived, he had been goading and steering the oxen from behind while weighing down the sled himself.

"I thought farm work was going to be hard," I said, lounging on the sled. "I think I might just take a nap."

Yonaton laughed while spreading more grain on the ground before the oxen. "Go ahead. Enjoy your time on the sled. We'll be winnowing soon enough."

"In the meantime, I'll lend you my weight." I closed my eyes, my body vibrating as the flint blocks on the underside of the sled cut into the grain beneath.

Yonaton slowly led the oxen around the threshing floor twice in silence. When he spoke, his voice was tight. "One of Yambalya's priests came by this morning."

"What?" I sat up, my eyes wide. "When?"

"Not long before you came. One of the Queen's soldiers was with him too."

"What soldiers?"

"You remember all those soldiers that came down from Tzidon with King Ethbaal for the wedding? I guess he left some of them behind. I recognized the cedar tree symbol on his tunic."

"What happened?"

"The priest was happy that we were bringing in the harvest early. He said we were showing proper fear of the mighty Baal. Then he pulled out a statue and told us we should humble ourselves before Baal so that he would hold off the rains until we finished."

"You didn't, did you?"

"No. My father didn't either. The priest wasn't pleased, but he didn't say anything. The soldier kept fingering his sword, but he never pulled it out, just spat on the ground and followed the priest away. As soon as they left, my father told me to start threshing."

I thought back to my conversation with Baruch—now it made more sense. Yes, the clouds were gathering unusually early, but apparently that wasn't the only thing pushing him to salvage whatever grain he could.

☙ ☙ ☙

My mind kept returning to the priest of the Baal and the soldier of Tzidon as I settled down in my spot under the pomegranate tree the next morning. Would they also come to this valley? Surely they would know to steer clear of a prophet of Yisrael. Wouldn't they?

Though the music was better when I played with Daniel, Zim, and Yonaton, my bond with the disciples strengthened now that I was alone. At a nod from my master, I launched into my opening *nigun*. Although I had played it countless times before, I immediately sensed something different. The rhythmic breathing of the disciples rippled through the air, the space around them seeming to contract and expand with each breath. As the *nigun* came back around to its opening note, the sun shone through a break in the clouds, and the disciples collapsed as one, quivering and shaking as if a great wind tossed their bodies like dry leaves in a storm.

My jaw dropped. Uriel stood above the disciples, his face angled upward. "For so many souls to rise together is rare, but it does happen. You felt them go?"

I nodded without a word.

Uriel peered deeply into my eyes. "What is the shadow on your heart, Lev?"

The two of us had hardly spoken since my return three days earlier, but my master was right. Following the tears, my heart was no longer blocked—it ached instead. The aching wasn't just painful; it felt as though my heart wanted to speak to me, but in a language I did not understand.

"You can put down the *kinnor*. They can no longer hear you."

I placed the instrument on the ground slowly in order to gather my thoughts. I pictured Yambalya drawing his knife across his chest and the faces of the farmers the following morning at the wedding. Baruch had the same expression yesterday. They all reflected the same thing: fear.

A priest came to my house with the most important man in the community, but assured Uncle Menachem that bowing down was his own free choice. Now another priest visited Yonaton's family with a soldier at his side—they were getting bolder. As their power grew, would they tolerate resistance? Yambalya's booming laughter rang in my ears.

"Master, the power of the Baal is spreading throughout the Kingdom. What will the people do? What will happen to those who refuse to bow? What will happen to you and the rest of the prophets?"

The old *navi*'s face conveyed an unexpected message. I had thought that my master might be afraid, but his eyes betrayed no fear. I thought my question might anger him, but there was no anger there either. I saw only sadness. Uriel sighed. "I do not know what will be, Lev, not for the people nor for the prophets. The visions I have received lately have all been of the present. I see nothing of the future."

"What will you do?"

"As I have always done."

"But won't they try to stop you?" I asked, my voice sharper than I intended. "Queen Izevel has her own soldiers. I saw them in Shomron. They're traveling around with the priests, trying to scare people into bowing down to the Baal. Do you think they'll allow you to travel and speak against them?"

"For now, yes. Their power is only growing, even while the prophets are yet free to travel and denounce them. Open conflict would force the people to choose between us, and they are still seen as foreigners. They will not fight openly until they are certain that they hold the hearts of the people. If a struggle is to start before that, it will be because we begin it."

"And you don't think that will happen?"

"Pitting fear against fear will not bring us the goal we seek."

"What do the other prophets say? Does Master Yosef agree?"

Uriel hesitated. "He is less inclined to this way of thinking than I. But I believe he too would prefer to avoid a conflict. For now."

"So then what will happen?"

"I do not know, Lev."

How could a prophet not know?

My master's wrinkled hand rested on my shoulder. "Lev, you must know that there is only one truth. The same hand that fashioned the light also made the darkness."

We remained in silence while the breeze shook the leaves of the pomegranate tree and the disciples rattled with the strength of their vision. The image of Queen Izevel bowing before the Baal came to mind, beckoning with her long hands to King Ahav. "Why would the Holy One create darkness?"

Uriel sighed. "Without darkness there is no choice. Our bodies may grow without darkness, but our souls cannot."

"But if there is just darkness—"

"Then we could not grow either. There must be a balance for our choices to be real. That is why the disciples have progressed so quickly since the wedding. The soul is a spark, but sparks do not shine in the bright light of day. As darkness deepens, the soul reveals its hidden light."

The disciples began to surface from their visions. As I watched, their trembling ceased and the tension of life returned to their bodies. Two of them rose unsteadily to their feet, two remained sitting, and one fell flat on his back, exhausted. "What did you see?" Uriel asked softly.

"The rain will come in three days' time," one of the standing disciples replied.

"Did you all receive the same vision?"

The others nodded in agreement.

"Very well. Lev, you are excused from playing for us for the next few days so that you can help Yonaton's family complete the harvest."

I grabbed my *kinnor* and raced toward the farm.

👜 👜 👜

By the third day, the winds whipped across the fields, stripping leaves from trees. The family's cattle bunched on the leeward side of the stone cottage, their great eyes wild.

Yonaton's father wasn't complaining—we needed wind for winnowing, and better too much than not enough. Normally, they winnowed on the threshing floor, the highest point on the farm. But this time, we hauled the grain down to a more sheltered area so that the gusts wouldn't carry away the harvest.

The effort of winnowing more than made up for the ease of riding the threshing sled. The winnowing fork reached above my head. With it, I hoisted the threshed stalks of grain and threw them as high as I could into the air. The wind did the rest; the heavy kernels of grain fell to the ground first, while the husks and chaff blew further away, where Yonaton's sisters gathered the debris to use for animal feed and fuel.

Between the back breaking work and the whistling wind, Yonaton and I gave up trying to talk. When a flash of lightning blazed against the dark skies in the distance, we exchanged a knowing glance and stepped up our pace.

The lightning had barely faded from our vision when Baruch ran over. "Stop winnowing. Gather as much grain as you can. Get it in before it gets wet." Baruch took the fork, tossing the threshed stalks by himself while the rest of us gathered grain and carried it to shelter. I kept gaping at Baruch working the grain pile, tirelessly throwing it into the air, getting through twice as much by himself as Yonaton and I had together.

When the first drops fell, only a small mound remained of the grain pile, and most of the winnowed grain was gathered. I didn't mind working on in the rain, but as the lightning drew nearer, Baruch ordered us all in the house.

I turned around just before entering to see Baruch lingering beside the pile, the winnowing fork on the ground at his feet. We saved most of the harvest, but whatever remained would now be lost. Baruch glared at the dark sky as drops rolled down his cheeks.

"Master, is it true that one must be wealthy to become a prophet?"

Though I could not see my master's face in the darkness of the cave, I felt his amused smile. "It is true that one always finds wealth with the nevi'im, but it is not essential to us. It is simply part of our Way, as are strength, wisdom, and humility." He paused as I absorbed his words. "Take care with what you hear from the uninitiated, my son, for even the truth they speak is lacking."

"How so?"

"Tell me, who is the wealthiest man in the Kingdom?"

"The King, of course."

"And is the King satisfied with his wealth?"

My first impulse was to say I didn't know—but I stopped myself. I was familiar enough with my master's questions by now to know I would not be asked anything I couldn't answer. Was the King satisfied with his wealth? How should I know? I thought back to the choices that the King had made in the past year, particularly those that drove us into hiding. By the King's own admission, they were all made to bring greater prosperity to the land. "No, the King is not satisfied."

"Indeed, whoever can be swayed by wealth does not have enough wealth to become a prophet, yet even a poor man, satisfied with what he has, is wealthy enough."

"And the other traits, are they what they appear? What about strength, master?"

"The strong man's will is more powerful than his desires."

"Wisdom?"

"The wise learn from all."

"And humility, Master?"

"The humble man knows that all is one. Even we the hunted are not distinct from those who pursue us. We are but two rays emanating from the same sun."

Rabbi Yishmael said: Do not judge alone, for only the One may judge alone. Do not say 'accept my view,' for it is for them to decide, not you.

Pirkei Avot 4:10

13

Yericho

The next two months were the quietest of my life. The ceaseless downpour, at times a drizzle, at times a gusty torrent, dampened my desire to speak. But it wasn't just my need for conversation that was subdued, the chatter in my head also diminished. I worried less about the future, finding comfort in the fact that I had chosen a master, letting the burden of deciding both of our paths fall upon him.

Yonaton and I stole away to the old musicians' cave with our instruments whenever he wasn't busy with the grape harvest. Now that it was just the two of us, I grew almost as familiar with his music as with my own. He harmonized wonderfully, but struggled to lead. So I became the leader of our duo, developing over time the sense of when to give him free rein and when he needed shepherding. I pushed myself to play crisper notes, and started to rely on small movements of my head, and especially my eyes, to signal changes in the music.

As I grew quiet, other voices emerged around me. I learned to distinguish one birdsong from another, and to discern the direction of the wind by listening to the water dripping off the cave roof. But I wasn't just becoming more sensitive to sound. Silent languages also revealed themselves. Even though I barely spoke with the disciples, my awareness of their moods heightened; I was able to sculpt my music to their needs, playing softer when their eyes were tight, faster when their heads drooped.

Yet, even as I became more peaceful, tension built in my master. The time for the planned ending of the gathering came and went, yet the prophet did not leave the valley to resume traveling. As the *Sukkot* festival drew near, he became fixated on the rain, standing for hours at a time at the mouth of his cave, observing the windswept clouds churn in the sky. When he wasn't teaching or searching the skies, he spent most of his time in the darkness at the back of his cave, even taking his meals alone.

On the first night of the weeklong festival of *Sukkot*, my master stood with me and the three remaining disciples staring out into the gloom while streams cascaded down the cliffs. A flash of lightning illuminated our rickety *sukkah* getting battered by the wind. A swirling gust rocked its wooden frame to and fro. Rain as hard as hail pelted the few cut palm fronds that remained on top. The *navi* sighed in disgust and returned to the back of the cave where a table of holiday dishes awaited. "Rain on *Sukkot* is a curse; you feel like a servant who brings his master a drink, and his master throws it back in his face." He broke the pitch seal of a wineskin and filled his goblet for the sanctification. "The rains will not stop in time for us to eat in the *sukkah* tonight. We will celebrate the festival here in the cave instead."

It was not a warm invitation to a feast. Despite the succulent aroma of roast lamb, my appetite dwindled as I sat down. Apparently, the disciples felt the same way. The meal was brief and silent, and when it was over, most of the food was left on the table to grow cold.

I woke in the middle of the night, heart pounding, sweat beading on my forehead. I knew the signs well—the old nightmare. It had visited me twice since Shiloh, each time depositing in my memory a little bit more, just small details. Once it was a shawl pulled across my back, another time a sword striking a shield. Now I lay still, trying to remember more, knowing that as soon as I moved the vision would evaporate.

There was a knife, my father's knife. Also, I felt my master's presence, as if he was there with me, helping me decipher the clues. Lying in the dark, suspended halfway between sleeping and waking, it struck me; until I first met the *navi* in Levonah, the nightmare had always been sealed, like a lockbox of memory. But now details were starting to leak out through cracks in its wood.

I sat up and pulled my sheepskin tightly around my shoulders. The dying coals cast a faint glow, enough for me to just make out the curled-up bodies of the disciples. We had taken to sleeping in the same cave since the rains, as much for company as for warmth. But my master's bedroll lay empty against the far wall. Where could he have gone? I turned to the mouth of the cave, where he had sat for weeks watching the rains, but I saw only gray mist creeping up from the valley.

I stepped to the mouth of the cave, shivering in the damp, cold air. The full moon penetrated the clouds enough to emit a dim, silvery light, reflected by the mist that blocked my view of the valley. Unable to see, I closed my eyes and listened—there was a rhythmic splashing coming from somewhere down below. I opened my eyes and peered into the haze, trying to locate the source of the sound. With a sudden gust of wind, the mist parted.

The old *navi* danced barefoot in a puddle of rain, his steps slapping out a wet rhythm. The prophet's linen tunic clung to his skin, and even from my distant vantage point I felt the raw power in his legs. After weaving several wide circles in the downpour, his feet grew silent. Uriel held his hands out wide, tipped his head back toward the heavens, and shook with laughter. He passed both hands over his face, like a child waking from a dream, and started back toward the cave.

I ducked inside and stirred the coals of the fire back to life. Uriel entered, dripping wet and singing quietly, shivering from the cold, but his face shining. He did not stop his song even as he rubbed his hands together over the blaze. His voice woke the disciples, and all gathered together around the fire. "There is no sorrow on *Sukkot*. It is a time of joy," Uriel began. "The Presence comes to dwell with us inside the *sukkah*, just as the bride joins her beloved under the wedding canopy. But such a union is possible only in joy. If we cannot rejoice in the *sukkah*, we may not enter." Uriel paused and met the eye of each listener in turn, holding mine the longest. It was a piercing gaze that cut right through to my heart. *Did he know I had watched him dance?* "But joy is a path to union wherever we sit. So we shall delight in our festival despite the rains. And perhaps we will merit to enter the *sukkah* before the holy days end."

🪕 🪕 🪕

On the fourth day of the festival, a new noise filled the cave. It took me a moment to realize that it wasn't actually a sound at all, but rather the lack of one: the rains had stopped. Outside, the wind blew wisps of dark clouds across the skies far above us, but there was no hiss of falling rain. A stillness pervaded the cool, clean air down below. Two disciples rushed out of the cave, waving for me to follow. When we reached the *sukkah*, one dropped to his knee and I climbed onto his shoulders—as the lightest one, the roof was my responsibility. The other disciple handed up the fallen branches one by one and I laid them across the top, creating a roof thick enough to provide shade but not shelter. When we had finished, I examined our rebuilt *sukkah*. The ground was soaked with mud, the walls were battered and barely holding together, and the waterlogged roofing dripped into the interior. Yet, I never felt happier to have a *sukkah*.

The one remaining servant prepared a feast, serving each of us individually, as he had since I returned. Midway through the meal, Uriel's hand paused on the way to his mouth. He stood quickly without explanation, exited the *sukkah*, and strode up the hill that bounded the eastern side of the valley toward the road. The rest of us continued to eat, but our eyes followed the prophet. It was not long until we saw what our master had sensed: a donkey trotting along the hillside.

The *navi* reached the road just before the rider passed, and he flagged him down. The man stopped, spoke briefly to Uriel, then continued on his way. There was a shadow on my master's face as he dropped back into the valley, but no trace of it remained by the time he entered the *sukkah*. He stepped inside and, ignoring his meal, burst into song. The rest of us joined in, but though I knew the tune well, I struggled to harmonize. My master sang a bit too fast.

The break in the rain didn't last, and we never returned to our *sukkah*. The eighth day that capped the festival marked the beginning of the rainy season. The ground was already bogged with mud and rain still fell in torrents, but Uriel declared that the prophets had prayed for rain at the end of *Sukkot* ever since Yehoshua led our people across the Yarden River, regardless of what the skies held. We gathered at the chilly opening of the cave, wrapped in all our clothing and sheepskin sleeping mats, to hear the prayers of the old prophet as he stood just outside the mouth of the cave, arms wide, calling out in a raw voice.

"Master of the World! For the sake of Avraham our father, who ran to bring water to the tired and thirsty, do not withhold rain from his children."

A gust of wind stuck Uriel's drenched tunic to his body and tossed his hair wildly. "For the sake of Rivka our mother, who ran to bring water to a stranger, and watered even his ten camels, do not withhold rain from her children."

Uriel cried out each petition in turn, rain rolling down his face; at the end of each one, we all shouted, "Amen."

"Holy One! For the sake of Moshe our Teacher, father of the prophets, who stood before you forty days without water, do not withhold rain from his disciples!" The *navi* stretched his hands upward toward the heavens as we drew in closer.

He clenched his hands in the frigid air as the winds rose to a howl. "May the rains come as a blessing and not as a curse!"

"Amen!"

"May they come for life and not for death!"

"Amen!"

"May they come for abundance and not for scarcity!"

"Amen!"

"Master of the World! You and only you cause the wind to blow and the rain to fall!"

"Amen!"

When he turned back from the rain, my master's eyes were aflame. In that moment, I saw the wild dancer in the rain within the old prophet. Uriel pulled two disciples out into the mire and began to dance. The rest of us joined in, finally relishing the drops on our faces. For the first time they tasted of blessing, not of bitter curse.

No sooner had the sun set that night, marking the close of the festival, than Uriel drew me aside.

"The first day we met, when I was entering Levonah, you were speaking to a boy leading a donkey. Do you recall?"

"Yes, Master."

"There was an emblem on his saddle bag from the city of Yericho."

"That was my friend Seguv. His father Hiel is rebuilding the city."

"Yes, I know that Hiel of Beit El is rebuilding the city; I wanted to know if your friend was his son." Uriel sighed and his body again appeared as it had before the festival: heavy, as if every movement was an effort. "I'm sorry to tell you that Seguv died six days ago."

Hot tears stung my eyes—they came so easily now. "Is that what the rider told you?"

"Yes, he was on his way to bring tidings to the King."

Seguv told me that the King had invested heavily in the rebuilding of the city—of course he would want to know that Hiel had lost another son. But I cared little now about the King or Yericho. My thoughts were on the warm smile, the friendly face that always stopped to greet me whenever he passed through Levonah, bringing the wider world into the small circle of my life. I wiped my cheeks with the back of my hand, "Why did you wait to tell me?"

"*Sukkot* is a time of joy."

Blood rushed to my face. *That's all he had to say? He knew I had lost a friend and had held it back for…joy?* "You should have told me," I nearly spat out the words.

"I know it feels that way."

Uriel's words only made me angrier. "Joy isn't always the right feeling. We need to feel other things, too."

"Not on *Sukkot*. Don't think joy is so simple—I'm not talking about the empty celebrations of fools. Real joy takes work, inside and out—more than any other emotion."

I avoided his gaze, but the *navi* pressed his point. "On *Sukkot*, we attach ourselves to the Presence, which we can do only in a state of joy. We choose to rejoice even when we don't feel joyous. That's why there is no mourning on *Sukkot*. The mourning period for Seguv will begin now and last for one week. His family will receive anyone wishing to visit."

Uriel paused, but I remained silent. "If you like, you may go."

Now my eyes met his. "You said we would begin traveling immediately after *Sukkot*."

"True. But I will wait for your return. The loss of a friend is a deep wound, and it must be mourned if it's to heal." Uriel let out another long sigh. "There is no time to go and return before Shabbat. If you go, leave early on the first day of the week. You may take Balaam to hasten your journey. You can let me know your decision in the morning."

I walked to the back of the cave and unrolled my sleeping mat. I removed my tunic, laid down, and pulled it over me, not up to my neck as I normally did, but up over my head. Thoughts of death were nothing new to me, but this was different. I knew Seguv; I never knew my parents.

With Seguv there was no lockbox of memories—they all seemed to rise to the surface of my mind at once: Seguv and his brothers laughing as they led their donkey into Levonah; Seguv holding out the afarsimon oil; Seguv standing in the throne room, presenting the oil to King Ahav; Seguv lying on his back, his eyes dark and vacant.

Lying in the darkness, hidden under my tunic, I felt the pain of my open heart. Tears came and I didn't hold them back. They streaked my face with loss. The disciples could hear me sobbing, but I didn't care. My tunic wasn't over my head to hide me from the disciples, it was to hide them from me. I couldn't bear to see pity in their eyes.

When my eyes finally went dry, I pulled the tunic down and saw that all the others were asleep. The ache in my chest gave me my answer to my master's offer. I would go to Yericho to mourn my friend.

ꙮ ꙮ ꙮ

I reached Yericho on the second day of my journey. In better conditions, I could have made it in one day, but muddy and washed-out roads made for an uneasy ride. I spent the night in a cave so shallow that it was really just a crevice, barely sheltered from the winds and relentless rain, unable to light a fire for lack of dry tinder. As I shivered through the night, I wondered if my decision to go had been rash—I was traveling farther than I had ever gone, to pay respects to people I never met, on the death of a friend I saw only a few times a year. Yet, the emptiness I felt when I pictured Seguv's smiling eyes pushed me forward.

On the morning of the second day, I descended into the great valley of the Yarden River, where the ruins of Yericho lay just north of the Salt Sea. Halfway down the mountains, the air grew lighter, the clouds thinned, and the rain dwindled to a light mist that barely reached the ground. As I descended further, the roads dried, and the sun glittered off streams of water running down the mountainsides. At the base of the mountains, the road flattened and passed through a grove of tall date palms, where a dozen camels—animals rarely seen in the cooler mountain plateau—grazed in their shade. There were also rows of newly planted trees whose species I didn't recognize. These must be the balm trees Seguv told me about, the source of the afarsimon oil, the justification for rebuilding the destroyed city despite the costs.

The dry air of Yericho drew the wetness from my clothes, and I was grateful to be spared meeting Seguv's parents stinking of soaked wool. No guard sat at the newly erected gates to direct me, but I had no trouble finding Hiel's house. It was the largest one and stood at the highest point in the city—much as the King's palace towered over Shomron. I tied Balaam to an olive tree out front, its trunk thick and gnarled, showing its age, a remnant of the great city destroyed hundreds of years before. I took a deep breath before passing the threshold, filling my lungs with clean air before entering a house tainted with death.

I took in the whole room with one glance. A middle-aged couple sat on the floor, barefoot, their clothing torn and their heads dusted with the ashes of mourning. Four men sat opposite them, but no one spoke. I paused at the threshold, then stepped as softly as I could to an empty stool, not wanting to disturb the stillness.

Sitting down among people I didn't know, I wondered again if I should have come. I wanted to give comfort, but it was not my place to break the silence—and what would I say, anyway? The couple on the floor must be Hiel and his wife, but where was Onan, Seguv's older brother? Could he have died as well?

I realized I was staring and turned my attention to the other guests. Two of the men, wearing dirty work clothes, resembled each other so much that they must have been brothers. A third sat rigidly in his chair. His posture and spotless linen tunic reminded me of the scribes in the throne room of the King. The fourth sat in the corner, eyes on the floor. Whatever he was staring at must have been absorbing, for he did not stir at all when I entered. His whole appearance bespoke nobility. His hair and beard were trim and neat. He wore a thick belt made of sheep hide— something I had never seen, even when visiting Shomron. Despite the heat, a vivid crimson mantle was wrapped tightly about his shoulders.

"Were you a friend of Seguv's?" Hiel asked me.

I stole my eyes from the nobleman in the corner. "Yes sir, I was."

A hungry expression entered Hiel's eyes. "How did you know him?"

"I live in Levonah. He came up to sell dates."

"You came all the way from Levonah?"

"No sir, I was in Emek HaAsefa when I heard."

The nobleman with the mantle snapped up his head, examining me. I could feel the heat of his gaze, his black eyes glowing like coals in the heart of a fire.

Hiel also sat up straighter at the mention of Emek HaAsefa. "Are you of the *bnei nevi'im*?"

I gave a weak smile, then thought better of it. "No, sir, I am a musician."

"Oh, you are that shepherd boy that…that Seguv spoke of." My smile almost broke through again when I heard that Seguv spoke about me, but Hiel's voice cracked on his son's name.

"Did he…I mean, were you…" Hiel was foundering.

Without warning, the nobleman with the fiery eyes rose to his feet, drawing Hiel's attention. "Are you leaving?"

The nobleman motioned with his chin toward the entrance. In the doorway, flanked by two guards, stood King Ahav himself. The other guests and I immediately jumped to our feet. Hiel and his wife attempted to rise from the floor, but Ahav stopped them with a gesture.

"No need to get up, my dear Hiel. The mourner needn't stand before the King. I was broken-hearted when the news reached me." The King pulled my vacated stool toward himself and sat down. "You may wait outside," he said to his two guards. I wasn't sure if I should leave as well, but followed the lead of the other guests and continued to stand respectfully.

The King ignored our presence, his attention fixed on Hiel. "I blame myself, of course."

Hiel's hand rose in protest. "You must not my King. I knew the risks involved. The dangers of the waters here are well known. I was proud to take on the mission of rebuilding a great city in Yisrael. Our losses have been tragic, that is true. But we hold you blameless."

King Ahav dropped his eyes and fingered the tassel on his belt, replying quietly, "I'm not talking about the waters. I'm speaking of the curse."

Hiel's eyes grew wide. "My Lord, I thought you did not believe in the curse?"

"Well, I didn't. It seemed so ridiculous. Just a story told to children and the ignorant to frighten them away. But now that it has come true, can we continue to deny it?"

"What curse?" I slapped my hand over my mouth, but the question had already leapt out. One didn't just speak in front of the King—certainly not to interrupt such an intimate conversation.

The King turned to me, and for the second time that day I had the impression that I was being examined. But while the nobleman's gaze penetrated to the heart, the King seemed to be weighing my value. "You look familiar," he said at last.

I dropped my hand from my mouth, but did not reply.

King Ahav's eyes held me. "You may speak."

"Thank you, my King." I bowed my head, avoiding looking him in the eye. "I am a musician. I played at the King's wedding."

"Ah yes, I remember." Ahav leaned back with the satisfied smile of one who has made a good purchase. "Yes, the curse. When Yehoshua conquered Yericho over five hundred years ago, he declared, 'Cursed is the man who will rise up and build this city Yericho. With his oldest son he will lay the foundations, with his youngest son he will erect its gates.'"

Hiel and his wife both started to wail. I shrank back against the wall—I shouldn't have asked.

The King turned back to the couple on the floor. "It's so strange that the curse would come true," he said, a tone of pleading in his voice, but their sobbing only grew louder. "Who would imagine that the curse of the disciple would materialize, when the words of his master failed?"

"And what does that mean?" The air in the room pulsed as the nobleman with the fiery eyes stepped forward, his frame seeming to expand as he stalked out of his corner toward the King. The hard tone of his voice sounded familiar. I had heard such a tone once before—from Yambalya.

The King snickered. "Come Eliyahu, you know the story better than I. Moshe pronounced a curse on the people that if they worship idols there will be no rain. Go on, recite it for us."

Eliyahu's nostrils flared as Ahav waved a hand for him to speak, but he did not argue with a command from the King. He drew his mantle tightly around him and declared: "Guard yourselves, lest you turn your hearts and serve other gods and bow down to them." Eliyahu's voice shook with rage. "Then the wrath of the Holy One will blaze against you. The heavens will be restrained, there will be no rain, the ground will not give its abundance, and you will be lost from upon the good land the Holy One gave you."

I had known these verses from the Torah since I was a young boy, but this was the first time that they made me tremble.

The King appeared unmoved. "You see," he said, again facing the bereaved couple, "It makes no sense that this curse would come upon you, my dear Hiel. Look around you. The people seek the Baal more every day, yet in my entire life I never remember the rain being so plentiful. So why should the curse of Yehoshua cause your family so much misery, when the curse of his teacher Moshe has foundered?"

Eliyahu stepped closer to the King. He would have towered over Ahav even if the King had not been sitting. Had the guards been in the room, they surely would have removed Eliyahu to a respectful distance—but they were outside. For the first time, the King shrank as he stared up into Eliyahu's fiery gaze.

I could barely breathe—the air grew heavy, like a gathering storm. Then Eliyahu spoke, his voice barely above a whisper. "As the Holy One, the Lord of Yisrael, before whom I stand, lives…there will be no dew nor rain during these years except by my word."

A shudder ran down my back. No one moved as Eliyahu locked eyes with the King. The silence pressed down upon us all. Then Eliyahu spun and strode out of the room, his mantle flying behind him like a banner of war.

Both guards rushed in. They could not have heard his declaration, but must have been alarmed by the fury on Eliyahu's face. "Is everything well, my King?"

"Fine," the King rasped. Clearing his throat loudly, he shook himself and added in a commanding tone, "You may continue to wait for me outside."

The guards bowed and left, and the King turned back to Hiel and his wife. "Always been unyielding, Eliyahu has. He's quite wise, really, but once he gets an idea into his head there's no reasoning with him."

"Well, he's certainly gone too far this time," Hiel said, no longer crying.

"Nonsense, he's harmless enough. With people like that it is best to just let them be."

An awkward silence descended on the room.

"And how is the King finding married life?" Hiel asked.

"Ah," Ahav smiled, his posture relaxing with the change of subject. "Izevel has been doing wonderful things with the palace. For my father it was a symbol, you know, and for me it's just a home. But she insists that a palace should be a place of devotion. She brought down a beautiful Ashera tree all the way from Tzur to plant at the gates. Are you men leaving?" The two brothers had stepped forward, and the King gestured them ahead, pausing in his description to allow them to take their leave of Hiel and his wife.

I thought this was a good opportunity to slip out as well, and stepped forward once the brothers turned to leave. I leaned down toward Hiel and his wife and repeated the line that Uriel made me memorize before I left. "May the Holy One comfort you among the mourners of Yisrael."

Hiel and his wife both lowered their head. I bowed to the King the way the farmers had, and respectfully backed out of the open door.

Mounted on Balaam and on my way, I inhaled the fresh air eagerly. I peered up at the mountain trail once outside the city gates. The return trip would be more strenuous than the downhill journey had been. A roof of black clouds hid the mountain tops, and I hoped the impending rain wouldn't prolong my ride. The distance from my master suddenly felt daunting.

I kicked Balaam into a trot and we were soon back among the date palms again. The patchwork shade upon the ground made the field a blend of light and darkness. As I watched the trunks flow by, a flash of red caught my eye. Eliyahu's mantle was crumpled at the base of one of the trees. Its owner lay beside it, head between his knees, gripped by the spirit of prophecy.

14

The Key of Rain

"What happened?" My master sat perched on a boulder at the turnoff to Emek HaAsefa as Balaam and I hobbled up the trail. Whether he had been waiting for me since daybreak or had arrived just in time to meet me, I could not tell. He showed no weariness, only quiet, complete attention. "I want every detail."

The return journey passed faster than I expected. The roof of black clouds lifted ahead of me as I ascended the pass above Yericho, and I made it back without encountering any rain. Ragged patches of blue could now be seen through breaks in the gray sky. Uriel led me to his cave where steam rose from a covered pot simmering over glowing coals. I had eaten my last hard loaf the night before and was eager to break the day's fast, but the urgency on my master's face told me that recounting what I saw would have to come first. Uriel filled a bowl full of fragrant lentil stew and placed it on the table. I sat at the empty spot and prepared to tell my tale while my master ate.

"No, no—sit here," the old *navi* gestured. "Eat first, then speak."

The prophet said nothing while I ate, though he supervised every mouthful as if measuring my progress. Why was he so anxious? He had waited much longer to hear my report after the royal wedding. Though still hungry, I pushed the half-eaten bowl of lentils away. "The road there was all mud and rain, but the plains of Yericho were dry. I could smell the balm trees from the foot of the mountain, though they're not yet in flower." I described the newly built city, its massive walls and buildings of fresh-cut stone. I told how Hiel had placed his house on a hill, as if he were king of Yericho. "When I entered, I didn't know what to say to Seguv's parents, so I just sat."

"You did well," Uriel said, breaking his silence. "Words rarely pass through the fresh pain of loss." He nodded for me to continue.

I described the house, the visitors, Seguv's parents. Uriel nodded as I spoke, saying nothing. I cocked my head at him when he finally interrupted to question me about Eliyahu's mantle. "Why is that important, Master? Who is he?"

"I might ask you the same question. Continue."

I recounted King Ahav's entrance, how I had been moved by the King's descent all the way to Yericho to comfort his faithful servant.

"And no doubt to strengthen his resolve. The King has much invested in the rebirth of Yericho and its balm." Uriel closed his eyes and waved me on.

I described Seguv's mother wailing as the King conveyed his wonder at the fulfillment of Yehoshua's curse.

"Yes," the prophet said, drawing out the word. The interruption gave me pause. I saw pain cut deep folds down my master's face. The thread of my story frayed and Uriel opened his eyes. "Why do you stop?"

I told how King Ahav forced Eliyahu to recite Moshe's words. These verses were part of a longer passage that my aunt used to recite with me every night before bed, as she still did with my younger cousins, and I recited them with ease. "Guard yourselves, lest you turn your hearts and serve other gods and bow down to them. Then the wrath of the Holy One will blaze against you, the heavens will be restrained, there will be no rain, the ground will not give its abundance, and you will be lost from upon the good land that the Holy One gave you."

I cleared my throat. "I have said Moshe's words many times, but until Eliyahu said them I never realized they were a curse."

"Not exactly a *curse*." Uriel bit off the last word. "But I do not expect this King to grasp the difference. Go on."

I described Eliyahu's fury. Uriel's hands trembled on the table as I repeated his oath, seared word for word into my memory, "As the Holy One, the Lord of Yisrael, before whom I stand, lives...there will be no dew nor rain during these years except by my word."

When I shared how I took leave of Hiel and his wife, Uriel's patience finally waned. "And once you left Hiel's home, what happened?"

"I mounted Balaam and rode through the gate. Then, as I was preparing for the ascent up the mountains, I saw…Eliyahu."

Uriel pushed his hands flat on the table, leaning in closer. "And what exactly did you see?"

"He was lying in a date grove at the side of the road, trembling."

"With the spirit of prophecy?"

At my nod, Uriel closed his eyes and leaned back. I eyed my half eaten meal, the smell of warm lentils teasing me as my master mulled over my story.

Then the prophet's eyes snapped open. "But he didn't receive prophecy in the house?"

"No…" I pressed my hand over my eyes, recalling the scene. Eliyahu towered over Ahav, the room shrank around them. The metallic ring of the oath echoed in my ears. That was not prophecy. Could Eliyahu have received a prophecy just before speaking out, while I was focused on the King? "I think…I think he received prophecy only after he left the city."

"You *think*, or you know?" Uriel's eyes bored into mine.

"It wasn't prophecy." I sat taller. "I would have noticed if he went into prophecy. And then he was standing there in front of the King…" My voice trailed off, having no words for the experience.

"After you saw Eliyahu in the date grove, what did you do?"

"I continued riding up the mountainside. I knew how long it took me to get there. I was worried that I would not get back before sundown tonight."

"And the King?"

He and his soldiers passed me soon after. They were all on horses."

"Did anything happen as the King passed?"

"No. I dismounted and stood to the side of the road." I rubbed a rough spot on the table. "The King didn't even look my way as he passed."

Uriel sighed deeply. "You have done well in your tale. It explains much—though one mystery still remains."

"What does it explain, Master?"

"It explains why the heavens are trembling and why the gates of prophecy have swung wide."

I frowned at Uriel. *Prophecy had gates?*

"Eliyahu has taken one of the forbidden keys."

I shook my head, "The keys?"

"Yes, the keys." Uriel nodded as he spoke, as if I understood, then in one quick motion he stood. "Do you recall the sisters we met on our first day traveling together?"

I nodded, remembering the anguish of the older sister who wanted to conceive.

"I explained then about the three keys that forever remain in the hands of the Holy One: the key to the womb, the key to the grave, and the key to the sky. Eliyahu has taken the last one—the key of rain—in many ways the most powerful of the three."

"Taken it?"

"Well, I should say he was given it. Who can take a heavenly key by force? But at the time you stood in Hiel's house, I was taken by *navua* here in Emek HaAsefa. I saw Eliyahu's soul rise to the highest realms, to the Throne of Glory itself. There he demanded the key of rain. There was an uproar among the angels. It was enough that he reached such an exalted place—how could he demand one of the keys? But the Holy One granted Eliyahu's request."

I had never heard my master speak like this. "What does that mean?"

"It means that as long as he holds the key, Eliyahu will determine if and when we receive rain."

"And the prayers we're offering—?"

"Will not be answered. The Holy One will not bring rain as long as Eliyahu denies it."

"What about Yambalya and the Baal?"

"They are powerless to bring the rain."

I pictured the faces of the farmers standing in the morning rain at the wedding. "But I saw—"

"There is no Baal." My master spoke calmly, but his eyes burned, reminding me of Eliyahu's. "Remember, the same hand which fashioned the light, made the darkness as well."

Uriel lifted his eyes to the soot-darkened roof of the cave. "That hand has now granted the power to bring rain to Eliyahu, and to him alone. Neither myself nor Yambalya can do anything affecting the rain, other than pleading with Eliyahu."

I grinned at the thought of Yambalya and his priests cutting themselves and calling out to the Baal in vain. "So when Eliyahu swore that there would be no rain other than by his word, he knew that he held the key?"

Uriel observed me closely. "A well placed question, and one that I cannot answer. Did Eliyahu know he would receive the key when he made his oath? Did he already hold it? We may never know."

Encouraged by Uriel's praise, I pressed the point. "But if the key is never given to man, why would he think he could receive it? He wouldn't swear otherwise—he must have known."

"So I believed, that's why I asked you if he received prophecy in Hiel's house." Uriel stroked his beard. "But prophecy is not the only path of power. What the righteous decree, the Holy One carries out."

"The righteous can bind the Holy One?"

Uriel nodded, his eyes cast in shadow. "You yourself observed a woeful example of this."

"When?"

"I do not believe that the Holy One commanded Yehoshua to curse the city of Yericho—he was moved by his own spirit to bind the city in ruins forever. But once his lips spoke the curse, the Holy One gave it power."

The weight of Uriel's words slowly penetrated. "That's why Seguv died?"

Uriel nodded. "Hiel's family has been destroyed by a curse uttered five hundred years ago."

I swallowed the lump forming in my throat. "That's what happened with Eliyahu?"

"Perhaps." The cave filled with a whiff of acrid smoke as the morning lamp burned out. Uriel rose and pinched the smoldering wick.

I could see the muscles of my master's shoulders knotted beneath his tunic. "You don't agree with what he did, do you, Master?"

Uriel turned back to me, his eyes cold. Had the question gone too far? "It's not for me to agree or disagree, Lev." His voice was calm, though his body remained tense. "Eliyahu must be an extremely powerful prophet. To wrest a key from the Holy One is something that has never happened; something I would have said was impossible."

Uriel sat down stiffly on his stool. "But it is true that his way is not my way."

"His way?"

"Eliyahu is willing to take a path I will not tread. The people fear power. You saw this in their reaction to Yambalya. Eliyahu wants to show them that the Holy One is the only power to fear. By this he hopes to win back the heart of the nation."

"Isn't that what you want as well?"

"Indeed."

"But you don't think it will work?"

"It may work—but will it last?" He rose and stepped toward the mouth of the cave.

I sensed Uriel's impatience with my questions. He preferred to be alone to ponder everything I told him, but I yearned to understand. "Why wouldn't it last?"

Uriel turned back toward me. "Because fear will not bring the devotion that the Holy One seeks. And will the people truly fear the Holy One, or just Eliyahu? Someday Eliyahu will go the way of all flesh and the darkness will remain. Then what will the people do, if we have trained them to fear?"

"Return to darkness?"

Uriel nodded. "This is why I left the path of fear. It is a tool most fit to the hands of darkness. The powers of darkness always appear to be greater in number, and often in strength as well." Despite the daylight outside the cave, shadow dimmed the prophet's face.

"But Master, why should darkness be more powerful than light?"

"Darkness is not more powerful than light, but in this world it seems to be so. Who would choose night over day? If light and darkness were seen in balance, there would be no real choice between them. The true power of light is masked, to enable us to choose."

I thought of Eliav bowing before the Baal. "But why mask it? Doesn't the Holy One want us to choose the path of light?"

"Of course, but it must come of true free will. This world exists so that we can perfect ourselves and creation as a whole; we can do this only through making choices ourselves. If the way is already paved before us, then even the right choice will yield no growth."

Uriel sat down again, but no sooner had he settled on the stool than he was back on his feet. "In the beginning, there was only the light of the Holy One—a light that shone so brightly that nothing else could exist." He took the extinguished lamp from its niche on the wall and set it down before me. "In order to create the world, the Holy One withdrew this light, leaving a space of darkness behind. Only a single ray of light shone into this void. But even this fragment of Divine light filled the emptiness with such radiance that a world of choice could not exist. So the Holy One made the lamp of darkness as well."

I fingered the clay lamp on the table. "A lamp of darkness?"

"A lamp that radiates darkness. A lamp that covers the light as night covers the day."

"But why?"

"As I told you, so that we can grow. The world is oil and we are the wicks. As we grow, we draw creation through us and reveal the hidden light."

"But you said the Holy One does not desire too much light."

"That is true. The more light we shine into the world, the deeper the shadow cast by the lamp of darkness. But that is not our concern—our task is to create more light, no matter the cost."

"Why create light if the lamp of darkness will only cover it up?"

Uriel's lips spread in a sad smile. His shoulders sank and his pace slowed. "When a child first learns to walk, his father might stand only one or two steps away. But as the child progresses, the father steps farther and farther away, not to punish the child, but to allow him to grow."

In my exhausted state, the image of a father teaching his son was too much for my newly awakened heart. I dropped my eyes to the table, all curiosity about Eliyahu or the lamp of darkness extinguished. I'd never thought of it before, but I must have known how to walk before coming to live with my aunt and uncle. *Had my father taught me? What else had he taught me before he left the world?*

Uriel reached over and touched me gently on the underside of my chin, forcing my moist eyes to meet his bright ones, nested in a bed of wrinkles that attested to age and wisdom. "Your father gave more for you than you can imagine."

I smiled through the tears.

The *navi* stepped to the back of the cave. "The lamp of darkness is now casting a powerful shadow. Since the gathering began, there has been a great rise in idolatry in the land. Traveling among the people has never been more important." He lowered himself onto a reed mat on the floor. "The remaining disciples left while you were in Yericho. The time has come to resume our travels. Play for me and I will seek our path."

It was my master's voice of command—the time for questioning had passed. As my *kinnor* was still in the musicians' cave, I drummed on the table, tapping out a complex rhythm I had learned from Zim at Shiloh. I closed my eyes and chanted softly between the beats.

The sound of chattering teeth alerted me that Uriel had ascended—the prophet could no longer hear my drumming—but I did not stop. I raised my voice even louder, no longer worried about distracting my master, the stone walls throwing my tones back at me. As I let myself be swept away by the flow of the music, sweat beaded on my forehead and my hands stung, the tightness in my shoulders releasing with each slap against the hard wood.

My throat was raw when I felt Uriel's gaze upon me. I broke off my chanting and opened my eyes. My hands faltered on the table. My master's face was clouded, his brow hanging low over pensive eyes.

"Where are we going, Master?"

"Nowhere."

"Nowhere?"

"Nowhere. We are to stay here through Shabbat and begin traveling on the first day of the week."

"Why?"

"I do not know. I did not merit a reason in the vision—I thought our work here was finished. All the disciples have gone and very few people live in the surrounding valleys. But perhaps someone is coming to us. Either way, we will know soon enough."

Hillel saw a skull floating in the water. He said to it: Because you drowned others, you were drowned. And ultimately, those who drowned you will be drowned as well.

Pirkei Avot 2:7

The Battle

For days we practiced patience, Uriel sitting in silence while I searched my *kinnor* for new sounds. My master said perhaps we awaited a visitor, one important enough for the Holy One to delay our travels in order to assist him. Yet, except for Yonaton, who came to visit often, not a soul entered the valley. As first light seeped through the trees at the dawn of the following week, I again asked, "Master, where are we going now?"

The prophet sighed. "I do not know," he lowered himself onto the cave floor. "Please play." No sooner had I reached for my *kinnor* than a rush swept past me, as if the cave had exhaled its contents. My master's body trembled on the ground; this time, his soul ascended faster than I had ever seen. Ignoring my instrument, I hitched our things to Balaam.

As I tied the last bag to the donkey, Uriel stepped out of the cave, his face ashen.

"Have you received instruction?"

"Yes. We must go now." The quiver in his voice silenced any further questions.

I led Balaam up the hill toward the road.

"Not that way," Uriel said, pointing down the hill toward a narrow track that wound north across the valley floor and snaked up the far ridge. "This way," he insisted, already moving as he spoke.

I touched my father's knife, concealed beneath my tunic. Shimon disappeared down that path right after telling me not to use my knife, and had not reappeared since. I shook my head to clear the image of Shimon's scarred face, and turned Balaam to follow Uriel.

A voice called out behind me, "Wait! Don't go yet." Yonaton weaved down the rocky hillside, his sister Yael trailing behind. "My parents sent provisions for your journey." Yonaton pulled two large loaves and a cake of pressed figs from the skin slung over his shoulder. Yael struggled under a massive, green-skinned melon.

I untied the top of one of the donkey bags and carefully added Yael's melon. Yonaton placed the bread and figs on top of the swollen fruit. Even though we had parted only the night before, I was glad to see my friend one more time. We embraced quickly.

"Go in peace. And take care of Master Uriel."

Uriel still descended moving down the trail, heedless of the gift we had received. I squeezed Yonaton's hand one last time. "I'll see you next year," I said, then led Balaam at a trot after my master.

Early grasses and mud-filled hollows slowed our progress. We traveled all that day along the overgrown trail, encountering no one. When the sun dropped below the horizon, Uriel pointed to a cave on the hillside. As we ascended through the trees, I gathered an armful of firewood. The prophet inspected the shelter while I arranged the wood outside its entrance.

"No, Lev," Uriel said, emerging from the darkness within. "Tonight, we light the fire inside."

I gazed up at the cloudless sky—it was a shame to spend the night in a smoke-filled cave when we knew there was no chance of rain. Did Uriel think that Eliyahu had relented already? I turned to ask, but my master's gaze was fixed on the breeze whispering through the oak trees below, and I couldn't bring myself to disturb him.

Uriel sat outside, gazing out into the darkness as I cooked dinner. When I finished, Uriel accepted a bowl of wheat porridge without a word, laid it beside him, then turned back to his contemplation.

The two of us had hardly spoken since leaving that morning. I knew that he preferred to be left to his own reflections, but questions filled my mind. "Master?" I said quietly.

Uriel turned toward me, firelight flickering in his eyes. "Yes?"

"I've been thinking about Eliyahu. Won't his curse also hurt those who don't bow to the Baal? Like Yonaton's family?"

"Indeed," he said, his eyes shining in the reflected light. "A curse brings suffering without making distinctions. It falls upon the guilty and the innocent alike." Tears welled in his eyes. "Even the one who called down the curse is not spared its destruction." He turned back to the darkness, his bowl of porridge untouched, congealing in the cool night air.

I thought of Seguv, dead soon after coming of age, never married, never a father. He didn't fall in battle or struggle for his life. He was the victim of a curse uttered five hundred years before he was born.

Yet, it wasn't Seguv's death that brought tears to my master's eyes. Was it Eliyahu's curse? Did he feel the pain of farmers like Yonaton's family, who would suffer without rain despite their loyalty to the Holy One? Was he thinking of Eliyahu himself? I didn't think so. These were not the quick and hot tears of anger or pain, they were the seeping tears of deep sadness. I cried this way when I finally accepted that my mother would never come back for me. These tears sprang from a well deep within.

But it was not my place to pry. I turned to serve myself and caught sight of Balaam, grinding his teeth at the side of the cave, our bags still hitched over his back—how had I not noticed that he was still burdened? My uncle would have sent me to bed hungry for such callousness. I moved to unload him, but Uriel stopped me with a grunt and a single shake of his head. Apparently, the donkey would have to sleep ready to travel. I left my master to his thoughts and returned to the cave to eat alone.

🐂 🐂 🐂

I dreamed of stars, my shadow floating across the jeweled sky. In the darkness, a mountain rose before me, a palace perched on its crown. Silently, the air shifted and I flew forward on the breeze. The palace grew until it filled the night sky. A dim light flickered through a window set high in the outer wall. I glided onwards, landing on the sill of the window.

I knew the room below by its tall columns, carved like date palms, marching in two lines down the center, their bases lit by torches, their tops lost in shadow: the throne room of the King. Two thrones presided over the room, just as I remembered; the King's was empty, but Izevel sat arrow-straight upon the one crafted for her father. Her hands gripped the heavy wooden arms of the chair, her olive skin glowing in the torchlight. Even though the throne dwarfed her small frame, the fire in her eyes and her air of command made it seem as though it could barely contain her force.

"You summoned me, my Queen?" The deep voice echoed through the cavernous room. In the firelight, Yambalya's violet robes looked nearly bloody, and they swirled as though carried on a wind as he approached.

"Yes. Have I acted too soon?"

"No, my Queen." Yambalya bowed before her, exposing the laddered scars on the back of his neck. "You were right to act now."

"And the people will not protect them?"

"They are sheep. They will not rise against us without the leadership of their king."

"That they will not have." She moistened her lips with her tongue and curled them in a serpentine smile. Her eyes narrowed as she watched the priest closely. "Baal has not informed you where he is to be found?"

"No, my Queen. The movements of one man, no matter how bold, are not a matter of note to mighty Baal."

Izevel leaned forward, her tapered fingers white on the clawed arms of the throne. "But he stopped the rains."

The cords of Yambalya's neck grew taut. "Yes, he stopped the rains. Their god is still strong in this land. But when their prophets are gone, the people will learn to fear Baal."

"Their prophets, yes. Most of their prophets are weak. But as long as he remains alive, he gives the people strength. We must find him."

Yambalya's eyes burned in the torchlight. "The servants of Baal seek him even now. They have never failed in the hunt. He has not been seen since casting his curse. We believe that he has fled the land."

Izevel laughed. "There is nowhere for him to flee. I watch the roads, and I have sent word to my father. He rules the sea. We will find him."

"Indeed we will, my Queen. I have read his future in the stars."

Izevel bent her head forward, close to Yambalya's. "What have you seen?"

"Eliyahu will not die the natural death of men—to this I will swear."

Izevel settled back in her throne, her face flushed with pleasure. "Excellent. I will hang his body from the walls of Shomron for the crows to devour. Let his death be a message to all who would stand against us."

"Yes, my Queen. It will be done."

Uriel shook me awake before the sun, the image of Izevel still looming in my mind in the half light. I wanted to ask my master about the dream, but his distant eyes still defied interruption. As I stepped out of the cave, the old prophet stared back up our path in the direction we had come. He sat down on the earth, placed his head between his knees, and was soon trembling with the spirit of prophecy.

By the time my master returned, our bedrolls were repacked and Balaam ready to travel. Uriel swept past me, stepping out of the cave and down toward the trail. "We have to move quickly. There isn't much time." He didn't elaborate as he dropped into the brush below our camp. Balaam trotted to keep up.

The *navi* kept to a driving pace all day. Daniel once told me that Uriel did not concern himself with taking the shortest or fastest paths, that his goal was to travel among the people. Yet, this time too we met no one along our path. What had changed?

The late afternoon sun had already reached the western ridge when Uriel finally stopped with a raised hand, gazing back up the trail. I spotted a man in the distance running toward us. Uriel increased his pace, but in that brief pause a sad smile had flit across my master's face.

The runner drew closer, but Uriel did not slow or turn again. I kept glancing back over my shoulder, measuring the runner's progress as the trail rolled up and down between the hills, gently climbing toward the west. When our pursuer reached the hilltop directly behind us, he paused and bent forward, hands on knee to catch his wind, then straightened and resumed running down the hill. In that moment, the dying sun illuminated his features and I realized that he was not a man at all, just a boy: Yonaton.

Uriel did not pause until Yonaton caught up with us. Gasping for air, he tried to speak, "They're looking—"

Uriel cut him off with his own skin of water. "First drink. You've had a hard journey—it was brave of you to come." The tenderness in Uriel's eyes contrasted with the rigid impatience of his body.

Yonaton gulped down the skin of water, and began again to deliver his message. "Yesterday afternoon they came looking for you. They were part of the Queen's personal guard. I recognized them from the wedding. They heard that I played during the gathering. They came to my house and had me lead them to the valley, where they searched all the caves with swords drawn. They asked me where everyone had gone. I told them that you were the last ones to leave that morning. They asked which direction you went, and I pointed them toward Yericho." Exhausted by the flood of words and gasping for breath, Yonaton doubled over.

My mouth went dry. I pictured the long column of soldiers that had escorted Izevel to her wedding. How many had remained behind?

"How many were they?" Uriel asked.

"Four," he forced out. Yonaton held up as many fingers without standing straight.

"You saw them go toward Yericho?"

"Yes. I wanted to come and warn you immediately, but it was already too dark, so I came at first light." I thought of the fire inside the cave and Balaam remaining burdened all night, ready to travel—had Uriel known?

"You brought nothing with you?"

"When I finished my food and water, I dropped the skins so that I could run faster."

My feet ached in sympathy. I had a hard enough time keeping up with Uriel; I couldn't imagine trying to overtake him. Yonaton stood barefoot—had his sandals also slowed him down?

Uriel sighed, turned his eyes to the sky, and shook his head. "Again, that was very brave of you. I doubt you can appreciate how much you risked coming after us. You will need to stay with us now. It is no longer safe to return."

"Why? They don't know I've come."

"They do. You were followed."

Yonaton and I turned as one, but saw nothing other than the wind playing over the low hills in the distance, stirring the brush.

"You won't see them," Uriel said with a shake of his head. "They will stay out of sight until they are ready."

I gazed up at my master. "Ready for what?"

"Surely you can reason that out for yourself?" Uriel started again up the trail. "Come, we must go on."

Despite the prophet's words, Yonaton was too drained by his run to do more than trudge along. When the sun set, we were forced to a crawl. Our trail wound through a steep ravine, already deep in shadow. Balaam brayed as he struggled to find footing on the loose rocks. After one particularly loud protest, Uriel laid his hand on the donkey's nose. "Peace, old friend." He gazed up at a rocky outcrop on the hillside above us. "Stay here. I want to examine that cave."

Uriel displayed no sign of fatigue from the day's march as he climbed up the steep slope and disappeared between the shadowed boulders. Moments later he reappeared and yelled down to us, "Come up. This looks like a good place to spend the night. Lev, see to the donkey. Yonaton, gather wood."

It took all of my skill to coax Balaam up to our resting spot. By the time I finished tying up and watering him, Yonaton came back with a double armful of wood. "Build the fire inside the cave," I whispered. "That way it won't be easily seen."

"No, build it outside tonight," Uriel corrected, then turned away before either of us could question him.

I struggled to prepare the evening meal—a large crack at the back of the cave drew the wind right through the hollow, turning our shelter into a chimney. My eyes stung as smoke swirled in the cross-draft, and the fire licked my fingers from every side. Any feelings of security brought about by finding cover faded with the dying daylight. Our pursuers couldn't be far behind Yonaton. I stared out into the night as I cooked—listening.

Uriel hummed softly to himself in the back of the cave, unpacking and repacking our gear, while Yonaton snored between us. I gazed up at the stars. Was it really less than three months since Dahlia and I lay on the wall watching them, wondering what the future held? Was I now gazing at them for the last time?

Uriel finished packing and came to the mouth of the cave. "Take the food off the fire, it is time to eat."

My eyes watered from the smoke. "It's not done yet, Master."

"We have given it as much time as we can afford. Take it off and wake Yonaton—he must be famished."

Yonaton indeed ate as much as Uriel and myself combined. Once we had finished, I picked up the pot to scrape it, but Uriel put up his hand. "There is no time for that. In any case, we cannot take it with us. Yonaton, throw the remaining wood on the fire. As long as it is burning high, it will appear as if it is tended. There will be no attack until they think we're asleep." I could see the whites of Yonaton's eyes as he stared around out into the darkness. "When you're done, we'll leave."

A column of sparks twisted up into the darkness when Yonaton dumped the last armload of wood on the blaze. Uriel led us to the back of the cave and handed us each a pack. "I've gone through and separated out only the most essential things. We'll need all our strength."

"What about Balaam?" I turned back toward the donkey, tied at the entrance.

Uriel sighed. "He stays. Leaving him tethered in front is the best sign that we are still in the cave."

I opened my mouth to protest.

"You think this poor payment for hard service?" Uriel raised his eyebrows. "Fear not. Men do not kill a beast of burden without cause. Balaam is wise. He will make his way with a new master. Or perhaps find his way back to his old one."

I appraised the pile of belongings to be abandoned. My *kinnor* rested on top. I trusted Uriel that we would need all our strength, but the *kinnor* wasn't a drain on my strength—it was a source of it. "I won't…" I insisted, "I can't…" I picked up the instrument, cradling it against my chest. "I'll carry it, the extra weight won't slow me down. I promise."

The fire sent shadows jumping and dancing on the cave walls, reflecting crimson on Uriel's tunic. "I'm sorry, Lev." He pulled the instrument from my weakly resisting hands and tucked it on top of a high rock cradled by a furrow in the cave wall. "It is well hidden there. May we merit to retrieve it."

I swallowed the bulge lodged in my throat, avoiding Yonaton's eyes. I laid my index finger to my father's knife beneath my tunic, suddenly grateful that I kept it on me at all times—would Uriel have made me leave that behind as well? Probably not. Shimon's dagger jutted through my belt, and he hadn't mentioned it.

But Yonaton's attention wasn't focused on me anyway. He peered into the crack at the back of the cave that began along the floor and rose into a narrow channel, splitting the cave wall to the ceiling. "You don't expect us to get out this way, do you?"

"There is no other path. They are watching the front."

"But it's too narrow—even Lev won't fit through."

Uriel approached the wall, running his hand up and down the fissure. Behind him, the new logs burned down, the gathering darkness urging us to hurry. How much longer would our attackers wait? Uriel's eyes rolled back in his head, his voice echoing in the close cave. *"You split the rock for Shimshon at Lehi, bringing him water and restoring our spirit. Only you can open our way and bring us out into life."*

The prophet's hand rose above his head like a general's in war, then came down with force, striking the rock with his staff. Nothing happened.

"You opened the mouth of the well for Yisrael, sustaining us in the wilderness. Open now our way and bring us out into life." There was a sharp crack as Uriel swung again, with the same result.

Yonaton stared at the dirt floor, his shoulders tense. Balaam brayed in the silence. Was he just restless, or did he sense someone approaching?

Fists now clenched, Uriel leaned in close to the wall and hissed between clenched teeth, "*In the name of the Holy One, I say this is the moment for which you were formed!*"

A low rumble shook the cave. I grabbed Yonaton for support. His bulging eyes met mine as our hands trembled within each other's grasp. When the tremor stopped and the dust settled, the opening at the top of the crack had grown to twice its width.

Uriel led the way. As his feet disappeared, I gripped the rock and pulled myself upwards, taking shallow breaths as I wormed after my master in the darkness. The channel narrowed; sharp rocks scraped my arms and cut into my fingertips. Dirt rained down upon my hair, and the welcome smell of moist earth reached my nose.

When I emerged into the moonlight, Uriel's arm thrust out like a beam across my chest, holding me back from a deadly misstep. We stood on a slender ledge, overlooking dark tree-tops. Yonaton squeezed out behind me, and I put out a cautionary arm to protect him as well.

We were on the far side of the hill. The half-moon hovered above the horizon in the western sky, casting a silvery light across a different valley than the one we had hiked that morning. We climbed down the cliff at a slug's pace. At first, I placed my hands and feet wherever my master did, but soon Uriel's long legs carried him over a patch of jagged rocks that I had to scramble through. By the time I bridged the gap, the prophet had disappeared.

The night air blew across my sweaty forehead; I shivered with the chill. I reached out with my right leg, searching for a foothold in the smooth rock. My body tensed, and my knee began an odd jumping motion. Even if I found a foothold, would my leg hold me? I reached farther down, straightening my quivering knee. My moist hands were slick against the rock. My foot slid and I felt my grip loosen. A call for help died in my throat as I fell.

The ground was rough, but it was only a handsbreadth beneath my foot. The shock of so sudden a landing choked the cry in my throat. Uriel's strong hands kept me from sliding down the slope. Regaining my feet, I saw the prophet in the moonlight beside me, a finger to his lips.

Climbing down in the dark seemed easier for Yonaton. He crouched at the bottom of the cliff, probing with his foot, and then dropped lightly to the ground.

We weren't down yet. The ground was a patchwork of brambles and sharp-sided heaps of stone. Awkward as I was descending the rock face, endless days spent chasing sheep over this terrain allowed me to slip smoothly down the hillside. At the bottom, Uriel dropped into a muddy streambed at the base of the hill. I sat down on the edge, swung my feet forward, and landed softly next to my master. A muffled cry came from above. Yonaton slithered down the side of the streambed, hitting the ground with a scrape and a hiss.

Uriel pulled Yonaton into a patch of moonlight to examine his leg—a dark gash marred the white of his hairless shin. Uriel grabbed the end of his own linen cloak, tore off a long strip, wrapped the cut and pulled hard on the ends. Yonaton winced and bit his lip as the prophet tied off the bandage.

We crossed the narrow streambed and picked up a faint trail. Despite his limp, Yonaton scurried uphill, his boyish features set with determination.

Voices drew my attention back toward the opening on the opposite hillside. In the darkness, the remnants of our fire sent a flickering, red glow through the crack that had freed us. It blacked out for an instant as a body slipped through the light's path, moonlight glinting off the sword stretched out before him.

Uriel clamped our shoulders with a grip that urged silence, forcing us to squat on the ground.

The soldier leaned across the ledge and scanned the hillsides. Was the pale moonlight sufficient for him to pick us out among the scrub and boulders? Did his roving head pause when it reached the spot where we crouched? I pictured him sniffing the earth, like the wild dogs in the hills above Levonah. They always found the injured sheep before the shepherds.

The crack blacked out again as the soldier reentered the cave. Yonaton and I exhaled, but Uriel yanked us to our feet and spun us by our shoulders. "Come, we must move quickly. They'll circle around the hill. It will be faster for them."

"Where are we going?" Yonaton whispered, touching the wet wrapping on his leg, where the blood was already seeping through.

Uriel didn't answer.

The moon dropped beneath the horizon, obscuring the uneven ground, forcing us to slow our pace even further. But I didn't mind the darkness: it concealed us as well.

I stumbled again and again. Yonaton limped along behind me, grunting whenever his shin brushed against obstacles on the unseen trail. Uriel pushed on ahead, surefooted and silent in the near-total darkness.

Uriel held up a hand, tipping his head back as if sniffing the wind. "Get down," he breathed. We lowered ourselves softly between the boulders at the side of the trail. I turned my head as I lay, my eyes glued to my master. With my ear pressed against the dirt, I felt a pulsing rhythm in the earth. Hoofbeats.

An impossibly tall figure appeared against the stars. As the shadow drew nearer, it revealed itself as a soldier on horseback. The animal stepped slowly between the boulders. Its questing gait indicated that the soldier didn't know our location. The loud breathing drew closer and a soft whinny sounded at our side.

I swallowed my breath, willing my heart to beat more quietly in my chest. The rider, sitting so far above the ground, could not see what lay at his feet. But how much did he trust his horse? How much did he understand it? The soldier could hear nothing above the heavy breathing of his steed, but would he surmise from the horse's agitation what the animal already knew: that three people lay on the ground before him?

Our faces remained pressed to the dirt as the soldier continued past us without breaking stride. Once I could no longer hear the horse's steps, Uriel rose again to his feet and increased his pace. *Where was he going?*

With the moon set, only the slow rotation of the stars marked the progress of the night. The Bear began the night high in the sky, but was almost at the horizon when Uriel rasped for the second time, "Get down." This time, I could barely hear the horse, and it never came close enough to see. Lying on the ground, I wondered what we would do once the sun rose. At least Uriel seemed to have a destination—but would we arrive in time?

We pushed forward, rushing toward the new day, which already made it easier to see pitfalls on the path. Now it was a race. When I saw a faint glow in the darkness ahead, brighter than the dawn quickly emerging behind us, I knew that we had won. The glow of a welcoming fire grew ever closer. Uriel picked up his pace and we matched him easily, drawn on by the promise of safety. Yet, as we drew nearer to the warm light, it became clear that this blaze would offer us no protection at all.

Had we walked up the trail two days earlier, we would have crossed a clearing to a large house, at least three times the size of Uncle Menachem's. Now, with the roof gone, it seemed even larger. The walls still stood, their stones black with ash. A red glow radiated from the burnt remains, still smoldering from their destruction.

Uriel staggered forward with a low moan, no longer restraining his voice. He dropped to his knees at the side of a dark figure on the ground, and I flinched as a high-pitched cry broke from my master's lips. The firelight reflected off the silver beard of the corpse, which Uriel stroked lovingly as he wailed. I stepped closer, recognizing familiar wrinkles around the mouth that sang so beautifully it never required words. Tzadok. Other shadows dotted the clearing around the ruin. We had arrived at the scene of a massacre.

A ram's horn blast split the dawn: a soldier with dark, hawk-eyes had reached the edge of the clearing.

The eerie silence following the blast was marked only by a last mournful wail from Uriel. I expected the soldier to kick his horse into a charge, but he just sat, watching us from a distance.

Uriel rose from Tzadok's side, his eyes now dry, radiating calm and power. "You two run. It's my blood they want. They'll take yours as well, but if you get far enough away, they won't bother giving chase."

Yonaton trembled, but his eyes were resolute. He straightened his shoulders and met my gaze with a short nod. We would not leave the prophet alone to die. "There are three of us," I said. "We'll fight."

Uriel gripped his staff in one hand, the other flexing rhythmically, his muscles growing tense as he eyed his enemy. "If he were going to attack on his own, he would have done so already. He's just watching us until the others arrive. Then it will be one old man and two unarmed boys against four soldiers with swords and horses." He spun us away from the soldier and gave us each a hard push in the back. "Go!"

Uriel barked the command with so much force that my legs reacted before I even considered disobeying. We darted across the clearing, past the destroyed house, and into the cover of thick pine trees on the far side. Our dark shelter gave me a renewed sense of safety, and I stopped for a last glimpse of my master.

Uriel rose to his full, imposing height; he twirled his staff above his head as the soldier circled, well out of striking range. A second rider charged up the trail. Would they wait for all four, or would the two attack? I staggered back toward Uriel, but Yonaton grabbed my arm. "He told us to get out of here!"

I bit my lip, tasting blood between my teeth. Yonaton was right, there was nothing more we could do for the *navi*. We dodged between the trees, crashing through branches and stumbling on the uneven ground, no longer caring about keeping quiet, or even where we were going. When the ground dipped onto a trail, we sprinted in earnest, knowing that our lives depended on putting distance between ourselves and Uriel. There was no way he could hope to defeat four armed soldiers with just his staff, yet when I glimpsed back before disappearing into the trees, he was still swinging that staff over his head, keeping the soldiers at bay. I realized that this meager defense, which could not preserve his life for more than a few extra moments, was not for him at all—it was for the two of us, buying us time to escape the certain death he faced.

A boulder blocked the trail ahead, and we swung around it at full speed. Our haste made us careless: We almost ran straight into the third soldier, riding hard up the trail. He reined in his horse and a wide grin split his sharp cheekbones, his eyes falling upon Yonaton. "Thought you'd have a little fun with us chasing shadows down to Yericho, didya? Knew you were lying. Knew you'd bring us right to him. Ought to thank you, I should. But the Queen says no survivors—no prophets, no disciples. Anyone who'd run to warn a prophet sounds like a disciple to me." He kicked the horse's belly and charged.

We dove to opposite sides of the trail, and the soldier pursued Yonaton. "Run!" Yonaton screamed as the soldier raised his sword.

I took one step down the trail, then froze. I may have left my master to face four soldiers, but I would not leave my friend to fight one alone. I snatched a sharp stone from the edge of the path and flung it with all my might at the rider's back. The rock missed its target, but came close enough to the soldier's ear to make him flinch. That was enough—Yonaton rolled back onto the trail as the sword plunged into the vacated ground.

The soldier reared his mount and turned, now facing me. I threw a second rock. He ducked it, then raised his sword for the strike. My legs were rooted to the spot. Even if I had run for the trees, I wouldn't have reached them in time. But the thrust never came—he lurched forward on the horse, hands clutching for balance as bright blood stained his tunic below the shoulder.

A man jumped out of the trees.

My mouth dropped. It was Shimon, his face livid, with dried blood obscuring his scars.

"Give me the other one!" he screamed at me.

I stared, uncomprehending. Shimon ran toward me with hand outstretched, reached into my belt, and pulled out the dagger that he had given me months before.

The soldier was wounded, but not badly enough. He recovered his balance and kicked his horse forward. Shimon threw the dagger, but the soldier ducked low over his knees to avoid it.

The horse thundered toward us. The rider raised his sword, then screamed out in pain as Yonaton's rock struck his injured shoulder. He checked his mount and swiveled his pale face back and forth between us. He was still better armed, but now it was three against one, and none of us was his intended victim. Pulling up his horse, he turned and thundered back up the trail.

Shimon reached out a quivering hand. "Give it to me."

This time I knew exactly what he meant, as if expecting the request all along. I pulled my father's knife from under my tunic, and handed it to the man who told me never to use it.

Shimon gaped at the knife in his hand. Then he closed his eyes, pressing the flat of the stone blade to his forehead. Tears squeezed out from under his eyelids. When he opened his eyes, his face was transformed. The burning anger was gone, replaced by peaceful clarity. Without a word, he bolted up the hill after his injured enemy. The look in Shimon's eye pushed all thoughts of flight from my mind. I took off after him, waving for Yonaton to follow.

All four soldiers now circled Uriel like wild dogs, jabbing at him with their swords, hemming him in. He held the end of his staff, swinging it in broad sweeps, keeping them at bay. They cantered just out of reach, knowing that he could not keep up his defense for long, waiting for the opportunity to strike. They would take the easy kill.

Shimon bounded from the trees, unnoticed, and leapt onto the closest horse. It reared and kicked as his weight crashed down behind its rider. Shimon threw a powerful arm around the neck and wrenched his enemy into a chokehold. With an upward thrust of his other hand, Shimon drove the knife through the soldier's back. A choking scream escaped the rider's throat as the tip of the blade broke through his chest above his heart. Shimon yanked the knife back out, and shoved the soldier's limp body off the horse.

The other three turned as one at their comrade's cry—a mistake. Uriel stepped forward and brought his staff down with a sickening crunch on the knee of a stocky soldier. The rider let out a howl and turned to fight the prophet, while his companions closed in on Shimon.

Two soldiers charged from either side, swords flashing. Shimon turned the first strike aside with the flat of the knife and threw himself backward to dodge the second. He dug his ankles into the horse's belly and it leapt forward. He rode in a broad circle around the clearing, two riders giving chase while Uriel dueled the stocky one in the middle.

Yonaton and I waited in the shelter of the trees, gripping rocks. As Shimon raced past, we threw. I missed the hawk-eyed soldier's head by a hairsbreadth, but Yonaton's fist-sized chunk of stone hit his companion just above his left eye.

The rider buckled on his horse, losing his balance and lurching to the side. He struggled to regain control of his mount, and we saw the sharp cheekbones and a blood stain below his shoulder—the same soldier we'd faced earlier. He recovered his balance and took off after us, blood streaming into his eye.

Again he pursued Yonaton, who eluded him by ducking in and out of the trees ringing the clearing. I chased after them throwing rocks, aiming high to avoid hitting Yonaton. I missed twice, but my third throw connected with the back of his skull with a resounding thud.

The soldier screamed out, and then spun his horse around to face me. Yonaton seized his chance. Jumping out, he grabbed the horse's tail with both hands and pulled down with all his weight. The horse reared its front legs high in the air as its neigh echoed through the trees.

The soldier fell backward, his sword tumbling from his hand. The combined force of Yonaton's weight and the soldier's desperate attempt to grip its mane caused his steed to lose its balance, and it too fell back on its haunches. The rider hit the ground first. The horse followed, landing on its rider and Yonaton.

The animal was the first to rise, kicking its legs and rolling to regain its footing. Yonaton struggled up as well, having absorbed merely the weight of the horse's hind legs in the fall. The soldier absorbed the hardest blow, falling from a height and crushed by the full weight of the horse's heavy body. Blood bubbled from his mouth as he scrambled for his fallen sword.

I dove past Yonaton, arms outstretched, reaching the sword before the soldier could grab hold of it.

I stood over my unarmed enemy, the hilt warm in my hand. The wounded soldier pushed himself upright, and let out a raspy cough, his face twisting in pain. I stared down at him, feeling the weight of the iron. My hands trembled.

Yonaton laid a hand on my shoulder. No longer attempting to fight, the soldier opened his mouth to speak and blood gushed out. I expected him to beg for his life, but the only words that escaped were a whispered plea. "Make it fast."

I pressed the point of the sword to the soldier's chest and squeezed my eyes shut, not wanting to watch. I always turned away when my uncle slaughtered the sheep. I drew the weapon back to gather more power, but my arms froze there.

"Do it!" the soldier cried, the effort forcing out a bloody cough. His chest gurgled—the soldier was dying. The most merciful thing would be to end it quickly. But I couldn't bring myself to deliver the final blow.

A hand closed over mine. I peered into Yonaton's eyes, afraid of finding pity there, but seeing only understanding. Yonaton took the sword and plunged it into the soldier's chest. The man twitched on the end of the blade, then went still.

The body slumped to the ground. I gawked at the bloody sword, then crashed to my knees. The little food I had eaten the night before came up first, followed by heaves of bile.

"Come on!" Yonaton pulled at my tunic. "There are more of them." He yanked the heavy weapon from the corpse and sprinted back toward the heart of the battle.

I pulled myself upright—my master needed me. Wiping the mess from my face, I ran after Yonaton.

We stopped again at the edge of the trees. Even with a sword we were no match for mounted opponents—we would wait for another opportunity to strike.

In the clearing, the hawk-eyed soldier still chased Shimon. Uriel smashed his staff into the nose of the stocky soldier's horse, and the rider grabbed at the reins to keep his balance as the horse reared. While he fought to get the horse back under control, Uriel slipped in closer, pummeling blows upon them both. Once the soldier regained his seat, he brandished his sword to hold off Uriel's assault.

But the stocky soldier's focus was diverted from the rest of the battle for a moment too long. Shimon saw the opening and veered toward the center of the clearing. The hawk-eyed soldier giving chase called out, but to no avail— all his comrade's attention was fixed on fending off Uriel's attack. He spun at the sound of a horse bearing down on him, but too late. Shimon jammed my knife into the soldier's neck. His eyes bulged and his jaw sank as he looked down upon the hilt of the knife protruding from his throat. He toppled sideways off the horse as the animal broke free.

The hawk-eyed soldier shrieked at the sight of his companion's collapse. He swiped at Uriel as he rode past, but the prophet blocked the blow easily with his staff. He rode on after Shimon, who was now unarmed.

Yonaton called out, "Here!" holding the blood-stained sword in his hands. Shimon's horse leapt forward, and I launched a rock at the soldier to keep him at bay. Shimon snatched the weapon from Yonaton's hand, and spun in time to block a thrust from the hawk-eyed soldier's sword.

Now Shimon had no need to run. He closed in on his adversary. Shimon's sword descended like a bolt, and the soldier raised his blade to block it. The clang of iron on iron sounded through the clearing as the soldier's sword broke off its hilt from the force of the blow. Shimon swung his sword in a wide circle around his head, then struck true. The soldier tumbled from his horse. His body slammed to the ground with a thud, followed by his head, which rolled to a rest at Uriel's feet, hawk-eyes gaping up at the old prophet.

Hillel said: Be among the disciples of Aharon, loving peace and pursuing peace, loving people and bringing them closer to Torah.

Pirkei Avot 1:12

Yochanan's Secret

"I don't understand." Shimon groaned as he and Uriel laid one of the slain prophets beside the ruined house.

"Tell me everything, from the beginning." Uriel approached the next of the fallen.

"I've been here since I left you. You were right, it was better for me here among the masters than it was among the disciples. The Queen's soldiers rode up at sunset, eight of them. Three of us went out to greet them with food—we had no idea. Foolish as it was, that probably saved my life. I don't think that anyone in the house managed to—Lev, no!"

I jumped back at the rebuke. Yonaton and I had approached one of the bodies—why shouldn't we try to help? Did Shimon think we couldn't carry the body? And why did he yell only at me? Yonaton was a bit stronger, but not by much.

Uriel edged over to my side, making himself a barrier between me and the dead. "Yes, why don't the two of you gather wood for the morning meal. We will need all of our strength."

My master's tone was softer than Shimon's, but his command no less clear. I bit back my response, and the two of us retreated from the line of bodies to the first row of trees, where we gathered sticks in silence so as not to miss a word.

Shimon hovered over another of the fallen prophets. "The details of the battle are not important. You see the results before you."

"Did anyone else survive?"

"I think not. We'll know for certain once we have gathered everyone." He studied the blackened corpse at his feet. "I hid in a cave last night."

Uriel placed a hand on Shimon's shoulder. "Flight is also courage when it holds hope for return."

Shimon nodded. "The ram's horn roused me. I wasn't sure if the blast was from friend or foe, so I crept back, keeping to the shelter of the trees. Then I saw one of them go after the boys, so I attacked. I managed to plant my knife in him, and he rode off. Coward. I knew he must be going after you. I couldn't help you barehanded, so I asked Lev for Yochanan's knife."

Shimon limped to the body that still had my father's knife protruding from its neck. He placed a foot on the soldier's back and grasped the hilt. The knife slid out with a jerk. Shimon plunged it into the soft earth a few times to remove the blood, then wiped the blade with his palm and brought the weapon to Uriel.

Uriel examined the knife. "Yes, Lev has shown it to me. For the second time this blade has saved your life."

"Indeed. But it is a tool of peace, not war. It should never have been used to kill a man."

Uriel rotated the knife, as if examining it for flaws. "It hardly seems you had a choice."

Shimon's forehead sunk toward the ground. "No, there was no choice. Not this time, and not when Yochanan used it to save me." Shimon sighed. "You know, just before it happened, I...I saw him."

Neither of them heard the branches fall from my arms.

Uriel fixed his eyes on Shimon. "You saw Yochanan?"

He nodded once. "I touched the flat of the blade to my forehead and closed my eyes. I recalled that day years ago. My fear, his sacrifice. I was filled with death, the injustice of Yochanon's murder, the horror of yesterday's massacre, and the evil of them trying to kill you now..." Shimon's posture straightened to the height of that morning's battle. "And that's when it happened."

Uriel's eyes bored in on his disciple. Even Yonaton stopped pretending to gather wood. "What did you feel?"

"Power, like nothing I've ever felt. Yesterday I injured my ankle running away, but when I took off after that soldier, I felt no pain—and I ran faster than I ever have." Shimon's hands stretched out in wonder.

"Clarity." Shimon closed his eyes. "I could see every needle on the trees, feel every whisper of the wind. When I charged into battle, I didn't have to decide what to do. My body just…knew. I leapt onto the back of that horse as if it were a pony!" Shimon's eyes popped open, cutting creases across his scars.

"Did you feel anything else?"

"Courage, no fear at all. Last night, I couldn't sleep, despite my exhaustion. I shook all night, petrified that they might hunt me down. But this morning, I wasn't afraid anymore. And so strong. I snapped that soldier's sword in two—I can't do that."

"How did it end?"

"When the last soldier fell, I felt it just…flow out of me. The fear hasn't returned, but my leg is throbbing, and well…" he glanced at his hands, "I won't be shattering any more swords."

Uriel managed a weak smile. "You have sought *navua* for many years, but it always eluded you. Most disciples either succeed or abandon their path—but you persisted. Now you taste the fruits of your commitment."

"This was prophecy?" Shimon's eyebrows furrowed. "This isn't like any *navua* I've ever seen."

"But I've seen far more than you have, Shimon. One can receive the Presence in many ways. There is a level, close to prophecy, which can come in a time of crisis. One sees injustice and rushes to act without considering oneself. When your heart, mind, and will move you in this way, you can become a fit vessel for the Holy One."

The words made little sense to me, and Shimon didn't seem to understand either. The lines on his forehead only deepened.

"Learn from Shimshon," Uriel continued. "Drawn after his eyes, he could never receive full *navua*. But when he seized that donkey's jawbone at the battle of Lehi, what filled him in that moment?"

Fear? I asked myself.

My master continued, not waiting for an answer. "The desperate need of Yisrael. He slew a thousand men that day. Despite his…flaw, Shimshon was a fit tool in the hand of the Holy One and merited to save our people from the Pelishtim."

"So the Presence brings you strength?"

"Not always. It is a spirit that fills you with the power you need at the moment. Shimshon, whose way was to fight alone, received the power of an army. King Shaul, who ran away from kingship, received this spirit in a different way, giving him the power to lead."

Shimon's face shone for a moment, then his eyes brimmed with tears. "But why wasn't I given this power yesterday? Why did so many have to die?"

"Do not take what you received lightly—it is a rare gift. Yesterday you were afraid. Today you were tormented by the massacre, in fear of another slaughter, and then remembered so vividly the sacrifice Yochanan made to save your life. The spirit didn't take you into battle. You were determined to fight, determined to succeed—you just didn't know how. That determination made you a fit vessel for the spirit. You didn't receive the strength of Shimshon or the leadership of Shaul. But it did bring you enough speed, strength, and knowledge to overcome these four soldiers. For that, I'm grateful."

My head throbbed. Between our journey, the flight from the cave, our march through the night, and the dawn battle, I was exhausted. Uriel's words knocked away my last restraint. I really grasped only one thing from the conversation: Shimon's transformation was connected to my father's knife—to my father's sacrifice for him. My father saved Shimon's life…*at the cost of his own?*

They stood there talking as if I were as deaf as one of the murdered prophets. They thought that I couldn't handle carrying the bodies—couldn't be trusted with the truth of my past.

It wasn't my place to interrupt, but they were talking about *my life*. I cut through the clearing in three strides, and faced Uriel and Shimon over the line of the dead. "What's this about my father?" I demanded.

Shimon gasped—he hadn't heard me approach. He leapt over a corpse and grabbed my shoulder, drawing me back. I shook his arm free, but allowed him to lead me away from the bodies.

"Lev, I'm sorry. But you can't know. Not yet."

I glared at Shimon. He knew. If Shimon owed his life to my father, then he owed me an answer.

Uriel's voice was softer. "Lev, when you returned to me, you said that where I went, you would go. I was moved by the strength of your promise and held it as binding, though you are not yet of age. But even I did not foresee where it would lead. You offered your life this morning, even if it was spared.

"I have served the Holy One faithfully my entire life, but I am an old man. There are more soldiers seeking me, and even if I were not pursued, the time to lie with my fathers is drawing near. It matters not how my soul will leave my body, in sleep or in battle. But your life is ahead of you. I release you from your oath."

Would my master dismiss me rather than tell me the truth?

"The journey to Yehudah is now too dangerous for you to attempt. Even the smallest passes will be watched. If you wish to return to your aunt, tell her that it is with my blessing and she will welcome you home. Your uncle will help you raise a flock of your own. No one will seek your blood. You will marry and build a family. Grow old.

"Or you may continue with me. We will travel fast, eat little, fight if we must. If you go where I go, it may be to the grave before the week is done."

I stared down at the bodies of the massacred prophets on the ground. If I hadn't been there, Uriel could have lain among them. I raised my eyes up to my master's. "Where you go, I will go."

Shimon shuffled next to me. Uriel continued to hold my gaze. "So be it." He bent his knees, bringing his eyes in line with mine. "Then it's time to hear the truth about your father. The truth about yourself."

Shimon's mouth dropped open. Uriel held up his hand and it snapped shut. "I have hidden things until now because knowledge can be dangerous. But at this point, you could hardly be in more danger—now ignorance is a liability." The old prophet held out the handle of my knife. "I saw your father's courage in you today. Take the knife."

I asked for the truth, but hadn't expected to get it. My fingers trembled as I grasped the weapon with both hands. It felt warm in my palms, having absorbed the heat of Uriel's hands.

"Do you recognize the imprint?"

I traced a finger over the insignia on the hilt. How many times had I wondered about its meaning since leaving home? I saw it in my dreams. My vision grew blurry as I focused on the milky white stone, but no new insight came. I shrugged. "Claws of some sort?"

Uriel cocked his head to inspect the insignia, then emitted a short, nasal laugh—the first sound of mirth I'd heard in days. "True, it does look like claws now, doesn't it? Much time has passed since I saw it first. Yes, some definition has been lost, but the image is whole. Not three fingers, five. The thumb, two fingers held together, a gap, then two fingers held together. Does that help you?"

"No, Master."

"The *kohanim*, the priests of the Holy One, hold their hands forward just so when they bless the people. This knife was used by the *kohanim* for offerings in the Holy Temple. Your father was a *kohen*." Uriel drew my eyes up from the knife with a gentle touch on my chin. "Which makes you a *kohen* as well. You were born a priest of the Holy One."

Uriel's words seeped through my exhaustion. Fragmented images whirled through my mind. My special bread—my aunt always gave me the first piece of bread. Hadn't Uriel done the same when I came to the gathering, making sure that a portion was always set aside for me? Uncle Menachem taught me that the *kohen* receives the first bread and the first fruits—why had I never made the connection?

Yonaton stood at the edge of the trees, grasping an armful of branches, watching us closely. When the two of us tried to help care for the fallen prophets, only I was rebuked, not him. "Is that why I can't help with the bodies?"

"Yes, you are forbidden contact with the dead."

How many times had I pestered my uncle about my father's land? His response was always the same, that my inheritance had been lost—always using the word inheritance, never once mentioning my father's land or even his tribe. "And this is why I have no land?"

"The *kohanim* are from the tribe of Levi, who received the service of the Holy One as their inheritance. They have no share in the land."

I shook my head, then raised the knife between us. "And this?"

"That knife was used by your ancestors to slaughter offerings in the Holy Temple."

"Shimon said it was for peace, not war."

"Indeed it is. When the hearts of the *kohanim* are pure and the people are devoted to their service, there is peace in the land."

"Why was it dangerous for me to know what I am?"

"Did your uncle teach you about the splitting of the Kingdom?"

"Yes," I said, then added quickly, "...but only when I went home after the wedding." I wanted it to be clear that I hadn't understood about the Golden Calf when we were in Beit El. "He said that Yeravaum feared that the people would return to the Temple, so he created the calves and commanded the people to worship the Holy One through them."

"Yes, a new form of our old sin in the desert. The annual pilgrimage to the calves will be in one week, at the full moon, exactly one month after Yisrael should have gone up to the Temple for *Sukkot*. And did Menachem tell you that not all the people accepted this substitution?"

I shook my head.

"The tribe of Levi were the most adamant in their refusal. They rejected the calf in the wilderness, and were not going to bow to it here in the Land. The *kohanim* had a double measure of their tribe's indignation."

My chest filled with pride at my tribe's defiance.

"When Yeravaum replaced the Temple, he replaced the *kohanim* as well. New altars meant new priests, an honor bestowed upon one of the most powerful families in the Kingdom, assuring their loyalty to Yeravaum. Most of the *kohanim* in the northern Kingdom of Yisrael fled south to Yehudah. Only a few stayed, and their very presence provoked Yeravaum and the kings who came after him."

"Why?"

"Because the Holy One anointed Aharon and his sons as our priests for all time. The only way to serve the Holy One at the altar is to be a descendant of Aharon. As long as his descendants lived in the land, they were a perpetual challenge to Yeravaum and his mock priests."

"So the remaining *kohanim* were hunted down?"

"No. Most went about their lives quietly. They became craftsmen, shepherds, teachers of the young. Yeravaum saw no reason to disturb the peace by dealing harshly with them."

"So why was my father different?"

"Because your father refused to flee or conceal his identity. He wouldn't let the people forget. He traveled the Kingdom, teaching about the Holy One, and rousing the nation to correct its ways."

Pride blazed through me again at this new image of my father, strong and defiant, though I now knew how much his defiance had cost him—and me. "But you also do this. You were never hunted, were you?" I surveyed the soldier's bodies piled next to the ruined house, "...at least until now."

"True. Yeravaum had no desire to break the connection between the people and the Holy One. Just the opposite: he told the people that worshiping his calves was the surest path to cling to the Holy One. Opposing the prophets would have destroyed this illusion, so we remained free to live and teach in the land."

I stared at the severed head of the last soldier to die, still oozing blood, and suddenly the battle made more sense. "But Izevel wants to destroy the connection between the people and the Holy One. She wants them to worship the Baal."

"Indeed."

I wiped my eyes with the palms of my hands, feeling suddenly like a little boy again. But I couldn't give myself over to my feelings yet—there was more I needed to understand first. "Was I never to know who I am?" I searched my master's eyes.

Uriel ran his fingers through his grizzled, white beard. "That was to be a question of how you matured. Had you grown into a man who likes to avoid trouble, like the *kohanim* who abandoned their roots, I would never have burdened you with this knowledge."

I squinted at Uriel. "But how could you know which direction I'd take?"

"When we met under the fig tree, I was a stranger to you, but you were well known to me. I have walked the land for over fifty years—almost always alone." Uriel's lips rose in a half smile. "Your father was a rare friend; I would not abandon his son. After he died, I visited your uncle whenever my path brought me close to Levonah. It was I who gave you that *kinnor*, for music is a channel for the soul. I saw early on that you possessed a rare spirit—a spirit like your father's—but I still needed to know you better. The past can be such a heavy burden. I needed to be sure that you could bear it.

"That's why I hired you to accompany me to the gathering. There I was to make my final decision: to leave you in ignorance and allow you to sink into the people of the Kingdom, or to smuggle you to Yehudah once you came of age. There you could learn the ways of the *kohanim*, and one day serve in the Holy Temple. Your uncle knew this, of course, but he long ago yielded to my desire for secrecy."

"But, Master, I thought that you hired me for my music?"

"Your music is beautiful, Lev—it is an expression of the spirit of which I speak. But I didn't need a musician badly enough to take you from your uncle's flock. I sought to know you better. And you needed to taste your father's world before facing the choice: whether to remain here a shepherd, or join me on the journey to Yehudah to learn the way of your tribe."

For years I grappled with the prospect of a life I hadn't chosen and didn't desire. Yet, all that time, another option lay hidden beneath the surface, waiting for me to take hold of it. Unlike the paths that Zim and Daniel had encouraged me to walk, this path was destined for me from birth; it was the path that my father had walked, and his father before him, all the way back to Aharon the first high priest. This realization broke through my last restraint. Tears coursed through the filth on my face, but I didn't wipe them away. The truth ripped open an old wound, but I preferred pain to the numbness I felt during all those years of mystery.

"And what now, Master?"

"Everything has changed. My days of walking the Kingdom are over. We are quarry now—we'd be hunted down within days. The watch on the passes will be doubled as well—the way to Yehudah is sealed."

My sense of safety brought on by that morning's victory slipped away. "Where will we go?"

"I don't know. Despite the delay, I must seek vision. Please play for me."

The ancient prophet's knees cracked as he lowered himself to the blood-stained ground. He closed his eyes and dropped his head between his knees, but there was no music. The wind rattled the trees along the edge of the clearing and Uriel gazed back up, deep lines cutting his face. "I forgot that we left your *kinnor* behind. I will attempt it on my own."

My master hunched on the ground, shoulders slumped with exhaustion, neck taut with the tension of a hunted man, while his brother prophets lay silently in a row next to him, awaiting burial. I couldn't imagine harder circumstances to open his heart to prophecy. I might not have my *kinnor*, but I still had my voice.

I searched for a *nigun*, for some music that could escort Uriel into the state of joy necessary for prophecy. Nothing came. Smoke from the smoldering building burned my throat, my eyes. Where was the joy in this place?

Shimon gently wiped the faces of his masters and set their clothes aright. Had he shown my parents' bodies the same tenderness? The idea of their death was nothing new to me, but now I knew the reason. For the first time, I felt more than just an ache at the thought of my parents' deaths, but a rush of admiration as well. They died because my father was a *kohen*—a *kohen* who wasn't content to flee or hide. I was also a *kohen*. If I ever made it to Yehudah, I could serve in the Holy Temple. What did the music in the Temple sound like?

I closed my eyes, picturing King Solomon's Temple, with its white walls and crown of gold. I imagined playing my *kinnor* there, before the altar of the Holy One, in an act of true devotion. A melody rose in my heart. I sang through the *nigun* once, my parched lips cracking as I opened my mouth wide to the music. As I returned to the beginning, an arm wrapped around my shoulder, and Yonaton's voice joined with mine, picking out deeper tones in the melody.

Shimon stretched an arm around my other shoulder. His voice was raw, and his harmony just awful. Still, there was something stirring about singing with this strange man, who had carried me to safety as a child and had just now saved my life once again.

The prophet's head remained bowed between his knees for a long time—I couldn't imagine the shadow that he was trying to lift from his heart. Uriel sat up, eyes open—was he giving up? He beheld the three of us, swaying before him, attempting to sing away his sorrow. He managed a sad smile, and dropped his head again, rocking his body to our music.

A wellspring of emotion bubbled up from the core of my heart. Ten years of emptiness and of longing for answers raged like lions. I held them and watched them melt away under the soft glow of the truth. For the first time, I knew who I was. My song broadened, deepened, flowing out like a river. The arms around my shoulders tightened their hold and the air seemed to crackle with tension. When the tension burst, I didn't need to open my eyes to know that my master had ascended.

♆ ♆ ♆

By the time Uriel stirred, Yonaton and I had built a fire and warmed our stale bread. Curious as I was to question my master, he had not eaten since the previous night and my first duty was to him. I handed the prophet a piece of toasted bread and bit my tongue to restrain myself from asking about the vision.

"Thank you, Lev," Uriel said in a weak voice, accepting the food. "But you should not continue to serve me this way."

"Why not, Master?"

"The *kohanim* serve the Holy One, not man."

"But I want to serve you."

Uriel shook his head. "The laws of the *kohanim* are many and complex. Sadly, we have no proper time for your education. I will serve myself, and Shimon is here if I need assistance."

Yonaton popped up at this. "And me."

Uriel again shook his head. "Yesterday you could not go back to your family because of these brutes, but they will tell their tale to no one now. You may safely return home."

The blood rose in Yonaton's cheeks. "I want to stay."

"Lev's uncle handed him into my care. Your parents made no such choice. They are expecting you, worrying over you."

Yonaton dug his hands into his hips. "When I told my parents that the soldiers were looking for you, my father told me I had to come. My mother packed me food. They wouldn't want me to leave you." He added quietly, "Not if I can help."

Uriel's tired brow knitted in thought. "There is a way you can help. Very well, you may remain as long as you are needed."

No one spoke as the prophet ate, but all eyes measured his progress. When he swallowed his last bite, Shimon could no longer contain himself. "What did you see?"

"We must contact Ovadia. He is still loyal, and in his position he'll know how to advise us."

"Ovadia?" Shimon threw his hands up. "How are we supposed to reach *him*? He's in Shomron, the heart of the Kingdom, right under the eye of Queen Izevel. We need to get you to safety. Wouldn't you be better served leaving the Kingdom?"

"No. You forget that King Ethbaal has the largest fleet on the seas. There's no kingdom with whom he does not trade, no end to his reach. The people have not yet accepted Queen Izevel's reign here, but once I leave the land, no one has reason to shelter me. I'd be given over immediately."

"And Yehudah?"

"Indeed, I would be safe there. But that is where Queen Izevel will expect me to go. She'll concentrate her power on the border." Uriel stood up and leaned upon his staff. "In any case, I have no intention of fleeing. Do not concern yourself with my safety. My last days will be here in the Kingdom, serving the Holy One in any way that I still can."

"Excellent, so we'll resist. But don't throw your life away going to Shomron."

"I didn't say we need to go to Shomron, we just need to contact Ovadia. It will be less dangerous for him to come to us."

"But how can we contact him without going to Shomron?"

Uriel cocked his head and scrutinized Yonaton and me, and his features molded into a grimace. "The boys. The only soldiers that we know can connect us with the boys lie right here. You and I are hunted, they are not. Hopefully none of the Queen's other lackeys know the connection between us."

"So what do we do now?"

"We need to find a place to hide until Lev and Yonaton return. We can't remain here the night; it's too well known as a gathering place. Just because it has been destroyed does not mean that they will not return to pursue others who may flee here."

Hillel said: In a place where there are no men, strive to be a man.

Pirkei Avot 2:6

The Steward's Wife

I burst to the surface of the frigid water, the skin on my arms rising in goose-flesh.

"Immerse again," Uriel said. "I saw your hair floating on the water."

I ran a hand through my curly hair, which had not been cut since high summer. Each time I dipped under the surface, it rose like a water lily seeking light. I pursed my lips and dunked again, tucking my chin to my knees and curling over in the narrow pool. When I came up, Uriel nodded.

"The impurity of the dead still clings to the rest of us," Uriel said. "We will not be fully cleansed until we merit to see the Holy Temple, where the *kohanim* can purify us with the ashes of the red heifer. But for you Lev, who have not had direct contact with the dead, living waters will suffice."

Through most of that morning, Uriel and Shimon had cleansed the dead prophets, laying them out in a nearby cave. There they would rest, like so many sleepers in a row, with their feet pointed toward Yerushalayim. At Uriel's insistence, the bodies of the soldiers were carried into a second cave. Shimon didn't object, but I suspected he would have preferred their flesh be scavenged by the vultures that already circled overhead.

Unable to help with the bodies, I returned to the cave to retrieve Balaam and the rest of our gear. My heart pounded as I stretched up to retrieve my *kinnor* from its hiding place. My grip relaxed as I ran my fingers over the strings, hearing its voice, a little surprised to find that it was still in tune. I was without it just one night, but it felt like greeting an old friend after a long separation.

Yonaton spent the morning working with the soldiers' horses, removing all the Queen's insignia and burning them in the fire, then setting the animals loose in the valley. Though the horses would have hastened our journey, Uriel felt they would draw too much attention.

"Where to now, Master?" I asked, as I shook myself dry.

"West. There's a cave not far from the King's Road where Shimon and I can hide."

Yonaton flushed. Between his run the day before and the horse falling on him that morning, he was struggling to walk. "I don't think I can make it that far."

Uriel shook his head. "Your legs have earned a rest. You may ride Balaam today."

It was not yet midday when we started our journey. Before long, our track cut through rolling hills like those around Levonah. I spent most of my life traversing hills just like these, but could not see any path that Uriel was following. Nevertheless, by late afternoon we reached our destination—a cave in a hillside just over the ridge from the King's Road, chiseled by hand like the caves at Emek HaAsefa. A towering carob tree hid the entrance from view.

It had not rained since my return from Yericho, but a cold north wind bit into my bones and I craved a hot, hearty meal. Yonaton, who managed to sleep much of the afternoon while riding Balaam, offered, "I'll go look for—"

"No fire tonight," Uriel interrupted.

I surveyed the broad valley that we had just crossed. Nothing resembling a soldier appeared anywhere on the horizon, but I hadn't seen the first group either. Were there more out there hunting us?

🪕 🪕 🪕

I rose before the sun after tossing and turning throughout the night. Shimon sat in the mouth of the cave, illuminated by flickering firelight. Sniffing at the smell of roasting meat, I untangled myself from my tunic and threw it over my head. I wrapped my sheepskin around my shoulders for extra warmth, and joined Shimon next to the small fire. "I was about to wake you to eat," he said. "The Holy One must truly love you. See what leapt right into my hands this morning?" A fat grouse dripped grease off its breast onto the smoking coals.

Shimon plucked the bird from the roasting spit and cut off a wing with his dagger. It was the same dagger that he had given me, the one that he threw wide of the soldier. Did he use this dagger because the other one, now tucked into his belt, had contact with the dead? Was this another one of the laws of the *kohanim* that Uriel wanted to teach me about? Shimon handed me the steaming wing, almost too hot to handle. "I envy you."

"Why?" The word was muffled by the crisp skin crackling in my mouth.

"You are walking toward danger, but at least your fate is in your hands. I…we…get to sit here and wait, praying that we're not discovered and hoping you're successful; knowing little and doing less."

I chewed the savory meat, keeping my mouth full so that I wouldn't have to respond. The hot meat warmed my throat, yet hadn't Uriel, who now slept after taking the first watch, warned us against making a fire? I was relieved when Yonaton appeared, rubbing his eyes. Shimon handed him the other wing and repeated the story of the grouse. Yonaton stared at him. "You're just a vessel for blessing, aren't you? First you save our lives, and now you fill our stomachs." The compliment brought a hint of a smile to Shimon's scarred face.

When we had finished eating, we tossed the remaining bones into the fire, wiped our greasy hands in the dirt, and descended to where Balaam was tied up for the night.

"You should ride," I told Yonaton. "I'll lead Balaam."

"I can walk."

"You can limp. Balaam can handle your weight, but both of us will be too much for him in the hills. When we reach the road, we'll ride together."

Yonaton sighed and shook his head, but climbed on.

"Be safe," Shimon said, his hand drifting down toward something inside of his cloak.

"What do you have there?" I asked.

Shimon pulled back his cloak, revealing the hilt of a sword. "It's the one Yonaton handed me during the battle, from the soldier that he killed."

"You kept it?"

"I was blessed to save us with it once. Perhaps I'll be so blessed again." Shimon watched us as we set off, ducking back into the cave only when we reached the ridge.

Yonaton shot a glance behind him. "Shame he's not coming with us."

I said nothing, just led Balaam on the path that Uriel pointed out to us the day before, which climbed gently until it intersected with the road in the distance. The footing was poor, and we trod along the path as the sun rose over the hillsides.

A figure on the far ridge caught my attention—a soldier on horseback. He sat on one of the hillsides overlooking the road, but he wasn't facing the road, he was peering out over the valley where our path crossed. He noticed us at the same time, nudging his horse forward and rising in the saddle.

My pulse raced. There was no reason to panic—we were just two boys with a donkey. I lifted my hand, hissing out of the corner of my mouth, "Quick, wave."

Yonaton glanced around until he too saw the soldier, and threw a friendly wave. The soldier waved back, then returned to his post on the hilltop.

Yonaton asked, "Was that a Yisraelite soldier or one of the Queen's?"

"I don't know, but there weren't any Yisraelite soldiers posted this far away before the wedding."

"You think he's watching the road?"

"He was facing the valley, so he could be watching both or—"

"Or he's keeping an eye out for anyone avoiding the road," Yonaton finished.

"If that's the case, we'll draw less attention on the road. We can cut over this hillside. It will be quicker, but I think it's too steep for Balaam to carry you."

Yonaton threw his leg over the donkey and lowered himself to the ground. "I can walk."

We saw no more soldiers as we made our way up, over, and onto the road. Both of us climbed onto Balaam for the ride toward Shomron. The donkey brayed in protest when I mounted behind Yonaton—we were quite a load for the old beast—but it nonetheless trotted forward faster than we could walk.

🪕 🪕 🪕

The evening breeze tickled the sweat on the back of my neck as we climbed the approach to Shomron. We passed six more soldiers on the road during our journey, two of them from the Queen's Guard, the other four Yisraelite. We lay down in the shade of a large carob tree during the hottest part of the afternoon. In order to draw less attention, we planned to enter the city just before sunset, when the gates would be crowded with those returning from the fields. But we underestimated the distance remaining to travel, and the first ram's horn blew before we reached the city. I nudged Balaam with my ankles, urging the donkey to trot faster.

The guard at the gates raised the ram's horn to his lips to blow the final blast before closing the gates. Yonaton called out, "Wait!"

The guard lowered the horn and waved us forward.

I jumped off and ran, drawing Balaam behind me. The guard blew the final blast, waited for us to pass, and pulled the outer gates closed. We couldn't have drawn more attention to our entry if we'd presented the guard with a sealed scroll emblazoned with our names. A second sentry, one of the Queen's men, also watched the gate. Fortunately, his attention was focused on the setting sun, and he was oblivious to two peasant boys.

The courtyards of the houses on Ovadia's street formed a high stone wall, punctuated with gateways and alleys. A deep shadow already filled the paved stone street when we arrived, and before long, Yonaton was glancing back over his shoulder, casting his eyes back and forth between the sides of the street.

"Did we miss it?" I asked.

"No. Well...you know, I'm not so sure." He twisted forward and back now, craning his neck to see the tops of the houses. It had been several months since we were at Ovadia's, but we had not anticipated any difficulty finding the house. "This is the street, I know it. Let's go back to the crossroad." Even Balaam groaned as we turned around in the fading light.

We passed the length of street two more times before Yonaton let out a loud "Ha!" and called a halt in front of a heavy wooden gate covered in fresh pitch, its stench stinging our noses.

"I don't remember any gate," I said softly.

"There wasn't one," Yonaton replied, "That's what confused me. But this is it, I'm certain. See, there's Ovadia's seal on the lintel."

The footstool carved into the lintel was indeed the same symbol that he used to seal his messages—I had delivered enough of them before the wedding to remember. I tried the gate, but it was locked.

Yonaton gripped a crude mallet hanging from the door post, and pounded out three solid blows. I flinched at each strike; they rang too loud in the silence of the twilit street. No one answered. We stared at each other. We'd invested all our energy in reaching Shomron, we hadn't even thought about what to do if Ovadia was away. I shuddered at the thought of sleeping on the cold stone street.

Yonaton swung the mallet once more, knocking louder. We stepped away from the gate, assessing the dark wall. A door opened, then quickly closed again. The gate swung silently outward on its hinges, and Ovadia stepped into the gloom, fastening the gate behind him. "Hello, boys. A bit late for a visit, isn't it?" He shifted from foot to foot as his eyes darted up and down the dark street.

I opened my mouth to respond, but Ovadia cut me off. "Well then, very good of you to let me know you're back. Come look for me at the palace in the morning, perhaps we can find work for you again. I recently heard Dov say he could use more musicians for all the banquets. Until tomorrow, then." Ovadia turned back to the gate.

I leaned in and breathed at his back, "Master Uriel sent us."

Ovadia whipped around, his eyes shooting up the street again. "Did anyone see you? Were you followed?"

"I don't think so."

Ovadia swept Yonaton, Balaam, and me quickly into the courtyard. He closed and bolted the heavy wooden gate, securing it without a sound, then coaxed Balaam over to a corner, tying him to a post near a watering trough and tossing him a pile of straw. Then he hustled us through the main entrance—I exhaled only when the door of the house was locked behind us.

Lamps burned in the main room where drawn shutters blocked the moonlight. Batya tucked a loose strand of raven hair under her scarf as her husband dropped us onto stools beside the hearth table. She poured out water in clay bowls while Ovadia paced. I gulped down the cool liquid, wiping my grimy lips only after draining the bowl.

Ovadia dropped onto a stool opposite me. "Uriel is still alive?"

I nodded.

"Is he safe?"

I nodded again.

"Where is he?" I opened my mouth to answer, but Ovadia interjected, "How did you get here?"

"He is safe," I replied. "He sent us to you for help."

Ovadia popped up and redoubled his pacing. "Help? So many need help. She's got eyes everywhere, you know!"

Batya offered us two hot loaves of flat bread. I tore off a hunk, cringing at the dark smudge my filthy hands left on the brown bread. I put the bread down and stepped toward the wash-basin.

Batya would not allow Ovadia to question us while we ate. Soon all four of us were seated at the heavy wooden table—even Ovadia's nerves calmed in the face of warm bread.

I contemplated the changes in Ovadia's house as I ate. Heavy blankets covered shuttered windows, a strange sight on a windless night. In the shadows, a new oven protruded from the wall on the inside of the house, just opposite the oven in the courtyard. I squeezed the warm bread in my hand—had they been baking at night?

Ovadia managed to hold himself back until the bread was gone, but when Batya rose, saying something about pressed figs, he leaned in close to us. "Where is he?"

I swallowed my last bite. "In a cave a day's journey from here."

"Well hidden?"

I nodded. "There's a tree blocking the entrance; I never would have known it was there."

"It must be one of Gidon's caves."

"Gidon's caves?"

"Built before Gidon's rebellion against the Midianites hundreds of years ago. Some, like those at Emek HaAsefa, were strongholds, others hiding places. Uriel has shown me several; no one knows them as well as he does. I've never heard of the one you speak of."

"That doesn't matter, we can guide you back."

"Me, leave Shomron, to get a prophet?" Ovadia put his forehead into his hands and snorted. "That's just what she's waiting for, an excuse to take off my head."

I stared at Ovadia—he was our only hope. We couldn't return to Uriel alone. What would we do then? Sit in the cave until we starved?

"Of course, you have no idea what's been happening here." He pulled his stool closer to us and lowered his voice. "The Queen has declared war on the prophets."

"We know," I said, an edge to my voice. "We've buried the dead."

The blunt words sank Ovadia into his seat, and he motioned for me to continue. I recounted the events of the last three days, holding nothing back, except Uriel's revelation about my father—I saw no reason to share this new knowledge. Yonaton leaned in close to me the entire time I spoke, but added nothing. As with our music, he seemed happy to let me lead.

When I finished, Ovadia met his wife's eyes with a groan. "It is worse than we feared." He cradled his temples in his palms. "We hoped that her power was limited to Shomron. Further into the hills, the people still love and fear the prophets. I thought they would protect them."

"The people love the prophets," Yonaton said, speaking up for the first time, "but they fear the sword."

Ovadia nodded. "Yet there are worse things than the sword, Yonaton. May you be blessed not to know them." He rose and faced Batya. "It seems that the fate of these boys is bound up with ours, yes?"

Batya gathered the remains of our meal. "You thought these boys were a tool in your hand. Yet, you see now, we are all tools in the hands of the Holy One."

I wondered what she meant, but was distracted by the sight of her collecting breadcrumbs from the table. During the wedding, I never saw her clean. "Where are your servants?"

A soft tear ran down her high-boned cheek. "They're attending to our land."

Attending to their land? Surely enough men attended Ovadia's land that he didn't need the house servants there as well? Perhaps for the harvest, but now? And even so, why should Batya weep over this?

I thought about everything I had seen since arriving: the gate blocking access to the house; a new oven, built inside the house instead of in the courtyard where it belonged; windows sealed on a still evening; hot bread past nightfall; and the servants gone. My eye fell on a waist high pile in the corner of the room, covered with a woolen blanket.

I rose from my stool. All eyes watched me go, yet neither Ovadia nor Batya hindered me. Lifting the edge of the blanket, I peeked beneath, discovering just what I realized must be there: a stack of freshly baked loaves of breads.

Ovadia approached and took the edge of the blanket from my hand. "Your eyes are starting to open, Lev. That is good. You will need them in the days ahead. All our servants, as you must have guessed, are gone. Our hired workers were dismissed even before the wedding, that was one reason I relied on you boys so much. Now even our slaves have been sent away to work our land in the Yezreel Valley. No one can know what we're doing."

A lump rose in my throat. "How many are there?"

"Thirty prophets and disciples. Hidden in a cave outside the city."

Batya gasped and clasped her hand over her mouth.

"As you said, Batya, they were sent by the Holy One. We must trust them." She nodded without removing her hand.

Yonaton stirred. "But why us?"

Ovadia raised his eyebrows. "Uriel sent you."

"Not now—during the wedding. You said you dismissed your workers and depended on us instead."

"Ah, yes." Ovadia's expression relaxed. "Even then I wondered if you would ask. Did it not seem strange to you that the King's steward, with all the servants at my disposal, was relying on two unknown boys to do my errands?"

"You told us that everyone was busy with preparations."

"Indeed they were—like bees in the hive. But I still saw to the most important details myself, and as you know, I often needed help. I commandeered dozens of slaves and servants, but always kept them at a distance."

"But why us?" Yonaton asked again.

Ovadia shifted his focus from Yonaton to me. I felt the challenge in his gaze to figure out this puzzle as I had about the bread. Ovadia dismissed his hired workers and relied instead on two country boys, both plucked from serving the prophets. The answer was suddenly clear, as though inked on clean parchment. "We were safe."

"You were safe," Ovadia agreed. "From the time of the engagement, the King was constantly on the lookout for anyone who could be disloyal."

"But you were not disloyal then," Yonaton said, "Were you?"

"No, I have always served my King loyally."

"Until now," I added with a grin.

"Even now." Ovadia jerked out of his seat and strode to the covered window. "This is the Queen's war. *Her* soldiers are after the prophets; the Yisraelite soldiers haven't been brought into the hunt. The King is doing his best to ignore the Queen's attacks, neither helping nor hindering her."

"But if you're not disloyal," Yonaton asked, "Why dismiss your servants?"

"The very innocence of the question is what made you so valuable."

"Why?"

"I'm known to have relations with the prophets. I'm foreign born. I'm a natural target."

"For who?"

"For anyone hoping to advance by setting me up for a fall. It makes no difference whether the accusations are true or not. I directed hundreds of servants, but I never let them get too close and never let them deliver my messages."

"Then why us?"

"As Lev said, you were safe. Uriel told me that neither of you had ever left home until you came to play for the prophets. You knew nothing of what was happening here in Shomron, and you were hardly looking to make names for yourselves in the court." Dark circles of exhaustion stood out below Ovadia's eyes in the lamp light. "But that was before. Then I had nothing to hide, and feared only lies."

"What changed?" Yonaton asked.

"I don't know. Something happened when the King went to Yericho a week and a half ago. He came back white-faced and silent. He told me nothing, just summoned the Queen to the throne room. Whatever she heard sent her into a rage, and she called in Yambalya. She emerged determined to kill the prophets and their disciples."

"And no one knows why?" Yonaton asked.

Ovadia shook his head. "The King is keeping his hands clean of the blood of the prophets, but there is someone else that he commanded me to find. I expect it is connected to him."

"Eliyahu," I said.

"Yes." Ovadia's eyes narrowed on me. "How do you know about Eliyahu? Did Uriel have a vision of what happened in Yericho?"

"He didn't need to. I was there."

"You were in Yericho?"

"Yes."

"Then do you know why we're hunting him? Did he confront the King?"

My face flushed at the memory of Eliyahu's wrath, and of the King cowering under his fiery gaze. "He did."

"Over the Baal?"

"Yes."

"You see Batya, I knew it. The Queen is proud. Eliyahu standing against the King must have prompted her to act before she was ready."

"Ready for what?" Yonaton asked.

"It was clear at the wedding that she intended to draw the people after the Baal—Yambalya wouldn't have coerced the guests to bow down except on her orders. Her influence has only grown stronger since then. Much stronger. But not enough to strike against the prophets. In her rage, she acted rashly. If we can reach Uriel, the resistance will have the leader it lacks. Under him, the surviving prophets can rouse the people to throw off Izevel's yoke."

"And the King's?" Yonaton asked.

Ovadia shook his head. "The King is more dedicated to the people than he is to the Queen. Even rebuilding Yericho and marrying Izevel were, in his mind, done for them. If the people rise against the Queen, I believe the King won't stand in their way."

Ovadia studied my face with sharp eyes until I began to shift in my seat. "To think that I brought you into my home because you were some innocent boy who knew nothing of the Kingdom or the court! You're finding yourself in the middle of too many events for it to all be chance. There is more to you than you are sharing, Lev, more perhaps than you know yourself."

My hand went to the bulge in my tunic that marked where my father's knife lay. Ovadia was correct that I was holding something back. *He need not know that I am a kohen, though. It has nothing to do with what we face right now.*

Ovadia broke into a sudden smile. "Uriel would never have led the resistance on his own. He would have put off war as long as possible, allowing Izevel to grow stronger and stronger. But now that Eliyahu has forced his hand, he will have to lead us."

Ovadia stroked his trim beard. "Unless Eliyahu expects to lead—he started this fight. Lev, did it sound to you as though he was planning to lead the people against the Queen? Tell me exactly what he said."

Blood pulsed in my neck, heating my cheeks. I pronounced his words firmly, with only a trace of the fire that had filled Eliyahu's voice at Yericho. "As the Holy One, the Lord of Yisrael, before whom I stand, lives...there will not be dew nor rain during these years except by my word."

Batya gasped.

Ovadia staggered back against the hearth. "He tried to stop the rains?"

I nodded.

"I've never heard of such a thing. Can he do that?"

"According to Master Uriel, the Holy One indeed gave him the key of rain. The heavens are sealed until Eliyahu relents."

"The Holy One gave him the key? That must be why the Queen summoned Yambalya. He would know if Eliyahu spoke the truth—the dark priest is filled with wisdom of their abominations."

Ovadia's eyes closed in, tightening his brow. "What you said didn't sound like prophecy though. It sounded more like an oath. Or..."

"...a curse," I finished.

Silence fell over the room.

I asked Ovadia, "You said Eliyahu wasn't one of the prophets. He is, though. I saw him receiving prophecy after he left Hiel's house. Was he not known as a prophet before?"

"I do not know. In his youth he was among the last disciples of Achia, Uriel's master. I do not know if he ever achieved prophecy before. I have known him only at the court. He has always been respectful of the monarchy there. Did anything happen in Yericho before he spoke?"

I shifted uncomfortably on my stool. "The King told Hiel that he blamed himself for Seguv's death."

"As he should," Ovadia said, planting himself opposite me. "To hire a man to rebuild a cursed city…. Of course, Hiel himself is also responsible for agreeing to do it. Did he say anything else?"

"The King thought it strange that the curse of Yehoshua would work."

"Why did he think that strange? Few prophets were as great as Yehoshua."

"Because Moshe said that if the people worshipped other gods, there would be no rain."

"What does that have to do with Yehoshua?"

"The King said that the people have turned after the Baal, yet he could never remember having so much rain. He wondered why the curse of Yehoshua would work when the curse of his master Moshe failed."

"What!" Ovadia leapt to his feet again. He drew his hand across his clammy forehead. When he spoke, his voice trembled. "Eliyahu invoked the curse of Moshe?"

I remembered Uriel saying that Moshe's words were not quite a curse, but they certainly seemed like it to me. "Yes."

All eyes were on Ovadia as he paced the room. "I had it all wrong. This is not a battle—it is a siege."

Yonaton looked confused, "But the battle has already begun."

"By the Queen, yes. But Eliyahu brought a drought. It may take years for its effects to be fully felt." He turned to Batya. "This changes everything—our plan will not work. We need to think of something else."

"But this should make our resistance even stronger!" Batya exclaimed.

Ovadia shook his head. "It cannot be done."

"Batya is right." I rose to my feet as well. "The Holy One gave Eliyahu the key of rain! What better weapon could we have? As you said, the Queen acted too soon—the people are still more loyal to the prophets than they are to the Baal. Why change the plan now?"

Ovadia shook his head. "Because the Holy One did not give Eliyahu the key of rain to fight Izevel."

"Then what is it for?"

But Ovadia's thoughts were elsewhere. "Nothing, nothing is as we thought."

Batya approached his side. "Tell us what you mean."

"It is the people. The Holy One's wrath will fall on all those who have turned to the Baal—and on all those who have been loyal as well."

Batya took his hand in hers. "But isn't the Queen the cause of their turning away?"

"Maybe. Yes." Ovadia shook his head. "It does not matter. Either way, Izevel will be the last to feel the lack of rain. The poorest will suffer first."

I couldn't understand why Ovadia was suddenly losing resolve. "But won't that rouse them against the Queen and the Baal?"

"Perhaps. But the Queen will tell them that this is not just a temporary stop to the rains, it is a drought, brought on by Eliyahu, a prophet. She will claim that he's a tyrant, that she has come to rescue the nation from his grip. In their misery, the people could turn against the prophets themselves."

Tears rolled down Batya's cheeks. "Then what do we do? Nothing?"

"We have thirty prophets already hidden. We'll hide as many more as we can."

"But how will we sustain them? We have sufficient barley for the hidden ones only until the new moon. What will you do then, sell land to buy grain?" Terror lit her eyes. "And you're being watched. How long can we keep this up before someone discovers what we're doing?"

"I don't know." Ovadia slammed his fist on the table; our bowls bounced with a clank. "But when it is known that a drought is coming, at least buying a store of grain will not appear suspicious. We must continue hiding the prophets—I see now that any battle will not succeed."

"But why not?" Batya cried.

"Didn't you hear the boy? Eliyahu evoked the curse of Moshe. There will never again be a prophet of Moshe's strength."

"But shouldn't that make victory even easier?" I asked, but even as the words left my mouth, I recalled Uriel telling me that the forces of light and the forces of darkness had to exist in balance. The more powerful Eliyahu's curse, the more powerful the counteracting forces would be. Perhaps if Eliyahu were leading us into battle our strength could prevail, but with Eliyahu in hiding, could any force that we set into motion be strong enough?

As if answering my thoughts, Ovadia said, "If this war is won, it will not be by ordinary men like me, nor even by the prophets of today. If we send the prophets out of the cave now, we send them to their deaths. We just have to do what we can, help as many as we can, for as long as we have bread. If we fail, we fail."

Ovadia sighed. "We'll need to find a way to get Uriel and Shimon here without being detected."

"Bring them *here*?" The words leapt out of my mouth.

"Yes, here. There's nowhere else I can sustain them."

I shook my head. "Master Uriel doesn't want to hide. He would support your original plan."

"We can save his life!"

"He said he will spend his last days serving the Holy One in any way he can. I don't think he'll go meekly into a cave."

"Shimon won't either," Yonaton added. "He'd rather fight."

Ovadia slapped his palms on the table and bore into my eyes. "Listen to me—it is crucial that Uriel survive."

"He won't want it. He says he doesn't have long to live anyway."

"Uriel must live. In the struggle between Eliyahu and Izevel, he may prove pivotal."

"If Eliyahu fails?"

"No, if Eliyahu succeeds. It may take the wrath of Eliyahu to defeat Izevel. But it will require one like your master to rebuild the nation—and there is none other like him."

"Why?" Yonaton asked.

But I thought I knew. "Master Uriel believes that we must turn to the Holy One from love, not fear."

"That's part of it," Ovadia said. "But Uriel is not the only prophet dedicated to the path of love."

"Then why?"

"You're too young to understand what Uriel has been through. Tell him whatever you must, but get him to me."

"And what about Shimon?" Yonaton asked.

"Shimon is loyal to Uriel. If he thinks that his help is needed to save Uriel, I expect he will do what he must. But once Uriel is hidden, Shimon may do as he pleases."

"Even if he agrees to come, how will we get him here? You said you can't travel."

"No, I cannot. The Queen is investing all her efforts into amassing power. Allegiances shift and swirl around her at all times. Those in her favor are advanced, those who are not…" His expression grew sour. "She distrusts me because I will not bow to her abominations. This is not yet required, but refusal is enough to draw her wrath. The King leans on me for many things, so I am safe at present. But I am watched. If I go to Uriel it will mean the death of us both."

"But what can we do without you?" My heart raced at the thought of traveling the King's Road with the prophet, and I saw my fear reflected in Yonaton's eyes. We were counting on Ovadia's authority to get the *navi* past the soldiers.

"You saw the Queen's soldiers on the road?"

I nodded.

"Perhaps we can risk it anyway. There are many ways into Shomron. It is not the people we have to fear—they are not yet corrupt enough to hunt a prophet—it is only the foreigners. There are many paths that they may not know. No one knows these mountains as Uriel does. It was he who first showed me the cave."

I shook my head. "They have lookouts on the hilltops. They're watching the valleys as well as the roads."

Ovadia groaned. "You see, Batya, a craftsman can have the finest tools, but he's an oaf without a plan." He drummed his fingers on the table. "Perhaps at night?"

I recalled our flight from the soldiers two nights before and shuddered. To reach Shomron in the dark, on footpaths, would take three nights at least. That meant finding hiding places during the days on top of the hardship of the night trekking. "Even if we could make it, we'd never get into the city. The Queen's soldiers watch the gates."

"The cave is not in the city. He will not have to pass the gates."

I didn't like the plan, but what choice did we have? "All right. If we can convince Master Uriel, we'll try at night."

"No you won't." Batya stood, hands on her hips. "You'll go during the day."

This was too much. Hadn't she been listening? "The valleys are watched."

"You won't walk the valleys. You'll take the King's Road."

Ovadia gaped at his wife. "How will they do that?"

A flush rose in Batya's cheeks. "With the crowd returning from the festival."

The edges of her husband's lips curved up in a smile. "Brilliant."

I stared back and forth between them. "What's brilliant?"

"The annual festival of the Calf is in five days," Ovadia explained. "The King will be there, along with all the nobility of Shomron."

"But if the King is there," Yonaton said, "There are sure to be soldiers as well."

"The King's guard will escort him, but he moves much faster than his subjects. Besides, those are Yisraelite soldiers—the Queen's guard won't dare attack while they're around. Once the King rides past, Uriel and Shimon can mingle in with the crowd."

"He won't agree."

"I told you, Lev, your master must reach that cave. And I have known him far longer than you have. I do not believe that he wants to die."

I bristled. "If you know my master so well, then you must know his loathing of the Calf. He hasn't even set foot in Beit El for sixty years. Even if he agrees to hide, he won't do it by pretending to be a Calf worshiper."

"It's the only plan we have." Ovadia reached across the table to seize my shoulders. "The Holy One has chosen you to serve your master. Now you must save him. Whatever you need to do, you do." His grip tightened. "Swear to me that you will get Uriel here alive!"

"He's my master, I'm not his."

"I am offering to save his life. Now swear."

Ovadia's eyes locked on mine, sapping my power to resist. "All right, I swear," I said, wondering how I would stand up to a *navi* when I couldn't even stand up to Ovadia.

"But we'll still have to get past the Queen's soldiers on the road," Yonaton protested.

"Yes."

"But how?"

Ovadia released my shoulders and turned to Yonaton. "Once I was traveling the hills of the Bashon alone, on a mission for the King. Just at sunset, I came upon a pack of wild dogs."

I wondered what this had to do with saving my master. Yonaton asked, "What did you do?"

"I sat down in their midst."

Yonaton's eyes grew large. "Weren't you scared?"

"Terrified."

"I don't understand," I said.

"If you run from a dog, it will give chase. But if you act like its master, it will grovel. You are not going to run from the Queen's soldiers, nor will you hide. You will pass them in the middle of the day, in a crowd returning from a festival for the Golden Calf."

My stomach rumbled, and though I knew that the navi was tired, I also knew that the wise never left their questions unasked. "I have one more question, Master."

"One more then."

I could tell from the direction of his voice that my master was lying down. Suddenly my curiosity felt out of place, and I struggled for the right words. "It's about food."

"The righteous eat to satisfy the nefesh."

"Is that why the prophets don't cook their greens properly?" I almost said "didn't cook their greens properly," but caught myself. Just because it had been months since any prophet I knew had tasted a vegetable, did not mean they had given up hope.

I rarely heard my master's laugh these days, though its dry rattle did not convey much humor. "What did you notice about the meals in Emek HaAsefa?"

Despite the total darkness, I closed my eyes to summon up an image of the gathering. "The vegetables were barely cooked; their colors were very bright."

"You saw well. Of all creation, it is only man that cooks his food. The colors tell us when it is ready to be eaten. Leave it on the fire and the color fades, because its vital force is sapped."

"Vegetables tell us when they should be eaten?"

"Indeed. The nevi'im see a generous creation which guides our growth—we need only listen."

Rabbi Yannai said: We cannot grasp the tranquility of the wicked, nor can we understand the suffering of the righteous.

Pirkei Avot 4:19

Shimon's Tale

We left the house before first light, before any prying eyes could take notice. Ovadia instructed us not to speak until we reached the main road, yet even there, neither of us broke the silence. When the ram's horn signaled the opening of the gates, we pushed our way through, practically invisible within a group of farmers heading out to their fields.

Ovadia's words turned over in my mind. *Eliyahu's curse evoked the power of Moshe. That power was not directed solely against Izevel and the Baal, the battle that Ovadia wanted to fight. The drought would hit all of the people of Yisrael, those who bowed to the Baal and those who did not. The power of the curse meant that even a prophet like Uriel couldn't alter its course. Trying to change it would only lead to his destruction.*

Ovadia believed all this, believed Uriel must hide until the devastation passed, and I had sworn to bring my master to him. But would he agree? If Uriel thought that Ovadia was wrong, I was stuck between two oaths; one to Ovadia and one to my master. I shuddered at the thought of what just one oath had done to Seguv and his family.

"Soldiers," Yonaton whispered, his chest pounding against my back.

"I can't see more than their heads," I said, craning my neck to see into the stone tower that stood above us. The hilltops surrounding Shomron were all topped with such strongholds, the outer ring of the city's defenses. "Are they Yisraelite or the Queen's Guard?"

"Can't tell."

The soldiers hardly glanced at us, but as we passed under the shadow of the watchtower, a feeling of disquiet rumbled in my stomach. Since swearing to Ovadia, my thoughts had been focused on Uriel, but a bigger problem just occurred to me.

"Yonaton?" His name caught in my throat.

"What is it?"

"Ovadia said that Master Uriel must get to Shomron—at any cost. But what about Shimon?"

"What about him?"

I hesitated. "Well, it's just that…I'm not sure. Do you think he's safe to travel with?"

Yonaton snorted. "Safe? I can't think of a better person to travel with. When was the last time you shattered your enemy's sword?"

I twisted around to face Yonaton. "Yesterday morning he lit a fire."

"He built it to roast us a grouse."

"I know, but Master Uriel told us not to. And Shimon complained about waiting in the cave. It sounds crazy, but I wonder if he wants to be found."

"You think he wants to die?"

"Not to die, to fight."

"The way he fights, I don't blame him."

"But that's not the way he fights—three days ago he ran from battle."

"You heard what Master Uriel said, he received a spirit from the Holy One. Like prophecy."

"Exactly, a spirit like prophecy, which he's pursued for years, and which he lost as soon as the battle ended. You saw the look in his eyes when he told Master Uriel about it. It was hungry."

Yonaton stared at me. "You don't trust him."

I turned back to face the road. "Ovadia made me swear to bring Master Uriel to Dotan. Master Uriel might listen to me, but will Shimon?"

"If Master Uriel agrees, Shimon will come along to make sure he's safe."

"That's what I'm afraid of. The plan is to sneak past the guards, not confront them. If Shimon won't enter the cave, we're better off without him on the road."

"Tell him that. Tell him that if he's not willing to hide, he shouldn't make the journey."

"He thinks he's protecting Master Uriel."

"Tell him *you'll* do that."

"He won't listen to me." I kept my face forward so that Yonaton wouldn't see my shame. "He knows I couldn't kill the soldier. He thinks I'm a coward."

Yonaton shook his head. "He's glad you didn't kill the soldier—the last thing he'd want is for a *kohen* to kill. You heard what Master Uriel said, that *kohanim* are forbidden contact with the dead. Think of the debt he owes your father. He wants to protect you."

"Exactly, which means he's not going to listen to me."

"Listen, I think you're worrying about nothing. You ought to be more concerned about convincing Master Uriel. Will he agree to act like a Calf worshiper and then retreat to a cave?"

"I doubt it, but we have to try. Perhaps we shouldn't tell him about hiding? Whether the plan is to fight or hide, he still needs to get to the cave. Let Ovadia convince him to stay put once we're there."

Yonaton snorted. "He's a prophet, don't be a fool. But if you can convince Master Uriel, I'll work on Shimon. Twice he's told me how I impressed him at the battle. I think he'll listen to me."

Yonaton's willingness to deal with Shimon lightened my breathing. "So you think it's better to bring him along?"

"Shimon's not stupid—he won't fight unless he has to. And if we have to fight, there's no one I'd rather have on my side."

üü üü üü

The full heat of the day was just starting to subside when we saw the great carob tree blocking the cave. Ovadia warned us to enter the cave only after dark, so we tethered Balaam by a spring a short distance away and waited.

The first thing I noticed as night fell were flames backlighting the tree. Had Uriel bowed to Shimon's recklessness?

I approached the cave first, lurking in the bushes while I spied out the situation. There was no sign of the prophet or Shimon. The blaze illuminated the cave, casting an eerie glow behind the carob's dancing leaves. A charred cooking pot lay at its edge. From my hiding place, I inspected the cave for any signs of a struggle.

Stones crunched under footsteps and I snapped my eyes to the path. By the fire's orange glow I saw Yonaton stepping toward the cave—but he was not alone. A shadow broke away from the darkness and rose behind him. I let out a strangled cry at the sound of metal hissing against a leather sheath. A sword rose behind Yonaton.

The arm froze and then dropped. "You have returned." Shimon sheathed his weapon as he eased into the firelight. His scars twisted in a tight smile.

A second figure slipped from the darkness into the cave. "You succeeded." There was no question in Uriel's voice.

I stepped out from my hiding place. "Yes, Master."

"Where are we to go?"

"The cave of Dotan, Master."

Uriel nodded solemnly. "A choice with wisdom. How many are already assembled there?"

"Thirty."

"There will be more."

"Dotan?" Shimon said, digging his heels into the rocky soil. "That's north of Shomron. Did Ovadia say how we are to get there?"

I swallowed. "Yes."

Yonaton stepped toward the entrance. "We shouldn't leave Balaam where he could draw attention. I'll retrieve him."

Uriel waved his hand in answer. "Balaam is fine where he is. It was wise to approach on foot." His eyes grew narrow. "Now the plan."

I had rehearsed my speech at least ten times in my head on the ride back from Shomron—but the words evaporated in my master's presence.

Uriel fixed me with a piercing stare. "Are we to join the pilgrims returning from Beit El?"

My chest froze, anticipating the prophet's angry protest. "Ovadia says it's the best way. Hopefully no one will—"

Uriel cut me off. "Very well. So we will do."

My breath seeped out in relief. That part at least was easier than I feared.

Shimon's hand grew white on the hilt of his sword. "We will be considered among those who bowed to the Calf!"

Uriel shook his head. "I will walk hooded and cloaked. You may do the same. No one will know us. If any do, the faithful judge the prophets with favor. They will understand that we are seeking the cover of the crowd. But even if they do believe we bowed, it is worth the risk. As Lev said, it is the best way."

"I agree, Master Uriel, that we must reach Dotan," Shimon said, "but perhaps you should seek vision before you decide how. The Holy One may grant us guidance whether this path is really the—"

"It is not the time for vision."

"But why not? Couldn't—"

"I never use prophecy to question my heart. This is true now more than ever. We are being carried by a powerful stream of events—ascending now could make me deaf to the voice of my own heart."

"Which is what?"

"We were told to seek Ovadia—we must heed his advice. Traveling with those returning from Beit El is the safest way to get to Dotan."

Yonaton sighed in my ear, but Uriel wasn't done. "The only difficulty is the delay. It is essential that we get to Dotan quickly. Even now they may be forming plans to resist Izevel. They will need our guidance."

I sucked in my breath again.

The sound drew Uriel's attention. "Is there more, Lev?"

There was no need for Uriel to know the next part until we reached Dotan, but Yonaton was right—Uriel would know if I was hiding anything. "They are not seeking guidance, Master."

"Then the resistance has already begun? All the more so, they will need leadership."

"No, Master, they seek no leader."

"No leader? What then?"

My throat clenched, so tight I could barely answer. Uriel studied me as I sputtered. "There is to be no resistance."

"No resistance?"

"No, Master."

"Then why assemble in Dotan?"

I swallowed hard. I needed Ovadia here for this.

Uriel held my gaze. "To hide?"

"Yes, Master."

The prophet shook his head. "I am too old to bury myself in a cave. There is no point in dying hidden. Even being struck down by the sword is better than that; then the people might see the brutality of their so-called Queen and rise up against her."

Shimon stepped between the prophet and me. "Then what shall we do, Master?"

"You were right—I must seek vision. Lev, your *kinnor*." Uriel lowered himself to the stone ground.

I hesitated. Two oaths: one to serve Uriel, one to bring Uriel to Dotan. All that day I pondered what I would do should those two vows conflict. I felt my master's presence, firm on the floor. Was he set on resistance even if his death would only be a symbol? At the very least, Dotan would extend my master's life, whether he wanted that or not. And what if Ovadia was right? What if my master would prove pivotal once the war was over? I saw now why Ovadia made me swear; the oath's power tied me to his purpose. I swallowed again and made my choice. "No, Master."

Uriel raised an eyebrow.

I gripped my tunic in my fists. "You said it yourself, Master, now is not the time for vision. There must be others resisting Izevel, but the Holy One did not send us to them. We were sent to Ovadia—we should heed his advice."

I felt the heat of Shimon's glare—he would welcome another fight. But I didn't return his gaze, just focused on my master, still crouched on the ground.

The fire rose in Uriel's eyes, flashed, and then extinguished. "Perhaps you are correct, Lev, and I should heed Ovadia's word without pursuing further guidance." He stared down at his hands, limp between his knees. "And perhaps you are wrong."

The uncertainty in my master's voice unsettled me. Uriel reached out to Yonaton to help him to his feet. "You boys have traveled far today—I have demanded enough words for now. To sleep. Let us each seek the counsel of our dreams."

🪕 🪕 🪕

The exhaustion of my body overwhelmed the restlessness of my mind, and I quickly fell into a deep slumber. Riding Balaam, it took much of the day to travel from Shomron, but my dreams returned me there in an instant.

The throne room glowed. Oil lamps surrounded the Queen and ringed Yambalya as he knelt before her. It could have been daylight if not for the nearly full moon shining through the eastern windows.

"We killed their prophets and still they resist!" Izevel's voice was shrill.

"It takes time, my Queen, to uproot a people's connection to their god."

"It is Eliyahu. And this drought."

"The people know nothing of Eliyahu, my Queen, nor do they yet realize there's a drought. Once they do, they will have all the more reason to turn against their prophets."

"Or perhaps they will see Eliyahu as stronger than Baal?"

The priest glared at Izevel, eyes smoldering.

"What of the hunt? You claimed that your servants have never failed."

"They are Baal's servants, not mine. And they will succeed. I told you, I have seen Eliyahu's future in the stars."

Izevel sat back with a snarl. "Yet, for now, they still resist."

"Yes, my Queen, but I have a plan."

Her chest thrust forward, black hair shining like a mirror. "A plan? What will you do?"

"If her Majesty will be guided by me, then before the moon wanes, half the stubborn ones in Shomron will bend their knees before Baal."

Queen Izevel wet her lips, her face burning yellow in the lamp-light.

Pale light filled the cave when I woke the next morning. Shimon and Yonaton still slept beside me, but Uriel's mat lay empty. My eyes scanned the back of the cave—Balaam's saddlebags were gone. My heart leapt as I pulled my tunic over my head.

Yonaton stirred. "Where are you going?"

"Master Uriel's gone."

Yonaton sat up. "His sleeping mat is still here."

"The saddlebags are missing."

"So?"

Why didn't Yonaton understand? "So Master Uriel would take them only if he intended to travel."

"Without us?" Comprehension filled Yonaton's eyes, and he rose to his feet.

Uriel took the saddlebags and left without waking us, without even taking his cloak, which Yonaton used as a sleeping mat. Had he decided to journey alone so as not to endanger us? And if my master were headed for a place of safety, would he have left so many of his possessions behind? Uriel said last night that it was better to be struck down than hide. Was he riding now toward a final meeting with Izevel's soldiers? Would he even raise his staff to defend himself this time?

We ran down toward the spring where we left Balaam the night before. From a distance, we saw Uriel tying the saddlebags into place. We were not too late.

"Master," I called, "Don't go!"

Uriel stopped his work. "Lower your voice, Lev. If you are seen with me—"

"Master, Ovadia can protect you."

"I have given much thought to Ovadia's plan, Lev."

"Ovadia made me swear to bring you to Dotan."

Uriel lifted an eyebrow at this. "Ovadia is very devoted." He placed his hand on my shoulder. "As are you."

I saw the resignation in the prophet's eyes. "It's not just that, Master. The people need you alive."

"I can do little for the people hidden in a cave, Lev."

"But this war will not last forever."

"Not forever, no. But Eliyahu has not attacked with iron chariots. He brought a drought—it may be years until its end."

"You must live. Ovadia says you can save the people."

"Where is the salvation in hiding?"

"When it's over," I urged. "Ovadia said it might take an Eliyahu to defeat Izevel, but we will need you to heal the people."

Pity curled his eyebrows. "Ovadia is mistaken. He has wisdom, but is still young. He has not seen what I have."

"Which is what, Master?"

"The Holy One always creates the remedy before bringing the malady, though it remains hidden until its proper time. The nation will not be rebuilt by an old man crawling out of a hole. My time has passed."

Yonaton broke his silence. "My father taught me that the prophets never lose faith. How can you give up your life? Master?"

Uriel started at the word "master." Only Uriel's servants and disciples called him simply "master," rather than Master Uriel. I had been calling Uriel master since returning to him months earlier, but this was the first time that Yonaton had declared him so. Uriel peered into Yonaton's eyes. "Give up my life? Certainly not. My life may be the only thing I have left to offer the people, but I will not hand it over needlessly."

"But Master," Yonaton said, "You saddled Balaam and left your sleeping mat behind."

"That is because I must travel a road that he cannot follow." Uriel took Balaam's lead rope and placed it in Yonaton's hand. "And neither can you. I cannot be your master, Yonaton, not now. There are two pieces of bread and a skin of water in the saddlebag. It should be enough to get you home."

We both stared dumbly at Uriel. A chill passed through me as the meaning of my master's words struck my heart. *He was sending Yonaton away. Yona-*

ton, who ran an entire day's journey to warn us, who killed the soldier when I could not.

Yonaton's eyes dropped to the rope in his hand. "But I want to come with you."

"I know," Uriel's expression softened. "You have a strong heart. I promised you could stay with us as long as you could help. You have done much, but you can do no more. You are not yet of age and your family is waiting. Your path lies with them now."

Yonaton's eyes fell to the ground, and I knew that he would not raise his voice again in protest.

I turned away, not because I still considered his sorrow indecent, but in order to give him the privacy to grieve. I felt grateful for being allowed to continue, though it was Yonaton's path that led to safety.

Uriel scratched his donkey behind his remaining ear. "Take Balaam for me. He has been my faithful companion, but he can no longer accompany me."

The significance of his words hit me. "Does that mean we're going to Dotan, Master?"

"Yes, to the cave."

"But you said that Ovadia was mistaken?"

"Indeed, I believe so. But you were correct last night—I was told to seek Ovadia. There is a power at work beyond my own. I must follow the direction I was given."

Uriel shot a glance toward the sun breaking over the horizon, then back at Yonaton. "Tonight is Shabbat. You must leave now to be home before sunset."

Balaam inched forward and nuzzled Yonaton's hand. Yonaton scratched him behind the ear the way that Uriel had a moment earlier, then turned to me, his eyes spilling tears.

I spread my arms and embraced my friend, knowing that it might be for the last time.

"The Cave of Dotan," Yonaton whispered as he tightened his hold around me. "When I'm of age, I'll find you."

"Don't," I replied. "Stay and help your family. There's nothing you can do for us now."

"I...," but Yonaton stopped himself short, released me, and pulled the old donkey toward the road. As he had brought no belongings, there was no need for him to return to the cave. I stood watching until he was out of sight. It was only after he disappeared that it occurred to me—I would now have to deal with Shimon on my own.

That evening, before sunset, Shimon and I built the fire high so that it would keep on burning into Shabbat. Our gear lacked for any luxuries, except for the last drops from a wineskin which Uriel used to sanctify our meal. Reclining after we ate, Shimon glared at me across the glowing embers. "It seems that we're following you now."

"We're following Ovadia," I responded, "Just as the Holy One instructed Master Uriel."

"The Holy One sent us to Ovadia, but we're following his guidance because of you."

I didn't want to admit it, but Shimon was right. Uriel had said nothing since Yonaton's parting that morning, as if his remaining energy was sapped by the decision to hide. He stared at the flames, motionless. "You think I'm leading us astray?"

"What I think doesn't matter, the decision has been made. I will help in any way I can."

Shimon's sword leaned against the wall of the cave, the cedar tree emblem on its hilt reflecting the amber firelight. "Then perhaps you should leave the sword behind," I said.

"Why?"

"It's too easily recognized."

"It will be out of sight. Until needed."

I knew Shimon would refuse, just as I balked at Uriel's suggestion to leave my knife behind during the wedding. Yet, if Uriel had insisted, I would have yielded. But that was the prophet; in Shimon's eyes, I was a child in need of protection. If Yonaton had been with me, perhaps together we could have pressed him. But how could I persuade him on my own that his eagerness to fight was a danger to all of our lives?

Shimon answered my unspoken thoughts. "Even if your plan is to sneak past the Queen's soldiers, it's best to be prepared." I leaned in to argue, but he wasn't done. He braced his back against the wall of the cave and shot words sharper than arrows. "Had your father been so prepared, you might be dining with him now in Yehudah, rather than hiding in this cave."

The old prophet's eyes opened wide for the first time since Yonaton's departure, and shot up to meet Shimon's.

"What do you mean?" My gaze jumped from Shimon to my master. "You said that my father was murdered for preaching against the Golden Calf?"

"He was," Shimon answered. He had brought up my father to win the argument about the sword, but now he was stuck—we both knew that I would not let the matter drop until I heard the whole story. His posture, so defiant a moment earlier, deflated as he leaned in toward the fire. "It was during the Civil War. King Ahav's father, Omri, was locked in struggle for control of the northern kingdom with Tivni. The armies fought with arms, yes, but mainly the battle was over the hearts of the people. Omri considered the people's reactions to every step that he took, and many of them admired your father. Sending soldiers to his house would have driven many into the arms of Tivni."

"But then why kill him at all? Did he support Tivni?"

Shimon turned to Uriel for guidance—did he not know the answer, or was he questioning how much to reveal?

Uriel broke his silence. "Your father supported neither, but both saw him as an opponent."

"Because he was against the Calf?"

Uriel shook his head. "Because he was for real kingship. He dreamed of a reunification of the two kingdoms. To him, only a descendant of David had the right to rule."

I remembered my conversation with Uncle Menachem about the splitting of the Kingdom. Hadn't I also questioned how the Kingdom could split when the House of David was granted an everlasting throne?

Shimon sighed at Uriel's answer. "Omri aimed to catch your father in an act of rebellion."

"My father rebelled?"

"It was only the appearance of rebellion that mattered to Omri. He knew that Yochanan traveled to Yerushalayim to serve in the Temple for each of the three pilgrimage festivals. The roads were well guarded, but your father would lead anyone that he could convince to join him through the mountain passes. Everyone knew that the penalty for crossing was death. If Omri caught your father crossing, he could be rid of him without provoking the ire of the people."

"And my mother?" My voice trembled.

Uriel said, "Your father sought my counsel the week before he died. We agreed that it was best for you to be raised in the Kingdom of Yehudah, with his brethren. This is why both you and your mother were with him at the border when the King's soldiers fell upon him."

Shimon fidgeted. "I'm sorry, Lev. I shouldn't have spoken."

"No," I said, wiping my eyes with my palms. "I want to know. Please, tell me."

Shimon again searched Uriel for direction. The prophet nodded, giving permission to finally lift the cloak that had covered over my past for so many years. Shimon lost his gaze in the fire, staring into the burning coals rather than face me as he spoke. "I was sixteen, making my third journey to Yerushalayim with your father. I walked up front near your parents and heard their last conversation."

"What was it about?"

"You."

Something stirred inside me. I knew suddenly that this was the story that had haunted my dreams since age two. Yet, now that I was about to hear the truth, a strange thing happened. The locked box I had built to secure the memory all these years could no longer protect me, so it opened on its own. As Shimon spoke in his deliberate way, images unfolded in my mind, matching him phrase for phrase. It was as though I had returned to a crisp autumn day ten years before.

"Lev's cold," Mother said, *tightening the shawl that bound me to her back, drawing me closer to her body and shifting me a bit higher. Lavender wafted from beneath her headscarf.*

"This isn't a place to stop," Father replied, *his sharp eyes scanning the mountains on either side of the narrow path. He was older than I imagined, the sides of his beard fully gray, but he stood tall, almost at Uriel's height, with a muscular build.*

"How much farther?"

"See that ridge up ahead? Once we pass there we'll be out of the inheritance of Ephraim and into the territory of Binyamin. Then we'll be in the Kingdom of Yehudah."

"And then we'll be safe, Yochanan?"

"Omri's soldiers aren't supposed to cross the border. Still, I never feel safe until I get back on the road." Father *gazed into her teary eyes, so much like Aunt Leah's. She was much younger than he, and had never made the trip before.* "I'm sorry, Sarah, I don't mean to scare you."

"It's not that," she collected herself, *but her eyes were wet.* "I was just thinking that I might never return."

He sighed, peeking over his shoulder at the twenty men following him through the mountain pass. "You're going to be all right?"

I grabbed at Mother's ear, and she caressed my small hand in hers, turned her head back toward me, and drew my hand to her mouth to kiss it. "I just need to remember that I'm doing this for him."

Father continued to scan the surrounding hillsides, eventually spotting a lone soldier mounted on horseback. At first he laughed, for there was nothing a single soldier could do against twenty men. The soldier grinned back at my father, raised a ram's horn to his lips, and blew three short, soft blasts.

I stared at Shimon across the fire. "Soft blasts?"

"Yes, soft. It was the softness that alarmed your father. Blasts like that could never be heard all the way in Mitzpah, where the soldiers were garrisoned. As soon as he heard the blasts, he knew it was a trap."

Father turned back to his followers and screamed "Run!" He grabbed Mother's hand and pulled her along behind him, dragging her toward the safety of the border. The pounding of hoofbeats thundered behind us. I saw no horses, but the panic and rush set me squalling.

One of the men following behind screamed, "No, this way," and ran back into the Kingdom of Yisrael. The other followers hesitated, then followed their new leader, separating themselves from my family and the border.

Five soldiers broke into the gap between the two groups. Though Mother's shawl must have blocked my vision of the soldiers, somehow I could still see and hear them in my mind. So my dreams were not just memories. As Master Yosef said, they must contain a drop of prophecy as well.

The officer leading the small pack of soldiers reined in his steed and surveyed the situation. "The two of you, pursue the large group, but don't catch them. It's enough that the dread of King Omri fall upon them." Two soldiers stalked the group fleeing back into Yisrael, one banging his sword onto his shield, creating a racket that echoed in the mountain pass while keeping his horse at a relaxed trot. The officer addressed the remaining two soldiers. "You follow me," he said, kicking his horse after us.

Father still ran, moving as fast as he could while pulling us behind him. Turning back, he saw that the three soldiers would overtake him before the border. Pushing Mother ahead of him, he yelled, "You run! It's me they're after. Save yourself and Lev. Get him to my brother's family."

"Yochanan!" she called, standing frozen as her husband stepped with forced ease back to meet the horses.

"Run, Sarah! If I can follow, I will." He waited until my mother, with me on her back, began running again toward the border, then walked toward the approaching soldiers. Though armed, he did not reach for his knife. Perhaps if he came to them unarmed, not resisting, they would have mercy upon him.

The soldiers pulled up their horses, surrounding him, with their officer mounted squarely between Father and the border. "Why do you pursue me, Yoav?" Father asked.

"But he must have known why," I insisted.

"Of course he knew," Shimon replied. "But your mother was still running for the border with you on her back. The longer he could keep them talking, the greater chance she would have to reach safety."

"Where were you?"

"Hidden. I couldn't decide which group to follow, and found myself stuck in the middle. Just before the horses arrived, I ducked behind a boulder."

A fiery rage rose against him for not standing by my father's side. Then I remembered he was only sixteen, not much older than me. I myself ran away from Uriel when the Queen's soldiers came to take his life. The anger evaporated, and I said nothing, waiting for Shimon to continue.

"*You know what this is about, Yochanan,*" *Omri's officer said.* "*I've warned you myself against defying the King's orders.*"

"*You've already won, Yoav. You've scared away all those following me. Now it's just me, my wife, and my son, and we're leaving Yisrael, going to join my brethren in Yehudah.*" *As he spoke, his eyes flitted between Yoav and my mother, who had reached the ridge, passing safely into the Kingdom of Yehudah.*

"*Oh? Never to return?*" *Yoav sneered.*

"*I vow, if you let me go, I will never return.*"

A joyless smile spread across Yoav's face as he drew his sword. "*You lie!*" *The officer drove his weapon forward and Father dove onto the ground to avoid it. He rose to his feet clutching his knife in his hand. Lunging at Yoav, he drove the blade into his leg, just above the knee. Yoav screamed in pain and brought down the hilt of the sword on top of Father's head, knocking him to the ground.* "*You never know when to quit, Yochanan HaKohen. The rest of your tribe fled to Yehudah long ago. They knew it was over for them here, but you refused to go, always defying us. Now your time has come to an end.*"

"*I'm leaving, I swear. You don't need to kill me.*"

"Did my father intend to return?"

"He was moving you and your mother to a safer place, but he had no intention of abandoning the faithful of Yisrael. Though now that he was caught, I believe he would have given up on his mission in exchange for his life. I never knew him to break a vow."

My head fell forward into my hands, tears streaming through my fingers.

"I'm sorry, Lev. I've said too much."

My palms muffled my voice. "No, please. I want to hear."

My request met only silence.

I raised my face to Shimon's. "I beg of you…"

"Very well. Your father lay pleading for his life. Then Yoav spoke the words that will bring a chill to my heart until I enter the grave. '*I'm not going* to kill you,' he said. 'I'm going to let my soldiers kill you. I'm going to make sure the Kingdom of Yisrael never has to suffer you or your seed ever again.' And though by this time your mother had already crossed the border, he kicked his mount after her."

"And you did nothing? This whole time?" I couldn't keep accusation out of my voice.

"While Yoav was there, I didn't dare. I would have been throwing away my life."

I nodded, hating my judgment. Who was I to question Shimon's bravery? Yet, when he returned to the tale, I glared at him across the fire, and could not go back into the vision.

"When Yoav rode off, your father howled and chased after him. One of the soldiers slashed at his back, carving a deep gash across his shoulder blade. He collapsed and the soldier drew back his sword for the final blow, his arm trembling like a leaf. Perhaps in his heart he feared the Holy One's judgment. His fear gave me courage. I hurled a rock with all my might, striking him in the ear. His thrust missed its target, hitting the ground instead of your father's neck.

"But now I was exposed. The other rider turned on me—there was nowhere to run. My best cover was the boulder, so I stayed put. Yochanan staggered to his feet, somehow ready to fight. He couldn't beat a mounted soldier, so he attacked the horse, slashing its throat. It fell over sideways, crushing its rider's leg against the rocky ground. Your father left him struggling under his mount, and came to help me.

"I was unarmed, so I kept the boulder between myself and the soldier, forcing him to dismount to get at me. The only thing I had to fend off his attack was my sleeping mat, but reed doesn't hold up for long against iron. That's how I got these." Shimon pointed to his face and pulled back his sleeves to show more scars laddered up his arms. My anger with him disappeared now that he had joined the fight.

"When I saw Yochanan approaching, I screamed as loud as I could. The soldier thought I was yelling out in pain or fear, but I did it to cover your father's footsteps. I'll never forget the look of surprise on the soldier's face when your father planted that knife in his back."

My hand glided over my leg, feeling the bulge of the knife hidden under my tunic.

"By this time, Yochanan's tunic was soaked with blood and he wobbled on his feet. He said to me, 'Come…Sarah and Lev.' I seized the soldier's sword and mounted his horse, pulling your father up behind me."

Shimon's bottom lip trembled. He steadied it between his teeth.

"Go on," Uriel whispered. "He should know this part as well."

Shimon swallowed the bitter taste in his mouth. "We had not ridden far when Uriel appeared before us on the trail. He held you screaming in his arms."

I turned to my master. "You were there?"

"I also traveled to Yerushalayim for the festivals, but I knew my way, I did not need your father's guidance." Uriel's eyes never left the fire. "I was ahead on the path when the ram's horn sounded. I turned back when I heard it. After that, I followed the sound of your cries."

"Will you continue the tale?" Shimon asked.

"No, you should. Now that you've started, he needs to hear it all."

Shimon nodded. "Your father slipped off the horse and took you in his arms—he could barely hold you, he was already so weak. We heard hoofbeats and Yoav appeared, bearing down on us with his sword drawn. Uriel stepped in front of your father, and Yoav pulled back to avoid trampling him.

So this was it—the reason that I recognized Uriel that first day, the reason I had felt so on edge when I saw him. He must have visited my nightmares for years. The vision tugged at my mind again, drawing me back in.

"*Stand aside,*" Yoav screamed.

"*I'm going where he's going,*" Uriel replied. "*Won't you kill me as well?*"

"*King Omri grants you passage, but I have my duty.*"

"*And I have mine,*" Uriel said, still standing between Yoav and my father, his staff firmly planted on the ground before him. "*I have two messages, one for you and one for your master.*"

Yoav's eyes jumped from Uriel to my father to Shimon, who still sat on horseback, sword drawn, then back to Uriel. Outnumbered, Yoav sheathed his sword. "Very well, navi. Give me my master's first."

"*In two years' time Omri will be victorious. Should he turn away from the path of Yeravaum, opening the road and purging idolatry from the land, then his will be an everlasting kingdom. Otherwise, his will be as the kingdoms of Yeravaum and Bassa, and dogs will lick the blood of his children.*"

Yoav's face was set like stone. "And the message for me?"

"*Ride home to your wife, for the child comes.*"

"*But it is not yet time!*" *Yoav's face faltered. He took a deep breath and straightened on his mount. "It is no matter. The child will come with or without me. I cannot leave my post.*"

"*The child you will never know, and your wife is already beyond your help. I am offering you a chance to say goodbye.*"

Yoav tensed in his saddle. "Goodbye?"

"Goodbye." Uriel drew himself up to his full height, eyes blazing and voice thundering like Eliyahu's in Yericho. "As you judged, so are you found wanting. You struck down Yochanan's wife and son. The lives of your wife and unborn son are forfeit in turn."

"A son?" Yoav beheld me, wailing helplessly in Father's arms. "But Yochanan's son lives!"

"Yes, he lives, but not from your mercy—you left him to die!" Father crumpled to his knees, almost dropping me as he fell. Uriel lifted me from his arms.

Yoav dropped his eyes to the ground. "What if I have mercy on him now?"

"That is not mercy, it is desperation. You think only of yourself, not the child."

"Then she will die? And my son?"

"So it will be."

Yoav studied Father's dying body, his blood raining onto the dry ground. "And what of me? Is my life forfeit for Yochanan's?"

"Your future is in your own hands. You are a man of strength. Turn your strength inward, conquer your anger, and live."

"And if I don't?"

"Then your greatest act of valor will be your last. King Tivni will die by your sword, but you will fall as well."

"Quill," Father said, his voice raspy. All eyes fell upon the kohen, kneeling in a puddle of his own blood. Uriel retrieved a quill and a scrap of parchment from Balaam's saddlebag, and steadied Father's hand as well as he could, while Father dipped the quill into the ready pool of red dye at his feet and wrote. "Take," he gasped, handing the scrap of parchment back to Uriel.

Uriel received the scrap and turned back to Yoav. "Yochanan is dying. Let me take his son to his brethren in Yehudah."

Yoav lifted his eyes to Uriel, then turned at the sound of approaching horses. The two soldiers that he had sent after Father's followers came to a stop behind him. Yoav straightened himself and faced Uriel, the tone of authority returning to his voice. "I have my duty. King Omri allows you to pass, but no one else."

"Does your duty include killing children, or may he return to his family in Yisrael?"

Yoav eyed the two soldiers behind him, then turned back to the prophet. "King Omri is just. He does not desire the blood of children. He may return."

"Shimon, take the child," Uriel said, advancing on Shimon, still on horseback. Then dropping his voice so that Shimon had to bend down to hear him, he said, "Take him to his uncle in Levonah, Menachem ben Yitzchak." But Uriel did not hand me to

Shimon, he carried me back to Father. "It is time to say goodbye to your child, Yochanan Hakohen."

I reached out. Father reached back, not to take me, but to lay his strong hands upon my head. Our eyes met as he blessed me for the last time. He kissed me on the forehead, leaving a small, crimson mark. At the same time, Uriel, whose body shielded me from the three soldiers, tucked the parchment into my garments.

I threw my arms around Father's neck, not wanting to let go. Even with Uriel still supporting me, my weight was too much for the dying man. The pressure on his chest brought on heaving coughs, each one forcing his eyes closed. "Take him. Don't let him see me die."

Uriel tugged, but I screamed, refusing to release my grip on Father's neck, dragging him forward. Uriel pulled my hands apart and drew me away, cradling me up to Shimon. Shimon placed me straddled on the horse in front of him, but struggled to keep me there as I writhed and screamed, reaching out for Father. "Hold him tighter," Uriel said. Shimon wrapped a quivering arm around me, pulling me closer into his body, and pinned my arms to my side. "Now ride. He will calm down once we're out of sight."

"Wait!" Father called, holding out his knife. "Take this. It is his birthright."

Uriel passed the knife up to Shimon. I pried one of my arms free and grabbed for it, but Shimon held it out of reach and tucked it into his belt. With a last command from Uriel to "Go!" Shimon kicked the horse, handling the reins in his left hand, my protesting body with his right.

Yoav turned to his two soldiers. "I'm going to follow him, make sure he doesn't make another try for the border. Wait here until Yochanan dies."

"And Uriel?" one of the soldiers asked.

"King Omri grants the prophets leave to go where they will." Yoav kicked his horse to pursue Shimon, but as soon as he was out of sight of the others, he turned his horse and galloped toward Mitzpah.

I scowled, feeling no sympathy for my parents' murderer. "He got what he deserved."

Uriel's cheeks were lined with wet tracks, though tears no longer flowed. "What he deserved? Perhaps. But could any of us survive in a world where we receive that which we deserve?"

"Wouldn't that be justice?"

"Yes, it would. But when the Holy One created the world in strict justice, it could not stand. Where only judgment reigns, creation crumbles."

"So Yoav lived because there is no justice?"

"There is justice, but tempered with mercy. We stand on the merit of what could be, and are not judged solely by what is."

My fists clenched. "He killed my parents."

"Indeed, and I cursed him for it."

"So where was your mercy then?"

Shimon flinched at the question. This was not the way to address my master, but at the moment I didn't care.

Uriel held out his hands to me. "You must understand, we are all vessels for the light of the Holy One. As we expand mercy in ourselves, it expands in the world. So too the opposite. As we judge, judgment increases in the world, and we are often the first to be searched out by its strictures." Uriel dropped his hands and turned back to the fire.

The blaze had collapsed into a pile of glowing embers. In the silence, Uriel's words held me. During Shimon's tale, I had been focused on myself, hardly noticing the prophet's pain. I assumed that Uriel cried for my father, his lost friend. But in the silence that followed, I began to understand.

Ovadia said two nights earlier that it was essential to rescue Uriel. Not because of what he could do, but because of what he had been through—because of what he had become. Had this been the transformation? Had Uriel grown from a vessel of strict judgment to mercy? Was this the reason that he, alone among the prophets, could heal a nation shattered by Eliyahu's judgment?

I remembered Uriel's words from earlier that week. "A curse brings pain without regard to who receives it. It falls upon the guilty and the innocent alike. Even the one who invokes the curse is not spared its destruction."

Back at Shiloh, sitting with Zim the morning after the festival, I was shocked to learn that Uriel's son served the Golden Calf that his father despised. Didn't Zim say he left his father's path ten years ago, exactly when I lost my parents?

"Master?" I trembled. "When you cursed Yoav, were you judged as well?"

The prophet's composure broke as a sob shook his chest. "Indeed." His head dropped between his knees and he shook with grief.

Shimon's mouth stood agape—he must not have known this part of the story.

"At the same time that Yoav's wife died, my wife left the world as well. By then, I had reached Yerushalayim and did not know until I returned weeks later. My son was forced to bury his mother alone."

Comprehension dawned on Shimon's face. "That is why he left the Way and turned toward the Calf?"

"So he says. As you know, I spent my life traveling among the people. I was often away, and he resented it. He said that burying his mother alone was the final act that compelled him to leave my path. But even he doesn't know the full truth, that it was my curse that drove him from me."

"But, Master," I said, "You are not from the family of priests that Yeravaum appointed to replace the *kohanim*, are you?"

Uriel shook his head.

Shimon explained, "This was during the Civil War. Remember what I told you about King Omri. He deliberated on the people's reaction to each of his decisions. Having the son of the great prophet as his priest would increase his stature in the eyes of the nation and help him achieve the throne. When Omri learned that Master Uriel's son Gershon had separated from his father, he moved quickly to offer him the position, before King Tivni could win his loyalty."

The prophet's wail echoed from between his knees. "Three families destroyed on a single day!"

Hillel said: Do not believe in yourself until the day you die.

Pirkei Avot 2:5

The Final Journey

The full moon blazed like a beacon in the western sky when we set out from the cave. Three days had passed in silence, each of us lost in contemplation in some corner of the small cave. For me, the time was spent digesting Shimon's tale, dwelling on the panic etched on my parents' faces, the eerie sound of their voices, and the image of their brutal deaths—details I had never before been able to recall. The rebound of Uriel's curse upon his own family struck Shimon harder than I would have imagined. He no longer handled or even examined the captured sword while we remained in the cave. Nevertheless, when it was time to depart the cave for our journey toward Dotan, he retrieved the sword and sheathed it around his waist.

Once on the road, we would just be pilgrims traveling home from the festival, but in the hills we were potential prey. We trekked under cover of night to limit the risk of detection, but the cloudless sky and the moon's silvery brilliance exposed us to prying eyes in any case. There was nothing we could do about that: the festival always fell at the full moon. Uriel scanned the hilltops as we walked. I likewise searched the dark horizon for the outline of a soldier, but saw nothing.

We stopped well before dawn, hiding a stone's throw from the road in a thick clump of bushes. I lay down, my eyes heavy with drowsiness, my fears of discovery insufficient to hold off sleep.

A steady rumbling in my ear woke me, sounding like the echo of a thunderclap off distant hills. I opened my eyes to sunbeams filtering through the thick branches above. "What's that noise?"

"Horses," Uriel replied. "Thirty at least, from the sound of it, being driven hard. The King and his escort."

"Ovadia will be with them?"

"I expect so. You may go back to sleep, we still have a long wait."

I sat up and pulled on my tunic. Anticipation had set in; sleep was no longer an option. The rumbling grew louder until the troop of horses thundered past, their dark shapes barely visible through gaps in the leaves.

Other horsemen followed the King's escort, riding past in ones and twos; then those on donkeys reached us, ambling past in small groups. The sun hung mid-sky when the first walkers appeared, at first just a thin stream of hardy farmers, in a hurry to return to their fields. Before long, the road was thick with travelers, gathered in groups that passed by in waves, ranging from boys newly of age to old men, talking and laughing as they went.

Uriel finally broke our silence. "It is time."

I crept out of the bushes, then circled around and sat beneath a tree on the roadside, resting my back against its trunk. A group of men passed, and when the last of them disappeared, leaving the road in front of me empty, I ran one hand over the strings of my *kinnor*.

Uriel and Shimon appeared beside me. Small groups of walkers flowed by as we ate our midday meal, appearing like three travelers stopping for a rest. When a large group of men appeared down the road, Uriel said, "We will let them pass, then join in from behind."

The sun beat down upon us once we left the shade of the tree. As we fell into stride with the group, my hair stuck to my forehead and sweat pooled beneath the rolled up sheepskin slung over my back. Images of the cool spring near my uncle's house danced in my head, but Levonah was behind us on the road—ahead lay Shomron.

We mingled in at the back of the crowd, moving past the very rear where we might stand out. My eyes flickered to the hilltops above the road, occasionally picking out a soldier stationed on a peak, but my breath remained steady. These were no longer the soldiers we feared—from above they would see nothing strange in this throng returning from Beit El.

The masses moving north on the road thinned throughout the day as men turned off toward home. In the late afternoon, we rounded a bend and the road dropped into a long decline. We were close to Shomron now, the destination of most of those still walking. We approached a cluster of men stopped ahead, just before the shade of a large carob tree.

"What's going on up there?" Shimon asked.

Uriel stood to his full height. "Soldiers."

"Yisraelite or foreigners?"

"Foreigners."

I glanced at Shimon, and my heart thumped in my chest. This was the encounter I was dreading. Would he seek conflict with the Queen's soldiers? I was relieved to see no hunger for battle in his face. His expression was calm, almost serene. Learning of Uriel's curse rebounding upon himself seemed to have changed Shimon—as if for ten years he had hungered to hold the prophet's power to curse, and only now realized its cost. He said, "A roadblock. Should we turn off?"

Uriel nodded toward the sides of the road. "They have soldiers stationed along the hillsides. They will be watching for anyone trying to avoid them. We are better off walking through."

I followed my master's gesture. At first I didn't spot them—they were not like the lookouts sitting mounted on the hilltops. These watchers were further down, in the shadows, where they could see without being seen.

Shimon's body tensed as he studied the soldiers bordering the roadside, and his eyes lost their quiet. His hand slipped under his cloak to the hilt of his sword.

I inched closer to him and whispered, "Remember, Master Uriel must reach Dotan."

Shimon regarded his hand, appearing surprised to find it grasping the sword, as if his battle-hungry instincts had acted of their own accord. He released the hilt and placed his hand on my shoulder instead. "I know the plan."

We drew closer to the roadblock. Uriel said, "There's a priest as well."

"What?" Shimon asked.

"A priest of the Baal. Under the tree."

I craned my neck to see. Sure enough, I caught a glimpse of violet robes in the shade of the carob tree. One soldier stood on each side of the road, while a third blocked the path in front of the waiting men, forcing them to pass through the shade one at a time. A man in a gray cloak was waved through.

He stepped under the tree, approached the priest, then dropped to his knees and pressed his forehead to the ground.

"Clever," Uriel said.

"What's clever, Master?"

"Izevel is most powerful in Shomron, but many are opposed to her, even there. So she waited until all the men of the city left for the festival, then placed a Baal on their path home. Now she can see who will bow and who will resist."

I peered under the tree, trying to glimpse the statue. "We must get through, Master."

"I will not bow before the Baal."

"Even to save your life?" Yet, the words rung hollow, Uriel placed too little value on his life. I changed tactics, appealing to his sense of mercy instead. "Even to save my life?" This too failed.

"Some things are more precious than life, Lev. We are commanded to choose death rather than bow to strange gods. Even you must be willing to die rather than bow."

Shimon's hand sought the hilt of his sword, not absentmindedly as before, but with the same blazing intensity in his eyes as when he first leapt out of the trees to save us the week before. "You see, Lev, I was right to prepare for battle."

"There are three soldiers ahead and at least five more on the hillsides—you can't fight them all!"

"Shimshon killed a thousand in a single battle. You heard Master Uriel, Lev. The spirit I received was the same as Shimshon's."

"You don't know if you'll merit that power again."

"No, I don't. But even if I don't, I won't be fighting alone."

"There's not much Uriel or I could do against all these soldiers."

"It's not just the three of us. It's easy to scare the people one at a time, but in their arrogance they've become reckless. The crowd is moving through too slowly. There are fifty men waiting and more coming up behind us. If we resist, we will draw much support—especially if it's known that we are led by a prophet."

I wanted to believe him, but recalled the fear on the faces of farmers just like these at the wedding. "But these men aren't armed. They will run at the first sight of blood."

Uriel shook his head. "It matters not if they are armed. Izevel is seeking to strengthen her support, not to spark a rebellion. Her soldiers will not fight so many, even if they could."

My mind raced. The Queen ordered her soldiers to hunt down every prophet in the land. Perhaps Uriel could lead the crowd through the road-block without bloodshed, but the soldiers were sure to notice that this was no ordinary man at their head. They were sure to follow him, and call others to their aid. Any violence would mean abandoning the plan, and I had sworn to deliver my master safely to Dotan.

We were close enough now to see the statue, a larger version of the one now resting in my uncle's house. Cast in bronze, its long helmet ascending toward the sky, a jagged sword raised, ready to strike, it stood perched on a wooden pedestal beneath the tree. Another farmer stepped forward, and he too bowed before the Baal. A thought occurred to me. "Master, if Izevel is afraid of a rebellion, then her soldiers cannot be killing all those who refuse to bow, can they?"

Uriel shook his head. "No, Lev, you must be correct. There are still too many in Yisrael, even in Shomron, that would refuse."

"So what happens to them? Are they allowed to pass?"

"Let us watch. There are fifty or more who still stand before us—I would expect at least ten to refuse."

One after another the soldiers waved the men forward. Some bowed quickly, falling to their knees and touching their foreheads to the ground, others hesitated, then bent at the waist, like the men in Yericho bowing before the King. Yet, each and every one of them humbled himself in some way before passing through the shade of the carob tree. The soldiers on the sides of the road barely watched as the travelers passed through.

Hardly ten men now stood between us and the tree, though the newcomers behind us continued to maintain the crowd's size. Shimon's eyes darted back and forth between Uriel and the soldiers. "If we're going to fight, we need to warn the men. Are we agreed?"

Shimon was right. If we were going to act, it must be now. My throat constricted and sweat ran down my forehead. I trusted Uriel's instincts—there was no sign that the soldiers were killing those who refused to bow. If they were, where were the bodies? But no one refused, so I couldn't know for sure. My vow to Ovadia rang in my mind. There was only one chance to prevent the violence that would ruin our plan.

"I'll go."

"What?" Shimon started.

"I'll go to the head of the line. I'll refuse to bow. If they let me through, you follow with Uriel. If they…if not, then fight."

"Wait, Lev, I don't think—"

But I didn't wait to hear what Shimon thought. My small size allowed me to slip easily through the crowd. A few men peered at me in annoyance—probably impatient to get through the roadblock and make it home—but perhaps because of my youth, no one stopped me.

The soldier at the front put out his arm, blocking me from advancing until the man under the tree passed. Like all the others, he too bowed down before the Baal.

The soldier's arm dropped, and I stepped forward.

My eyes were on the priest, but my thoughts were on the soldiers.

The priest approached. "Bow. Then go on."

I stood silent and still, holding my arms tight so they wouldn't tremble.

The priest insisted, "You bow. Do it now, then go."

I held my breath steady, stared back at the priest, but didn't move.

The priest moved closer. "You not bow? Baal angry. Curse the rain."

My mouth filled with a metallic tang. One knee trembled and I dug my toe into the dirt to still it. One of the soldiers turned to watch me now. But still I didn't move.

The priest leaned in and spoke in a whisper. "Don't bow. Just pick up and go." He rotated his body, positioning himself between me and the waiting crowd, at the same time dropping a copper piece on the ground before the statue.

A laugh bubbled up from my belly—I swallowed it back with effort. Uriel was right; not all the men ahead of us were willing to bow. That's why they were only allowed through one at a time. Most men, seeing those ahead of them bow, would bow as well. Those who refused just had to pick a piece of copper off the ground. Those behind—who were not watching closely enough to see the precious metal—would think they were bowing from the waist, just enough to humble themselves.

"Pick up. You keep copper."

Questions flashed through my mind as I peered at the shiny metal. Hardly anyone among the men returning from the festival of the Golden Calf would refuse to pick up the copper. But what about those who refused to give even the impression of bowing? Was that the real point of the roadblock? The Queen's soldiers had already attacked the gathering places of the prophets. Now that the faithful were scattered, there was no way to distinguish them from the rest of the people. Was the roadblock intended to weed out the most devout? To find the prophets and disciples hidden among the commoners?

What about Shimon and Uriel? Would they pick up the copper to save their lives?

One of the soldiers stepped in toward me—I had delayed for too long. I could pick up the metal and get past the Baal, but needed to do it in a way that Shimon and Uriel would realize I wasn't bowing. I stepped to the side, then bent down and picked up the copper. Anyone watching closely would see that I wasn't even facing the Baal, but it was enough—the priest waved me through.

Once out of the shade of the carob tree, I turned around to watch. Neither the soldiers nor the priest paid me any mind—to them, I was just a boy waiting for his father to pass through.

The next man scowled at me as he bowed, annoyed at me for jumping ahead of him and then passing so slowly.

Easy as it was to pass through the roadblock, would Shimon still refuse? Shimon objected to even walking among those returning from Beit El—would he be willing to give the impression that he'd bowed to the Baal? If it was just his life, I was certain that he would rather fight than pick up the copper. But would he do it to protect Uriel? I caught Shimon's eye and gave him the slightest of nods, the most communication I could risk with the soldiers so close. But Shimon just glared back, his eyes resolute.

Three more men passed through the roadblock, two dropping quickly to the ground, the third bending to pick up the offered metal. Shimon drifted ahead of Uriel, placing several men between them. When he reached the front of the line, my hands clenched. A farmer under the carob tree pressed his head to the ground, begging loudly for Baal not to withhold the rains. When he rose, Shimon stepped forward.

The soldier on the far side of the road looked up as Shimon approached— his scars distinguished him from the crowd even without the fresh wounds. The Tzidonian's nostrils flared as if smelling him for blood. Four of his comrades had failed to return from duty the week before. Was he on the lookout for their killer?

Shimon stepped up to the priest.

"You bow. Then go on."

Shimon's voice was calm, yet pitched to carry. "The people of Yisrael do not bow to the Baal."

A murmur rose from the edge of the waiting pack. One of the soldiers left his post at the side of the road and stepped into the circle of shade under the tree. His hand rested on the hilt of his sword, and black dots marched in a tight pattern across his cheeks, becoming jagged lines at his throat before disappearing into his tunic. I'd heard rumors of the coastal people's tattoos, but had never seen them before. The ink gave his face a bestial look.

Shimon met the soldier's gaze.

With a rustle of violet robes, the priest waived the soldier back. He retreated, but kept his eyes on Shimon. The priest leaned close and whispered, dropping a piece of copper to the ground. Shimon peered at the metal, but did not move.

I wanted to scream at him to take it. I bit my lower lip until I tasted blood. How stupid I had been. An old man and a boy would have passed through easily. Shimon had no desire to hide. He had accompanied us only to help Uriel reach safety. And yet with his scarred face and unyielding nature, he was our greatest danger. Once Uriel had agreed to join the crowd returning from Beit El, the time had come to part ways. I should have confronted him, even without Yonaton. What would happen to my master if Shimon refused?

The soldier stepped forward once more, this time loosening his sword in its sheath. The priest again waved him away, but the soldier retreated just halfway. The priest pulled another piece of metal from his pocket, this time silver. He didn't just drop the silver on the ground, but rolled it to where Shimon could pick it up without even bending in the Baal's direction.

I tried to catch his eye, but Shimon glared at the idol. *Don't look at the statue Shimon. Just pick up the silver and move on.*

Shimon turned from the Baal. For a moment, he locked eyes with the soldier, whose sword was now half drawn. Then he broke eye contact and bent down to pick up the silver.

As Shimon bent over, his cloak parted in front. The hilt of his sword peeked out between the fabric, revealing the cedar tree emblem engraved on the handle. The priest was no longer watching, but the tattooed soldier was.

The soldier leapt forward, drawing his sword in a smooth motion. Shimon grabbed for his own weapon, but in his bent over position his enemy was faster. The sword flashed in an executioner's cut. Shimon threw out his empty left hand to block the blow, but bone is no match for metal. His arm shattered, just like the soldier's sword in our last battle. The tattooed soldier aimed another blow and Shimon fell limp to the ground.

My teeth sliced my lip—I must not scream. I swallowed to hold back the tears. Shimon was beyond my help. I must save my master.

The priest ran forward, screaming in his guttural tongue. He slapped the soldier's face and gestured wildly at the men waiting to get through the roadblock. But he was no longer in charge.

The tattooed soldier called to his comrades lining the hillsides flanking the road. They were eight in all, and the tattooed one seemed to be their leader.

He pointed to Shimon's body, and another soldier ran forward, grabbed Shimon's arms, and dragged him to the side of the road.

They may have been heavily outnumbered, but the Tzidonians were the only ones armed. They bunched together under the carob tree, backs to the trunk, ready to defend themselves.

Though shock and anger flashed across the faces of the Yisraelite men, their fear prevailed. No outcry cut through the stillness of the rolling hills at Shimon's murder; no one advanced to attack. The only serene face was Uriel's.

Seeing that they were unchallenged, the soldiers broke their defensive position. The tattooed soldier pushed the priest back toward the Baal. Then he screamed at the man in front of the line, "Come. You bow now!"

The man dropped to the ground, his eyes avoiding the blood stained earth. The priest reasserted himself, waving the soldiers back to their positions. One soldier returned to the front of the crowd, the others remained clumped under the carob tree.

Another man stepped forward. Uriel stood next in line.

This farmer groveled in the dirt before the Baal. A soldier grew impatient and kicked his hip. The farmer didn't need a second urging to move on; he jumped to his feet and ran toward the open road. Uriel approached.

The prophet stepped up to the priest.

"You bow. Then go on."

Uriel's face had none of Shimon's defiance—it was radiant, his eyes distant, heedless of the priest.

The priest stepped closer to whisper in Uriel's ear, and dropped a copper to the ground.

The smile on Uriel's face stretched as he bent his head forward. My heart leapt—he was bending down to pick up the copper! But Uriel merely brought his chin to his chest and held it there.

At first I didn't understand what my master was doing. I could barely contain the urge to scream, *Take it! Take it!*

Then I understood.

The prophet would neither bow nor pick up the copper. He wouldn't fight or resist. He was offering the back of his neck to the sword. Uriel would give up his life quietly, a martyr before a mass of witnesses. His death would be a symbol of the brutality of the Baal and the Queen. Just as he desired.

I squeezed my eyes shut. Why hadn't I let Shimon fight? He was already armed and surrounded by fifty men. The priest's reaction showed that the soldiers' presence was intended to evoke fear, not to kill. Would they have melted away before an organized resistance?

And Shimon may have received the Divine spirit again—then nothing could have stood before him. But now he lay dead on the side of the road, because he listened to me, while Uriel stood with his neck exposed, awaiting a similar fate.

The tattooed soldier remained by his post at the side of the road, but had still not sheathed his sword. Another group of pilgrims reached the roadblock, swelling the number of Yisraelites observing the scene to more than sixty men.

I reached under my tunic and gripped the handle of my father's knife. *If I fight, will I receive the same spirit Shimon had? If I'm determined to succeed, will the Holy One give me the strength to battle these soldiers?*

The tattooed soldier advanced toward Uriel. The priest stepped between them, pointing back toward the side of the road. The soldier pushed him out of the way.

I loosened my blade in its sheath, my fingers whitening on the hilt. If I was going to act, the time was now.

A surge of energy tingled through my muscles. As I drew the blade from under my tunic, Zim's voice rose in my heart. "Remember, if you believe it, it's true."

The soldier raised his sword above Uriel.

I sheathed my knife and ran forward screaming, "Grandfather, Grandfather!"

The soldier's arm stopped.

I grabbed Uriel's hand, placing myself between my master and the sword.

"He's not right in the head," I begged the soldier, loud enough for all the Yisraelite men to hear.

A shadow of doubt dimmed the tattooed soldier's eyes.

"He'd bow to your sandal if you wanted him to, but we'd never get him up off the ground."

"He bow." The soldier swept his arm across the waiting crowd. "They all bow."

"He's just an old man," I insisted.

Murmurs of protest rose from the waiting men. They watched Shimon die, but were now starting to rouse themselves. A tall farmer at the front of the line shoved his chest against the arm of the soldier holding him back. "Let the old man go through!"

I turned to the priest. "Could my grandfather have one of those pieces of copper? It would mean so much to him."

The priest stepped forward, pushing the tattooed soldier back. "Go," he said. "Don't bow, just go." The priest thrust a piece of copper into my hand and pushed the two of us through.

Uriel allowed me to guide him out of the shade of the carob tree, past the remaining soldiers. The radiance departed from his face. He said nothing as we fled, just walked on in silence.

As the roadblock shrank into the distance behind us, the reality of our situation settled in. My success sealed our fate: we were heading into hiding. We would live in the darkness of the cave until redemption came.

Shimon's scarred face hung above me. He had saved my life, stood by my father when no one else had, and followed me to his death. Had I been wrong to fight him? Or if I had given in, would Uriel and I now lie beside him?

And how many others suffered a similar fate? Tzadok was gone, Shimon was gone. The enemy had attacked the known gathering places of the prophets. Had they struck Beit El? It was one thing to kill prophets in the remote wilderness, but had they become so bold that they would strike in the middle of that city? What about Yosef and Raphael? Were they even still alive?

I thought about Eliyahu—pursued more than any of us. I had never seen drought myself, but the elders of Levonah spoke of its terrible suffering. How many dry seasons would it take for the people to stand up to the tyranny of Queen Izevel?

Then Dahlia's face rose in my mind, tight russet curls clustered around her smiling hazel eyes. Would she already be married by the time I came out of hiding, those curls forever tucked under a scarf in the way of married women?

As the sky darkened, the number of people on the road continued to thin. The nearly full moon rose above the horizon just as we reached the hills ringing Shomron. Still silent, my master pointed toward a small path that turned off the road, winding through a sloping valley. We pressed on through fields and clumps of trees until the moon was directly overhead and we came to an orchard on a steeply terraced hillside. Saplings leaned at odd angles and the scent of freshly dug soil hung in the air. The hillside rose to a cliff above us.

The trail swung to the right at the base of the hill, and Uriel paused before the first terrace. I couldn't see any markings, but my master found what he was searching for. He climbed upward, feet crunching in the dried earth. We wove back and forth across the terraces, climbing steadily higher, until we reached an old olive tree, its roots wrapped around a boulder at the base of a cliff. Uriel stepped behind it, disappearing from view. I followed, slipping sideways through a crack in the cliff wall.

Darkness engulfed us. I crept forward, my fingers brushing the stone walls that squeezed steadily inward. Without warning I stumbled, nearly falling. The echo of my footsteps reverberated in an open space.

A flame emerged in the distance. It grew from an orange glow to a yellow point, revealing itself as a lamp. A man with a short gray beard smiled when he saw Uriel, placing one finger to his lips. The lamp illuminated a three-way junction. The lamp-bearer turned to the right and we followed.

We descended a broad passageway, the floor smooth underfoot. Every now and then I felt a draft from the side as we passed openings in the darkness. Once I heard snoring and once the sound of deep and slow chanting. I paused to listen to the complex rhythm until our guide waved me forward.

I quickly lost track of direction. I had never been in so intricate a cave before, with so many caverns and passageways. Ovadia was fortunate to find such a place to hide the prophets. Was this another one of those caves carved out in the time of Gidon?

Our guide stepped into an empty chamber, and Uriel had to duck to avoid striking his head on the cavern roof. The lamp bearer touched the flame of his lamp to another that sat in a niche cut into the wall, igniting it. Then he bowed to Uriel and stepped back into the darkness.

I surveyed the chamber in the wavering light: my new home. The events of a week had uprooted everything I knew. There would be no sunshine in the cave, no Yonaton, no Dahlia. Yet I was still alive, which was more than could be said for Shimon or Tzadok.

Drained from the journey, I laid out my sleeping mat. Uriel knelt down in front of the lamp, contemplating the flame with unblinking eyes.

Despite my exhaustion, I dared to break the silence we had maintained since the roadblock. "What do you see, Master?"

"All things above are reflected below. So it is with the lamp of darkness, reflected in the flame."

"You see darkness in the flame?"

"Look closely at the center. Darkness surrounds the wick, consuming it, emitting no light."

I moved closer, examining the flame as my master spoke.

"That is the shadow of the lamp of darkness. Beneath the blackness is a thin layer of sapphire, the color of the Throne of Glory, on which the Holy One sits. The darkness appears greater than the blue, but does not dim its brilliance."

The flame filled my vision. At first the blue jumped and faded, but as I concentrated, it grew in depth and radiance. "It's the other way around. The darkness makes the blue seem even brighter."

"Indeed. So it is with our world. No amount of darkness can destroy the light, no matter how deep the darkness grows."

Uriel sighed. "The order of the world has flipped. Once, light dwelled above and shadows filled the caves. Now darkness will reign over the land and light will retreat underground."

My master turned away from the lamp to face me, the fire reflected in his bright eyes. "It appears, Lev ben Yochanan HaKohen, that we have the time to begin your education after all."

Dear Reader,

As an avid reader myself, I treasure the feeling of connection with an author that I get from reading a book. But now that I'm an author, I'm struck by the one-sided nature of that relationship: all readers get a glimpse into the mind of the author, but rarely does the author hear back from the readers. With your help, I'd like to rectify this.

The subject matter of this book is a real passion of mine. In fact, it was the vision of one day being able to share this passion with readers such as yourself that drove me through the six years of writing The Lamp of Darkness.

I'd love it if you would take a moment and share a bit of yourself with me as well. I'm so curious to learn who my readers are, where they live, what they do, and what their passions are. I'm also constantly trying to improve my writing, so it would be a great help to me to know what you liked about the book and what you didn't. If you're really willing to engage, please include a picture of yourself holding the book (or your digital device loaded to the book cover). Just note, I intend to post some pictures online, so let me know if you want yours private (and nothing explicit please). My personal email is Dave@ TheAgeofProphecy.com, and it's my aim to respond to all who contact me.

Personally, when curious about a new book, the first thing I do is check out reader reviews, normally on Amazon and/or Goodreads. Until recently, I almost never left reviews myself, but then I realized that the more I partici-pate, the more I can help other readers, and the better the entire system works. Before you move on, please take a moment to leave a review online so that others can benefit from your insights as well.

It has been a privilege to share this journey with you.

Dave Mason

P.S. Those of you hungry for more will find an ever-growing library of resources at TheAgeofProphecy.com. Sign up for the newsletter to receive ad-vance notice of new materials, specials, or the next book release.

Also, connect with us at:
Facebook.com/TheAgeofProphecy
Twitter.com/AgeofProphecy
Google Plus (the url is crazy long, so just search for The Age of Prophecy)

Glossary

Ahav: Also known as Ahab.

Am Yisrael: The nation of Israel.

Avdei Canaanim: Non-Israelite slaves (plural).

Avadim Ivrim: Israelite slaves (plural).

Binyamin: Also known as Benjamin.

Bnei Nevi'im: Literally the children of the prophets, figuratively their students.

Dvekut: Cleaving to the Divine.

Eliyahu: Also known as Elijah.

Emek HaAsefa: Literally, the valley of gathering. A fictional location.

Eved: Slave.

Eved Canaani: A non-Israelite slave.

Eved Ivri: An Israelite slave.

Halil: A straight flute.

Hevron: Also known as Hebron.

Ish Elokim: A man of G-d.

Izevel: Also known as Jezebel or Isabel.

Kohanim: Priests (plural).

Kohen: A Priest.

Kinnor: An instrument that most resembles an ancient lyre.

Labneh: A sour, spreadable cheese.

Malkosh: The late rains.

Matnat Ro'im: The shepherd's gift.

Navi: Prophet.

Navi'im: Prophets.

Navua: Prophecy.

Nefesh: The lowest level of the soul.

Neshama: A higher level of the soul.

Nevel: An instrument that most resembles an ancient harp.

Nigun: A melody, usually without words.

Niggunim: Plural of Nigun.

Pesach: Passover.

Shalom: Peace, also used as a greeting.

Shavuot: Also known as Pentecost or the Feast of Weeks.

Shomron: Also known as Samaria.

Sukkah: The temporary huts built during the festival of Sukkot.

Sukkot: The Festival of Booths when we build and live in temporary huts.

Tefillah: Prayer.

Tikun: Fixing.

Totafot: Also known as Tefillin or Phylacteries.

Yericho: Also known as Jericho.

Yerushalyaim: Also known as Jerusalem.

Yisrael: Also known as Israel.

Yoreh: The early rains.

Yovel: The fiftieth year, called Jubilee year in English.

About the Authors

Dave Mason   Mike Feuer

Dave and Mike have led bizarrely parallel lives. Born just four days apart, they both grew up in secular, Jewish, suburban communities, then found their way to Colorado College. Despite having friends, interests, and even one class in common, they remained complete strangers. Dave then backpacked through over a dozen countries including Syria, China, and Cuba, while Mike lived in the woods for two years, immersed in wilderness therapy with at-risk youth.

Later, both turned their attention to the environment. Dave went to NYU Law and subsequently became a litigator for the Natural Resources Defense Council (NRDC). Mike studied desert agriculture and water resource management, but ultimately found his calling as a teacher.

Fifteen years after first becoming classmates, the two finally met as part of a core group formed to create a new kind of Torah study institution in Jerusalem, called Sulam Yaakov. There, they became study partners, close friends, and both became ordained as Orthodox Rabbis. Dave was blown away by his studies about the inner workings of prophecy, and was surprised at how little exposure he had to this crucial part of his tradition. He decided to create The Age of Prophecy to bring this world to light for others like himself.

Mike joined the project initially as a research assistant, bringing an expertise in the terrain, history, and stories of the Bible to the book. His deep involvement earned him contributing author status, though Mike prefers the term creative co-conspirator.

Professionally, Dave is a businessman, social entrepreneur, and business strategist. He and his wife Chana live in the eclectic Nachlaot neighborhood of Jerusalem, where they homeschool their son, Aryeh Lev.

Mike lives with his family outside of Jerusalem, at the edge of the Judean wilderness.

Made in the USA
Lexington, KY
12 March 2014